tangled BOND

the Holly Woods files #2

tangled
BOND

the Holly Woods files #2

EMMA HART

Interior Formatted by Tianne Samson with E.M. Tippetts Book Designs

emtippettsbookdesigns.com

books by

EMMA HART

The BY HIS GAME series:
Blindsided
Sidelined
Intercepted

The CALL series:
Late Call
Final Call
His Call

The WILD series:
Wild Attraction
Wild Temptation
Wild Addiction

The GAME series:
The Love Game
Playing for Keeps
The Right Moves
Worth the Risk

The MEMORIES series:
Never Forget
Always Remember

The BURKE BROTHERS series:
Dirty Secret
Dirty Past

The HOLLY WOODS FILES series:
Twisted Bond
Tangled Bond

chapter ONE

"**I**'M-A worried about-a your blood sugar."

"Why?"

"You eat-a all of-a the cup-acakes!"

I roll my eyes and look at Nonna. "When it passes the level my blood pressure reaches when you go all cupid on me, then we'll discuss this. Until then..." I dip my finger in the frosting of my cupcake and suck it off.

"You need-a a man-a!" She scowls at me, and quicker than should be right for a woman of her age, she leans forward and attempts to swipe my cupcake.

Attempts is the important word there. Pssh. She's an amateur if she really thought she could get it away from me.

"Nonna, I love you, but no woman needs a man. We already get periods—why the hell do we need something else in our life that's going to force us to eat copious amounts of ice cream?"

"You should-a be married!"

"I should be working," I mutter, peeling the case away from the cake.

"Noella!"

"Nonna!" I snap back. "What are you even doin' in my office?"

She hugs her wrap around her shoulders and tilts her head back slightly so her nose lifts. She looks down at me, the crow's-feet at the corners of her eyes more endearing than threatening as her gaze narrows. "I try-a to get-a you a husband!"

"I don't need a husband!" I sigh, finally setting the cupcake down. "I'm an independent woman. I don't need anything other than what I want. Least of all a dang husband!"

"Who will-a put-a your-a shelves up?"

"If I can't use a drill after all my gun training, I shouldn't be allowed to own a house." Or a gun, for that matter.

"Build-a your-a furniture?"

I tilt my head to the side as a triumphant smile stretches across her face. "Trent, Devin, and Brody," I reply. "You know, the crazy-overprotective brothers who still treat me like I'm six unless I bribe them with barbecued pork and beer."

"What if-a someone breaks-a into your house?"

"Then I'll chase them off with my gun. Again," I add pointedly.

So what if I cried after that little incident? Tissue and blankets would have the same effect as crying into Detective Drake Nash, I'm sure.

It'd be a hug without abs and biceps…and a sexy, frustrating attitude.

"Is-a not-a safe!" Nonna fumes. "You need-a a man!"

"Nonna. I do not need a man. Thank you for your concern, but I still have nineteen months until my birthday, and that is enough time to find a *boyfriend*." I take a bite out of my cupcake and look back at my computer screen.

I have no idea why she's in my office except to bug me. Maybe she got off at the wrong bus stop.

"You need-a a man!"

"Nobody *needs* anything unless they actually want it, and I won't settle for anyone less than perfect for me just because you're afraid I'll become a *zitella, comprende?*"

"You are-a a pain, Noella." She huffs and heads toward the door. "You will-a be-a the death-a of me!"

I smile when she opens the door and shuffles through it. "*Ti amo,* Nonna."

She pauses and glances over her shoulder. "*Ti amo, bella.*"

My smile grows even as she turns fully and meets my eyes again. So I resist the urge to roll my eyes like a petulant teenager, but same thing, right?

"What-a about-a Detective Nash?"

My smile drops. Holy hell, what'd she have to bring him up for?

"Don't worry about him."

"You been on-a that-a date yet?"

"Nonna. I said don't worry."

"Is-a no," she mutters with a heavy sigh. "I book-a you a table!"

Good luck getting that past Drake.

She closes the door behind her this time, and I get up to lock it. No more random drop-ins from her, thank you. Least of all when she has a bee in her bonnet. No—screw this. Where Detective Drake Nash—my sexy, pain-in-the-ass nemesis and guy I owe a date to—is concerned, Nonna has a swarm of freakin' hornets in her bonnet.

There's a small chance I may be ignoring his calls. And texts. And e-mails. And hiding in the bathroom under the masquerade of being "busy" whenever he drops by unannounced.

See, here's the thing. There's nothing wrong with the man. Physically.

He's pretty. Real pretty. He has the awesome dark hair that's floppy and fingers-running-through-until-forever soft and silky. He has the most arresting smile I've ever been faced with, not to mention that quirky little smirk that's both sexy and intimidating. And the jaw... Oh, the jaw. That perfectly carved specimen of a jaw that's always covered with the right amount of stubble. Let's not forget the eyes now—the eyes that would give a snow queen a run for her money with her iciness. And that's just the color of them. The emotions the man can portray in them are unreal. Anger, frustration, happiness, determination... Heat... Desire... Lust... Pleasure...

I shake my head. *Snap the fuck out it, Noelle.* Screwing the man on your kitchen table is not a case for repeated dreamy blackouts at lunchtime. Well, if we want to be technical, *he* screwed *me,* and what a damn fine screw it was.

So what is my problem?

Him.

We're oil and water. Chalk and cheese. Snow and sun. Equally, though, we're fire and gasoline, burning matches and fireworks, kindling wood and a bonfire. We're opposite but explosive. Opposite but unhealthy. Opposite and possibly a little bit toxic.

A lot toxic, because the man riles me up like no other.

He's arrogant and infuriating and oh-righteous-me. He's the definition of Mr. Right, except he's Mr. 50% Wrong At Least.

This I know, because when he's wrong, I'm right.

I'd raise this to seventy-five percent, but I figure I have to give him some kind of personality trait.

Ugh, Noelle, you bitch.

I grab the cupcake and shove it in my mouth. The man makes me want to eat all the cupcakes and skip the treadmill. Put simply: I have no idea how I feel about Detective Drake Nash. And that's scary.

Mostly because I'm scared of finding out how I feel, and the only way that's going to happen is if I see him. But... Hell. It is so easy to avoid him, even in a small town like Holly Woods. My brothers have stopped telling me when he's working, sure, but I'm a smart woman. I simply avoid the police station on the way to and from the station, and if he drives past me, then he's gonna have to flash those nice little blue lights of his to make me stop.

I rub some frosting from my lower lip and open my e-mail. Nonna's turning up to give me lecture number one hundred and fifty-six of this year—in April—has thrown me off. My inbox is filled with promotional e-mails from Coach and Louboutin and Victoria's Secret. It pains me to click the little boxes and hit the delete button, but I'm being strong and resisting the urge to buy all the things.

Hey—I can always go into my trash folder and read them tonight when I'm curled in front of my TV with a burrito or two.

I finish the cupcake as an e-mail from Natalie Owens pings into my inbox. I narrow my eyes. We went to high school together, but despite us both being on the cheer team, she barely ever said two words to me. Now, I have a blank-subject-line e-mail from her.

I want to ignore it, just to be a bitch, but my nosy side ultimately wins out and I open it.

Dear Ms. Bond,
I'd appreciate if you could inform me of your earliest availability for a consultation appointment.
Yours sincerely,
Natalie Owens.

Well, how polite of her.

I could probably learn a thing or two.

I reach for my planner and flick through it to this week, noting an empty space tomorrow afternoon. Although… There's every possibility I have something there that I forgot to write down. I grab my phone and dial the extension to Grecia, my Mexican assistant-slash-receptionist-slash-personal burrito-recipe-giver.

"Hello," she answers simply. Good thing I know that her phone flashes with my name.

"Do I have anything at two o'clock tomorrow afternoon?"

Papers shuffle at her end. "Yes. You have an interview with Carlton Hooper for the tech job."

Bastard. I forgot about that. Of course I'd have to replace Marshall. My deceptively sweet ex-tech guy is currently in the county jail awaiting trial for the murder of his old stepmom, her bit on the side, and her best friend and the attempted murder of his own cougar ex-girlfriend.

Not to mention the whole illegal weapon thing. The same one he pulled on me before I shot him first.

"How about after? Someone e-mailed me about a consultation. Does anyone else have any space?"

More paper shuffling. "If you can be done with the consultation in thirty minutes, I can reschedule with Mr. Hooper for half an hour later and tell him you have a family commitment."

"Grecia, you're wonderful."

"I know. You tell me every day."

"That's because I mean it." I grin although she can't see it. "Um, could I get a copy of my schedule for the rest of the month to cross-check with my planner?"

I can hear her smile as she says, "I'll bring you coffee and collect your planner."

"You really are wonderful."

She laughs and clicks off. I e-mail Natalie, somewhat prematurely, about the appointment tomorrow afternoon with a line about squeezing her in quickly, and I've just clicked send when Grecia opens my door and strolls across the room. Her black hair is pulled into a ponytail on top of her head, her dark, olive-toned skin making her brown eyes glitter brightly. She's short even with four-inch heels on her feet, so she has to bend right over when she puts my coffee mug on my desk.

She grins knowingly as she grabs my favorite Erin Conden planner from next to me and strolls out.

I still can't believe she's dating my ex–FBI investigator, Mike. I shudder at the memory of walking in on them dry-humping in his office. That said, there hasn't been so much as a hand-brush since I threatened them with their jobs.

I don't pay people to get themselves off on my time.

"No!" Grecia shouts.

I stand up, my chair rolling back. Grecia's yelling "No!" that angrily only means one thing.

Detective Drake Nash is here.

"All due respect, ma'am, I'm here on business."

Aw, shit! I frantically look around my newly decorated duck-egg-blue office. From the potted plant by the door to the tub chairs in front of my antique-style desk to the flycatcher on my windowsill waiting for its lunch.

I have no time to run across the hall to the bathroom and lock myself in there.

Crappy crappy crap.

Who said that this avoiding thing was a good idea?

"She is busy!"

"I have a warrant."

I clap my hand over my mouth and quickly turn the key in my door. I lean against it, breathing heavily.

Sweet fuck. I'm a grown woman. Has my vagina shriveled up into my bowel and died?

"Ms. Bond." Drake raps loudly on my door. "If you're in a meeting, I'm afraid you'll have to cut it short. I'm here on official business."

My phone screen lights up on my desk. I dart across the room—as quickly as one can in four-inch heels—and grab it. I open the message from Bekah, my best friend and first employee.

Official business, huh? I call bullshit.

Uh-huh, I reply.

"Ms. Bond! I have a warrant and will break your door down."

You're in trouble. BIG TROUBLE.

Captain freakin' Obvious.

I fist my hand and hold it against my mouth, quietly putting my phone back down.

"Open the goddamn door, Noelle!" He bangs on it again, and I sigh, reserved.

Prepare your ovaries and gird your womb, Noelle. You're gonna have to let him in.

I straighten my nice, new, red pencil skirt, make sure the girls aren't popping out of my black blouse, and make my way to the door. I twist the key in the opposite direction and the lock clicks. Calmly, I open the door, and meet his raging, blue eyes.

"Good afternoon, Detective. Can I help you?"

His face is hard, and his eyes aren't just raging. No—they're stormy, a tsunami waiting to be unleashed. He barges past me, his elbow knocking mine, and I purse my lips.

"Why, come on in, sir. Can I have my assistant get you a coffee with your apology for your rudeness?"

"Don't fuck with me," he warns, turning and pinning me with his gaze. "Shut your door."

"I think you mumbled your 'please.'"

He retraces his path until he's standing over me. He reaches above me and pushes the door shut, the handle easily falling from my grasp as it swings shut with a bang that ricochets through my office.

"Please," he adds as the echo dies.

I glare at him, and yes. Now, I remember exactly why we don't get along.

"Take a seat, Detective, and tell me all about your *official* business with your w*arrant.*"

"I prefer to have my discussions standing." He grasps my arm—not tightly, but strongly enough that I'd have to insert my Louboutin into his ballsac to get him to release me.

"From experience, you prefer most things upright."

Slowly, his lips curve to one side, his smirk both sexy and infuriating. His eyes flash with the memory. "Especially where you're concerned, Ms. Bond."

I drop my eyes to his belt, allowing them to linger on the buckle before falling another inch or two to his crotch. "Don't tell me you dropped in for a midday booty call."

"Are you offerin'? Since you're holdin' out on me, I think you owe me."

"Excuse me?" My eyes snap up to his, and the smugness reflecting in his gaze tells me that I fell for his trick.

Son of a bitch.

"Our date? It's been two weeks since you agreed to go out with me, and call me obsessive, but I'm counting nine missed calls, ten missed texts, and five missed visits to your office."

"You counted? Hell yeah, that's obsessive."

"Maybe I just really want to date you."

"Or you want to return the favor of a bullet through the foot."

His arm rests on the weapon at his hip. "That can be arranged right now, if you'd like to call it even."

My fingers curl around the handle of the one at his other hip. "And I'll up the score just as quickly."

Drake laughs, his anger seemingly gone, and leans in. "Go ahead. It'll give me the reason to get you in cuffs I've been waiting for."

I'm ninety-nine percent sure my blood pressure has gone batshit crazy at his words. Hell, my pulse is much stronger than it was thirty seconds ago.

"Five minutes ago, you were yelling about a warrant," I breathe, swallowing the burst of desire bolting through me. "Your official business seems far more personal, though, if you don't mind me saying."

"Not at all," he replies. He takes my hand from his weapon, but instead of releasing it, he keeps his grip. "I'm surprised you didn't reach for your own gun."

"And tell you where it is? I'm no amateur, Drake."

"And still, I underestimate you."

"Rightly so." I remove my hand from his and reach up my skirt. Then I pull my favorite Tiffany-blue Glock from my thigh holster. The muzzle presses against his upper thigh, but to his credit, he doesn't even flinch at the contact.

"I underestimate you," he murmurs, his fingers brushing my waist. "But I don't take you for stupid. You won't pull that trigger. Not there. It's too close to the part of me you like."

"You assume far too much, Detective." I drop the gun anyway and dart around him, strolling to my desk and setting it down softly on top of my latest case folder.

Drake comes up behind me, reaches around me, and rests his hands next to mine on the desk. I briefly close my eyes as his hard body melds against mine, because the man has one fine fucking body. I can feel it now—all muscle and tone and pure, hard strength. His biceps brush mine, except his are way more…bicep…than mine. Like, seriously, how does he fit those into that hot-as-hell white shirt?

This is what happens when he touches me. I go all giggly schoolgirl. Sweet Jesus though. It's hard not to.

I know what that body looks like and feels like and acts like, and those memories can't be erased. I can't erase the memory of his body, slick with sweat, tensed with determined pleasure, moving against mine as I took everything he had to give me.

I take a deep breath, but despite my efforts to inhale slowly, it fills my lungs in a rush that jolts me. Drake feels it, because he drops his face to the curve of my neck exposed by my sleek topknot. Every part of me wishes I could unravel the hairbands and pins, but still, his lips against my collarbone… Oh, hell. They feel so good. So sweet and hot.

"This is highly unprofessional," I manage, unwillingly tilting my head to the side and exposing my neck to him. "For your official business, I mean."

He trails his lips up to my ear, where they brush the lobe, curving into a smile. "You are my official business, Ms. Bond."

"Are you trying to seduce me into that date?"

"Is it working?"

Yes. "No."

"Okay." He straightens, the quick blast of cold air between us sending a shiver across my body. Just as quickly, though, he grabs me and turns me so my butt is perched on the desk and he's right in front of me.

Oh, hell no. The last time we were in this position, cock-in-pussy and hell-yes-Drake-right-there-more-please happened.

I squeeze my legs shut although the chances of him parting my legs in this skirt are questionable. Mind you, I did have a gun successfully hidden up there…

Instead of parting them, he shoves them to the side so he's coming at me side on, but his arm around me ensures that my breasts are still planted against his chest.

"Trying," he says in a low voice. "Cute. Real cute."

"Sure are, ain't ya?"

He covers my mouth for a second before lowering his hand so only his thumb is pressed against my lips. "You should know by now that, if I'm tryna seduce you, cupcake, I'm gonna fuckin' well do it. Right now, no, I'm not, but by the looks of your pretty little red cheeks, it wouldn't be hard. What I am doin' is collectin' on the debt you owe me. And you owe me a date—so a date you're gonna give me, whether you damn well like it or not."

"Nonna called you, didn't she?" I groan.

"I didn't answer." His eyes sparkle with laughter. "But since I've tried to get you for two weeks and you've been hidin' in your bathroom to avoid me, I figured I'd force my way in."

"You lied to me."

"You lied to me," he counters.

Damn, I hate it when he's right. I huff.

"So. That date?" He smiles.

"Really? You're gonna barge in here all alpha and start demanding things?"

"In case it escaped your notice, sweetheart, I am an alpha, and I'm not fuckin' afraid to take your tight little ass over my knee and prove that."

I want to glare at him, but instead, I clench my legs together.

This better be Mother Nature messing with my hormones.

"Fine!" I snap. "As long as Detective Alpha knows he's takin' Ms. Alpha P.I. on a date."

He leans in, and his grin is evident as he touches his mouth to mine. It's a simple sweeping brush across my lips that somehow seems to send a thousand lightning bolts through my body.

"Noted, ma'am."

"And no ma'ams. I'll ma'am your testicles."

"Noted, Ms. Bond," he corrects himself, his hand curving around my hip and pulling me against him despite my legs still being to the side. "I'm off the day after tomorrow. Is that good for you?"

"Umm." I hesitate.

He laughs, stepping back. "Call Grecia."

Am I that predictable?

I pick my phone up, staring at him in frustration, and dial her extension again. "Am I busy the day after tomorrow?"

"You have an interview at three," she replies.

"I have an interview at three," I repeat.

Drake snatches the phone out of my hand and lifts it to his ear, his eyes focused on me the whole time, the icy blue cutting through me. "Ms. Bond is otherwise preoccupied on Thursday and will be indisposed all day. Please rearrange all her appointments for another day. Thank you, Grecia." He hangs up without waiting for a response, I'm guessing.

"I… You… Did you…" I sputter, staring at him in disbelief. I'll be "indisposed?" "Otherwise preoccupied?" What the hell is wrong with him? "Did you seriously just do that?"

Drake grabs my hands and forces me to stand, his arms easily going around me as my hands press against his chest. One of his hands finds its way from my back to my butt, and he pulls me into him there, too.

"Yes. Indisposed, all day. Completely and utterly preoccupied. You owe me a date, Noelle, and I'm collectin' in approximately thirty-six hours."

"This is ridiculous."

"Agreed. But I want to see if we can last more than two hours without a fight."

"I'm going into this passionately, so that's unlikely."

"You mean pissed off."

I scowl. "Passionate. I'm part Italian. I get passionate, not pissed off."

He dips his face, grinning. "Sure. Passionate. I can think of plenty of other emotions for you to apply your 'passionate' to, but whatever."

"I swear to God, I will—"

Do absolutely nothing, because he kisses me to shut me up. And fuck, he kisses me. It's nothing more than a point-prover and a point-scorer, because it's hard and hot and his lips move across me with such speed that I can barely comprehend where his kiss starts and mine ends.

My fingers are curled into his formerly crisp, white shirt, and his are digging into me in an almost desperate yet sinfully hot grasp that has goose-bump-filled shivers steaming across my skin until every hair is standing on end.

He releases me, leaving me gasping for air, angry, pissed, high on his formidable kiss. "Ten a.m. Thursday morning. Be ready, Noelle."

"Like I have a choice," I murmur as he releases me with a light tap to the ass and opens my office door. "Asshole," I add more loudly.

He stops, turns. That smirk is back, and his eyebrow is curved upward in his amusement. "Bitch," he counters. "Bring that on Thursday. It's kind of hot."

I reach for the nearest item—a hot-pink Sharpie—and launch at him seconds before he shuts the door. The loud laugh reassures me that I've hit him, and I allow myself a second of smugness before the silence envelopes me and reality hits.

I really have to do this—a date with Drake.

Jesus.

I need a miracle.

chapter TWO

DATES on Thursday are bad. And not because Thursday is tomorrow, but because it's the day before freakin' family dinner.

If I thought I could get away with it, I'd totally call Drake and rearrange, but I don't even think a Friday night interrogation by my grandmother will pass as an excuse. Besides—I can't put it off any longer.

Two weeks is kinda, sorta, really freakin' ridiculous.

And it's one date. That's all I agreed to.

That's the settlement I came to with myself last night after two margaritas too many and definitely one cupcake too many. One date isn't that bad, really, right? Especially if the kissing happens.

Wait.

I didn't agree to *that* with myself…

My eldest brother shakes his head at me across the table. "I think you need help."

"What I need is to skip town," I mutter, dipping my nacho into the sour cream and shoving it into my mouth.

"What made you agree to date my superior?"

So there's a chance Trent still doesn't know about my and Drake's little romp in my kitchen. There's an even higher chance that he *never* will. Because yuck.

"Temporary insanity?" By way of orgasm.

This is a thing.

He raises his eyebrow.

"Oh, come on. It could be worse, right? I could be going out with Giorgio Messina again."

Instantly, Trent's expression sours. "I find myself oddly thrilled about Drake over Giorgio."

"Wow. What a blessing." I snort, dipping another chip into some guac. "Look. I agreed. I'm going. Then I'm taking a vacation to Easter Island or somethin.'"

Trent shoves two sour-cream-and-salsa-covered chips into his mouth and considers this. "Huh," he manages through a mouthful of food. "I don't trust him."

"You trust him to find a murderer but not take me on a date?"

"Big-brother logic."

"Is ridiculous," I add, grabbing the empty box and shoving it in the trash can next to me. I sigh and rest my elbows on the desk. Then I run my fingers through my hair. "This whole situation is ridiculous."

"Agreed. You two can't even say hello without fightin'. Hell, y'all fight and skip straight over hello. Your goodbye is, 'Fuck off.'"

My lips twitch to the side. I'm almost ashamed to admit that he's right.

"Which is why, as much as I don't like it, going on a date makes sense." Trent grins when my smile drops. "Nonna and Nonno, remember? Fought like cat and dog but loved the shit outta each other."

"You tryna tell me I'm in love with Drake?"

"Dunno. Are ya?"

"Like I love stepping on your son's Lego whenever I babysit."

Trent laughs, redoing his tie before grabbing his coffee from the desk. "Thank God—I don't have to worry that my boss will be my brother-in-law. That would be awkward."

I roll my eyes as he leaves without saying goodbye. How the heck did he make the jump from first date to brother-in-law? I bet Nonna called him, too. I'm quite honestly torn between wanting her to know so she gets off my back about dating and wanting it to be a secret from her so she doesn't set us a wedding date and book me an appointment at the nearest wedding boutique.

Alas, this is Holly Woods, and she probably knew when the date is right around the time I did. Hell, she probably knows exactly where the date is, and I don't even know that.

Crap. I have no idea where he's taking me. How the hell can I prepare for it if I don't know where it is?

I reach for the phone and stop before I lift it up. If I call him, it'll look like I'm thinking about it, but if I don't, how do I know what to wear? I pick the phone up. Put it back down. Pick it up. Put it down.

"What in the shit are you doin'?"

My eyes cut to the door where Bekah is tying her auburn hair into a ponytail and eying me with thinly veiled amusement. "Obviously, I'm trying to decide whether or not to make a call."

"You don't know what to wear tomorrow, do you?"

"Fuck off," I reply, fighting my grin. Goddamn it. I hate that she knows me this well. "Yes. Okay."

"You did this with Gio, too, remember?"

"Yeah, yeah," I mumble, tapping the corner of the phone against my mouth. "But at least I knew where we were going…"

"So call him and ask." She shrugs. "I would."

"No, you wouldn't. You'd make me do it."

Her grin is wide. "True. Want me to do it for you?"

"You will?"

"No. Do it yourself, you pussy," she laughs.

I flip her the bird before she walks down the hall.

The phone rings and I scream, dropping it. I hear Bek's laughter from her office two doors down and flip another bird through the walls as I reach down to grab the phone. "Hello?"

"Your two-o'clock is here," Grecia says. Then she lowers her voice. "She looks antsy. Like she shouldn't be here."

Jolts of intrigued worry make their way down to my spine, making me sit bolt upright, and I stand up. "I'm coming down." I hang up before she can respond, and after straightening my dress and wriggling my feet into my heels, I go downstairs.

The fact that this building is a converted, spacious, four-bedroom house and not a traditional office is something I've always loved. I can be downstairs in seconds, and the banister that follows it down is the very same one that was installed when it was built in the eighteen hundreds, restored to keep its beauty.

I brush some dust off the bottom and peek into the empty meeting room. Color charts from my meeting with Jason, the decorator I've hired to freshen up the building, are strewn across the table where I can't be bothered to tidy them away. Instead, we're simply conducting our now twice-weekly meetings on the top of them.

Changing the meetings from daily to twice weekly is my way of "cutting down" on cupcakes.

Spoiler: it isn't working.

A stunning woman with short, blond hair cut into a stylish bob is sitting on the new, red sofa outside Grecia's office. She's flicking through a glossy magazine, completely immersed in the content between the pages, and I feel a little rude interrupting her, but hey.

"Natalie Owens?" I ask hesitantly, because although we went to school together, we run in totally different circles and always have.

She looks up, her dark-brown eyes framed by long, curled eyelashes that look like they brush the skin above her eyes. "Noelle!" She immediately deposits the magazine back on the stack on the glass coffee table in front of her and stands. The smile stretching across her face is bright, but the dull fear sparking in her eyes belies her apparently happiness.

I accept her embrace with a little—all right, all right, a lot—of awkwardness. "How are you?"

"I'll be better if you can help me." She glances away and clears her throat before offering me a nervous, high-pitched laugh.

I touch her upper arm and guide her toward the stairs. "Let's talk." I precede her up the staircase and open the door to let her pass into my office.

She sweeps past me gracefully, but I can almost smell her nerves.

Nerves aren't a new thing in this job. Every client I see has an element of nervousness to them when they walk into my office. After all, they're asking me to find out information they probably aren't going to like hearing. It's usually something simple like a rub to the back of the neck or picking at their fingernails.

Natalie far surpasses this. As soon as she sits down, her knee bounces and she attempts to still it by rubbing her hands down her thighs. As I close the door and lock it, she scrapes her hand through her hair. Then, as if it's a knee-jerk reaction, she reaches up and smooths the locks back down into their pristine style.

I resist the urge to narrow my eyes, because then I'll lose myself in cop mode and watch her for her lies instead of actually helping her.

Damn Marshall, murdering Lena and fully reawakening my cop instinct.

I slowly lower myself into my seat and look at Natalie. She's nibbling on her bottom lip now, and honestly, I want to whisper for fear she'll bolt if I speak too loud. Abusive, cheating boyfriend?

"What can I help you with, Natalie?"

She runs her tongue over her lips and takes a deep breath. Her fingers brush together, and she leans forward. "I think I'm being stalked," she says quietly.

Oh, okay. That's new.

I grab my pen and poise the tip above my notebook. "Elaborate."

"My boyfriend and I broke up three weeks ago. He cheated on me, and I refused to accept his apology. He's been begging me to take him back ever since."

Inwardly, I wince. "That's closer to harassment than stalking."

"I know." She exhales slowly but loudly. "But it's not only the calls. There are…messages. Threatening ones. With my mail, texts, tucked under the wipers of my car. And sometimes, it just feels like I'm being watched, you know? I can't go anywhere without feeling like I'm being followed."

"Okay. And when did it start—the messages?"

"Four days after we broke up. I forced him to move out the same day I found out."

Her jaw ticks, and she licks her lips again.

Lying.

I nod, ignoring the nudge from the back of my mind. "And the feeling of being followed?"

"The day after."

"Okay." I underline that on the notepad, set the pen down, and look at her. "Natalie, you do realize that this is probably a matter for the police, don't you?"

"I have issues with figures in authority." Bitterness flickers across her face, and her lip curls in disgust. "The hoops they have to jump through for simple things is ridiculous. The local PD are so busy making sure no one tries to kill the damn mayor that my gut feelings won't be enough for them to go on."

Wow. She really doesn't like authority, huh? I knew someone like that in Dallas. Not for long, though, because he pulled a gun on my partner and ended up getting himself killed. He was more trigger-happy than I am…

Not that I'm saying she'll get shot. Just that, you know. Respect and all that.

"You think the person following you is your ex-boyfriend?" When she nods, I continue.

"So, what if I find out? Then what do you do with that information?"

"Then I take it to the police and they have to arrest him."

I sigh and sit back in my chair. "They'll do their own investigation and bring me in for questioning over it, even if my brothers make up half the detectives on the squad. That doesn't exempt me from the procedures." I hesitate as fear flickers across her delicate features. "But," I add, "and I mean but, if you agree to report this to the police, I promise to take this and get to the bottom of it."

Natalie inhales quickly, her eyes widening as my words hang in the air between us. She wets her lips then tugs on the bottom one with her teeth. Her dejected sigh is accompanied with slumped shoulders, and I have only one thought.

I would really, really love to play this chick at poker. The last time I saw someone this expressive was when I was sixteen and wanted to see why my brothers loved porn so much.

"What if they see?" she asks quietly, all bitterness completely removed and replaced with resignation.

"The stalker? Call from here and request that a plainclothes officer comes to you in an unmarked car if you're that worried." I open my drawer and pull a new contract out. "Here's my basic contract. My flat-rate fee is on there as well as a breakdown of my process and what I need you to get for me. I'll have one personalized for you drawn up once I've seen a copy of the police report. Take your time with this." I slide it across the table.

She shakes her head. "I'll have it to you tomorrow. With the report," she replies.

"I'm out of the office tomorrow, but I'll get to it first thing on Friday morning." I glance at the clock. "Without being rude, I have another appointment in five minutes." I offer her a smile and stand.

"Of course." Natalie folds the contract and tucks it into her purse before getting up and joining me at the door. "Do you mind if I use your restroom?"

"Sure don't. Head down the hall and you'll see it. It has a sign on the door." I shake her hand then close the door as she disappears into the bathroom.

My phone rings before I can process that meeting, and I dart across my office to grab it.

"Noelle Bond?"

"Your next appointment is here," Grecia says. "He's cute," she adds in a hushed voice.

I fight my laugh. Great—that's what I want to do. Hire a cute tech whiz so her boyfriend, who happens to be an ex–FBI investigator, can see her little doe eyes whenever he walks past.

"Bring him up in five minutes, okay? I need to get ready."

"Sure." She hangs up.

I put the receiver down and pause. What's one minute out of five to make a phone call? I grab my cell instead of the office phone and bring up my call log. Then I scroll to Drake's name and hit *call*.

"Detective Nash," he answers, his voice gravelly but distracted.

"I have a question."

"Better than a dead body."

I laugh. "Shut up. Okay, so this date thing tomorrow."

"Date," he says. "Just date, Noelle. No date thing."

"Fine." I roll my eyes. "For this date, what am I supposed to wear? Where are we going?"

There's a small crackle on the line, and I swear it's him smiling.

"Not sayin'. But wear clothes. Course, if you wanted to wear lingerie and high heels, I can rearrange my plans."

"Um, I'm thinkin' I'll stick to the clothes. But that doesn't help, Drake. Do I wear jeans? A dress? Shorts? Boots? Heels? Flip-flops?"

"Sweet fuck, cupcake. I think you just gave me a brain aneurism." He chuckles. "Wear whatever you want. Preferably something that shows your leg and a hint of panties when you bend over."

"Will I be bending over?"

Another chuckle. "If you ask me nicely."

I bite the inside of my lip although I can feel my cheeks heating at his insinuation. Or is it an offer? Knowing him, it's an offer. Or a

19

promise. Whatever.

All I know is that, right now, I have an image of me bending over the end of a bed while he fucks me from behind.

I clench my legs together and take a slow, deep breath.

"Noelle? You still there?" Smug—that's what he sounds like.

"You're a head-screwing little shit," I half snap at him. "Nice try, Detective, but you won't be seeing my panties. And to think, I just spent the equivalent of a mortgage on two new pairs."

"You did what?"

"See you tomorrow." I grin and hit *end call* as he yells out a "Wait!"

I've barely put the phone down when it rings again, his name flashing on screen. I let it ring to voicemail then put my phone on silent.

There are three rapid knocks at my door, and I call out, "Two seconds!" then scuffle in my papers to find Carlton's résumé. Upon finding it beneath my electric bill and a ten-percent-off coupon for Victoria's Secret, I grab it and shove the bill and coupon into my top drawer.

Whoops.

Carlton Hooper. Twenty-six years old. Two degrees that don't make much sense to me, but Dean reassured me that they mean he's more than qualified for the job. And apparently cute.

I shrug and get up yet again to go to the door. I'm gonna start leaving the damn thing open, I swear.

"Noelle, this is Carlton Hooper. Mr. Hooper, this is Noelle Bond, the owner of Bond P.I. She'll be interviewing you today," Grecia says, and, oh, she has a point about the cute thing.

Dirty-blond hair swept to the side—think a teenage Justin Bieber hairstyle but rougher and messier—piercing, dark-blue eyes, and enough muscles hidden under his white shirt that he'd send a whole college of girls into cardiac arrest.

Dear California, you're missing a surfer, but Texas has decided to keep him. Thanks.

"It's a pleasure to meet you, Ms. Bond." He holds his hand out, and I put mine into his. Nice, firm handshake.

God, what a male ought to have. Nice, firm handshake. Shouldn't I be thinking that but about his ass?

Wait. Oh, never mind. Nothing wrong with eye candy in the

20

office.

"Come on in and have a seat." I motion to the tub chairs and glance at Grecia. "Thanks, Grecia. If Bek's in her office, route all incoming calls to her and take your break."

She smiles thankfully as Carlton walks past me and sits in one of the chairs. I close the door and stroll to my side of the desk, aware of his eyes on me. Shouldn't have worn the tight dress today…

Then again, I wasn't expecting to interview Mr. Cute here, was I? Ugh. I'm going to start asking for headshots for prospective employees.

Image is everything and all that.

I sit down and smile at him. "Tell me about yourself, to start."

"Uh…" He glances at the résumé like he needs a script prompt. "I'm twenty-six, from Berkeley in California."

Nailed it.

"I have two degrees, one in computer programming and one in graphic design, and…"

I nod as he continues his monologue. It's refreshingly random and unscripted, so I think he thought I was going to dive straight into the questions. When it becomes clear he's running out of steam and clearly on the verge of talking me through every pet he's owned since age three, I stop him and start on the list of questions Grecia and Bekah helped me draw up.

I freaking hate interviewing. It's the worst part about this job… Which is why I picked someone young when I hired Marshall.

I hope my next employee isn't a murderous idiot.

I spend the next thirty minutes with Carlton, and by the time I'm asking him the last question about flexibility, I'm almost certain he's not violently inclined. Well, I'm really hoping he isn't, not only 'cause of the cute thing, but because he is absolutely perfect for this role.

"Thank you," I say, standing and walking around my desk. "I'll be in touch next week. Thanks for coming in, Carlton."

"No, thank you for the chance, Ms. Bond. You obviously run a successful business, and it would be an honor to be part of your team."

I open the door and smirk. "Flattery will get you nowhere, honey, but cupcakes might just." I shake his hand again.

He laughs. "Bye, Ms. Bond."

"Goodbye, Carlton." I shake my head, smiling, and walk back to my desk, where I grab my phone. Turning it over, I see the voice message icon blinking in the corner of the screen, so I unlock it and dial the annoying robotic lady.

I don't have to be a genius to know that it's from Drake—and probably angry.

"I swear to God, Noelle Bond, you better not fuck with me tomorrow. 'Cause if you do, sweetheart, my restraint might snap and I will bend you over and fuck you into the middle of next week—and next time you tell me about your underwear then hang up and ignore me, I'm gonna get your ass over my knee and spank it until you come. Understood? Excellent. Ten o'clock tomorrow. Don't be late."

My jaw drops as the lady tells me that the message is over. He's going to—where? What? Sweet baby Jesus on horseback! I cover my eyes with my hand and drop the phone. My breathing is more than a little erratic right now, but hell if I know if it's because I'm angry or excited by that prospect.

Because, hell, I kinda wanna call him right now and do the panty thing to see if he will keep his threat.

Then again, I know he will... And Spanx aren't made for spanking. Ironically.

So, instead of baiting him further, I text him a simple, *I'd like to see you try,* and put my phone in my purse.

Oh—wait.

Never mind. I totally baited him.

I'm so in trouble tomorrow.

chapter
THREE

BRING *your gun.*

That was the text message I woke up to this morning. Actually, it was the one I woke up to at one a.m. while my phone was buzzing like a vibrator on high power under my pillow. Well, I say I woke up to it. What actually happened was a very unladylike word combined with "waffle" as I threw my phone into my pile of dirty laundry by my bedroom door.

Yeah. I'm not proud of the very rare c-word escape mission, but I'm not responsible for what I say or do when I'm woken up at one a.m. while dreaming about Gigi's. Really, Drake should have known better.

You never, ever wake a sleeping woman. Not even for sex. If we want sleepy sex, we initiate it. The last time my ex tried to have sleepy sex with me, I elbowed him on reflex and the whole Dallas PD thought he'd been hit in the face with a tree.

Again: not responsible.

I'm not shocked he texted me at that time of the morning—but, while I'm thinking of it, what was he doing texting me at that time? Was he awake? Working? Did he wake up randomly with a thought that he needed to tell me that? *Why was he thinking about me at one in the morning?* One. In. The. Morning.

Holy shit. I sound like a fucking thirteen-year-old hypothesizing about the cute boy who glanced at her in the middle of math. Does he like me? Was he really looking at me? OHMYGOD what if he was?

I need to seriously screw my head on tight and clamp up my vagina or this date is a bust—mostly because Drake Nash will own me entirely.

Damn, being a woman is so freakin' hard. I'd bet anything he isn't sitting at home right now, feeling like he wants to throw up all the elephants line-dancing in his stomach. Neither is he worrying about his fucking underwear in case his dress blows up and shows it. You know, for all the wind right now, but no one wants a Marilyn moment.

Because really, why did I wake up at five a.m. to read that message? That wasn't even the first time I'd woken up. Like the ten millionth, and I haven't even slept since.

Hell. Drake Nash is ruining me. Worse? I'm pretty sure I like it.

I need psychiatric help if, only weeks ago, I hated the man and, now, I'm all in a twizzle about a date with him. A date I'm only going on so my grandmother stops getting all up in my business.

Sure, Noelle. You tell yourself that.

Ugh. I'm a fucking moron.

But my gun. Why on Earth would the man I shot in the foot tell me to bring a gun to our first date? Perhaps he's the crazy one. Perhaps he and the rest of the world are stuck in a never-ending ball of insanity and I'm the normal one.

Yeah. Definitely shouldn't have added that sugar to my cereal earlier.

I twist the bangle at my wrist. Around and around and around and around until it pretty much spins by itself.

God, where is he?

Why am I doing this to myself? I am a strong, independent, kickass woman. I've been in situations where my life was absolutely at risk. I've held the fates of others' in the palms of my hands, and I've stared straight down the barrel of a gun. But can I go on a date with someone without wanting to throw up everywhere? Can. I. Hell.

The knocks at my door are loud and confident. Can knocks even be confident? Or is it intimidating? Like a big boom-boom-boom that rattles windows and doors and sofa cushions and oh my God this is so ridiculous.

Someone take a frying pan to my face. Seriously. For real. Right now.

If I call my brothers, maybe one of them will shoot me and put me out of this misery. Hell, I'd take being knocked out right now.

Hello? Someone? Anyone?

The last time I felt this nauseated, I was waiting for my period after I'd lost my virginity.

Crap.

I nibble on my thumbnail, and hell, I need to shove this ridiculous nervousness the heck down, because it's not like it's a blind date Nonna set up. It's not like I don't know Drake. I know him better than I possibly should.

And maybe that's the problem.

I know how dangerous this man could be to my heart. The most fiercely guarded part of me—not because she knows pain, but because she fears it. And if anyone, *anyone,* could inflict real pain on her, it'd be Drake.

Two more knocks sound at the door, and I stand up, feeling my own butt up to make sure my dress isn't caught in my panties. Not that there's much panty for them to be caught in. I mean, they're definitely in the porn-star area of the panty chart.

I grab the door handle and open it. Or try to. Apparently, I didn't think to unlock the door at any point this morning, so all the door does is nudge until it bangs against the frame, where the lock is still sticking into the frame.

Fuck my life in all the positions of the *Kama Sutra.*

I twist the key, and when the door clicks with the unlocking motion, I pull it open.

And set off my alarm.

It screeches through the house. My scream is short but loud as the high-pitched sound assaults my ears, and I drop my keys as I turn toward the alarm system block right by the door. I see Drake's laugh rather than hear it on account of the noise reverberating off the walls, and if that smile wasn't so fucking hot, I'd wipe it off his face with my boot.

I key in the code and the alarm dies. The silence is strangely deafening compared to the awful alarm. And just like that, the awkwardness hangs between us. At least, it does for me. A lot for me.

All for me, okay? All for me.

"All right, cupcake?" Drake's grin is lopsided, and he's leaning against the doorframe. His ice-blue eyes are oddly warm, glittering with the laughter I know he's struggling to keep inside. And the navy-blue Dallas Cowboys T-shirt he's wearing clings to every part of his upper body, from his shoulders to his waist to his biceps.

And oh man. He makes them look good.

"That isn't a great start to this date. That damn nickname drives me insane."

His grin straightens and grows. "I know, but you ain't allowed to be mad at me today. Nice, remember?"

"That's askin' a real lot," I mumble. "Wait there."

I turn into the front room, and with a little more tremble in my hand than I'd like, I grab my gun and lift my dress to slip it into my thigh holster. I know I could put it in my purse, but I feel more comfortable having it about my person. Drake has his at his hip, after all, and he's off duty today.

"Gun between your tits?" he asks as I grab my purse and throw my phone into it.

"Perhaps," I reply, stepping outside to join him on the top step. I slam the door shut and shove the key into the hole despite the elephants still raising a circus in my belly. "I'll never tell you my tricks, Detective."

"Drake." He slips his arm around my waist and pulls me into him. He breathes over my shoulder since my head is still down from locking the door, but his firm hold squeezes my heart tight. "We ain't workin', Noelle. First date equals first names."

"You say 'first date' like you know there'll be a second."

His fingers twitch against my hip. He ghosts his lips across my pulse until they hover at the curve of my collarbone. "I do. And a third. And fourth. And fifth. We'll have so many fuckin' dates you're gonna lose count."

His confidence is like whoa sexy.

"We'll see," I whisper. "Let's get the first out of the way, shall we?"

"If you insist," he murmurs, grasping me and turning me toward his truck. "You brought your gun?"

"I'm insulted you have to ask."

"Good." He pulls the door of his truck open and sweeps his arm for me to climb in.

I raise my eyebrow at him, because isn't he supposed to help me in?

"Noelle, if I helped you in, you'd castrate me."

"So a ten percent chance it's wrong?"

The quirk of his eyebrow mirrors mine. "I'm tempted to take my chances."

"This is a date." Drake sweeps his arm around my waist. His fingers brush against the side of my stomach, and flutters erupt in the pit of my tummy when he uses his other hand to help boost me up and into the cab.

My butt brushes the edge of the seat, but he expertly deposits me onto it, and instead of releasing me when I'm safely seated, he leans in. The grin stretching across his face is smooth and sexy.

"Plenty of places I can think of lifting you like that."

"You already did," I drawl dryly. "Like my kitchen table."

He pulls back, roaring with laughter, and trails his fingertips across my lower back as he lets me go. Damn those frickin' shivers that cascade across my skin and through my pussy.

"Oh, babe," he says, still laughing, paused at my door. "It's gonna be a long fuckin' day."

"No shit," I mutter, grabbing my seat belt as he shoves the door shut.

A really, really long day.

"Can you tell me where we're goin' yet?"

"Nope." He smacks his lips together as he says it, starting the engine.

"Please."

"No."

"Pleeeeease."

"Noelle," he says with a sigh, but his lips are twitching. "Have I ever let you down?"

I open my mouth only for no sounds to come out. Well, no. He hasn't. In fact, he's always done more than what's been expected of him. I shake my head.

"Then trust me." He flicks his fingers against my thigh. He glances at me, his eyes piercing, and the secret they hold bugs the hell outta me.

Patience is a virtue. Obviously one that wasn't bestowed upon me. Ever.

"Fine." I mutter it and fold my arms like a petulant child.

He laughs—again. I'm pretty sure that, whenever Drake Nash writes his to-do list, he writes *Fuck with Noelle* at the top in big, black, capital letters. And adds a fucking smiley face after it, too.

"Nice weather," he comments, still smiling from his laughter.

"If you like your weather hot and humid."

"We live in Texas. What other kind of weather is there?"

"Storms…"

"Which are still hot and humid."

"Then I like my hot-and-humid weather with a dash of lightning and a sprinkling of rain." I click my tongue. "And asking about the weather, really? What are you, British?"

"It's a conversation starter."

"No. What's your favorite movie? Or beer? Or animal? Or cupcake? Those are conversation starters. The weather is that awkward conversation you have when you're forced to use the counter in the bank because the ATM is out of order."

His eyes flick my way. "You go to the counter?"

"Don't be ridiculous. I hate people. I go to another ATM."

"You hate people but work as a private investigator?"

I shift in the seat so I'm facing him. "My job is the reason I hate people. Do you know how many cheating spouses we found last month? Twenty-three. Twenty-three!"

"Okay, okay. Let's talk about your acceptable conversation starters instead. What's your favorite movie?"

"What's yours?" I shoot back, grinning.

"*Goldfinger.*"

I want to say that my heart doesn't stutter, but it does. Totally. Like a great, big freaking cough, actually. Possibly a full-blown choking fit.

How is my favorite movie his favorite movie?

"Noelle? Favorite movie."

"You stole my answer," I huff. "So I'm going with *Ten Things I Hate About You.*"

He turns off the highway, and his rich laugh fills the truck. "Because I didn't see that coming."

"Don't flatter yourself, Detective. My list for you is way longer than ten."

He pulls up in a parking lot and rests his arm across the top of the steering wheel, turning to me. "I'm not sure how I'd cope if you actually liked several things about me."

Oh, I do. Your eyes. Your arms. Your butt. Your cock.

His eyebrows slowly go up, and his lips form a smirk. The pure amusement etching its way across his features has blood rushing to my cheeks.

"I said that out loud, didn't I?"

He nods. Smugly.

"Well, this date was great, but I'll be catching the bus home. Like, now. Thanks." I unclip my seat belt and go to open my door when his opens. I've barely pushed mine away when he appears in the space and leans into the truck, that smirk still curved on his lips.

"For equality's sake, I happen to be very fond of four parts of you. Your mouth—as long as it's kissing and not talkin', that is—your tits, your ass, and your pussy. Now, we're even, and the only ride you'll be catching is one with me, so get your extremely hot ass out of the truck and do as you're told for once."

I snort. "You do realize who you're talkin' to, don't you? The day I do as I'm told is the day I'm rendered incapable of doing my own thing."

"I keep handcuffs in my truck when I'm off-duty. Don't tempt me into using them."

"You've threatened it at least five times. You're all no talk and no damn action, aren't you?" I sniff and jump out, my breasts brushing his chest as my feet hit the floor. "I'm not afraid of a little metal. If you're gonna whip them out and fuck me, get the heck on with it."

"Quite the proposition for the first date," he murmurs, smiling.

"Either you handcuff me or I'll do it to you. But I'll likely attach you to a lamppost or something, so you wanna get on that."

"The lamppost? Will you be against it and naked?"

"Uh, unless said lamppost is in either my house or yours, that'll be a negative."

He wraps his arm around my shoulders and pulls me away from the truck he can close the door. His chest is vibrating from his laughter, and I have to choke back my own because his is so damn infectious.

"Why are we in the middle of a random parking lot?"

"Not random," he says quietly into my ear. He spins me and slaps his hand over my eyes.

"Oh my God. What the hell are you doing?" I grab his hand and try to pry his fingers away from my eyes, but he simply takes me by the wrist and stops me.

"Trust me, remember?" He runs his lips along the curve of my earlobe, and his exhale ghosts across my jaw.

"Fine, but only because I know I can reach my gun."

Another laugh. Jesus. Why is his laugh so fucking perfect? I wish he'd be like laugh-chuckle-snort once in a while. And not even a derogatory snort. One of those great, big freakin' snorts that means you need to blow your nose ten times after.

They aren't attractive at all.

"Where are you taking me?" I ask as he nudges me into a walk.

"If you keep asking, I'm gonna dump your ass by a river and then you'll never know."

"You're such a bastard."

"But you like my cock, so it works."

"Most bastards have nice cocks. It's not exactly a trait exclusive to you, you know."

"I'm offended that you think my cock is *just* nice. Spectacular, amazing, godly—those I can understand. But nice, Noelle? Really?"

"Hey—put that really in front of nice and you've almost got a compliment."

"You're impossible."

"At least I'm trying. Do you know how hard it is for a people-hater to be nice to people?"

"I'm sure you're real traumatized," he drawls. "Stop. Stop, Noelle!"

"Stop what? Talking? Walking? Breathing?"

"Fuck, I'm gonna spank that sass outta you in a minute."

I lean forward, sticking my ass against him, and wriggle my hips. He promptly drops his hand from my eyes, steps back, and smacks his palm across my butt. I gasp, jumping away from him and grabbing my poor butt. Oh my God.

He actually spanked me.

And I liked it.

"I should put a bullet through your foot, you bastard!"

Oh. My. God.

He. Spanked. Me.

He laughs, grabs my hand, and pulls me into him. "I got other places for you to put your bullets, cupcake."

"Like your *balls?*"

He spins me by my shoulders, and I blink a few times before where we are sinks in.

"Holy shit," I breathe. "Are you insane?"

"I'm on a date with you. You don't want me to answer that." He slides his hands down my arms, and strong and certain, he grasps my waist. Then he pulls me back into him. He wraps his arms around my stomach, but I can't breathe, because this isn't your usual date.

This isn't fucking flowers and dinner. It isn't a picnic in the park or a walk on the beach.

This is the fucking shooting range.

"Surprise," he whispers, the word holding so much. Just so much.

"You brought me to the range. For a date," I whisper back. "Holy shit, Drake. Why?"

"Because, if I took you for dinner, I'd have a glass of wine down my shirt within five minutes."

"I'd never be that careless with my wine. Maybe yours, but not mine." I smile, dropping my chin to my chest, because holy crap. All the holy craps and shits and fucks.

"True. But I brought you here because it's your favorite place. And it's legal, unlike your father's backyard range."

My smile becomes a full-fledged grin, and I can't do anything but laugh. "You realize that, the last time we were at a range together, I shot you?"

"I still have the scar, so yeah. But I'm fucked if we're sharin' a booth. You're on your own there, cupcake."

I drag my teeth across my bottom lip. "Probably for the best."

He slowly moves around the side of me, taking my hand. "Let's go. I booked us two booths."

"You can book booths?"

"You can if you're the leading homicide detective who solved the first murder in town in twenty-something years."

"Did you take my credit?"

"Absolutely."

"Dick." I hit his arm, smiling, then stop. Because his eyes are so bright right now. They're so arresting and intense, and his fingers are sliding through mine without an ounce of fear.

No. I lied. I can see the fear. There isn't much, granted. His confidence far outweighs his fear, but there's a spark of it in his eyes. The tiniest amount everyone else would miss. But for me, it mixes with his confidence and arrogance and makes him seem more human. Makes him dangerous.

Beneath his sexy threats and cocky smirks, there's a very real fear simmering. And you know what?

I have the very same fear.

That this date will be the worst in history. That, in a couple of hours, we'll realize we've made a huge mistake. But through it all… If I have to make a giant dating mistake, I want it to be him. 'Cause then I'll know that my mistake was a good one.

Because he's really not that bad.

I take a deep breath as his lips part. He blinks once, and when our eyes meet again, *something* moves between us. I can't put my finger on it, but I don't think I want to.

"Let's go," he says softly.

I nod and let him lead me into the building. The shots ringing out are muffled by the heavy door separating the range and reception areas. We're booked in by the tattooed, bored-looking man behind the counter, handed two sets of ear defenders, and given a flat-toned rundown of the rules.

I think the man needs a cupcake.

Eventually, Mr. Monotone shows us to our booth—not two, like Drake said—and leaves us to it.

"You know, I haven't been here since my sweet sixteenth." Yes, I did have it at the shooting range…followed by cupcakes. Obviously.

"Was that byb choice, or did they ban you?" Drake cuts his eyes to me and pulls his gun off his belt.

"How many times do I have to apologize to you, huh? I followed the rules—you were the one being a dick, and I didn't even mean to shoot you!"

Amusement dances across his face. "Oh, I'm sorry my foot got in the way of your bullet shot at the floor!"

"If you're still that sore about it, why did you bring me here?"

"Because, if you do it again, I can arrest you. I hadn't even graduated from the academy back then."

I lean against the side as he lifts his gun, knocks the safety off, and lifts it higher. He locks his arms into place, and sweet hell. Those weapons are deadly enough without having a gun attached to the ends of them. My eyes flit over his upper arms, pure muscle twitching and dimpling as he pulls the trigger and the shot booms out.

When he's put the gun down, I say, "You weren't a cop then?"

"That year," he answers. "Trent and I were a couple months out of the end."

I frown, but yes. He is right. Trent got his badge between our birthdays.

"Okay, but you could have gotten me arrested," I say.

"Nah." He turns to me, grinning. "Why would I do that? One, it was your birthday, and two, I'd never have lived that down. Whining because a sixteen-year-old girl accidentally shot my foot, and not even dangerously?"

"Another half inch and they would have needed to reattach your toe," I remind him dryly.

"And that woulda been dangerous." He laughs. "It's fuckin' bad enough as it is. I'm never gonna hear the end of it from your brothers."

"But you're their superior."

"But I only have power over Trent, and he's got one helluva right hook I'd rather avoid."

Now, I laugh. True that. Trent's right fist has dished out more than one or two black eyes in the last few years. I guess that's what happens when you insist to your wife that the punching bag stays in the basement and the brand-new artificial Christmas tree she bought last week can go fuck itself.

Fortunately, that's a skill he did teach me. Right before I left for training in Dallas. Something about overly handy college-aged bastards who lose their ability to hear when the word *no* is uttered. I mean, kicking them in the balls works just as well, but the punch straight after was purely for my entertainment.

"You know I have the same right hook, right?" I ask Drake with a coy smile after I take a shot.

"Naturally. I'm almost certain you'll never need to be saved by a man."

"I'm no damsel in distress." I wait as he fires again, hitting the target dead-center.

"Noelle, sweetheart, you're probably the reason damsels get distressed. Your badass gene is unparalleled. Is there anything you are afraid of?"

I smack my lips together. "Spiders."

Drake stops, and as he slowly turns his face to me, he arches one eyebrow in disbelief. "You're afraid of spiders."

"Of course I'm afraid of spiders. Honestly, there is estrogen mixed with my badass gene."

"You're afraid of spiders," he says again, his disbelief even more evident in the way his eyebrow drops and his eyes widen.

"I'm hands-up, jumping-on-the-table, screaming kind of afraid of spiders."

"Please," he mutters. "Please call me if you find one in your house."

"Why? So you can video me brandishing a hairband as a weapon and put it on YouTube?"

"No. Good idea though." He laughs and, with his gun set down, comes to me. He stops right in front of me, and as always, his proximity makes my heart race.

I put my own gun down again and resist the urge to wipe my hands against the skirt of my dress. My tongue flicks across my lips when he softly touches his hand to my chin and tilts my head back.

Our gazes collide. Laughter and satisfaction glitter back at me from the icy-blue abyss that is his eyes. I could get lost in his eyes so easily... It would be so easy to stand and stare at him and forget everything else, even the gunshots happening around us.

"I want you to call me if you have a spider in your house because, yes, I want to see you be scared, but not for my amusement. You're the hardest person I know. You are so...unbreakable, Noelle. For anyone who doesn't know you, *you* are fuckin' terrifyin'. Someone breaks into your house, you go search with a gun. Someone does the same to your office, you go on a warpath and go out for blood. Someone holds a gun in your face, you shoot them first."

He releases my chin only to trail his fingers down my neck to my collarbone then over my shoulder and the thin strap of my dress to my arm. Then lightly, oh so lightly that there's nothing but electrical sparks where his fingertips are brushing my skin, he drops his hand down to mine.

"I want to see you feel fear over somethin' that is so ridiculously small and harmless and far more terrified of you than you are of it because I want, more than anythin', to see the softer side of yourself you rarely let out to play."

I swallow. Hard. But the lump in my throat doesn't go anywhere, so I fight it by taking a deep breath. His words swirl around my mind, and I want to argue, to fight his ridiculous fucking statement, but I can't. Because his ridiculous fucking statement is one hundred percent true.

Damn righteous pain in my backside.

Blood rushes to my cheeks, and I look away from him. It's like the flutters in my stomach have changed to something much more quivery and uneasy. I still want to rebuff his statements. I wanna yell that he's being stupid, because I am totally soft. I cried at a rescue shelter commercial two days ago. I want to remind him that, after I checked my house for the intruder with my gun, I broke down and sobbed uncontrollably. *Into him.*

I know what he's asking. He's asking me to drop my guards for him when, three weeks ago, I could barely stand to be around him. God.

"Fine," I whisper then clear my throat, bringing my eyes back to his. "For this date. I'll be the flouncy, little girly damsel you want me to be, but then, after that, I'm going to pull out my highest stiletto and do unspeakable things to your crown jewels with them."

His smile is slow and sexy and so, so heart-stopping with the way a tiny dimple appears in his cheek and his eyes light up. "Right. You're gonna last another couple of hours without cussing me out, back-talking me, or threatening more bodily harm?"

I open my mouth and then close it again. "You're the one who wants me to be demure."

"For the record, cupcake, I happen to find your feisty side sexy as fuck. And I never said demure. I said it's okay not to be a hardass sometimes and let the men in your life be the men."

"Are you callin' me a man?"

He drops his eyes to my chest, which is hugged by white lace, and lingers there. "Sure. I dream about fucking men with tits as great as yours all the time."

"Aw, I think that was a compliment."

He winks and closes his fingers around my hand. "Come on."

"Where?"

"Right here." With a laugh, he spins me so I'm facing the target and steps behind me. He pushes me forward until I'm where I need to be standing to shoot and moves so close to me that there can't be any space between our bodies.

"What on Earth are you doin'?" I ask, turning my head so I can look at him.

He reaches around me, grabs my gun, then positions his mouth by my ear. "I'm being the man on this date and teaching you how to shoot properly."

"I'm assuming you're going somewhere with this."

"Well, yeah. It doesn't exactly help my masculinity when my date can shoot better than I do." He takes my hand and places it on the handle of my gun. He closes his over mine, his fingers bringing mine up to the trigger.

"You're not using this as a ploy, are you? Like, you're not gonna suddenly drop the gun and shoot me, are you? My boots are expensive."

"Obviously you're worried about your boots. Not a bullet in your foot. Your priorities are real fucked."

"Hey. I'm a woman. My boots are my babies."

"And so are your sandals, and your high heels, and your slippers…"

I take my hand off the gun and elbow him. "Are you saying I have an unhealthy relationship with my shoes?"

"Yes. Fuck, yes." He laughs, and the way his chest vibrates against my back suddenly has me hyperaware of how very close we are.

"Well, look at that. We agree on something." I take the gun again and ignore the intense warmth of his palm over the back of my hand and the way his fingers stroke mine. And the way his body is so hard and toned and so very against me. "This position is incredibly uncomfortable."

He touches his mouth to the back of my head and I feel his smile. "If you think you're uncomfortable…"

"You put us here."

"I wasn't thinkin."

"No, but another part of you is." And good Lord, I am so very tempted to wriggle my butt against him right now.

"Wriggle your ass and I can't promise this bullet will hit the target."

I won't be wriggling my ass. "You're a pain in my ass, Detective." And a literal kinda one if he doesn't get his erection under control.

"Jesus, Noelle," he breathes. "Shut the fuck up and shoot so I can let go of you."

"And if I don't?"

"Kiss your fuckin' cupcake goodbye."

Well, now. That's quite the threat. One I am so not willing to risk.

"Okay, Mr. Instructor. Teach me how to shoot this load. I mean, the gun. The gun."

"Noelle," he growls. He lets gun go and grasps my hips.

My dress bunches under his rough touch, and I inhale sharply at the jolt it sends through me. His warm breath flutters across the back of my neck when he reaches up and moves my hair away. And it gets warmer, and warmer, and warmer, until oh shit, that's not his breath anymore.

His lips, soft and red hot, press against the base of my neck. Bursts of heat shoot right through my body at the very simple touch, and my blood pumps harder and faster until all of me is on fire.

Drake drags his mouth across my skin, peppering tiny kisses between firmer, longer ones. I can't think. At all. There's just his mouth on my skin and his hands on my hips and his erection pressing against me. I can't breathe right. I want to close my eyes and forget everything and savor his touch.

"Pull the trigger," he whispers against the side of my neck. "Now." I do.

Completely uncontrolled by me, my finger pulls and the gun goes off.

The bullet doesn't even hit the rings of the target.

"You're a prize bastard," I breathe, putting my gun down and breaking free from his hold.

He steps toward me, pushing me against the ledge where our guns are, and grips it on either side of my body. "I know," he whispers, dipping his face down to mine.

My mouth goes dry as his eyes drop to my mouth. His hard cock is pressed against my lower stomach, and my breasts are heaving against his chest as I still struggle to control my breathing. The best I can manage right now is short, sharp bursts of air. They don't even qualify as breaths, in all honesty.

They're more like the physical embodiment of my desire right now. And so is the intense throbbing between my legs. Jesus, he could free his cock, slip my panties to the side, and fuck me right here in the middle of the range and I don't even think I'd care at all.

In fact, right now, I'd welcome it.

"We need to leave. Right now," he says gruffly, grabbing his gun and moving off me.

I quickly nod in agreement and grab my own, putting it back into my thigh holster. I take two steps past him, but his fingers clasp my wrist and he pulls me back into him.

"Next time you look at me like that, we won't be walking away from the situation."

"Like—like what?" My voice is as scratchy as my throat feels.

"Like you want me so far inside you we become the same person, 'cause, Noelle—I'm absolutely not afraid to fuck you until you forget that we are different people."

I want to say something cocky. Something that'll throw him off. But I can't. He has me tied up in fucking knots.

"Noted."

Noted. Fucking noted. Is that really the best I have?

"Let's get you your damn cupcake." He lets me go and stalks past me.

I catch him up by the doors. "Just to clarify, by cupcake, you mean an actual cupcake, right?"

With a deviously sexy glint in his eye and his lips tugged into the most confident smirk I've ever seen, he hits me full force with his gaze. "Sweetheart, if I mean I'm going to fuck the hell outta you, I'm gonna say it, not use a cupcake as a euphemism."

"Unless you're going to use cupcake frosting as an added extra."

"I don't even like cupcake frosting that much," he admits, grabbing his door handle. "But shit. Now, I want to handcuff you and lick the frosting off your body."

I blink at him. "That escalated quickly."

"Agreed. So shut up and get in the truck before something else fucking escalates."

chapter FOUR

"OH! Can you stop outside the office?"

Drake flits his eyes to me. "You're gonna work?"

"No. I had a new client come in yesterday and I want to see if she brought the contract and retainer yet. She was supposed to report it to the police."

"Okay, I'm gonna try to keep a level head here, but what the fuck?"

I sigh and summarize my meeting with Natalie. "I told her I needed a police report, because then, if I happen to see the guy stalking her, I can call the cops there and then."

"And you want to ask me about the ex-boyfriend."

I suck my lower lip into my mouth and release it on a smile. "Maybe."

His heavy sigh beats mine, and he makes the turn toward the office. "Fine. Then we're going to Rosie's for cupcakes."

"Rosie's?"

"If you think I'm driving almost an hour to Gigi's while my cock is still semi hard, you can think again."

"Boo. Is this how you normally treat your dates?"

"Don't date."

"You don't date? How do you not date?"

"Cop."

"So was my married father. My married brother is, and my newly-engaged brother is, too. The other, well… He whores, mostly. And I dated while I was a cop."

"Homicide cop," he tries again.

"I'm sorry. I must not know about the part of town where people are dropping likes flies due to murder."

"Not everyone has to date, Noelle." He pulls up outside the office. "I made a choice not to after I left the academy and settled in at home."

"So, you haven't dated for, what, ten years?" I turn in my seat.

"I whored. One or two dates and that was it. I wasn't interested in more."

I can't help but think that this is rather deep for a first date. "So, what? You're gonna take me on one more date, pin me against a kitchen counter again, then that's it? You won't be interested in more?"

"Believe me, if there were any way I could not want more, I'd take it."

"What on Earth does that mean?"

"It means that, if I want more with anyone, it's you."

"If? How very reassuring." I unclip my seat belt and, with my hand on the door, look at him. "Well, when you decide, Drake, be sure to let me know what you actually want." I shove the door open.

Fuck him. I blew off a whole day of work for this goddamn date and for what? A possibility of something more from a guy who admits on said date that he's always shied away from more?

How about he shies away and kisses my ass as he goes?

His car door opens and closes with a slam, but I'll be fucked if I'm gonna turn back and listen to him. If he wants more? If? If? I'm not a fucking chocolate cake that's kind of sickly after a slice or two. I'm a goddamn human being, and either you want more of a relationship with somebody or you don't.

Ironic considering that, three hours ago, I didn't know what I wanted. And now that possibility is an if from him, I'm pretty sure I'm erring on the side of wanting him.

Because fucking obviously.

"Fuck me," Drake calls. "Women. Y'all are always overreactin' over somethin'."

"Oh, no!" I turn on my heel, my foot actually stomping on the ground as I face him, and storm toward him. "Women overreact? Are you for real? You bug the ever-lovin' shit outta me for two weeks about this date. Then you tell me on the damn date that you don't do more than two dates because you're a homicide cop in a town with two murders in twenty years? *Baciare il mio cazzo—*"

He yanks my body against his with one tug of my wrist, and before I can finish telling him to kiss my fucking ass, he slams his mouth against mine. Because I'm completely silenced and trapped against his firm body, my anger has nowhere to go except directly into him. Even as he fists my hair and bites my lower lip, making me gasp, I'm still real fucking pissed with him.

The anger fuels the kiss.

It's fast and furious. A total war of lips and teeth and tongue.

I grab his shirt too tightly, and he tugs my hair too harshly. I nip his lip; he bites mine harder.

It's the hottest fucking thing. Ever.

And in the middle of my work parking lot.

The fucks I give total zero.

"Women," he mutters against my tender lips. "Always overreactin.'"

"I swear to God—"

"I want more with you," he growls. "Even if it means we threaten to kill each other ten times a day and argue fifty. That's your definition of love. Hate so passionate it's real and tangible. And sweet shit, Noelle, I hate the fuck outta you more often than I think I even like you."

"Feeling's mutual, asshole."

"Think about it. I don't want a pushover. I want someone who'll challenge me on something as bullshit as how many sugars go in a coffee."

"Two."

"Three."

"Savage."

"Says you."

"This is so dumb."

Drake laughs, his hold on my hair changing from rough to gentle as he threads his fingers through it. My blood is still pounding, my chest still heaving, and my thoughts are so erratic that not even my heart can't keep up.

"Incredibly dumb," he agrees, his mouth hovering over mine. "Seriously. Think about it. I don't want a fuckin' damsel in distress. I want you."

I run my teeth over my bottom lip and release it quickly. "Fine. I'll think about it. More. As long as you answer all my questions about the stalker boyfriend."

He clicks his tongue. "Always a catch, ain't there?"

"Yep, and I'm only up to number three, so you've got another nineteen until catch twenty-two."

"Your attitude stinks."

I raise an eyebrow. "Like a field full of roses." I grin and extract myself from his arms. "Sweet and tempting—"

"And hiding a shit-ton of thorns."

"Oh, honey, I couldn't hide you even if I tried."

He pauses, grimaces, and punches the air. "Got nothin'."

"Yes!" I laugh, skipping toward the front door. "This is going down as one of my proudest moments: making you lost for words."

His grimace becomes a half smile right before I turn and push the door open. Our eyes connect briefly before my name is screamed by my apparently very angry receptionist.

"You aren't supposed to be here!"

"Oh, hush. Did Natalie bring in the contract and report?"

"The retainer check is locked in your desk." Bek steps out of the kitchen with a coffee mug in hand. "Are you here in the middle of your date?" She glances over my shoulder. "Please tell me this isn't the middle of your date."

Drake sidesteps past me, his hands up. "We made it out of the range without her shootin' me. I wasn't gonna risk it."

I whack his arm with the contract Grecia handed me. Son of a bitch. He disappears into the kitchen, laughing, and I pull the police report out of the envelope.

"So." Bek grins, sidling up with me with an innocent look over her face. Except her grin, of course. That's as devilish as her thoughts will be. "The range, huh?"

"Yep." I smack my lips together and flick through the report. Devin took it. Good.

"Kissing?"

"Outside," Grecia answers, filing the nail on her ring finger. "It was like watchin' a soap opera. She stormed off all pissed and he grabbed her and, oh." She finishes on a sigh.

I snap my fingers. "Hello? My life isn't a romance novel. There are too many guns and cheating fuckers for that. Go back to your book."

Grecia rolls her eyes.

"So, are you a thing now?" Bek perches on the edge of Grecia's desk.

"A thing? What is a thing?"

"Don't be a bitch. Are you seeing each other?"

"Only when we're in immediate proximity."

"Oh my God!"

"Jesus, Bek! It was one damn date!" I sigh, holding the papers up. "One. Date. Not a fucking marriage proposal."

"But are you a thing? Will there be a second date? Have you even finished the first?"

"I don't know, I don't know, and no, he owes me a cupcake."

"Obviously," she mutters. "You know, I don't even care if you're a thing. I'm calling you Droelle anyway."

I freeze. "Did you just give us a ship name?"

"Well, yeah. You're like Shamy, except he's not as mantis-y as Sheldon, and you're way hotter than Amy."

"You gave us a ship name."

"Who did what?" Drake walks out of the kitchen with a coffee in a takeout cup.

"Did you make a coffee in my kitchen and not get me one?" I ask him, staring between him and the offending cup.

"I gave you a ship name," Bek says. "You're now known as Droelle."

"Aw, hell." I look at my best friend. "Droelle is like fetch. Never gonna happen!"

Drake frowns. "The name or the relationship?"

"Put me on the spot, why don't you?"

"I don't know the answer, either," he points out, tilting the cup my way.

I grab it and sip. Holy shit, hot. Hot. Hot.

"Droelle is so gonna happen," Bek insists, getting up. "I might put it on a T-shirt."

"Why would you do that? What's wrong with you? Holy shit, I need a cupcake before my sugar-deprived brain shrivels up," I moan, walking toward the door.

"I ship Droelle!" Bek yells as I stomp through it, Drake's coffee still tight in my hand.

"I don't blame her," Drake adds. "Droelle is one of the better ship names. Could be Kimye."

"How do you even know anything about that?" I ask, stopping at his truck. "You know—no. I know the answer. The same way my brothers do, presumably."

His answering grin is infectious and reminiscent of the teenage Drake I find myself remembering. So, by the time I was thirteen, he was leaving Holly Woods to begin his cop training, but he was sweet then. The whole time. Just not to me. Mind you, I wasn't exactly sugar sweet to him, either.

I guess, though, back then, he was simply my older brother's mean friend who played football and soccer and baseball with him.

Insanity is being on a date with a man you've hated as long as you can remember and hoping that there will be a second, despite your reservations.

Our drive to Rosie's is quick, and I wait in the car while he gets out and enters the café. I know. I'm letting him buy me my cupcake. He'll probably come out with a joke sperm-flavored one or something, one he's planned out specifically. Or maybe he'll try...

And bring me one with bright-yellow frosting and a chewy lemon candy on the top. Complete with chocolate sprinkles.

It has to be hot in this car, because I think I'm melting.

"I'm impressed," I admit, taking the box from him.

Next to my lemon one is a triple-chocolate torte one, the rich frosting swirled into a perfect point, white chocolate chips buried within the dark depths of gooey chocolate.

Looks like we're cutting the cupcakes in half.

"Eyes off my cupcake," he demands, starting the engine again. "If you want a triple torte one, you should start hiding those in your desk drawer instead of lemon ones."

I open my mouth then... Fuck him. "I really hate it when you get stuff right, you know that?"

"I know, sweetheart. It's why I make a point of being right."

"Your house is closer to Rosie's," I point out, putting the coffee in the center console.

"I know, but since you don't have your car and there's cupcake frosting, I might never let you leave."

That chocolate frosting being dotted down my stomach to my pussy with his tongue licking it all up doesn't sound half bad. Neither does being stuck in that situation.

"Noelle."

That sharp, husky tone—it's not even a threat or a warning. It's a promise, pure and simple. When he says my name in way so controlled, with so much growly depth to it, I know I'm ten seconds from trouble.

"Sorry." I look out the window so there's no way he can tell what I'm thinking. Or so I hope. The man has a damn sexual thought radar.

He pulls up behind my car in my driveway, and I hand him the cupcakes without looking. Hugging the envelope tight to my chest, I grab my purse and fish my keys out.

Naturally, they're tucked between the laces of my Chucks.

"Ugh. Hold that." I shove the envelope at Drake and crouch down, extracting the sneaker from my purse and wrestling with the keys until they're free to the tune of his laughter. "Bite me," I snap back at him, shoving the key into the lock and turning it. I move to disable the alarm, but the absence of any lights on the box makes me freeze.

"You didn't set it," Drake breathes into my ear.

"Thank you, Sherlock." I walk through the hall and drop my purse on the coffee table, reaching for the remote to turn the TV on at the same time.

Drake shuts the door as I reach down to pull my boots off and change the channel. I lose my balance and fall sideways onto the sofa, but hey, my boot is off, and I'm already sitting down to tug the second off.

Drake shakes his head, sitting down. The cupcakes end up on the table next to my purse, and I reach forward to open them when he pulls the contract and report from the envelope.

"Here." He hands me the contract and keeps the report for himself.

I snort and snatch the report from him. "Uh, my case. You work homicide. This is Devin's."

He blows out a long, frustrated breath. "Fine. Then why am I here?"

"Because you got me a cupcake and you're useful?" I raise my eyebrows. "Now, hush up a second."

I tuck my legs beneath my butt and open the report. For the most part, it's exactly what Natalie told me in the office, just more detailed. Nothing I didn't already get from her though. I guessed that every threatening message had something to do with hurting her, but several messages have threatened sexual things. Not necessarily rape… Something about a tape, but Natalie insists in the interview that she has no idea what her stalker is talking about.

"This." I lean toward Drake, my finger at the start of the paragraph. "If the stalker is her ex, do you think it's a secret sex tape?"

His brow furrows as he reads it over. "How long were they together?"

"It was long term. She says she doesn't know."

His forehead wrinkles further. "Isn't that a female thing—dates and shit?"

I look at him and shrug. "What's today?"

"No idea."

"So it's entirely plausible that she doesn't know the exact date their relationship started—so you could argue that her boyfriend could have filmed in secret."

"Absolutely. Just because he's only stalking her now doesn't mean he wasn't obsessed with her before."

"I suppose."

Most obsessive tendencies come from a personal relationship. Stalkers this thorough are rarely total strangers. You have to know the other person's routine, when they'll be in certain places, eating, drinking—hell, even peeing. Without being presumptuous, I think the evidence suggests that it's totally her ex-boyfriend.

After all, if anyone knows her routine, he does.

"What do you know about a Nicholas Lucas?"

"That his name is fucking stupid because it's ass-ass?"

"As-as," I shoot back. "Don't be a dick. This is a working date."

"Remind me never to date another P.I."

"You say that with the inflection of someone never intending to date again."

"Maybe I'm not."

"This isn't on topic!" I shove the report at him. "I know that Devin won't give me the police report, and since he has no kids, I can't bribe him, so I'm playin' on your good character for information."

He cuts his eyes to me, but he grabs the report and focuses on it. His eyes flit over the numerous lines, and I know that, by the end of the paragraph, he's completely enraptured by the interview.

I guess I'll eat my cupcake, then.

I pull the sugary, soft goodness toward me and scoop the lemon candy through the frosting. Dropping it into my mouth, I focus back on Drake. He's a page further, and he's a much slower reader than I am. Maybe it's because he's the kind of guy who needs to know every single detail, whereas I'm the woman who skims it and makes her own decisions?

Hmmm. I dip my pinkie finger into the frosting and suck it off as his eyes continue to scour the report. Never once does he look up at me. Nope. One hundred percent focused on the papers in front of him—and for the first time, I see him in cop mode.

Not detective-my-career-depends-on-this mode. Cop mode.

The emotion across his face—that hardness, that solid determinedness—is nothing other than a desire to get to the bottom of a mystery.

If real life were Clue, he'd be the guy rolling the die every time, the conclusion written on the card tucked into his pocket.

"Not the boyfriend," he mutters, dropping the report back on the cushion between us.

"Really? You think that?"

"Do I think he's watchin' her? Sure. They just broke up. Guy's cut up. Wants to see if she is."

"You sound like you know what you're talking about."

He grunts. "Can I finish?"

"Sure," I half lie, 'cause his last statement was way too bitter for a guy who dates twice, fucks, then says goodbye.

Drake stands, tucks his hands in his pockets, and walks toward my window. "Sounds like he got obsessive during the relationship because *she* was unfaithful. And that obsessiveness… It carried over. Made him into who he is today. Into the kind of guy who would hurt the fuck outta her in revenge."

The paper crinkles as I grasp the report and set it on top of my contract. Old feelings rush through me, and it doesn't matter in the slightest that we've dated once. What matters is the fact that the elephant in the room, the one standing between us, is so decorated with the past and dreams and realities and imaginary happenings. And, God, it stands between us like a steel wall, because for all of our combined history, neither of us knows a thing about the time when I wasn't in Holly Woods.

"I think…" I pause, staring at my fireplace directly in front of me. "I think we're done today."

I hear his breath from here, and it takes every bit of strength in my body not to look at him.

"I agree," he says quietly. He shoves his hands in his pockets and walks to the door.

I focus on the almost-silent screen of the TV, because midafternoon TV is shit—let's be honest.

My front door opens.

I close my eyes.

"I'll e-mail you a full report on Nicholas Lucas," Drake says—loud yet soft, understanding in every sense. "If you're goin' up against a guy who got away with murder, you need to know."

I jump up, but he slams my door at the same time my feet hit the floor.

And I don't know what to consider first—that my client's stalker is an apparent murderer walking free, or that Drake walked out on our date, leaving his cupcake sitting on my coffee table.

I look at the dark-brown goodness, temptation filling me, almost beating down the deflated sadness from him leaving. But it feels… wrong to even consider touching that cake.

So I grab the stapled-together papers, my lemon cupcake, and go upstairs to my room, despite it being three in the afternoon.

Who the hell cares?

chapter FIVE

Y phone buzzes with the incoming text messages. In my half-asleep state, I pull it from the nightstand and open the blinking rectangle stretching across the screen.

Mayor chats shit at three, Bek texts.

As opposed to any other time? I reply.

Bless her for thinking the mayor doesn't chat shit at any other time.

Shut up. Supposed to be a debate with the guy going against him.

Alistair Harvey?

Sure. Him.

Ugh. The lack of fucks I have to give about this mayoral campaign are severely dismal. As in they amount to a big, fat fucking zero.

Mayor McDougall is the most corrupt person I've ever met in my life. Seriously—the man paid his way out of a cheating allegation twenty years ago, and I wouldn't be surprised if he's done the same since. Fact is, the good mayor of Holly Woods has more fucking fireworks up his ass than the United States of America set off on Independence Day. If only he'd light half of them...

He's been the mayor of Holly Woods for as long as I can remember. I think he even sat in the front row at my baptism way back when. He's like the political Simon Cowell. He changes his mind so often that the whole town has whiplash from his indecision. Like those flowers he approved for the local park? Yeah. Well, we can safely say he *forgot* to plant the damn bulbs.

So listening to him spout his total crap at a campaign speech? Excuse me if I don't sing his biblical praises at the top of my lungs. Hell, y'all would be lucky if I don't sing his hellish ignorance from my own level of hell.

Six a.m. is far too early to deal with the mayor and his stupid claims. I tug on workout clothes and make my way to the spare room, where my elliptical is sitting alongside my treadmill. I hesitate in front of the treadmill for a second before plugging my phone into the jack, hitting the workout playlist on Spotify, and jumping on the bitch treadmill.

We've never gotten along, but you know. Desperate love handles call for desperate early runs and all that.

My feet pound against the moving belt, and I breathe with each step. My head is bursting with pain, but that's simply the result of one more glass of wine than was called for last night. Actually, given the way my date ended, it wasn't nearly enough.

My phone rings, slicing through the music, and I tap the answer button. "Hello?"

"Noelle," Brody, my younger brother, says. "Are you going to the debate today?"

"I don't want to, but I'm assumin' this call is because Dad is gonna make us all."

"Yep. And he said your ass better be on the side of the mayor's."

"My ass might be, but my vote is on the other side."

"Obviously, it is. Do you need a ride? I can get you if you want."

Clearly, someone heard about my date.

"Brodes, I can drive."

"Are you sure?"

The protective tone of his voice makes me fumble. Damn my brother—actually, damn them all. They're pretty much the only guys I can't say no to when they go all sibling on me.

"All right," I acquiesce. "I'll take the ride."

"Of course you are. I was going to stop by anyway."

"Obviously." I smile.

"You sound out of breath. Did I interrupt some woman time?"

"Some woman time? You're gross. No. I'm running."

He pauses. "You're running? As in, actual running?"

"Yes." I grab my water bottle. "Is that all? You're killing my buzz here."

"Fine. I'll see you later."

"Bye." I hang up and hit the play button. The music starts back up, and I continue my run to a much better sound than my brother being equal parts prying and protective.

My family's finding out about the end to that date is the last thing I wanted. Hell, I still don't want it. I can imagine the private chat before Brody called this morning. Ugh—I don't even want to do this today. I want to take my moment to be my inner teenage girl and mope.

Wait. I did that into a bottle of wine last night.

Fact is, my date with Drake did the one thing I knew it would. It confirmed to me that there's more to him than the arrogant, argumentative, sexy son of a bitch I know. There's a fun side and that side is intriguing. I want to delve deeper into it, tear apart the layers that are Drake, and hang there a while. That's it. That simple.

Or it was until he got all bitter. Clearly, the good has himself some relationship hang-ups—and clear commitment issues—and that's bullshit to me. If he's been cheated on, well, newsflash, so have I, and you don't see me running toward the hills to avoid discussing it.

My ex was an unfaithful fuckhead who liked to dip his cock into many different pools. I could be a rare creature, because after the shock wore off, I didn't become an insecure wall-flower.

I reasoned that he wasn't good enough for my special brand of awesome in the first place.

And hey, true or not, it worked.

I block Drake from my mind and focus fully on the run. Except, now, my motivation has gone—and I've apparently been running for the last thirty minutes.

Whatever. That's some two hundred calories. That's a cupcake. In my dreams, at least.

With a heavy sigh, I set the treadmill to stop and hop off when it's slowed enough. The belt moves for another few seconds while I take my phone and water bottle and head into my bedroom. The elliptical stares at me through the wall with its imaginary eyes, so I give it the finger.

The last time I got on that thing I couldn't walk for an hour afterward. Leg-killing bitch.

After a quick shower, I tie the towel around me and squeeze every last drop of water out of my hair. I run a brush through it and grab my hairdryer. I'm approximately halfway through my long-ass necessary blow-dry when the machine sparks and I drop it. It stops blowing as soon as it hits the floor.

"Shit." I pick it up and flick the switch. Nothing. "Double shit." I pull the plug from the wall and put it back in, moving the switch again. Still nothing. "Triple shit with sprinkles." I drop it back on the floor carelessly, because, hey, it doesn't care that I now have to wrangle my half-damp hair into submission in the form of a bun or some crap.

At least my bangs are dry.

My phone rings on the bed, and in my naked state—screw it. I'm ignoring it. If it's important, there's a thing called voicemail.

I rifle in my drawers for underwear, then throw them on the bed before pulling out a royal blue pencil skirt and white blouse. I guess, if I'm going to this dumbass debate, I should try the professional look again this week.

I'm going to put shorts and a tank in my purse.

My phone rings again, and I clasp my bra, humming to myself. Panties next. Then my blouse. I'm doing up the final button when my phone rings for a third time.

I guess that's important.

I lean over, and the most recent number added is on the screen beneath the caller's name: Natalie.

Why is she calling me this early?

"Noelle," I answer the phone. "What's wrong?"

"Oh my God, finally," she says quickly. "I got another letter. This time through the mail. I'm scared, Noelle. They're threatening to hurt me, and my shed was broken into. There are chips on my back porch window and a couple of bricks beneath it. I think they left the note after!"

"Windows aren't as easy to break as everyone thinks." I tuck my phone between my shoulder and my ear and grab my skirt. "Are you still at home?"

"Yes."

"With the letter?"

"Yes."

"Called the police?"

"No."

"I'm calling Devin on my way over. Don't leave your house."

"But I have an important appointment!"

"If it's more important than your life, keep it. If not, reschedule." I tuck my blouse in and buckle the small belt as silence hovers for a moment.

"I'll be here," she finally says. "Please make sure he isn't in uniform."

"I don't think the Holly Woods police department owns a uniform past rookie rank, hon. You're good." I run downstairs, slip my feet into some black Jimmy Choo heels, grab my purse, and open my door. "I'm getting in my car now. I'll only be a few minutes. Make sure your doors are locked and you have something that can be used as a weapon if they're still there, okay?"

"I have a pan," she whispers.

"As good as anything," I reason. "I'll see you in a minute." I hang up and double back quickly to set my alarm. Once it's done, I lock the front door and get into my car, already dialing my brother's number.

"What?" Devin groans.

I pull out of the driveway. "Mornin' to you, too, grumpy-ass."

"Noelle, what the fuck? It's not even eight."

"I know, but someone broke into Natalie Owens's shed, tried to break into her house, and left a note."

"Why can't these assholes operate during normal hours? And why the fuck can't you call someone on duty?"

I glance at the clock. "'Cause I'm pretty sure you start in thirty minutes away, so it's probably a good thing I'm draggin' your ass outta bed."

"Shut the hell up." There's a rustling noise. "Shit! Amelia must have turned the alarm off 'cause she's off today. Fuck!"

"You're welcome." I snort. "And since I'm not on hands-free, I'll see you in ten minutes at Natalie's house."

Another shout of, "Fuck!" comes through right as I hang up.

My brothers. I swear. They're all pains in the asses—all I need is for Trent to step up and get under my feet and they have a full house in the Bond family sibling bingo.

I make the few turns to Natalie's house and drive slowly down her street. I guess that one of the perks of living in a place like Holly Woods is that you know where everyone lives, even if you haven't spoken to them for years. The perk of my job is the refresher when they fill my forms out.

Her street is quaint and very quiet—not the type of place you'd expect a stalker to roam or a break-in to be attempted. From the newly cut lawns to the perfectly trimmed hedges and houses with perfectly painted exteriors, it's the picture-perfect, stereotypical American street. But hey.

Beautiful lies hide ugly truths.

I turn into Natalie's driveway and park my little Audi behind her suave BMW. Her face appears in the window to the door as I get out of my car, purse in hand.

Shit. I left her file on my nightstand.

Still, I lock my car and go to her front door. She opens it before my feet have touched the steps leading up to it, and I offer her a wary smile.

"Anything?"

"No. I don't think they hung around after posting the note."

"Do you have it?"

She nods. "On the coffee table." She steps aside to let me in.

Although my focus is on the room to my right, which is clearly her living area, I can't help but glance around her house. Vintage-style, very rustic and full of charm. Cracked and scuffed photo frames adorn the walls of her spacious entry hall, and I recognize the people in the photos as her family and closest friends. Lena is even in a few, along with Mallory, and my stomach twists.

Lena, the woman I found poisoned and tortured to death not two months ago, and Mallory, her best friend and possibly the only person she ever really trusted in this world.

I swallow back the hard hit of emotion and walk through into the living room, which is much the same style. The same frames are hung on the walls, and even her furniture is very chaise-longue style with wooden legs. Her house screams pure class, and this girl either got lucky at yard sales or she has more money than most people in this town.

Oddly, I want to side with both options.

The note is lying on the coffee table, like she said, and I bend over to look at it. Aside from finger-sized creases in the corners, the note is perfectly crisp. There aren't even fold lines. And it's handwritten. The writing is messy but cursive, like the author really tried to neaten up their letters but went all kindergarten regardless.

Two sharp knocks at the door startle me, and Natalie screams, her hands going to her mouth. I get up and go to the window. Upon recognizing Devin's car, I nod to her that it's okay. Natalie opens the door, albeit hesitantly, and my brother walks through.

With his dark hair the exact shade of mine messy in an I-just-woke-up-in-severe-need-of-a-haircut style, cleanly shaved jaw, and his deep-brown eyes a smidgen darker than mine, my brother literally looks like he's walked off America's Next Top Model.

"That the note?" he asks gruffly, immediately going into cop mode.

"Yep."

He knows better than to ask me if I've touched it, as evidenced by his quick pull of gloves from his pocket. "I have forensics on their way."

"Forensics?" Natalie's bottom lip wobbles.

"Sorry, Miss Owens. I can't ask them to come unmarked." Devin lifts the note and holds it directly in his eye line. "When did you find this?"

"I called Noelle ten minutes ago, so maybe twenty minutes ago?"

"You hear anythin' before?" He puts the letter back down and walks through the door.

I follow him, cupping Natalie's elbow to encourage her to, too.

"The bricks, the shed…?" he says.

"No. I-I've been having trouble sleeping for a few weeks. My doctor prescribed me sleeping pills, and this is why I didn't know." Natalie sucks one of her cheeks in and crosses her arms tight. Her position screams defensiveness and defiance—but if she had any information, why would she hide it? Her fear was, and is, real.

"Okay." Devin unlocks the back door with the key sitting steadily in the hole.

I scoot past Natalie to follow him out. She's right. The window is chipped in two or three places. There's even a crack spreading out from one of them, but when I scrape my nail down the inside of the window, the surface is smooth. It doesn't go right through the glass.

Devin is questioning Natalie over by the shed. The door-less shed, because there's a hinge lying on the ground next to the wooden plank that is, or was, the door. Apparently, our would-be burglar thought taking hinges off would be easier than breaking the padlock—which is still attached to the door.

And why is there even a padlock there? Who locks sheds in Holly Woods?

Taking care to step around the bricks on the floor, I lean against the wall of the house, focused on my brother and Natalie. Devin stops to take a call, and a few seconds later, I'm joined by two forensics guys and a couple of other officers.

"Noelle," Officer Jake Dylan acknowledges me.

"Officer." I offer him a smile before moving out of their way.

"What do you make of this?" he asks, catching me before I can disappear.

"Someone tried to break into her house and left her a threatening note," I reply carefully. "I make that someone has a real issue with Miss Owens. Simple."

I'm not doing your work for you, Jake Dylan. Figure it out yourself.

This time, I move a little quicker to escape him. Devin is pointing toward the house and telling two other officers what to do, and I smile. I love seeing my brothers in control, doing what they do best… Unless I'm the one they're telling what to do.

Makes me think that Nonno would be real proud of his boys if he could see them now.

When the two officers disappear, I hover back a little more. Natalie's complexion has faded to a greyish tinge, and she has one arm wrapped around the top of her stomach. She looks like she's about to pass out, and a sliver of worry worms through me.

"Natalie?" I ask quietly when there's a break in the conversation. "Are you okay? You don't look too good."

She looks at me, her lips twitching unreassuringly. "I think the adrenaline has worn off. It's sinking in."

I know from experience that this is the worst feeling. I gently touch her arm and glance at my brother, and he nods.

"Come on," I tell her. "Let's get you inside to sit down. I'll make you a hot drink while you calm down."

Without a word, she lets me lead her back to the house and into her kitchen. She sits at the breakfast bar. I'd prefer the table, but hey, if she faints and gets a concussion, at least she'd be focused on that instead, right?

I fill the kettle on the stove and boil the water. By the time it screeches that it's done, I've managed to locate green tea and decaf coffee.

Who in their right mind drinks decaf coffee? Even when my sister-in-law was pregnant, she had one cup of weak caffeinated coffee a day. Her argument was that she put so much milk in it that it turned into a coffee milkshake, so the caffeine was vetoed. And hell, no one was going to go up against her. She was pregnant, and the Bonds aren't that stupid.

I hand Natalie her green tea. "You'll feel better after a hot drink. I promise."

She nods slowly and wraps her trembling hands around the mug. She's hunched in on herself, and she briefly looks up to meet my gaze. "Didn't you get broken into not long ago?"

"Too many times," I mutter. "It's awful."

"What did you do when you...you know. Found out someone had broken in?"

Grimacing, I reply, "Searched my house with my gun out."

She blinks. "Seriously? You didn't freak out?"

"Well, sure." I sip my coffee. Ugh. Yuck. "Even though my stuff was all over the place, it didn't sink in until after the police had left. I was mostly pissed at someone breaking in, but when that wore off, it was a total 'shit, someone broke into my house' moment, and I went crazy. I still don't feel totally safe in my house now and I have an alarm. It's hard knowing someone's been in your house without your permission."

Natalie shudders. "I'd be a total mess if they'd gotten in. Look at me now—I'm bordering on an anxiety attack from a brick at my window."

And the note. But I won't be mentioning that right now.

"Do you have an alarm system?" I ask.

She shakes her head. "I've been meaning to get one for a couple of weeks now, but something always got in the way of me making the call. I guess I have to do it now."

"I have the card for the company who did mine in the car. The cops rushed it through, so I'll speak to Devin later when I see him again since he's real busy out there right now, and I'll get him to contact them for you. They'll forward you the bill, but they'll have it done tomorrow."

"Really? That would be amazing." A little tension leaves her shoulders.

"Really." I flick my eyes toward the clock on the stove. "I have to go to the office now, but I'll write this up and see if I can find anything about your ex's location last night." I pat her hand. "We'll get this figured out. Don't worry."

"I know. I trust you."

I put the phone down and drop my head to my desk. Sweet Jesus. Nick Lucas, Natalie's ex, is the most elusive man in Texas right now.

Two hours of phone calls to a ridiculous number of people has wielded absolutely no information about his whereabouts of last night, and his phone rolls straight over to voicemail. These calls are after a staff meeting, a phone call from Dad confirming that he'll see me at three, signing off on a new contract for Mike, a random drop-by from my decorator about his inability to get the shade of pink I picked for the kitchen, an interview with an eighteen-year-old high-school almost-graduate for Marshall's job, and a text exchange with Devin about Natalie and her alarm system.

At least Bek brought me a cupcake at lunchtime. Which I haven't had a chance to eat, because well, I used the thirty-second break I had earlier to pee and yell desperately for a coffee.

I say yell. I begged. Unashamedly.

I sit back up and hit the space bar on my laptop to wake it up. I add to my spreadsheet of calls Bek insisted I make, and I hit save, then print. I close the computer once I have the list in my hand and tuck it into my file marked *Owens, N.*

The clock reads two thirty.

"Oh, someone give me a break," I mutter to myself, standing and heading for the bathroom.

I look like a bird made its home in my hair and a raccoon adopted me.

I grab the wet wipes from the cupboard and pull my spare makeup down, too. And here everyone laughed at me for keeping makeup at the office. My father would kill me if I turned up this afternoon looking anything less than one hundred percent professional, and not because he's harsh, but because the mayor is, unfortunately, a lifelong friend, and it's expected.

Put it this way: If my brothers aren't all in ties and button-down shirts, Dad will pull his spare sets out of his trunk and force them to get changed. Yes, this has happened, and I have it on video.

Ten minutes later, I have a fresh face of makeup that makes me look somewhat human. If my stomach could stop growling, too. That would be even better.

I grab the cupcake from my desk, and I'm about to pull the wrapper off when Brody walks into my office.

"What are you doin'? We gotta go. Now."

I groan. "I'm hungry!"

"It's just past lunch!"

"Which I didn't get because I've been workin' all day," I argue, taking my purse from the back of my desk. I throw it over my shoulder and pick my phone up. "So, long story short, I'm eatin' it in your car."

He pauses for a moment as we go downstairs. "Only because I'm in a squad car."

"Obviously."

"And you're vacuuming your crumbs after."

"In another life," I reply with a grin shot over my shoulder. "That's why y'all hire cleaners."

"Hours cut," he grumbles, opening the car. "Something about cuts the mayor wanted. Now, we have to clean up ourselves."

"Oh, you poor little babies." I snort as I get in. "Imagine having to clean up after yourself like actual adults! How horrifying for you."

"Hey, you have a cleaner."

"Who comes in once a week. Other than that, I keep a full set of cleaning equipment in the cupboard in the basement. We clean our own offices, thank you."

Okay, so I think Grecia does Mike's sometimes, but as long as it's tidy, I don't care if he's offering sexual favors in return for her vacuuming a couple of times a week.

"You wanna come clean my office? Charlotte's on my back because she had to empty my trash twice in three days."

"Charlotte, huh?" I take a bite of my cupcake as the police receptionist is brought up.

"Noelle, she's been crushin' on me for three years. If I were interested, I'd have fucked her already."

"Straight to the point as always."

He laughs and pulls up outside the Oleander hotel where the… whatever-the-hell kinda boring hour this is gonna be…is.

"You got crumbs on my seat," he grumbles when I get up.

"Apparently, you should take Charlotte up on her crush, 'cause you sound like you need to get laid." I bend over to brush the crumbs off. Most go outside the car, thankfully.

"Dad's gonna kill you if you go in there stuffing your face with cake."

"And I'm gonna kill someone if I don't get some food in my belly. I'm hangry right now."

"Hangry?"

"Hungry and angry."

"There's a ship name for that?"

I raise my eyebrows. "It's a very real thing. I'm hungry and angry, so I'm hangry. Really hangry."

"You're so fuckin' weird."

"This, from you."

"Do you two ever stop fightin'?" Dad interrupts us at the door of the hotel. "Noelle, why are you eating?"

"Because I haven't eaten a damn thing all day."

"She's hangry," Brody inputs.

"What's hangry?" Dad looks between us.

"Can't a girl eat her cupcake in peace?"

"Noella!"

"Oh, fuck it."

Nonna ambles up behind Dad and shoves him out of the way. With her silver-peppered black hair knotted into a bun on top of her head, she squints at me through apparently brand-new glasses and raps her cane against the floor.

"You-a eating cup-a-cakes again?"

I put the last bit of my cake into my mouth. "Eaten," I correct her around the mouthful of food.

"Ah! Is-a not your-a job why-a you single! Is-a your manners!" She proceeds to lecture me for a minute about manners in smooth Italian. Something about how men don't like women who have to pick crumbs outta their cleavage every time they eat a meal.

"Okay, Mamma. Let's get you sitting down before everyone rushes in." Dad clasps her shoulders and turns her before she starts on my lack of a relationship again.

Brody holds the door open for me and shrugs. "I don't see anythin' wrong with women pickin' crumbs outta cleavages. View's hella nice."

I laugh. Yep, Brody wins that one. Not sure where Nonna got her idea from, because it is a seriously tricky business to remove crumbs from the girls without flaunting them.

I follow him into the ballroom-like room. It has many purposes aside from this one—indoor hotel weddings, prom, parties. Its versatility means the Oleander will never go out of business, as someone will always need this room.

Devin and Trent are sitting next to Mom, suited like I knew they would be. I see that Alison, Trent's wife and one of my best friends, has gotten away with this. Probably because Silvio, their four-year old, will be done at daycare and Aria, their ten-year-old, will be done with school.

Next time this happens, I'm offering to babysit.

Dad takes the seat next to Mom, and Brody sits between me and Nonna. It's no coincidence that the Bond women are split up by the men. Nonna and Mom are one step past polar opposites, and I have more than enough of both of them in me that I'm pulled into every fight because they always think I'll side with them. That and no one wants one of their famous word battles to take the spotlight off the mayor.

I sigh and tuck my purse beneath my chair. Mom catches my eye as I sit back up and winks as someone takes a seat next to me. Nonna, seeing this, turns, but her gaze focuses on the person sitting next to me.

And by the thrilled glint in her eye and the way her grin becomes mischievous and intrigued, I know exactly who's sitting there.

"All right, cupcake?"

"Screw you," I whisper harshly at him.

Drake leans into me. "We need to talk," he says quietly into my ear.

"In my experience, us talking is the last thing we need to do because it always ends badly," I hiss back.

"I know, but I was out of line yesterday. I'm sorry."

"Apology accepted, and talking done." I shrug and fold my arms, my eyes on the chairs set up on the makeshift stage in front of us.

"No, it isn't."

I sigh and look at him. "You don't owe me an explanation, Drake."

"No," he agrees, his ice-blue eyes focused on mine. He brushes my hand with his. "But I owe you a do-over, at the very least."

I unfold my arms and shake my head. "You're crazy."

"We've established that, but I think your nonna has one up on me. She looks like she's planning a wedding in her head."

Jesus, Nonna.

"We're done talkin'," I say, giving the crazy old lady a hard look.

Seriously, Devin proposed to Amelia in Italian at family dinner last week, and Nonna cried. And not just happy tears. She spent the next two hours singing in Italian and praising God for blessing my brother.

Then she zeroed on me like a sniper. I could see it running through her head. Two down, two to go, and we're going in age order.

I Googled mail-order husbands that night. The fact that a lot were Russian only made it all the more tempting.

Brody had a fling with a girl with Puerto Rican heritage a couple of years ago, and when Nonna found out she wasn't Italian like he'd told her, she literally whipped his butt with her cane.

Got that on video, too.

"Nonna," Trent warns. "Put your bow and arrow away. You ain't Cupid."

Nonna cackles.

She was a witch in a past life.

"Still not done," Drake murmurs as the mayor and his opponent, Alistair Harvey, step out onto the stage flanked by their wives.

"Way done," I argue.

Slowly, he trails his knuckles down the side of my thigh. I shiver.

"You sure about that, sweetheart?" he asks.

"Touch me again and I'll put your balls into a blender."

He does it again, and I thump his leg.

"Noelle!" Dad scolds me in an angry hiss when the mayor starts talking on the stage.

Drake's shoulders shake with his silent laughter, and I glare at him out of the corner of my eye. Bastard. Total bastard.

Ugh. All the seats in this place and he picked the one right next to me. Of course he did. For what, to apologize? He could have sent a text. That way, Nonna wouldn't take a perfectly innocent seating arrangement and spin it into something huge that has me popping out babies within the next eighteen months, because that has to be what she's thinking.

She has wedding bells in her eyes and they have my name on them.

I've long accepted that she'll never understand my lack of desire to get married. Maybe my job has jaded it despite the fact that I've grown up with two stable marriages in the form of hers to Nonno and my parents'. And now Trent and Alison. The day they break up is the day the world ends.

But me… I don't see it. It's a piece of paper and promises said in front of loads of people. Hell, when I was six, I married Danny Bower in front of half of our class and we even signed our names on the wrapper of a Twinkie. We broke up three days later.

He was a total dick anyway. Still is.

Maybe, when I'm in a relationship with someone that's steady and stable and safe, I'll feel differently. Maybe I'll want that one day, but right now, I'm happy to be with someone.

I take a deep breath as Drake shifts beside me. Jesus, I cannot think about this crap when I'm next to him. It's total craziness. I have no idea what this is between us apart from totally screwed up.

On the stage, the mayor steps back from the podium, and the room breaks out into raucous applause. Brody elbows me, clapping, and I unenthusiastically join everyone else.

Drake leans over, clapping himself as someone whistles behind us. "How much of that did you listen to?"

"Not a damn word."

He laughs as the mayor calls for quiet so Alistair Harvey can say his piece before they go head-to-head. He does it with a shit-eating, smug look on his awful little face though, mind you. The man really needs to be told that men of his age can't get away with a short-back-and-sides haircut without looking like a mushroom-head.

A high-pitched noise breaks through the continuous clapping—loud enough to hear it, but quiet enough that it's indecipherable. Drake freezes next to me, his back straightening, and his hand moves to the gun at his hip with certainty. My body is reacting in the same way. I sit bolt upright, freezing mid-clap. And it's there again, the noise. Except this time, it's louder. Spine-chillingly intense. Even as it echoes through the closed door, it feels like pure pain. Total distress.

"Is that—" Brody starts.

"A scream?" I finish. "Yep."

As if it's synchronized, Drake, my brothers, and my father all stand up and turn toward the door. They storm past me, and I notice several other officers in the crowd running for the door, too. I grab Dad's hand for his attention.

"Noelle," he says, looking down at me. "You're not a cop. Sit down."

"Neither are you anymore," I shoot back and stand, making sure to get my purse from under my chair on the way. "Do you even have your gun with you?"

"It's in the car."

"Yeah, well, mine is in here." I release his hand to tap my purse. "Stay close to me, okay?"

"You are the only woman I'd ever let protect me," he mutters, laughing to himself.

I grin.

Dad closes his hand around mine and whistles to clear a path through the people rushing toward the exit. Typical Holly Woods—everyone has to know everything. And I do... But only from a professional standpoint. Yeah, I have a gun and can protect people.

I'm basically a pretend cop. Pow pow.

I run, somewhat awkwardly in heels, with Dad to where I can see the back of Drake's head. He's huddled with my brothers and some other cops in a small group, and I let Dad's hand go.

If there's a drama this big, the sheriff will be around. And if there's the sheriff, there's my dad. They're worse than me and Bek.

"What's going on?" I ask Devin when he breaks away from the main group.

"Mayor's daughter has lost it," he whispers back.

I frown and jog over to where Drake is. My heels click-clack against the wooden floor, and my instinct is screaming for me to pull my gun out.

Drake turns, presumably hearing me coming, and the look he gives me is enough to make me falter. His features are smooth but hard—his jaw is clamped tight, and his eyes have that ridiculously hot don't-fuck-with-me look in them.

"Madison McDougall," he says to me in a tight, gravelly voice. "See if you can find out what's wrong. She's crying too fuckin' hard for us to get anything outta her." "More like y'all men handle crying women with the finesse of a bulldozer," I retort.

He shakes his head, his jaw loosening as the twitch of his lips agrees with me. He rests his hand on my lower back and guides me through everyone to where Madison is sitting in the corner of the room.

Madison McDougall is the girl next door everyone wants to be when they're in high school. Waist-long, highlighted-blond hair, baby-blue eyes, sweet smile, and always the picture of composure and kindness.

Yeah, well, this version of her is *not* that one.

Her lips are cracked, evident through the smudges of her red lipstick, and her cheeks are stained with the black mascara she's cried off. Random lines disappear over the edge of her jaw and chin, some of them sweeping over the red shadows of her lipstick. And Drake's right. She's hysterical, gasping for breath between each sob.

"She's gonna need a paper bag. Now." I tap Drake's arm and approach her as he turns. "Madison," I say quietly, kneeling in front of her. "Madison!"

She chokes on her tears as she looks up.

"That's it, honey. I need you to calm down now."

With her eyes wide and panicked, she shakes her head and reaches for her neck with a frantically shaking hand. She's telling me that she can't breathe, and I'm not surprised in the slightest.

"I don't care if it's a damn tampon disposable bag. I need a paper bag!"

"Here." Drake pushes through the crowd once more and hands me one.

I help Madison hold it over her mouth and breathe my own sigh of relief when she inhales and the bag collapses in on itself. The wrinkling sound is much better than the questioning murmurs of the people behind us.

Slowly, the color from Madison's cheeks fades from red to a much paler pink, and Drake quietly asks someone to find out if there's anyone with medical training in the building and get the mayor and his wife.

"Okay, Madison." I take her hand. "I need you to tell me what's happened, sweetie."

Her blue eyes fill with tears, and she takes a deep breath in the bag again. The tension shoots up as everyone waits to hear what she has to say, and in this moment, with fear riddling her tear-filled gaze while she's curled into herself, she looks far younger than her twenty-five years.

"I-I went-went into her-her room." Another breath. "She-she didn't ans-answer. And she's-she's dea-dead. Na-Natalie. She's dead."

chapter SIX

RAKE moves into action immediately, confidently stepping forward. "Which room, Madison?"

But she's gone. Hyperventilating into the bag once more, each cry more traumatized than the last.

"Nurse," someone says behind me.

Someone kneels next to me, and I scoot over, focused on Drake. His shoulders heave as he takes a deep breath and turns his face. When our eyes connect, there's a hard determination glaring back at me. He holds my gaze for a second longer before turning to Trent.

"Secure the hotel. No one in, no one out, and I want every single fuckin' security tape they have." He flicks his eyes back to me. "You. Come with me."

It just doesn't sound as sexy when there's a dead body around.

He holds his hands out, and I place mine in his. He curls his fingers around mine and tugs me up, holding me until he's sure I'm steady.

Then he turns and stalks toward the reception. And I mean he *stalks*. Each stride is strong and confident, and his walk is nothing short of powerful. He screams that he's in charge and everyone better recognize that.

"Natalie Owens," he demands of the lady behind the counter. "I need her room number."

"I'm sorry, sir. That's confidential information."

Drake pulls his badge out and shoves it toward her. "HWPD. I've been told her dead body is in your hotel room, and I'm in charge of homicide. I suggest you get me her goddamn room number before the media get wind of this and your hotel turns into a media circus. And by suggest, I mean give me it right now."

Apparently, his words also scream that he's in charge and everyone better recognize that.

And. Ho. Lee. Shit.

He's really hot when he's bossy.

By the time I've gotten to the reception desk, the receptionist is handing Drake a spare key and he's grabbing my hand and spinning me.

"Oh!" I squeal when he doesn't let my hand go. "Why are you dragging me around like you're a cat and I'm the bird you just killed?"

I probably shouldn't have finished that sentence.

"Try to replace your brain-to-mouth filter, Ms. Bond," he drawls, pulling me into the elevator.

I don't even know that he pushed the button. Is he some kind of elevator wizard?

"I don't have a brain-to-mouth filter. The DNA strands responsible were drunk the day they were supposed to give me that."

"Drunk? I think they had an accident with a firework."

"Well, I am pretty at night."

He cuts his eyes to me, and I'm awfully aware that *he's still holding my fucking hand.* "I'm dragging you, as you put it, because you were one of the last people to see Natalie Owens alive—"

"I swear to God, if you pull me in for official questioning, I'm making it worthwhile and making good on my threat to shoot your other foot, too."

"—so you can give her a basic identification before forensics gets here and the team assembles downstairs," he finishes as the doors ping open. "Plus, you'd sneak your way up here anyway, and I have a feeling this is already going to give me a headache, so I'm picking my battles."

I smirk. "You're a smart man, Detective Nash."

"So they tell me." The curvature of his lips matches mine, and he lets me go to open the door. He slots the card in, pulls it, and when the light blinks green, he pulls the handle down and pushes. "Jesus."

"Is she dead? I don't think calling Jesus will help. He clearly isn't her biggest fan if she is."

"Noelle," he growls.

"Sorry. I'm hangry still, and it makes me a total bitch. And dead people make me uncomfortable, and I ramble when I'm uncomfortable."

He holds his hand up to silence me. "The only thing I need from you right now is: Is this Natalie Owens?"

He steps to the side, and as I move through the door, I freeze. Yep, it's Natalie Owens, all right, but not as I know her.

She's lying on the bed, her wrists and ankles bound by ropes to the posts at each of the four corners, and there's bruising coming up her skin from those restraints. New bruising, because I don't think I saw those this morning or when she came into the office. Thankfully, if anything about this situation is thankful, they resemble rope binds, exactly like the ones holding her now. Her legs are obviously wide open, her underwear nonexistent, and I swallow as I guide my gaze up from her most intimate parts and across her torso.

Lash marks decorate her taut stomach. They're red, raw, and totally fresh. Tiny spots of blood bead along some of the marks, and the ones across her breasts are even worse. Looking closer, I can see some lighter marks, too—ones that are obviously older.

But it's her face and neck.

I cover my mouth with my hand.

Her face is purple, her eyes so bloodshot that they're bulging and almost red. Her mouth is open, her lips swollen, as if she was crying for help in her last moments. A chill fills the air as I focus on the deep-purple tie knotted around her neck, cutting into her pale skin.

I swallow hard. Hours ago, I was talking to her in her home. Albeit a very shaken-up Natalie, but oh, hell. Shit. Fuck.

"Noelle," Drake says softly. "Is this Natalie?"

I nod and turn, walking into the hall. I lean against the wall next to the doorway and put my hands on my knees. Was this her important appointment? In the hotel where the debate was being held? And if so, who was she meeting? Who did this? Who knew this information?

Drake stops in front of me and cups my face. The palms of his hands are hot against my cheeks, and I breathe in again as he tilts my face up. His eyes, despite their hardness for the situation, are full of concern for me.

"If you want to go, no one will hold it against you."

"No," I whisper. "I just need…a minute. That's all."

"Are you okay?"

"I will be if you do your hot-cop thing and start demanding things of the people you work with."

His short laugh is weak. "Okay." He presses his lips to my forehead, the warmth lingering from his gentle touch even after he's stepped away and his phone is attached to his ear.

He does what I said so flippantly. Within five minutes, he's ordered the floor to be evacuated and cordoned off, called in almost every officer in the HWPD to get started on questioning everyone in the building, called Tim, the town coroner, for him to come in, and confirmed that the sheriff is on his way up with a bottle of cold water for me. And my father.

Excellent.

Trent and Brody are the first to arrive, closely followed by my dad and Sheriff Bates. Sheriff Bates is the sweetest gentleman I know, and he rarely wears anything other than a button-down shirt pressed to perfection. Today is no different, and as he approaches me with his pure-white hair slicked back from his face, a water bottle in his hand, I'm thankful for his calming presence.

"Drink," he orders. The word is soft, but the authority in it has me automatically unscrewing the cap and sipping. He's commanding in a grandfather kind of way, something I know we've all welcomed in the years since Nonno passed.

That's the thought I hold on to now as the hall is filled with security guards emptying rooms with little explanation, allowing everyone ten minutes to pack their belongings to be transferred to another The forensics team arrives, and they disappear into the room with Drake, Trent, and Brody before closing the door to preserve as much dignity as Natalie has left.

She could have exposed herself to as many people in life as she wanted to, but in death, she'll be respected in a way she perhaps never respected herself.

I can't wipe the images of her tied up, that tie around her neck.

Was the tie deliberate? A spur-of-the-moment act? It's clear to see that that's the way she died. She was strangled. Her appearance could tell even a CSI-loving amateur that.

I take another sip of the water as Drake reappears, closing the door behind him.

"We found identification inside her wallet," he tells Sheriff Bates, shoving him a white, leather wallet with his gloved hand. With his other, clad in the same type of latex glove, he removes her driver's license and holds it up for him to see. "Confirmed as Natalie Owens."

I knew it, but shit.

Drake puts the wallet into a sealable plastic bag and briefly opens the door to hand it to someone inside the room.

"What else is there immediately?" Sheriff Bates asks as the lock clicks.

Drake snaps his gloves off and shoves them into his pocket. "Marks on the body indicate an affinity for bondage. There are numerous burn marks across her wrists and ankles. Tim will need to spend more time with her body, but his initial thought is that it's beyond a dom-slash-sub relationship. Perhaps a serious sadomasochistic relationship wherein the dominant acts as her rapist and she struggles as such."

I frown. How could that be enjoyable for her at all? "Who would get pleasure from pretending to be that brutally attacked?"

"You'd be surprised," Dad answers. "Holly Woods isn't necessarily the town everyone thinks it is. Sure, it's real quaint and cute, but beneath, there are some dark secrets. This is, unfortunately, one of them."

"BDSM? Why would it be?"

"Because Holly Woods prides itself on being a 'clean' town. Meaning we have little crime, no controversy, and the bar that's exclusive, invite-only for the rich living within a fifty-mile radius."

"Are you telling me that D.O.M. is a sex club and not a…? Wait." I pause, rolling the water bottle across my lips. "Of course. The name itself…"

"Is obvious without being brash," Drake answers. "Put it this way: If you need to know about it, you do. The police department know because they need our services. I can count on one hand the amount of calls we've had to there in the last two years, but I'd bet anything that Natalie was a member, at least once upon a time."

"Would they condone that kind of thing though? The…pretend rape."

"Absolutely not," Sheriff Bates says sharply. "The rules are very clear. Even if it's consensual and both parties have signed the necessary contracts the club demands. There's no way for them to know if the participants are genuinely wanting it or being forced into it."

"Will they release any information about Natalie though? Surely a club like that would be reluctant."

Drake shakes his head. "I already have Brody preparing for a warrant for it, just in case, but here's the thing: BDSM is about safety, first and foremost. That's the whole reason for the contracts. You can't walk into D.O.M. and pick up some random person the way you can in a bar. You have to have met them before and whittled out every detail of your relationship. We've seen their contracts. They're tighter than anything I've ever read before."

"You think they'll hand the info over?" Dad asks him.

He shrugs. "Who knows? If she is, or was, a member, it won't look good when it's revealed that she was murdered in a sexual situation. Plus, if there's the risk of a murderer on their client list, they'll hand everything over to us. Thankfully, they stick to a select clientele of no more than fifty or sixty people, so it should be relatively easy to contact everyone."

Only fifty or sixty. Oh, yeah—that can be done by lunchtime. If you get up at four a.m. What the hell?

"So, what killed her?" Sheriff Bates asks. "I'm going to have to personally deliver a report to Mayor McDougall before sunset."

"Asphyxiation," Drake answers. "Given her…situation…Tim thinks it was erotic asphyxiation, but he'll know more when he's had a chance to carry out her autopsy in two to three days."

Erotic asphyxiation. The art of restricting oxygen flow to the brain during sex to heighten pleasure.

Risky.

Obviously.

"But that's consensual, isn't it?" I ask, looking between the three men. "He wouldn't have been able to do that to her without her agreement."

"She was bound to the bed and unable to move," Drake points out.

"But there had to be respect there. If she said no and he valued it, he wouldn't have done it, surely."

"Unless he didn't respect her at all."

"Then this…" I swallow and glance at this door.

"Then this isn't a sex game gone wrong." His eyes bore into mine. "This is murder."

Eight p.m.

I finally sit in my car after hours of being inside that hotel, waiting to be officially released by the HWPD. I've seen several breakdowns, a few anxiety attacks, more ambulances than I ever thought I'd see in one day, and more than one or two women preparing to sue the hotel for the disruption of their stay.

Yeah, because that's the real issue here—that people can't get their chosen rooms. And many have been upgraded free of charge.

People logic. Sucks.

All I really want right now is a big, fat pizza, a bottle of wine, and a hug.

Given the fact that my phone is ringing, yet again, that seems like a real long shot.

"Hello?" I answer the unknown number warily.

"Ms. Bond?" an unfamiliar female voice says.

"Speaking."

"My name is Ellis Law. I'm Mayor McDougall's personal assistant."

Oh, awesome. "What can I do for you, Miss Law?"

"Ellis, please."

"Then it's Noelle, please."

"Very well. Mayor McDougall would like you to come into his office immediately to discuss a pressing matter."

Even better. "Can it not wait until tomorrow morning? I've barely eaten today and I'm exhausted. I'd hate to give the mayor anything less than my full attention." Actually, I'd hate to give him any of my attention, but hey.

"My apologies, but it's incredibly important you come and see him tonight. I can arrange to have a meal of your choice either waiting for you or to-go when you leave. Mayor McDougall understands you've been at the hotel for several hours now and is more than happy to ensure you're made comfortable."

Free dinner?

Hello, Ellis. I'm on my way.

"Make it a Chinese chicken chow mein with egg fried rice and spring rolls to-go and I'll be there in five."

If smiles were audible, hers would be whooping in delight. "I'll let him know. See you soon, Noelle."

The line cuts out. My stomach rumbles, and I knock my fist into it.

"Hey, greedy bitch, dinner is free tonight. Pipe down." I put the car into drive and take the turn out of the parking lot. The one that leads to a late business meeting and a free dinner.

The Oleander is in the center of town, and Town Hall and the mayor's office can be seen from some of the rooms, so it only takes me two or three minutes to drive the few blocks distance and pull up in the almost-empty parking lot. Of course there would be a grand total of four cars here. Why would council officials be working the evening of the day when their head honcho's bitch fest was interrupted by a possible murder?

How unreasonable of me to expect that.

I sigh and get out of my car, slinging my purse over my shoulder. Damn me for getting tempted by free food. I want my bed. Still, I walk into the building and take the elevator to the fourth floor, where the mayor's office is.

Ellis Law is sitting behind a desk in the middle of the room, her pixie cut spiked and her sweeping bangs pinned out of the way as she types. She glances up when the elevator doors shut, her eyes tired, and smiles.

"Noelle?"

"Yes," I reply quietly. "Is Mayor McDougall ready to see me?"

"Absolutely." She gets up, readjusts the waistband of her pinstriped pants, and goes to the large closed door behind her desk. "Sir? Noelle Bond is here for you."

"Send her in," he barks.

Well, excellent. Everyone loves a mayor in a bad mood.

Ellis sweeps her hand toward the door with an apologetic smile. Looks like my dislike of the mayor has found a friend—for today, at least.

Mayor McDougall, a tall, brash man who's spent the last twenty years combing his hair over to convince us that the bald spot on the crown of his head is a figment of our imagination, is scribbling furiously on a notepad. He looks up with amber-colored eyes and points his pen at the chair.

"Sit."

I bite my tongue before a snarky comment comes out and do as he said. I set my purse down next to me on the floor and tuck my ankles beneath the chair, my hands resting in my lap.

The mayor keeps me waiting.

I clear my throat, and when he looks up, I quirk an eyebrow. "Surely you didn't invite me here to see you writing, sir. With all due respect, if this is going to take much longer, I'd rather come back tomorrow before the little remaining patience I have for today runs out."

His lips twitch up, and he sets the pen down. Slowly, he rests his elbows on the desk and touches his fingertips together. "Calling you in was the right decision, it seems. I was wondering if you were as sassy as your grandmother."

"Don't let her hear you say that. She prides herself on being the passionate one."

"I can't imagine why." He drops his hands and dips his head to remove his glasses. Clasping the arm between his finger and thumb, he looks at me intensely, sending chills down my spine. "I want to hire you."

"Excuse me?"

"More specifically, I want to hire you to work alongside the police." He gets up, leaving his glasses on top of the notebook, and walks to the window with his hands clasped at the base of his back. "You and I both know that many of the so-called detectives are incompetent fools, especially in homicide. Detective Nash and your brothers are some of the few I trust, and naturally, they are working on Natalie's untimely demise."

Untimely demise, indeed.

"An office space will be prepared for you in the department should you require it."

"I have a business to run first and foremost. I won't leave my staff to their own devices, not to mention other cases I'm working on currently." Like finding out if the guy who works in the hardware store is gay so my friend Alonso can ask him out. "And working alongside the police is a very vague statement. I need more than that before I can even consider it."

Mayor McDougall turns, loosening his tie. "I want you to find out who killed Natalie, Ms. Bond. This case must be resolved as quickly as possible to avoid the ramifications for all involved. My campaign is too high profile and at risk of a loss for the first time in over thirty years. I simply cannot have it overshadowed by the death of Natalie, no matter how sad it is. It behooves everyone for her murderer to be charged with as little investigation as possible."

Good Lord, this man is a crusty, selfish penis-head, isn't he?

My eyebrows shoot up. "With as little investigation? Unless forensics gives Detective Nash a thorough DNA rundown and it's matched with someone in the system, there'll be more than a little investigation."

"Which is why *you* need to work with them. It's no secret you solved Lena's murder, and now, I'm asking you to solve Natalie's. You'll be paid your standard fee plus extras by the council—gas money and the like—and a payment for your time here this evening at your average rate."

"I don't charge for consultations, Mayor McDougall."

"Perhaps not in your business hours, but I called you in your personal hours. Therefore, you'll be paid." He walks toward the desk and grasps the back of his chair. He leans forward, his fingers tightening, his look intimidating. "Ms. Bond?"

"Is Detective Nash aware of your intention to hire me? Sheriff Bates?"

"Sheriff Bates is on board with my decision. As for Detective Nash, it will be mentioned to him tomorrow when you attend the briefing at the station."

"When I attend? That's awfully presumptuous. I don't like to agree to cases until the prospective client has had a chance to read through the contract and issue any amendments. *However*," I add strongly when he attempts to interrupt me. "I will go to the briefing tomorrow after leaving a basic contract with your assistant. You'll have twelve hours to make any changes, including the addition of your previous statement regarding payment. I'll have my assistant draw up a new contract with that, providing I agree to your terms, and you'll have a further twelve hours after delivery of the amended document to have it signed and delivered to me including the retainer check."

If he's angered by my demands, he doesn't show it. In fact, he looks rather like he respects me. "I appreciate anyone who can get straight to the point, Ms. Bond, and the fact that you're a woman makes it even more amusing."

Wow.

"I'm going to pretend you didn't just insult me because of my gender," I say through gritted teeth, reaching for my purse and standing. "What time do I need to be at the station tomorrow?"

"Eight a.m. Sharp."

"You'll have a contract on your desk beforehand." I turn to the door and open it.

"Ms. Bond?"

"Yes?" I look over my shoulder.

"I mean it when I say this case needs to be solved with as little investigation as possible."

"And I mean it when I say this case will be solved with as much as necessary."

He pushes off the chair, making it swing around and bump into the side of the desk. His amber eyes narrow into catlike slits, and a tic makes his jaw twitch. "I've known Natalie Owens for many years. It's in the best interests of everyone's safety for you to follow my instructions."

"Excuse me for pointing out the obvious, sir, but safety is exactly why this investigation will take as long as it needs to."

"There are things about her you wouldn't like. Many things are best left undiscovered, Ms. Bond."

I meet his eyes and hold his gaze for a second longer than necessary. I'm not sure why he thinks he can intimidate me or that I'll roll over and beg for a belly rub like every other woman he works with, but he should probably try not to be a sexist bastard if he wants me to cooperate.

As it is, we have a verbally binding contract that will be on camera, and as soon as I start investigating, all bets are off.

I close his office door behind me, grab the takeout cartons from Ellis with a smile, and press the elevator button.

As little investigation as possible, indeed.

chapter SEVEN

I PICK a little watermelon seed out of the chunk and pop the delicious piece of fruit in my mouth. Not one part of me wants to stroll into that police station right now and be all, "Hi. I'm in your investigation. Surprise!"

I didn't even call my brothers last night to tell them. It sounds simple, but I know how pissed they all got when I ended up being involved in Lena's murder. Never mind that Natalie Owens is a client of mine—again. Something only Drake knows.

It's why I have her case file with me. One more thing for them to have. As it is, though, it doesn't matter. When I dropped my contract off this morning, Ellis informed me that the mayor has informed Sheriff Bates that I'm to have full access to all police departments and findings and I must pay them the same courtesy.

I don't think the mayor has any idea what he's doing.

I don't want to be thrown into the middle of a murder investigation again. I don't want to deal with this bullshit for the second time in almost as many months. I want to live my quiet little life with cheating couples and lost dogs and suspicious-acting teens.

I don't want to have the safety of people placed in my hands.

The day I quit the Dallas PD is still too raw. It's still too real even though it happened a couple of years ago. I can still remember the call I made, every gun shot, every cuss word as the engine started outside and the plain, white truck, still full of children, was driven away.

I can have a gun in my hands. I can shoot before I think. But I can't protect people. I learned that on that day.

I'm too naïve and selfish.

No.

I was naïve. I'm probably still selfish. But I'm not naïve anymore. I've learned from my past decisions, and I've made better choices since.

Unless you count every single decision with Drake, but somehow, I don't.

My window is knocked on three times, and when I turn, I see Devin's face in it. He turns his finger for me to wind it down, so I hit the button.

"What are you doing here?"

I breathe out, more a sigh than anything, and end up blowing a spit-less raspberry. "Because I literally cannot be bothered to explain right now: Guess who the mayor hired last night?"

Dev stares at me for a second before his lips form a grin and a huge belly laugh erupts from him. My lips thin as he continues laughing like he's two years old and watching Sesame Street or something.

"Are you done? Because guess who doesn't know the mayor hired me?"

"Fuck off," he shoots at me, still laughing. "Oh shit, sis. They're gonna go nuts."

"Yeah. Which is why I'm sitting in my car and not going in there."

"Can I come watch when you tell them?"

"I'm sorry. Are you a newly-engaged thirty year old man, or a fourteen year old boy waiting for next week's edition of *Playboy*?"

"Noelle, I don't give a shit how old I am. This is gonna be fuckin' gold. Wait—when you say they, do you mean Drake, too?"

Reluctantly, I nod.

Dev laughs again. "Let's go." He opens my car door. "This is too awesome to pass up."

I groan and take my purse from the passenger's seat. They're literally going to kill me, aren't they? They're sure as hell gonna tear me a new vagina after I reveal my purpose for being here.

God, it's gonna be like the high school football team welcoming the little geeky girl as their quarterback, isn't it?

I drop my keys into my purse and wriggle my toes in the end of my Louboutins. They're my absolute favorite shoes—mostly because their sleek, shiny blackness and blinding redness on the sole make me feel powerful. They're a look-the-hell-at-me kinda shoe.

Maybe not so much with ripped jeans and a tank top, but whatever.

Dev wraps his arm around my shoulder and briefly squeezes me into his side. I give him a wan smile, because honestly, I feel sick. I wish I were already in there, that this whole thing were over and done with. I know that Drake, Trent, and Brody will have expected me to call, but I was afraid to.

I was so fucking scared to call them and tell them that their investigative team was being expanded to me.

Jesus, Noelle. You're not a teenager stepping into a science project. You're Noelle fucking Bond, and if they have a problem with that, they can bend and kiss your ass.

But Drake.

This could ruin everything.

What is everything though?

What do we really have except for a ridiculous attraction and a history of apparently hilarious and explosive arguments?

What if something is waiting in the wings and the mayor's hiring me is the villain in our tentative love story?

What if we're the modern-day Romeo and Juliet—without the whole dying thing, but only destined to be together in another life where everything is simpler?

"Dev." I grab his arm and swallow right outside the building. "I can't do this. I can't storm in here and step in alongside them like I deserve it."

"You do." The door opens, and Brody steps through.

I turn to my baby brother, taking a deep breath. He knocks his fist into my cheek with the barest touch.

"Yeah, I heard. Drake and Trent don't know. But Noelle—you do deserve this. You know as well as I do that you deserve to be sitting in that fucking meeting room with the best of the best. You know that you should be one of the best detectives Holly Woods has ever seen, and you are. You just don't have the badge. Don't taint your present with your past. Now, get your ass into that fucking briefing room before we grab you and drag you in there."

"Brody wins the 'inspirational speech of the year' award!" Dev announces.

"How about you go fuck a chicken, you cocky bastard?"

"Ignoring that you're referring to my fiancée as a chicken, at least I have something at home to fuck that isn't my right hand."

"I'm left-handed, douchebag."

"Fine—I can fuck something that isn't my hand… Or bed slats."

"One fuckin' time, man. I saw it on YouTube."

"Why were you even watching bed slat porn?"

"Oh my God!" I snap, storming past them both into the main reception. "You slimy, antagonistic, sneaky little shits!"

They laugh and high-five as I storm down the hallway. Ignoring Charlotte's greeting, I take the single flight of stairs upstairs to the briefing room. I slam the door open, and instantly, Drake and Trent turn to me, as do the three other officers sitting in the room, who I recognize as Detectives Brown, Harper, and Johnston.

All men.

Fucking men.

What is this town's issue with powerful women?

Drake stands, Trent echoing his movement.

"What the fuck are you doin' here?" my brother asks.

I smile sweetly and hold my hands out to my sides. "Hi. I'm your new work buddy. Isn't it fucking wonderful?"

"What?" Drake growls, his eyes focused entirely on me and pulling at my gaze despite my best effort to look anywhere other than at him.

"Oh, yeah. Didn't you get the memo? The mayor hired me last night to work with y'all to find Natalie's killer, so surprise!"

"Noelle," Brody groans. "The attitude, sis."

"Is exactly what she needs," Sheriff Bates answers, entering the room right after him. "Brody, shut the door."

He does it, and the sheriff continues.

"Last night, Mayor McDougall called Noelle into his office in her personal hours and proposed that she work with the homicide department in solving Natalie Owens's probable murder. It's not a secret that he's not happy with the majority of our female officers, and in his eyes, Noelle's advantage is that she isn't a cop. Now, this goes without saying that it's confidential information." He scans us all. "Holly Woods will know in five minutes what the good Ms. Bond is up to, but they won't know who hired her, and that, gentlemen, gives us a total advantage. Now, some of y'all have personal ties with her." He stares harshly at Trent and Brody, and his gaze lingers for a moment too long on Drake, "But under no circumstances will that come between y'all and y'all's duty to your town."

"She's my damn sister!" Trent spits. "If there's a gun on her and it's her or the shooter, you seriously expect me to ignore that?"

"Three weeks ago, I had one pulled on me when I was all alone and I dealt with it perfectly fine, thank you," I remind him. "I'm not a goddamn princess, Trent. I'm the best detective this department has and I'm not even fucking employed by it."

"Not by my choice." Sheriff smirks. "And yes, Trent. Brody, too. I expect you to focus on apprehending a suspect, not saving your sister. Y'all know she's more than capable of saving herself. The only—and I stress, only—time that's acceptable is if she's unarmed and her life is in total danger."

"Whoa now," I reply, raising my eyebrows and putting my hands on my hips. I give no fucks about my diva status. "Would you say that if I were in possession of a penis, Sheriff? 'Cause if not, retract it, and I'll take the bullet like your guys do."

"You were so born with the wrong genitals," Brody mutters.

I punch him.

"Noelle." Sheriff draws my attention back to him. "Yes, ma'am, I would. If your colleague is unarmed and you can protect them, you do, even if it's at the cost of your suspect. None of y'all signed up to be a martyr when you went through your training. And as a cop, you know that."

"I'm not a cop," I remind him through gritted teeth.

"But you were." His eyes spark. "And you're as good as any I've got in this building. So let's be done with our new addition courtesy of the mayor and get on with our briefing. Any objections?"

Drake grunts his agreement, the expression on his face identical to Trent's.

Thunderous.

I can practically feel the anger vibrating off him. He's like a

84

ticking time bomb, and I swear that, if anyone so much as breathes in his direction, he'll bite their head off.

I knew this was a bad idea.

Brody pats my thigh twice and gives me a regretful smile. Hey, what can I do though, right? I'm here now. I'm being trusted by both the mayor and the sheriff—and my youngest brother. And, honestly, does it matter that Drake and Trent aren't impressed?

As long as Nonna doesn't get wind of this tonight at the rescheduled family dinner, not at all.

She'll implant a new pair of ovaries into my pelvis when she discovers this.

"Two days ago, Natalie Owens came in with stalking concerns. She expressed that she was forced to file a report before Noelle would work on it." Sheriff Bates scribbles on the whiteboard and draws a line under it. "Yesterday morning, she calls Noelle with concerns about being broken in to. In turn, Noelle calls Devin Bond, the detective in control of Natalie's case, and informs him of it due to the shocked nature of the victim." More scribbles and another line. "Forensics have, so far, delivered no clues as to who the would-be burglar or stalker is." Another line. "That's at approximately eight a.m. Just over seven hours later, Natalie Owens is found dead in a hotel room at the Oleander."

My toes curl inside my shoes, and I refuse to meet Drake's eyes as he looks at me.

"In those few hours, Natalie Owens had an important appointment which stopped her from staying inside her house and keeping herself safe. Natalie Owens willingly went to the Oleander and met someone who, at the very least, had sexual relations with her before she was killed. We don't need Tim's report to know that she was murdered. What we also know is that her murderer was someone she trusted enough to surrender her body to him. She knew her killer. She knew the risks, and if our assumptions are correct of her being a member of D.O.M., she had a contract with the killer." Sheriff looks at Brody. "Take Detective Johnston and the warrant on your desk to the club. I want every contract and member file they have on record."

Brody nods.

"Detective Bond," he addresses Trent, "you and Detective Harper and Detective Brown are tasked to finding out what Natalie did between the hours of nine a.m., when Detective Devin Bond's team left her house, until she was discovered by Madison McDougall at approximately three thirty p.m."

Oh no.

"Y'all can leave," Sheriff Bates tells them, zeroing in on me and Drake.

Everyone shuffles out, Trent shooting me a dark look as he does.

"And Detective Nash," Sheriff Bates says once the door has clicked shut. "You and Ms. Bond will cover everything else." He glances at me. "Madison is at home now following her admission to hospital for severe shock last night. Interview her and get an understandable statement from her. Then track down Natalie's ex-boyfriend. If he was her stalker, I want his ass in an interview room within forty-eight hours."

"Understood," Drake says tightly.

"I have her file with me," I add quietly. "We should be able to find Nick now and conduct necessary interviews."

"Noelle."

I focus on the sheriff instead of the window. "Yes, sir?"

"Within my building, you keep to legal boundaries. In your own, whatever y'all do is your business. I want this case solved."

What I don't know won't hurt me, he means.

"Absolutely, sir. I'm sure Mayor McDougall told you I refused his offer of an office in the department for the duration of the investigation."

"Yes, he did." He smiles slowly. "He told me many other things, too, and all I have to say is your father will be proud when I tell him."

I shrug. "I'm no pushover. I think he found that out."

"Don't tell me you pissed off the mayor," Drake growls, turning in his seat and staring at me. "That's the last thing we need."

"Of course I pissed off the mayor. I had a conversation with him."

"Well, that explains a fuckin' lot."

"Enough." Sheriff Bates steps forward. "I trust y'all to work together despite your personal relationship, whatever that may be this morning. A girl has been killed, and that far outweighs your personal issues. Work that out outside of my building. Now, get into Nash's office and work out your plan, y'all."

"Let's go," Drake says shortly, standing so quickly that his chair clatters to the floor behind him. His hard steps echo against the tiled floor as he storms his way to the door, and his bicep flexes when he grasps the handles and slams it open.

The knock of the knob against the wall is startling in its loudness, and as he stalks his way through the doorframe, I turn to the aging man before me.

"I sure hope y'all have soundproof walls, because it's about to go down."

"Well, you're your mother's daughter and your nonna's granddaughter." He shrugs.

I grin, grab my purse, and walk past Drake. Then I snake my way through the tables and down the stairs until I reach his floor. His office door is partially open, and I shove it open the way he did the briefing room's.

"Don't even," Drake growls, his fists on his desk, leaning forward. His eyes could slice diamond.

I slam it shut behind me and drop my purse on a chair. "What the fuck is your problem?"

"You bein' here!" he yells. "What the fuck, Noelle? You couldn't say no the mayor, huh? You just as gutless as everyone else he tramples on?"

"Gutless? I have more balls of eggs in my ovaries than you have sperm in your balls. Why don't you give me a little credit for once, huh? He hired me because I have a track record—"

"Because you solved one murder?"

"Because I'm good at my fucking job!" I shout, jabbing my finger at myself. "You think I wanna work with you? With all of y'all in this fucking building? No. I'd rather drive my car into a tree. I don't want to be working another damn murder case, but here I am, working with you, the very last person I wanna work with!"

"You think I wanna work with you?" Drake slams his fists onto the desk before straightening. "Like fuck do I, Noelle. I don't want your ass anywhere near my fuckin' case."

"Then tough shit, *cupcake*, because you're stuck with me."

He swipes his hands against his desk, knocking off several sheets and his pen holder. Every step toward me is angry but calculated, the anger etched into his features obvious and more than a little hot in its determined frustration.

Drake's body collides with mine, his hands cupping the sides of my face, his lips melding onto mine.

The door stops me from moving back another step, but he doesn't stop pushing. He moves against me until I'm flush with the door and every part of his body is connected with mine. He doesn't move a goddamn muscle except for his mouth as it explores mine with a hard-hitting intensity that has my knees weak and my skin tingling and my lungs constricting.

"We can't work together," he breathes, still holding my face. "It's the worst idea I've ever heard. Me, you, together nine hours a day? No, Noelle. Just no."

"Like I said," I reply as breathily as he was, "tough shit. If I had a choice, I wouldn't be here either. I'd be holed up in my office with my cupcakes and cutesy little lost-dog files and not-so-cutesy cheating-bastard files."

"Jesus." His thumbs brush across my cheekbones. "This—fuck. Do you not see how dangerous this is? Me and you, working together? I'd let a serial killer run for his freedom as long it meant you would be safe."

I lick my lips, refusing to look away from his eyes. "Our working together is no more dangerous than our being together, and you're all for that, aren't you?"

"That's different. If you were mine, you'd have to let me protect you. I know for a fuckin' fact that you'd pull your gun before I pulled mine in any other situation."

"You told me you didn't want a damsel in distress." I move his hands from my face. "So, surprise, Drake—I'm not. I never will be. If I ever need savin', it's on my terms, and you should know that. Working with me ain't gonna kill you or anyone else, so suck it up and get the hell on with it, because like Sheriff said, her dead body is bigger than us."

He stands in front of me, not touching me but somehow caressing every inch of my skin. "But that's the problem, ain't it? Nothing is bigger than us, Noelle. Especially when 'us' is barely even defined."

I take a deep breath, so deep that my breasts brush his chest. "It doesn't need definition. We're not a word in the dictionary. We're just…whatever we are."

"Whatever we are." He snorts, backing away. "Sounds about

right."

I shake my head as he moves toward his desk, turning from me. He reaches up and loosens his tie, throwing the released strip of satin on top of his keyboard when he's freed it.

"You know what? No. The mayor can kiss my freshly waxed vagina. I'm not putting myself through his shit because you've got your cock up your own ass."

I tug the door open, but Drake is quicker than I thought, and the force he shuts it with jars me into letting the handle go. He leans forward, our eyes colliding and connecting in a way so intense and irresistible that looking away simply isn't an option.

"Sit your ass the fuck down. We have a job to do. Regardless of the shambles that is us," he mutters, but each word is still somehow perfectly pronounced and filled with anger.

I reach into my purse, which I'm still holding, and slap Natalie's file against his chest. "Here. Read this. I'm going to explain to my team why I'm suddenly the mayor's bitch. When you're done with that, call me, yeah?"

This time, when I open the door, he doesn't stop me.

Cupcakes are waiting on the meeting room table.

Gigi's cupcakes.

And the gas receipt next to the box has the total scribbled out.

I guess they've heard… About everything.

"Cupcakes are on me, Miss Noelle," Dean says when I sit down.

I smile at him. Brawny and built, buzz-cut hair, yet sporting a new beard, Dean is made of marshmallow inside.

"Thank you, Dean. I appreciate it, especially today."

"We heard." Bek meets my eyes. "For real, Noelle? You're working with the HWPD?"

"In theory," I begin.

"In reality, you and Nash have already fought," Mike smirks.

"You know," I say to him, "if you didn't have, like, a hundred and fifty pounds on me and I hated cupcakes, you'd so be licking this frosting off your face right now."

"God." Bek leans forward. "Seriously? It's barely been an hour."

"Are we here to discuss our cases or my private life?"

"He is your case."

"No. He's an unfortunate partner. Now, get on with it and tell me what you've got." I pull a cupcake from the box and remove the wrapper, grabbing a fork from the holder in the middle of the table. Everyone lays out the basic info as they usually do, and I nod my way through it, shoveling a forkful of cake into my mouth every other sentence.

I'm not even ashamed when I reach for the second cupcake.

Bek, however, looks at me with the kind of concern only moms and best friends can muster.

"Okay. Y'all get on now," I tell everyone, scrunching up my second cake wrapper and throwing it toward the trash can in the corner. Ultimately, I miss it, but Mike bends down and tosses it in before he walks out.

"Noelle," Bek says quietly.

"I'm fine." It's unconvincing, I know, but maybe saying the words out loud will help.

There's been an odd kind of empty ache since I stormed out of the police station earlier.

"Right. Two cupcakes immediately and you're as fine as the new guy who served me coffee at Rosie's this morning." She snorts. "And don't even go there trying to get me to talk about him!"

"Wasn't gonna," I lie.

"What did Drake do?"

"Nothing. Not really." I rest my head on my hand. "He reacted… too much. Does that even make sense? Like, Trent going crazy? Okay. But Drake? There are levels of emotion, and that was not on the first-date kinda level."

"Maybe because you two never have been. You've always been all or nothing, and hell, y'all passed nothing a while ago. I don't know why you keep fighting him."

"Because of this. We fight. We are a *fight*." Drake and I…we're a bomb and a lit match. But when that match touches the fuse, it's sure to explode right before us.

"And your grandparents?"

"Shut up." Just because they fought every day for decades doesn't mean that's the key to a successful or even healthy relationship.

"I don't know why you fight it. It's okay to get your heart broken, you know?"

"At twenty-eight? Bek, I don't know. I don't want to give him my heart. I don't want to give him me."

"Then why are you so bothered? Why do you let him affect you this way?"

I meet her eyes, picking at the corner of the cupcake box. "Because I don't know how to not to."

"Well, you've gotta figure it out soon." She stands up. "Seriously, Noelle."

"I know," I say quietly, looking down. "I don't need you to tell me."

She shrugs and pauses at the door. "Just because you're forced to work together doesn't mean you can't have his second date is all I'm sayin'."

But it does, doesn't it? It means our relationship is way more professional than personal, and that's dangerous. I don't want that to get in the way of him doing his job. He's the best damn detective I've ever met. Even better than my brothers, honestly. And I don't want to be his liability. If we work together as more than detective and investigator, we're risking something. We're risking safety. We're risking answers. We're risking lives.

I know why Sheriff put us together. In his eyes, I'm far less of a liability with someone I've been on one date with than I am with people I share DNA with. Equally, I'm far safer with Drake than I am with detectives I last spoke to in the line at Rosie's weeks ago.

And I get it. I'm a woman. I'm automatically weaker than a man—I need someone who cares about me to protect me. Which is exactly why, in Sheriff Bates's eyes, Drake is the perfect partner in this.

But...damn.

He's wrong. He's not my perfect partner. How can I work with that man, constantly thinking about what has been and what could be and what might never be? How the heck does that make any sense?

I fold my arms across the table and bury my face in the nest they make. Good God. This whole thing is so screwed that I can't even stand it.

Another client murdered. A seriously tumultuous relationship with the lead detective. A contract that binds me to them both.

I just can't catch a break.

"Noelle?" Grecia says hesitantly, opening the door. "The mayor has the contract here."

I hold my arm out, my eyes still closed. I've been lying back on my chaise longue for two hours now, waiting for my phone to ring.

Spoiler alert: It hasn't.

A welcome reprieve but a hellish one at the same time. I know that Drake will be working. He'll be getting it done without me because that's the kind of asshole he is. This contract I'm holding right now be freakin' damned, right?

I open my eyes and scan over the amendments scrawled in red. "Fine," I say, handing it back to Grecia. "Can you type it up with the additions and send it back over?"

"Absolutely." She takes the stapled-together sheets and leaves my office.

I rest my hands on my stomach and stare at the ceiling.

Why did I walk out of his office earlier? I should have given him the file and then forced him to work with me.

No. I should have called him and warned him what was happening.

I should have called him and talked about it before I agreed with the mayor.

Actually, no. I shouldn't have. This is my job, my business, and the mayor is simply paying me to do that. And he's paying me a *lot*. The only person who should make business decisions with me is the reflection in my mirror.

But I still should have warned him.

Damn. Now, I feel guilty.

I'm not the one who lost my shit though. He is. I'll apologize to him when he does to me. If he does. Which he won't. Because he's male and can't possibly be wrong ever. And I'm far too stubborn to apologize without getting one in return, so we're at an impasse.

Both professionally *and* personally.

I get up, grabbing my shoes by their heels, and set my office phone to the answering service. Then I grab my copy of Natalie's file and my purse and head downstairs.

"I'm out for the rest of the day," I tell Grecia. "If anyone needs me, I'll be at home."

"Sure. Are you all right?" She looks at me with worry in her dark-brown eyes.

"Crap day." I smile wanly and head out, still holding my shoes.

The concrete parking lot is hot beneath my bare feet, so I run across to my car while I dig my keys out. Mercifully, I find them quickly, and I unlock my car and drop my butt to my seat, swinging my feet in before the soles of them burn off.

I dump my things on the passenger's side, barely glancing as my shoes roll off the seat and hit the floor with a thud. Instead of picking them up like a responsible adult, I pssh at them, shut the door, and start the engine.

My phone buzzes somewhere in the depths of my purse, so I turn the radio up to drown it out. It's not like I can answer it, but I'm pretty fed up with that damn buzzing noise.

The only thing that should buzz as much as my phone is a vibrator.

And there's no way a Samsung is fitting *there*.

And it's still buzzing when I kill the engine outside my house.

Lord help the little piece of crap or my heel might go straight through its screen.

I'll answer it—once I've had a chance to pee. My bladder has been seriously neglected in the last two days, and given that I hate cranberry juice, I'm not in the market for an infection right now. Or medical bills.

If I get the medical bills, I don't get the shoes. And I want the shoes.

I unlock the door then throw my purse to the side, dumping my shoes with them. I unbutton my jeans as I run up the stairs, sighing happily when it pops open and relieves the pressure on my bladder.

Jeans. They're the work of the devil, and I'm probably five pounds too heavy to be wearing this pair. Oh well.

I peel my pants off my legs while I'm on the toilet and leave them in a heap on the floor. Two mental online-shopping lists later, I pull my panties up, flush, and walk into my bedroom for some comfy shorts.

My front door opens. Loudly.

I finish tugging the neon-orange shorts over my butt and grab my gun from the nightstand. What the fuck?

And did I forget to turn my alarm on again this morning? 'Cause I sure as hell didn't disable it when I walked in a moment ago.

Wait—fuck that. Someone's in my damn house. Why am I contemplating the alarm?

Oh yeah. Because *someone's in my damn house.*

I hold my gun in front of me and slowly tiptoe down the stairs, my finger resting lightly on the trigger. If this keeps happening, I'm gonna have to go door-to-door to remind the residents of his town that I will shoot them if they come into my house uninvited.

Still, my confidence in my ability to use this weapon doesn't change the fact that my heart rate has picked up considerably and my body is flushing with uncertain, anxious heat.

A shadow moves in the doorway to my living room, and I stop on the bottom step.

It creaks.

I freeze.

"Fuck!" Drake steps back. "Put the damn gun down, Noelle!"

I drop it. "What the fuck are you doin' in my house?"

"You weren't answering your phone, and when I called the office, Grecia said you were here."

"So you decided to storm in and not knock? And you're surprised I had a gun pulled on you? Sweet Jesus!" I sweep past him, safely depositing my gun on the sofa. "Again: What are you doing here?"

"We need to talk."

"Ugh, you say those words far too much." I walk into the kitchen through the connecting door and pull a bottle of Pepsi from the fridge. "I don't have anything to say to you, but if you have that much to say, spit it out."

He stares me harshly as I unscrew the cap of the bottle and bring it to my mouth. Shivers waltz across my skin in waves, each one more intense than the last, because his eyes... God.

I hate his eyes.

I wish he would never look at me again.

They say everything he doesn't. They say everything he's said before and what he wants to say, and it's terrifying. Thrilling, but terrifying. I feel like I need to spill every sin I've ever committed even down to stealing a lollipop from the general store when I was four.

After three steps toward me, he takes the bottle from my hand, retrieves the cap from the other, screws it back on, and places it on the counter behind me. "Contrary to what you believe, cupcake"—he rests his hands on the edges of the counter on either side of me and leans in—"*we* have a lot to say."

"That's your opinion."

"It's fact."

"That's also your opinion." I push at his arm, but he doesn't relent.

In fact, he brings his hand closer to me and brushes an inch of exposed skin at my hip with his thumb. The movement is light, but my skin is burning from the contact.

"This would be so much fuckin' easier if you didn't have a job that means you seem to be smack in the middle of yet another murder investigation I'm controlling," he growls. "But you are, and I have no choice but to work with you unless I want to lose my job. Shut your mouth before you give me your sass," he adds, putting two fingers against my lips. "So we'll work together... Under duress. But before that happens, we have the big, fat elephant in the room that is the issue of you and me."

I smack his hand away from my mouth and spin out from him. "You keep going on like you and me being in a relationship would be something that would last longer than five minutes."

"Perhaps it would."

"Perhaps it would?" I lift my eyebrows and run my fingers through my hair. "Shit, Drake! We can't go a day without fighting. How fuckin' insane are you that you think that kind of relationship would be healthy? That it would be worth the inevitable collapse, huh?"

"Noelle Bond, you're so fuckin' in denial it's unreal."

"No, I'm realistic. That's the difference." I storm back into the front room. "This, you and me, is pure *insanity*. We've fought twice today and it's only one o'clock!"

"Then there's plenty of time to make up, isn't there?"

"Oh, you are so persistent, aren't you?" I spin and look at him, pushing some strands of hair away from my face. "Are you trying to verbally beat me into submission? Are you trying to drive me into craziness so I agree to what you want?"

"No." One word. Hard. Simple. Growly. "I want you to fuckin' want me. Is it that much to ask?"

"Yes!" I wipe my brow and look away, taking a deep breath. "Yes. It's asking the world, Drake. Do you get that? Do you get that it isn't as simple as you want it to be? If I want you, it's because I want you, not because you want me to."

His steps are certain as he approaches me and forces me to look at him with a touch to my jaw. My eyes settle on his, and I'm stripped bare completely.

I know the answer.

I know his question.

But I don't want to hear either of them.

"And do you? Want me?" His voice is softer now, but the hoarse tone is still there. "'Cause, babe, I ain't gonna lie. I'd burn down New York City for you if I had to."

The words catch in my throat, because yes, *I want you.*

I break away from him and run out of the room and to the stairs, taking them two at a time, my eyes focused on my room as soon as my open door comes into view. His steps thunder after mine, but he's quicker than I am and lodges his shoulder between the door and the doorframe, forcing me to let it go. I'm pretty sure a tiny, frustrated scream leaves my mouth as he grabs my arm, spins me, and tugs me against him.

His eyes are blazing. They're a fiery inferno of the absolute hottest temptation.

"No," he growls again, taking my chin in a firmer grip, his gaze refusing to relinquish its hold on mine. "No, you don't get to fuckin' flake on me now, Noelle. Yes or no. Do you want me?"

The words burn through me, pulsing through my bloodstream until they're screaming to get out, because there's no more running from this, and I think my heart knows it.

"Do. You. Want. Me?"

"Oh, I do!" I say roughly and harshly, shoving his hand away and turning. Two steps and I turn back to him. "I want you, but I shouldn't, because you piss me off so goddamn much! It's driving me absolutely fucking crazy, because I have no idea what to do with myself anymore."

He closes the distance between our bodies once again and wraps his arms around me until I'm trapped in his embrace. "Say it again," he murmurs. "Without the defiance."

"It's passion, actually, and it's one of my better qualities."

His laugh rumbles against me. "Sure is, cupcake, but how about a little less angry passion and a little more sexy passion, yeah?"

I sigh, but my lips curve up anyway. When I don't answer, he once again takes my chin between his finger and thumb and tilts it up. I inhale as his breath fans across my lips. Tension dances between us, its moves complicated and intricate, getting faster and faster until it's suffocating.

"Noelle—"

"I want you," I whisper. "God only knows why. But I do."

He smiles, sliding his hand up my back and into my hair. "Sweetheart, you've got me."

His lips are sweet and firm as they touch mine. I lean into the kiss, my fingers fisting the back of his shirt as Drake deepens it. I feel it everywhere from the tingles at the base of my neck and the flutters in my stomach to the weakening of my knees and the curling of my toes.

"Murder investigation," I breathe, leaning back. "This is a really inappropriate conversation for us to have had right now."

"Well, for one, you weren't willing to listen before." He grins, loosening his grip a little. "And two, the way this town has been in the last month, we'd be lucky to have had it outside of one. Especially with your stubborn streak."

I'm going to ignore that last comment. He's a fine one to talk. He does have a point though.

"Okay, but, uh, what exactly is this conversation? Like, specifically."

His grin drops to a half smile, but it's a hopeful one, and it sets another round of butterflies off in my tummy.

Sweet hell, I wish he didn't have to make me feel like a teenage girl all the time.

"You want me, so you got me. I want you…"

I make my smile match his.

"Don't leave me hangin' here, or I'll spank the answer outta you."

I dip my head to hide my laughter, but when I take a step back, Drake pulls me against him again and the giggle breaks loose. It's silenced by the burning way his lips collide with mine and his tongue unapologetically sweeps across the seam of my mouth. I gasp at the quick, dominant move, and then the kiss is all lips and tongue and quite possibly another gasp from my side. He kisses me until I'm dizzy and need to hold on to him to stay standing.

Hot. Damn.

Drake Nash is a walking, talking, highly irritating, spectacular kissing machine.

I wonder if he has a coin slot so I can get those world-stopping kisses to order.

"So?" he asks, his tone gravelly. "Do I have you, Noelle? Will you at least try for me? Are you mine?"

"Mine," I murmur, sliding my hands up his taut body to grab the crisp collar of his white shirt. "Real possessive, that, don't you think, Detective?"

"Oh, absolutely, Ms. Bond. 'Cause see here—that's nonnegotiable." His eyes sear into mine. "No two ways about it, *bella*. If I have you, you're mine."

Bella. Oh.

"Are you sure that's nonnegotiable?" I ask through the clogging of my throat. "I'd quite like to be my own on Tuesdays and Fridays between the hours of two and eight."

The annoyed darkening of his eyes is spoiled by the fight he has going on with his mouth. Ultimately, his smile wins out, but not without a frustrated growl.

"Twenty-four fucking seven, you little pain the ass. And now, you're fucking with me."

"I know, but it's *so* fun."

"You want fun, huh? I'll give you fun, Noelle." He spins me and shoves me back onto my bed.

I clap my hand over my mouth as a scream leaves me when I go backward. A shadow falls over me as he leans over my body, grabs my wrists, and secures them above my head with one strong hand. I breathe in sharply at the rough move even as a jolt of pleasure flies through my bloodstream, leaving a fiery trail behind that.

"Fun," he mutters, a darkly sexy smile on his lips. "No, fun is forcing that agreement off the tip of your tongue where it got stuck, sweetheart. But, because I'm a nice guy, I'm gonna give you one last chance to admit that you're mine before I flip you over and fuck it out of you."

I look up at him, ignoring the way my clit is throbbing at the brush of his erection against my thigh when he moves. Ignoring the way goose bumps have covered my body. "I'm not saying a thing."

"Good choice," he whispers right before he harshly tugs on the waistband of my shorts and kisses me simultaneously.

My legs bend of their own accord as he releases my hands and removes my shorts and easily. I crane my neck to kiss him harder and undo his top button. The shorts fall off my foot, and he covers my body with his, his hardening cock pressing against my panties and my clit.

His hands trail up my body, taking my shirt with him, and he cups my breasts as I finish undoing the buttons and yank the shirt from his waistband. I push it over his shoulders, my palms smoothing over his hot, tan skin, and he releases me for two seconds to shrug it to the floor. God—his body is so lean and perfectly toned. Sinfully ripped, even. With nothing but lust for him driving me, I want to touch every inch of him.

"Still not saying?"

I laugh breathlessly as he pulls my tank over my head and kisses along the curve of my breasts. "You're gonna need a scarier threat than this."

"You should be scared." He flicks the clasp between my breasts and pushes the cups to the side.

My pussy clenches as he brushes his lips across my nipple in a way that isn't really a kiss but feels completely like one.

"I'm barely getting started with you." Now, he closes his mouth over it, and I arch my back into him.

"Nope," I breathe. "Still not scared."

He smiles against my skin and trails his mouth down my stomach. I shiver when he kisses just above my panty line, because oh my.

"How about now?" His breath coats my clit through the thin fabric.

I inhale on a huge shudder that trembles my whole body. Tingles everywhere. Heart pounding.

Oh, God. This is so cruel.

He laughs quietly then lifts my hips and grasps my panties. He slides them down my legs torturously slowly, making sure his fingertips trail down the insides of my thighs. Then he teases across my instep, which is kinda tickly, but how can I laugh when I know I am totally exposed to him?

I throw my arm over my eyes, blocking him from my view as his fingers trace paths up my legs and he parts them. I can hardly breathe, and at this rate, I'm going to be a gasping mess before he lays another finger on me.

He rubs his thumb over my clit in a circle, firm enough that my legs jerk and air fills my lungs. He laughs again, and still gently stroking it, he kisses the inside of my thigh. "Your body is your worst enemy, Noelle. You won't say you're mine, but look how wet you are for me."

I don't have a chance to respond because he replaces his thumb with his mouth, and if this is his way of trying to get the words out of me, he stands no chance. I don't think I can breathe let alone fucking talk. I don't think I can think except for about what he's doing to me, how deftly he's moving his tongue and teasing me. How his exploration is making me writhe on the sheets and arch my back and tilt my hips closer to him while trying to move away all at the same time because it feels so good.

Holy shit, what is he doing to me?

I know what he's doing to me, but I don't. It's like my nerves have all come to life, sending heat flushing through my body. I'm hot but I'm shivering, and I bite my lip and moan as the tip of Drake's tongue flicks across my clit with the whisper of release.

But he moves.

I groan in annoyance, automatically bending my legs upward and closing my legs. He laughs, and I hear the clink of a belt followed by whoosh of fabric as it pools on the floor. Then, he deftly hauls me onto my side, making me shriek.

"What are you doing?"

"You ask too many questions." He taps my ass and lies behind me, grabbing my thigh and lifting my leg.

The end of his cock brushes against me, and I tilt my head back, my stomach tightening in anticipation. When his fingers twine in my hair instead of guide him inside me, I reach down, wrap my fingers around his hard length, and angle my hips so he eases inside me easily.

He grips my hair, pulling my head back so his mouth ghosts over my temple. My eyes flutter shut as he pulls out and thrusts back in, repeating the movement several times, each thrust harder than the last. I'm hypersensitive to everything, from his stubble on my cheek to his fingertips digging into my thigh. The rough smattering of hair on his chest, grazing my back. The twitch of his hand buried in my hair. The jerk of his foot hitting mine.

It's like last time, except it isn't. I remember, though, what it's like to have him deep inside me like he belongs there, what it's like to have him command my body so expertly that I'm virtually powerless. What it's like to have him touch me and tug me and fuck me until there's nothing but stars and blinding heat and utter satiation.

He's doing it now, our bodies moving together, and I'm reaching back to his neck so I have something to grab. He presses openmouthed kisses to my neck, his breathing harsh and heavy, and I grasp his hand on my leg, too, needing to touch him in every possible place.

He lifts my leg higher, kisses my collarbone a little harder, grips my hair a little tighter, and then there is nothing but bittersweet ecstasy.

chapter EIGHT

H E once told me that he can make a fuck punishment as well as pleasurable.

He wasn't lying.

It's been half an hour and a—lone—hot shower after, and I can still feel my knees jittering even as I sit at my kitchen table and watch him figure out the coffee machine. I chew on the side of my thumb as I consider what this…is. What it means. Because I still didn't say what he wanted me to.

Drake places a steaming mug of coffee in front of me. "Latte, cream, and half a sugar."

I smile as I curve my hands around the mug. "Thank you."

"You're welcome." He turns and throws out the empty pod, grabbing another from the pot.

I mean, okay. This shouldn't be confusing. He's made it clear what he wants, but he's also made it clear what he doesn't want, and that's me working with him. Something which truly is nonnegotiable. I just got a text from Grecia telling me that the contract is already back in the hands of Bond P.I., hand-delivered by one of the mayor's bitches, complete with a hefty check for me to cash tomorrow.

We don't work well together, as evidenced by the amount of times we butted heads during Lena's murder investigation. It was like constantly running into a brick wall only to be swallowed into the center of the brick and spat back out again when you were so angry that it became unbearable.

Which, incidentally, is what led to all the kissing.

Drake takes the seat opposite me, and I look out the window to my backyard. I don't have the greenest thumb in the world, so it's restricted to a shed, a dirty patio area devoid of a grill and table set, and overgrown grass.

I really need to call Brody to cut it.

Goddamn, it really shouldn't be this awkward between me and Drake right now. So we had a highly emotional discussion followed by some highly emotional sex in a very different context, and now, we're having coffee. That's what adults do, right? Talk, sex, coffee.

I guess it's only awkward if they didn't do the sexing before they finished the talking.

Dear Mom, I forgot how to adult woman right.

I click my tongue against the roof of my mouth, keeping my eyes off Drake. "So."

His smirk is still damn well visible to me. "So."

"So."

"This ain't so ping-pong. Spit it out."

"What do we do now?" I look at him. "Like… What are we? This? Working…and other…stuff."

"You're real cute when you're nervous."

"I'm not nervous."

"Why do you look like you're about bolt, then? I gotta say, seein' you runnin' down the street in that bathrobe would be somethin'."

I scowl. "Do you know how hard it is not to insult you right now?"

"If I answer with, 'As hard as my cock was an hour ago' do I get a bonus prize?"

"Good grief. You're really about twelve years old, aren't you?"

He winks, laughing. I roll my eyes at his easygoing manner. Although I guess it really is easy for him. He's already flat-out declared that his fine ass is mine.

"Listen." He leans across the table, his arms bulging from beneath his shirt. "You know where I am, babe. I've told you what I want. This is down to you right now. The ball is in your court entirely, but I need to know something. Whether it's yes or no or a damn maybe—I need

103

to know if you want this even a fraction as much as I do."

I swallow and pick at my sleeve. "Honestly?"

"Honestly."

"I don't know," I admit quietly. "We don't work well together, Drake. I don't want to throw myself into a personal relationship with you if our working one will make it suffer. And right now, we both know that the working one trumps our personal one, doesn't it? I'm a cop dressed up as a private investigator, because that'll always be in my blood."

He reaches across the table, his fingers toying with mine as he lifts my hand. "Then try," he replies simply, sliding our fingers together. "We can compartmentalize, sweetheart. The work relationship is left there. The personal one is left here."

"We both know that won't happen." Yet here I am, staring at our clasped hands, at his skin, which is tanner than my natural light olive. At his fingers, long and rough, strong as they hold our palms together. "We're both too...grudgey."

"Grudgey, huh? Is that another word for stubborn?"

"Shut up." I look away for a second but smile. Damn him. My eyes find their way back to his, and I suck my bottom lip into my mouth. There are hope and intensity and a glint so fucking bright that I can't do anything but take a deep breath.

Throwing caution to the wind is risky, but sometimes, it's the right thing to do.

"Okay," I whisper. "I'll try. But I'm warning you now, compartmentalization isn't my strong suit."

"I know, and I am completely prepared for you to tear me a new asshole next week for my behavior this morning."

"Which you still didn't apologize for, by the way."

"Nonna invited me to dinner tonight. If I come, does that count?"

Well... "Are we going together? Because if we are, then yes, because she'll pull out the wedding scrapbook for me she's had for the last five years and ask your opinions on various things."

Drake leans forward, his smile lopsided but mischievous. "Can I veto it all?"

"Even the Italian three-course dinner?"

"Even that."

I purse my lips to the side, but those butterflies are back again, and before I can do a thing, I find myself replying, "Go for it."

"Liliana!" Mom yells, something slamming down. "One day, you will let me cook dinner for my own children!"

"No! You-a no cook-a!" Nonna fires back. "You-a give-a packet pasta! Packet pasta!"

Oh, God, she's gone all shrill.

"There's nothing wrong with packet pasta! You're a food snob!"

"You cook-a *Italiano,* you cook-a it right-a!"

I look at Drake. "I feel like my asking this is getting old, but can you shoot me?"

He laughs. "It isn't that bad."

I grab the door handle. "Wait." I push down, open the door, and wince.

"Why I ever agreed to let you live with me, I don't know! You're a complete pain in my backside, Liliana!"

"You dis-a-respect-a my food!"

"Oh, I don't care about your food, just like you refuse to eat Southern meals! Why should I give a crap about yours?"

"Because it-a is-a *Italiano!*"

"Yeah, well, in the last lasagna you made, the mince was dry!"

Nonna gasps and screams, in Italian of course, "You take that back now!"

"No!" Mom yells, understanding but refusing to speak it.

I lean back against Drake. "Still think it isn't that bad?"

"Holy shit. Is your family secretly the inspiration behind Jersey Shore?"

"It's likely," I admit, stepping into the building.

"Where's your dad?" Drake asks as they continue to fight, Nonna yelling in rapid Italian and Mom deliberately shouting back with the most Southern accent she can muster.

"In the front room, watching television with my brothers, and pretending he can't hear them." I shrug and walk into the front room, where, to my incredible lack of surprise, the situation I just described is reality.

Aria, Trent's ten-year-old daughter looks up at me. "Nonna's sayin' bad words again, Auntie Noelle."

"Nonna always says bad words, baby," Trent responds for me. "Ignore her. You know better than to use them."

"*Cazzo!*" Silvio, his four-year-old, says. "*Cazzo!*"

"*Cazzo*, no!" Trent and I say at the same time.

I'm smart enough to clap my hand over my mouth and look away instantly as Alison sits up.

"Silvio! No. That's a naughty word."

He grins sassily. "I like it."

"It's bad. Say it again and I'm taking all of your stickers from today."

He opens his dark eyes, his long lashes only extenuating his shocked gaze. "Sorry, Mama."

Alison raises her eyebrows.

"Sorry, Daddy," he adds, looking appropriately ashamed.

Trent's eyebrows pull together in a guilty look.

Alison leans forward to grab his arm. "Don't you dare," she hisses.

"What did I miss?" Brody asks, slamming the door behind him. "Whoa—who let Mom and Nonna out on day release together?"

Dad snorts from his chair in the corner. "Satan got bored."

"Don't let Nonna hear you say that," I tell him. "Last time I mentioned the s-word, she lectured me for fifteen minutes on saying the devil's name."

"Did she miss the point where you called her Satan?" Devin asks.

"I'm still alive, aren't I?"

"Antonio, I'm going to kill her!" Mom storms into the living room. "Get that woman out of my kitchen right now!"

Dad focuses on the television, only the twitch of his fingers on his whisky glass giving any indication that he heard her.

"I'm sorry for this," I mutter back to Drake. "I got this, Mom."

She looks up, tucking hair behind her ear. "Drake! It's lovely to see you."

Just like that, everyone stares at us. Trent glares. Dad grins. Mom beams. Brody smirks. Devin lifts one eyebrow. Alison winks at me.

"I'm *really* sorry for this," I say, amending my statement before I grab his forearm and tug him into the hallway.

Nonna is muttering about pasta and sauces and the like in Italian, stirring the spaghetti with far too much vigor. If she isn't careful, she's going to take her own eye out with that wooden spoon.

"Hey, Nonna. Look who accepted your invitation for dinner."

She glances up, fire in her eyes, but it soon dissipates when she sees Drake standing behind me. Now, she looks like I told her that I'm getting married.

"Drake! Is-a lovely to see-a you!" She walks toward him, her arms wide open.

He glances at me in alarm as she wraps her arms around his waist. "Hey, Liliana." He returns the hug with one arm.

Nonna steps back, and with her dark eyes wide and her lips turned up mischievously, she looks between us. She does it so obviously that it's deliberate, and I lightly bite my tongue so I don't snap at her. I don't want to give her the satisfaction of knowing she's bugging me already.

I choose to grab a bottle of water from the fridge instead of continue her little eye games.

"So," she says to us, turning back to her cooking. "You come-a together?"

I choke on my water and thump my fist into my chest. "Excuse me?"

"Dinner. You come-a together?"

Unfortunately, I catch Drake's eye. He's grinning at me. Bastard.

"Yes," he tells Nonna. Double bastard. "We came together."

"So you-a dating? Noella! You-a dating?" She spins around quickly, the spoon still in her hand. White sauce splatters across the cupboards. "You-a really-a dating?"

"Dating is a strong word," I hedge, shooting a fuck-you look to Drake over the top of Nonna's head. "We are...trying not to kill each other every time we see each other."

"So you-a dating."

"Not every relationship has to be defined, you know."

"So you-a admit-a it is-a a relationship?"

"Not all relationships are romantic ones. Some of them really do come with murderous tendencies." I scowl at her, but it goes right over her head.

"Oh! Noella, you-a dating!" She drops the spoon and shuffles into the front room. "Antonio! Noella is-a dating!"

"You're dating?" Dad and Trent ask at the same time.

"You're taking the word of this crazy old woman? I'm already married inside her head!" Seeing her hopeful grin, I point my finger at her. "No. No. Put those wedding bells down, Nonna!"

"You're dating?" Trent repeats, turning on the sofa so he's facing us. "Really?"

"No!" I protest.

"We're apparently tryin' not to kill each other," Drake adds. "Which is a good start, I reckon."

"Well, if that's what you're callin' it," Mom sighs, "then no wonder she thinks you're dating. Her whole marriage was spent trying not to kill Nonno."

"She's crazy," I tell her. "Look at her. She can't walk to the car without her cane, but she's dancing—why is she dancing? Dad, make her stop dancing. That ain't right."

Nonna cackles and walks between me and Drake, humming the wedding march.

Devin looks at me sympathetically. "If you ever get married, you know you need to elope, right? Because she wasn't even that happy when I proposed to Amelia."

"Dev, if I ever get married, I'm eloping and I'm damn well staying there." I snort, perching on the arm of the chair next to Trent.

"Oh, no. I'm still mad at you," he says, shoving at me.

"Trent, get over it," Alison sighs.

"Why didn't you tell me you were workin' with us?" He looks up at me.

I shrug. "Because you'd have staged an intervention. Think about it this way though—I won't have to bug you for information because I'll have access to it. So that's a plus."

He holds my gaze for a moment. "Yeah, I'm sold."

I bat at his arm.

"How did it even happen?" Brody asks, leaning forward to see me.

I explain everything from the phone call to—

"You went for the free food," he surmises.

I shrug again. "I was hungry."

"What did he say to you?" Drake asks.

"He did the usual. I might have been too hungry to remain

completely polite, but he said something odd when I left."

Dad stills, but his eyes slide to me. "Odd? Odd how?"

"He told me that whoever killed Natalie needed to be found as quickly as possible but without much investigation. He said there are things about her that I won't like. Secrets and stuff."

"What kinds?"

"Well, if he told me, it wouldn't be a secret, would it?"

"How does the mayor know her so intimately?" Alison questions. "Isn't that odd?"

"No." I bite the inside of my cheek. "She was best friends with his daughter forever."

"It's more than that," Drake inputs. "I did some research earlier, and it turns out that Mayor McDougall has been grooming Madison to eventually take over as mayor—or at least the mayor's wife."

And after he made that bullshit sexist comment to me, too. I guess the good mayor believes that his daughter is a class above the rest of the women in the world, huh?

What a pig.

"But," he adds, "he was also teaching Natalie the same thing. I checked the council's employment roster, and she's on it."

"Huh." Brody scratches at his chin. "I didn't think she'd ever stepped foot in the building."

"Me either."

I frown, looking down. What could she have possibly done for the mayor that would mean she didn't have to go into the town hall building?

"Maybe she did online stuff she could do at home?" I suggest. "Like social media management or something?"

Drake snorts. "I don't think the mayor knows what social media is, Noelle."

"Well, I don't see you coming up with another idea."

"Maybe I haven't said it yet."

"Spit it out, then."

"I see not killing each other is going real well," Alison remarks with an amused twist of her lips.

"Hey," Drake protests. "We lasted, what, maybe two hours?"

"Give or take a few minutes, pretty much," I agree. "I think we're about due for a fight."

He laughs, and I hear Nonna's cackle from the kitchen. Then Drake's phone rings, and he pulls it from his pocket.

"It's Tim," he says, glancing at the screen. "Excuse me a second." He walks into the hall and opens the front door, saying, "Nash," into the phone.

Brody, Trent, and I all stop, our eyes meeting. Tim wouldn't call Drake on a Saturday evening about the autopsy unless something came up in it—something that could change this investigation. My stomach rolls as the minutes tick by and he doesn't come back in.

"Dinner is-a ready," Nonna calls.

We all make our way into the dining room where the long table is set, and Trent lifts Silvio onto his chair.

"Thanks, buddy," he says, wrenching the Innotab from his hands. Silvio narrows his eyes as he takes it and puts it on the top shelf of the bookcase.

My four-year-old nephew points his fork in Trent's direction and yells, "Pew-pew!"

A fork gun. Now, I've seen it all.

"Put the fork down, Sil," Alison orders. "The longer you play with the forks at dinner, the longer Mommy keeps your Nerf gun."

"No fair," he grumbles. "Everyone else has guns."

"Everyone else is grown up, pal," Dad reminds him. "And when you're grown up, you can have one too."

"Promise?"

"What the heck? Sure. I'll buy you one."

"Excellent," Mom drawls. "Another generation of gun-loving Bonds. There simply aren't enough of those in this family."

And everyone wonders where my sass comes from. Really.

"For-a once, I-a agree." Nonna sets the large bowl of creamy pasta in the middle of the table and scoops a portion onto Silvio's plate with a wink, then Aria's. "Too-a many guns. Noella, why-a do you need-a three?"

"Because I forget stuff all the time, and this way, I always have one I can get," I reply, digging my fork straight into the bowl and spearing a piece of pasta.

"No!" She taps my hand. "We-a wait for Drake!"

Devin grabs the spoon from her. "Don't worry, Nonna. If he's still on the phone, he's probably walked his way down to the station to carry his conversation on in person."

"I still don't understand why Bates moved the morgue to the station basement," Dad adds.

"Because the mayor cut the funding, remember?" Trent takes the spoon. "It was either his driver or the morgue."

"Why does the mayor need a driver?" Alison asks.

"More worryingly, why do his driver costs equal the morgue's?" Brody counters.

"Why does he even need a driver? You can walk anywhere in Holly Woods in five minutes. Hell, even Nonna can get across town in ten." I take the spoon from Trent and point it in her direction.

"Hey-a," she protests.

"Why do you have a car, then?" Dev asks me.

"Because there isn't a Gigi's in Holly Woods. Duh."

Dad is shaking his head in resignation when Drake comes back in the house. He enters the dining room with a grim look on his face, and Dad, my brothers, and I all look at him, frozen.

"We need to go to the station. Now," he tells us.

"What's happened?" Trent asks, already moving to stand.

"She was murdered," he answers. "That's all I can say here."

Brody and Trent get up, but Dev shrugs.

"Dev," Drake says. "You took her stalker call. We might need you."

"All right." He gets up without argument and follows the other guys to the door.

I kiss Dad's cheek. "I'll call you later. Promise."

He taps my arm. "I know."

I follow Drake out of the house and to his truck. He holds the door open for me, and I sit, but then I pause before he shuts it.

"Why do I get the feeling this isn't as simple as her stalker being her killer?"

"Because murder is rarely simple." He shuts the door and walks around the truck. When he's in and the engine has started, he continues. "Are you working tomorrow?"

"I wasn't planning on it." I guess it looks like I have to change my plans.

"You are now," he says, confirming my suspicions. "Natalie's house hasn't been searched yet. I want us there early tomorrow. Then we'll interview Madison and the mayor and try to track Nick Lucas."

There's an 'and.'

"Do you have a new tech guy?"

"I was going to call the last guy I interviewed on Monday and offer him the job."

"Have Grecia do it tomorrow. I think he'll be needed first thing on Monday if my suspicions are correct."

"You're being very cryptic, Detective, and I don't like it."

He smiles, looking at me. "Trust me. It's about to make a whole lot more sense."

He pulls up outside the station and parks in his usual spot. My brothers are right behind us in Dev's truck, and they part next to us in Trent's spot.

Drake takes my hand and holds it while I get out of his truck. He really needs to get a smaller truck or get me a stepping stool or something. I think it's a borderline monster truck.

I pull my hand from his as my brothers get out of Dev's truck. I mean, it's weird. Plus, he is Trent's closest friend.

God, that really is weird, isn't it?

Drake doesn't take offense though, merely shaking his head with an amused smirk on his face. I look away, nowhere near as amused as he is, and drop back to walk with Brody.

"It's hilarious when you get embarrassed," he whispers with light laughter.

"Shut your face," I mutter.

Dear teenage me, the whole relationship thing doesn't get easier. They lied. Love, adult Noelle.

We take the stairs down to the converted basement, where Tim is, and instantly, I'm hit with the smell of death. It's rancid and awful, and I force myself to breathe through my nose instead of my mouth. I hate the morgue. I always have. Knowing that beyond a door or two are the dead bodies of people stuffed into freezers has always seriously bothered me.

Tim is sitting at the desk in his office, holding his glasses to the side and pinching the bridge of his nose. He isn't a particularly young man, anyway—fifty-something. But right now, he looks like he should have retired ten years ago.

"Excellent," he says tiredly, looking up with gray eyes. "Is it party time?"

"When at Bond family dinner," I tease.

"Should have guessed." He smiles. "Take a seat…if you can all fit."

His office is tiny and packed with papers and various things I don't really care for—like that model of a torso with half of it showing its organs. Or the brain I seriously hope is fake in a jar. Or that hand curved on top of the bookshelf, which I also hope is fake.

Long story short, this is my first visit to Tim's office, and it's probably gonna be my last.

Drake grabs my shoulders and propels me into one of the chairs in front of Tim's desk while Brody takes the other. Drake stays standing behind me, leaning forward, with his hands on the back of my chair.

"Tell them what you told me," he orders, his voice gentler than normal.

Tim rubs the bridge of his nose once more before putting his glasses on. Then he looks at us all in turn, one by one. "Natalie Owens was murdered without a shadow of a doubt. While it isn't uncommon for autoerotic asphyxiation users to accidentally take it too far, it rarely happens with a partner. With her hands and feet bound, she was completely powerless to whoever strangled her under the guise of that particular fetish." He opens a brown envelope and pulls some Polaroid photos out. "She suffered numerous lashes to her body, some of which opened up old welts from previous whippings. Whoever Natalie was in public was not who she was in private, as is typically the case."

More photos are laid out, these ones under UV light.

"There are clear signs of sexual activity before her death. Ninety-nine percent of it is internal, but there are very light traces of semen on her stomach and thighs, which have been sent for DNA testing. Of course, that doesn't mean that whoever she slept with killed her."

"Sounds like it could have been anyone," Brody remarks.

"It could have. But we have more. I pulled skin from beneath her fingernails and swabbed in and around her mouth for saliva traces. The chances of us getting a DNA match for at least her last sexual companion is high, and they are likely to be her killer."

"Would they really be that careless though? To let her touch them and not clean her?" I ask.

"It could have been an opportunistic moment," Drake explains, brushing his thumb across the space between my shoulder blades.

I fight my shiver. "She was there… Tied… Too easy. If it were premeditated, then no, her killer wouldn't have allowed her to touch them at all."

"So, what does this mean?" Trent leans forward. "We have nothing to go on except a definite murder charge until we get the DNA results?"

"Which might not even show anything conclusive," Tim concedes. "But no. That's not all. You have another huge factor that threw me." He scoots his chair back and pulls another envelope from her drawer. "The first thing I did was draw blood from her and send it to Austin for testing with a rush from Judge Barnes. The results were…interesting."

"You didn't tell me this." Drake's thumb stills.

"No." Tim removes sheets of paper stapled together in the corner. "I was surprised, given the lashings she'd taken. I expected to see high alcohol or drug levels. Perhaps even poison, but I saw none of that. What she did have was an extremely high level of hCG in her blood."

I take a deep breath.

"What is that?" Dev asks. "Like a legal drug or something?"

"No," Tim says simply. "Natalie Owens was four months pregnant."

I pick at the banana muffin in front of me. I haven't eaten a thing since last night. After we left Tim, Drake gave me a ride home and left me at my front door with nothing more than a peck on my cheek and a reminder that he'll be here at seven a.m.

It's seven fifteen and I'm still waiting. He'd be late to his own funeral given half a chance. Actually, screw half. Give him the sniff of the possibility of a chance and he'd be late.

I hit his name on my call list and tap the speaker button, still aimlessly picking bits of banana out of the muffin and dropping them down onto the open wrapper. It rolls over to voicemail as the sound of a truck rumbles outside. I sit up straight and peek over my windowsill, and when I see his truck, it's the first time in my life that I've been thankful to walk away from cake.

114

I grab my purse and cell, set my alarm, and lock my door behind me. Dark sunglasses shield Drake's eyes from the sun peeking out from behind the clouds low in the sky, and the tight set of his jaw tells me that he's pissed.

Oh, goodie.

"Morning," I say softly, closing the door to the truck.

He grunts a reply.

"You were up all night, weren't you?"

He shrugs and starts the engine again.

I put my hand over his and he stills, turning his face toward mine slightly.

"Have you had coffee?" I ask. "Breakfast? I have muffins inside."

"Coffee and cake don't solve the world's problems, Noelle."

"No, but neither does going without them, so why not have them anyway?"

"Your reasoning is incredibly hard to argue with."

"I know." I smile. "Give me two minutes."

I dig my keys from my purse and jump out. I jog back to the front door and make sure to disable the alarm. Damn thing really is a pain in the ass for situations like this. Then I stop in the middle of the kitchen.

Crap. Natalie was supposed to get her alarm set up today on an emergency call.

I guess she won't be needing that.

Drake's footsteps echo behind me, and I turn to remind him, but before I can, he frames my face with his hands and presses his lips to mine. It's short and sweet and, oddly, completely welcome.

"Morning," he mumbles quietly, his sunglasses presumably left in the car.

I smile. "I see you woke up."

"Have you seen your ass in those shorts? They'd wake up the entire graveyard if you walked through."

I laugh and move my attention to the coffee machine. I pull two takeout mugs from the cupboard, 'cause, you know, doesn't everyone have those in their kitchen?

"You have reusable takeout cups in your kitchen?"

Apparently not. "Uh, yeah. I have to run out early a ton of times, especially if clients think their spouses are lying about where they're going. I once had to go follow some guy in my pajamas at six a.m. because his wife thought he was lying about his earlier flight to New York for some business meeting."

"Was he?"

"Yeah. He went and bonked his mistress before he went to the airport."

"It's a wonder you've never been arrested for invasion of privacy, you know that?"

I fill one mug and smile sweetly over my shoulder. Then I slide the cup along the counter to him. He picks it up and sniffs.

"Hey," I say to him, "Normal coffee, no cream or sugar."

His smile reflects in his eyes. "We already know how the other takes their coffee. Maybe there's hope for us yet."

I purse my lips, but he winks, exaggerating his smile, and I laugh at him. To be fair, Trent and Alison never really got it right until he finally learned how she takes her coffee on a morning before her shifts…and that took him eighteen months. So Drake does have a point there.

"What if one of us didn't drink coffee? Then what?" I ask, fitting the lid on my cup.

"Let's be honest here. You'd never be the one to not drink coffee, and if I didn't drink coffee, I wouldn't come near you before four in the afternoon. I wouldn't be brave enough to face you until you were falling asleep."

"I could so go without coffee," I argue, grabbing a muffin and shoving it at him. "I'm not that much of a bitch without it."

"Sweetheart, don't take this the wrong way, but you can be that much of a bitch *with* coffee."

I glance at the clock on my fireplace before I step outside. "Fifteen minutes into the day. I'm going to count myself as the bigger person here and not respond to that asinine comment."

"Oooh, asinine. Big word for this early."

I spin on the balls of my feet by his car. "Keep that sass up, Detective Nash…"

"And you'll shoot me?" His eyes twinkle.

"No," I say with a sassy half smile. "I can implicate a sex ban now. That's way more threatening than shooting you."

Drake snorts, getting back into the truck and putting his cup and muffin in the center console. "A sex ban? Yeah, all right, cupcake."

"I'm dead serious."

"Noelle, if you think your dumbass sex bans can stop me from touching you and turning you the fuck on whenever I want to, then clearly I need to fuck you again—and harder this time." He lifts one eyebrow, almost running a red light.

"You need to pay attention to the road," I scold him, but my mouth is dry.

Holy shit, and I thought I had no brain-to-mouth filter. Does Drake Nash spit out every sexy thought in that delightful little mind of his without a second thought?

Wait—delightful little mind? What kind of voodoo is this prick pulling on me?

Handsome, part Italian, a Catholic in theory, killer eyes, deadly kiss… Oh, that voodoo.

New Orleans, I need a cure, please and thank you.

"You're mutterin' to yourself, and you look like you have a headache. Are you thinkin' too hard again?"

"One more word," I warn. "One more word and I'm clamping your cock to your thigh."

"If you can find a clamp big enough, I'm gonna say go ahead."

"Cocky bastard."

He slows before turning the corner toward Natalie's street, and he looks at me with a grin that tells me that I walked straight into his trap. "I am, aren't I?"

I exhale loudly, looking away. "Okay. We're here to work. Let's try to be professional."

"Shouldn'ta worn those shorts."

"I should be able to wear whatever I like to work and not be lusted over. Especially when I'm being dragged along on my *day off.*"

"You don't get days off when people die, cupcake."

"I don't get them when they're damn well living, either." I jump out of the truck and slam the door shut. "It'd be real helpful if adulterers could schedule their trysts around my schedule."

"I don't think it works that way." Drake gives me a half grin and inserts the key into the front door.

My skin prickles when he opens it. There's a chill in the air, and if this were a horror movie, I'd say that Ms. Natalie Owens's ghost was haunting this house to stop us from entering and potentially discovering a myriad of her secrets.

I don't know whether Drake feels it or not, because he walks in as if he owns the place, while I'm still hovering on the threshold, a hand curled around the doorframe.

"What are you doing? Waiting for the spirits to cross from the other side and come answer your questions?"

I glare at him. "It feels…strange. Last time I was here, she was so scared and alive…and…alive," I finish lamely before swallowing hard.

Two days.

Two days ago, I was here, and she was sick, which I now know wasn't because of the breakdown. It was probably because of that sweet baby growing inside her.

A baby who'll never know life because its momma was killed. A baby who didn't deserve that ending.

Oh my God.

Oh my God.

"Noelle." Drake cups my face the way he did earlier. "One step. Inside. This isn't the time to be the sweet Noelle I like. Now is when your badass gene can kick the fuck in."

I divert my gaze while I swallow down the lump in my throat. He's right. I can't be emotionally connected to this. I have to come in and look at this house with a critical eye, even if that means being a bitch to him.

"I'm okay," I reassure him, forcing my arm to pull me inside the house. Then I briefly close my eyes, breathing in.

Work, Noelle. Forget everything else.

"What are we looking for?"

"Anything," Drake answers, shutting the front door. "Anything that seems out of place. Diaries. Planners. Calendars. Anything that might relate to her pregnancy."

I hold my hand out, and he passes me a pair of latex gloves. I wriggle my fingers into them because it's really not the easy snap the TV makes it out to be. I practically have my pinkie finger make love to its empty finger space before it goes in. Jesus. If someone wants to make hand-friendly latex gloves, it'd be real appreciated.

I do, however, snap the latex against my wrist. Because. I won't be doing it again though because it does kinda sting a little.

'Kay. A lot. Ouch.

"You take upstairs," Drake says. "I'll do downstairs."

"Got it." I put my foot on the bottom step and start slowly walking up. There are two bookcases on the U-turn of the stairs, each of them filled bottom to top with books. Some are fiction, popular romance and fantasy novels and the like, and others are nonfiction books.

How to Change Your Life in Ten Easy Steps. The Art of Feng Shui. Confessions of a Female Stripper. 50 Easy Recipes for Chicken.

Well, she had a varied reading taste, huh?

I comb my fingers across some of the hardcovers on the middle shelf as I walk past. Such a random mixture of books. I wonder if there's a parenting one in there covered by another book's dust jacket.

I stop halfway up the second set of stairs and turn back to the shelf. One by one, I pull each hardcover down and open the fronts of the dust jackets, leaving them in a haphazard kind of pile by my feet as I sit on the bottom stair.

"Come on, come on," I mutter to the books, starting on the second shelf.

"What are you talkin' to?"

I ignore him and continue on my quest. I'm going to look like a total dick if my gut feeling proves to be wrong.

Except it isn't.

So You're Having a Baby? is hiding beneath a dust jacket for homemade Chinese meals.

"Yes!" I fist-pump the air. "Sneaky!"

"What is?" Drake appears on the stairs, his face peeking out around the corner.

"This." I hold the book out. "She knew she was pregnant, for sure."

He takes it, briefly flicking through its pages. "So, why let someone whip her stomach the way she did?"

"People don't necessary want the babies they carry." I gather a few books and put them back on the shelf in the order I took them off in. "Maybe she was too afraid to have the baby but too afraid to have an abortion, too. Maybe she thought continuing on her sexual lifestyle, the whippings and abuse to her body, would kill the baby. It's not beyond the realms of possibilities. She could have drunk lots and taken drugs and done whatever to kill the baby in a way she deemed natural without having to risk the condemnation of nurses at the clinic…and the medical bills."

"What about the father?"

"He didn't have to know. She told me that Nick was cheating on her, but if she was the one cheating, then it'd make sense that there wasn't another man on the scene to help her."

"Do you think she was cheating?"

I slot the last book onto the shelf and pause. "I don't know. The only person who does is Nick Lucas, and he's annoyingly absent right now."

Drake nods. "Carry on up and see if you can find out anything else. Here." He pulls a couple of evidence bags from his pocket and hands them to me. "Just in case."

I take them and stuff them into my own pocket, focusing on moving upward. Her bedroom, the spare room, and the bathroom. The spare room gives me nothing, and her bedroom gives me nothing other than a tiny desk calendar with stars marked onto it and a half-eaten package of crispy M&Ms. With a huff, I take to her bathroom, pulling her medicine cabinet open.

Everyone has secrets in that thing.

And bingo.

Contraceptive pill packets are in abundance here. When I turn each foil strip over, each pill is labeled with the date. I look to the trash can, and one totally empty strip stares back at me.

Hmm.

I check each strip and finally find one with three days missing. The last day missing being Friday.

How did this get past her doctor? How was she prescribed the pill without being tested for pregnancy?

Of course, I know. You can go so many months without any kind of tests past blood pressure. And if Natalie had been taking this pill for a long period of time without any problems…

But if she was on the pill, how did she get pregnant? Antibiotics? A day missed? Carelessness?

Sweet shit.

I perch on the edge of the bathtub. All of these boxes—they don't even have her name on them. Some of them don't even have doctor's labels.

She wasn't being prescribed them. She was getting them illegally. To try to kill her baby.

Why wouldn't you take the easy route? If you don't want a baby, why not get a medically safe abortion? Or put it up for adoption? Or anything other than try to to kill your baby at home.

Illegal pills and stomach lashes.

I drop the strip to the floor and press my mouth against my upper arm. What on Earth could drive her to do something that drastic? I don't understand it, not for a second.

"Noelle?"

I squeeze my eyes shut for a moment, because I can't imagine the torture Natalie was going through—mentally or, indeed, physically. To do that… Gosh. It doesn't even make sense, does it?

No, *I answer.* No, it doesn't. It also tells me that the baby didn't belong to her boyfriend. Unless there was an underlying veil of abuse she never passed on to me at her interview, but I didn't get that feel.

The more I learn, the less certain I am that she was honest at all. Aside from the obvious in the form of her stalker. But who even knows if all of her claims were true?

I hate doubting people. I want to believe that every one of my clients has a spouse who isn't cheating or they aren't being followed or that lie their teenaged daughter told them was really a lie. I want to see the good in people, because where's the use in going through life seeing the bad? Why would you look at a dark-gray, stormy sky if you had the option to stare at one where the sun's light was filling it?

I'm sometimes harder than situations call for, but when it comes to truth and lies, I want to believe that lies don't exist. That everyone can be honest. That lies are merely made up of misunderstandings and fears warping together.

I'm cynical, too, though, and I know that, sometimes, lies aren't that simple. Lies can be intricate webs of deceitfulness so carefully woven that, soon enough, even the liar can't distinguish between real and make-believe.

"She has several appointments with her gynecologist on her calendar in the kitchen. At least I'm assuming so. And a star every few weeks."

"Her period," I say softly. "Mom used to do that—mark on the calendar approximately when it was due so she knew to be ready.

Except Natalie was marking when she should have been due. I don't think her ex knew she was pregnant, Drake." I turn my face and meet his eyes. "The pill strips—the last one taken was Friday, and none have her name on. She was trying to kill the baby."

I could say it a hundred times and it'd never sink in.

He leans against the doorframe, his eyes moving between the cupboard, the trash can, and the strip I've dropped between my feet on the floor.

"Shit," he breathes.

"We really need DNA on that baby." I drop my eyes to the pills. "This could change everything. She wanted that baby dead, Drake. *Dead.* But not so badly that she'd get an abortion."

"Which means the father wasn't her boyfriend, but someone who could change her life without it being too bad. But who?"

"That's the question, isn't it?"

A rock has settled in my lower stomach ever since we left Natalie's house armed with evidence that's already been handed over to forensics. The images we took are being copied and handed to Sheriff Bates to place onto his board.

I wasn't expecting him to be involved, but apparently, when the mayor's daughter is the one finding the body, it changes everything in the police hierarchy. The soft-spoken yet commanding gentleman who usually takes Sundays off to take his wife for dinner and dancing is dressed in a suit, wading through sex club memberships with my baby brother.

Meanwhile, Drake and I are on the way to the mayor's house, and I'm trying to stop feeling so sick at the news we discovered in her house.

I try Nick Lucas's phone again, and this time, it rings before heading to voicemail. "Hi, Nick, this is Noelle Bond of Bond P.I. I'm working with the Holly Woods Police Department on an urgent matter concerning your ex-girlfriend, Natalie Owens. It'd be real helpful if you could give me a call back at seven-three-seven-six-five-three-nine-nine-eight-zero as soon as possible. Thank you." I hang up and slap my phone onto my lap. "People shouldn't have phones if they won't answer them. Can't we get his address and surprise him? I'll bring the cookies."

Drake snorts. "I've had Brody and Trent both drop by his apartment today. Brody asked some questions and it turns out Nick hasn't been home in four days at least. According to his neighbors, he's gone to see his folks in Arkansas for a few days. They know to call us if or when he gets home."

"What about his parents? Can't we call and see if he's there?"

"Did Grecia call your new tech guy?"

"First thing this morning."

"Wanna pay him overtime and charge it to the mayor?"

I cut my eyes to him. "Am I allowed to do that? The contract said necessary extras, but this doesn't seem like it should be something necessary."

"It's not necessary to verify with a potential suspect's parents' if he's where he claims—in their house?" Drake smiles slyly. "Sounds pretty necessary to me."

"Oh, you are a bad influence, Detective Nash. I should tell the sheriff about your law-breakin'."

"I seem to remember him giving you permission to do what you need to for information as long as he doesn't know about it. I reckon he doesn't need to know about this."

Argh. "Okay. Detour to my office."

He does, and by the time we reach the empty building, I've already texted Grecia and had her ask Carlton to come in to see me. He arrives moments after Drake and I do, when Drake is unsurprisingly raiding my coffee stash in the kitchen.

Carlton pushes his dirty-blond hair out of his eyes. "What's up?"

"First, I'm sorry for dragging you here on a Sunday."

"No worries. You said flexible, and I was doing nothing except screwing around on the computer."

Speaking of computers... "Did you bring yours? Computer, I mean. My old guy had two laptops he'd bring in, and I'd like a chance to have Dean show you our system on the desktop in his office tomorrow."

"Sure. It's right here." He pulls the newest Mac computer out of his messenger bag.

"Perfect." I swallow and give Drake a grateful smile when he brings me a coffee. "Do you need a drink or anything before I get started?"

"No worries. I'm cool."

"Great. So…" I give him the need-to-know facts about Natalie's case. "This is a copy of the stalker case she opened with me before she died. It includes the details of her ex-boyfriend, the guy she thought was her stalker. I can't get ahold of him, and neither can the police, but we've managed to work out that he's at his parents' place in Arkansas."

"But you don't have their details and you want me to find them," he surmises correctly.

"Can you?"

"It might not be legal." He cuts his eyes to Drake.

He promptly leaves the room.

I look down, smiling, before returning my gaze to Carlton. "Doesn't matter. I do things my way in this building. My unofficial business tagline is 'what the Holly Woods PD don't know won't hurt 'em.' So, Carlton, can you do it?"

"What do you need?"

"Phone numbers. That's it."

"You got it." He opens the computer, slinking down in his chair until his face is completely obscured by the screen.

"I'm just gonna…" I say awkwardly, sliding my chair back and picking my mug up, "leave you to it."

He doesn't acknowledge me, his fingers moving across his keyboard at a lightning speed.

Anyone who can type that fast cannot be trustworthy.

I join Drake in the spare meeting room adjacent to the one Carlton is proving his worth in. Perhaps a dining room before, it contains only a two-seater sofa, a couple of armchairs, and a small coffee table as well as a picture of the Austin skyline at night, as seen from the Hyatt hotel. Drake is standing by the window, his arms folded, the sun casting a shadow across the back of him.

I pause by the door, bringing the rim of my mug to my mouth but not drinking. That white shirt—that fucking white shirt. He must have a whole store's worth of the damn things in his closet. It hugs every inch of his body, and the navy-blue jeans he's wearing fit way too perfectly to be legal in any of the fifty states.

"He doing it?" he asks, cutting through my moment. He looks

over his shoulder at me.

"He said so." I shrug and put my cup on the coffee table, sitting on the edge of the sofa. My elbows rest on my knees, and my fingers brush as my hands fall limply in front of me. "I hope so," I add. "Because, if not, I don't know how we're supposed to move forward unless we get the FBI to hunt him down."

Drake laughs quietly, leaving the window and joining me on the sofa. "That's a little drastic at this point in the investigation, cupcake."

"I know." I sigh when the sofa cushion dips with his added weight. "It doesn't matter though, does it? The chance of it being as simple as Nick being her killer is completely outrageous."

"You've watched too much TV."

Now, it's my turn to laugh softly. I knock my elbow against his. "No, I've seen too many investigations where the people figuring it out have gone around and around more times than an expertly twisted spinning top on a tile floor."

He wraps his arm around my shoulder, pulling me into his side. "We'll figure this out. You're the only woman on this team."

"No pressure, then," I drawl. "I don't know. Lena's investigation consumed me for weeks. I can already feel myself obsessing over Natalie's murder. Like, I'm seriously pissed off that this little bastard Nick has disappeared off the face of the Earth and that I can't grill the shit outta the mayor and his daughter until someone has found Nick. But then I want to scour through the club's membership files myself and retrace her steps from the time when my brother left her house to when she was killed. I want to do it all. Isn't that crazy?"

"No," he says simply. "You're an investigator, as much as it's a pain in my fuckin' ass."

I elbow him again.

"You wanna know everything and you wanna know it now. You're like a damn toddler with candy."

"Or a grown woman with cupcakes."

"I'll refer you back to my toddler comment."

I click my tongue against the roof of my mouth and knock his arm from my shoulders. "Prick."

"Pain in the ass."

"You already used that."

"I know."

"Y'all fightin' already?" Bek appears in the doorway.

"What are you doing here?" I look at her.

"Needed some files for that Jenner-Miller case. Caught Brody on his way back from McDonalds." She grins. "He had half the restaurant in his passenger's seat."

"I'm really not surprised," I snort.

"Uh…" Carlton appears behind Bek. "Sorry. I don't want to interrupt."

"Oh, you're not. Bek, this is Carlton, our new tech guy. Carlton, this is Rebekah, my best friend and another investigator."

They shake hands and murmur pleasantries.

"Did you find it?"

"The number? Yeah. And their address, all of their jobs, and the last used locations of Nick's credit card."

Drake gets up and holds his hands out for the papers. Carlton hands them over, and I get the feeling he's a little intimidated by Drake. There's no shame in that. I would be, too, if I didn't have a freaky hate-sex relationship with the man.

Drake's lips curve to the side, and he drops the papers on my legs. "Arkansas my fuckin' ass."

I frown and turn the sheet the right way up. My eyes fall to the credit card records from the last twenty-four hours, including transactions pending. It was last used in the sandwich shop next to the tattoo studio I thought closed four years ago. It's just outside town, and he apparently works there.

"Can you get the appointment list for there? For today?" I add, noting the opening times.

"I can try." Carlton disappears again. Two minutes later, he comes back with his computer in tow. "They don't use anything online. You have to call them."

"Okay." Drake looks between me and Bek. "Bek, I need you to go down there and see if they have anything for tomorrow with Nick. If they say yes, book something. If not, ask to see the appointment list for the rest of the week. Get a name of a woman scheduled tomorrow and we'll do the rest, all right?"

Bek looks at me. "Do I get paid, too?"

"Sure. The extras are coming from the mayor, not me." I shrug.

"All right," she agrees. "Lemme grab my files and I'll head down there." She disappears up the stairs.

"You want some homework?" I direct to Carlton, standing up.

"Sure. My roommate will only make me watch dumb reality TV."

"Perfect." Then I tell him exactly what I want him to do. With the promise of overtime pay, courtesy of Mayor McDougall, of course.

chapter NINE

AFTER we'd found the mayor and family not at home, we called it a day, and I went home alone for a hot date with the finding power of social media and a bottle of wine.

Now, I'm regretting the wine, but not my late-night soiree with Facebook and Instagram. Like the credit card reports, Nick has been in town the whole time. His posts on Instagram the last few days have all been of tattoos. Some of them were captioned as throwbacks, but the background looks awfully similar to one of the latest ones he noted as brand new.

Bek's visit to the studio also gave us our in. Their morning was open after only recently deciding to open on Mondays to make it seven days a week, which is why I'm out of bed by nine and driving out of town to the studio.

I don't think he did it. But you know. I wanna know if he was stalking her at the very least. And he does have the whole got-away-with-murder thing hanging over him. I didn't really pay much attention when Drake said it, but as it turns out, it was a pretty serious situation. He was eighteen, just graduated, and he and some friends broke into a store. The robbery was armed, but since there was no video proof he held, or shot, the gun, despite the testimonies of his friend—who the gun belonged to—he got away with a couple years in jail and that was that. He moved to Austin right after, then to Holly

Woods.

I pull up outside the building and notice Bek's car already here. She gets out when I kill my engine and mutters something about needing more overtime pay since it's on the mayor.

I laugh. Yeah, it doesn't work like that. Only on days off or he'll dispute my invoice.

The tattoo studio is small and run down. It's not exactly the well-kept establishment I envisioned when I found out they have to open seven days a week to keep up with demand, but hey. I'll reserve full judgment until I've been inside. I'll try to anyway, because the rusted sign proclaiming it to be Nick's Tattoo Studio screwed slightly wonkily into a wall covered with cracked, dirty, white paint doesn't do much for my confidence.

"Nice place," Bek tries, the twisting of her lips to her betraying her words.

"Yeah, if you come from the Amazon," I mutter, pushing the door open.

The radio is on low, and the scent of jasmine hits me. Thankfully, it seems like the outside appearance really isn't reflective of the interior. Tattoo designs line the walls, and a black leather sofa is in the corner in front of a glass coffee table covered with magazines. Hell, switch the sofa color to red and you have my waiting area. To our right is a waist-high reception counter, and sitting behind it is a guy with dreads that fall long past his shoulders, a septum piercing, and tattoos peeking up from his collar.

"Can I help you?"

"Uh…yes." Bek walks up to him. "I have an appointment. With Nick?"

"Name?"

"Rebekah."

"Sure," Dreads drawls. "Take a seat and—"

"I'm here. Come on in." Nick appears in the doorway, and. Um. Oh. Shit.

Nick is hot.

And I ain't talking about his body temperature.

I'm talking brown hair, green eyes, cheekbones-chiseled-into-next-week kinda hot.

"Sure," Bek replies, her voice cracking. She clears her throat and throws me a holy-shit look over her shoulder.

Holy shit is right. And I am *so* going to hell.

Nick closes the door behind us and leans against it. His eyes turn calculating as he sweeps his gaze across us, eventually settling it on me.

Uh oh. Busted.

"There's only one reason a Bond would walk into my studio, and since you're the only one without cuffs, I'll save you the awkward explanation about why you're here."

"I'm assuming you got my message."

"Yeah, I got your message."

"And you didn't return it because…?"

He laughs derisively. "Because I couldn't give a shit about my fucked-up ex. That's why."

I lick my lips. "Nick… You have heard, haven't you?"

"That someone bumped her off?" He raises one eyebrow. "Yeah. Not gonna say I'm surprised, darlin'. She messed with the wrong people in the wrong place."

I'm gonna come back to that one. "What do you know about her stalker?"

"That she was certain it was me, but not enough to leave me the fuck alone. Trust me, I've been tryin' for weeks to get her crazy ass off my damn back."

"Wait, what?" Bek asks. "She told Noelle she hadn't spoken to you since she ended your relationship."

"Since she ended it?" He laughs again. "Little miss fuckin' perfect strikes again, eh?"

I smile tightly. "Why don't you tell me what happened?"

"What happened is that Nat was a whore, pure and simple." He swigs from a bottle of Diet Pepsi. "She couldn't keep her legs shut. She had her membership at that stupid dom club when we met, but I made her stop going. She did for a while. Then she started again. Something about her sexual needs being more than I could give her. Whatever, yeah? We were happy otherwise, so I told her she could do that shit once a week if I could do what I wanted the same night. It worked. She got her sadist kicks and I got my cock sucked by someone who actually knew what to do with it."

Delightful.

"'Cept she got dumb. Started lyin' to me about where she was goin' and who she was lettin' tie her up or whatever the fuck it is they do in that place. She started screwin' people she had no business screwin' with. Took it past our one-night-a-week agreement. She got addicted to that place and her sick fetishes, so I ended it. Told her to keep her fantasies the fuck away from me."

"What about the baby?" I question, rubbing my bottom lip with my thumb. "Did y'all make arrangements for that? Buying things, doctor's appointments, what'd happen after she gave birth, stuff like that?

"Why would I?" He snorts. "She told me the kid was mine, but I ain't that stupid. I made sure we used condoms when I found out she was letting every Tom, Dick, and fucking Spartacus ride her pussy bareback."

Straight to the point, this one. He's so sour that not even Willy Wonka and his army of Oompa Loompas could sweeten him up.

"So, you aren't the father?" I frown. "Earlier you said she was messing with people she shouldn't have been. What did you mean?"

Nick runs his tongue over his teeth, his eyes hardening. "People you probably shouldn't be messin' with, either."

"Unless they're a branch of the mafia or a Mexican cartel, I think I'll take my chances, thanks."

His lips tug up. "She was sleepin' her way to the top. She craved power. She was a manipulator through and through. And that baby was her ticket to the top...to have power over the people already there."

"Call me stupid," Bek starts, looking at me.

"Oh I'd call you plentya things, darlin', but stupid ain't one of 'em." Nick grins.

I roll my eyes when a flush creeps up her cheeks.

"You're not making sense," she continues, despite her obvious embarrassment. "There isn't much power in Holly Woods, at least nothing worth having compared to other places. If she wanted power, why not leave?"

"Because she was set for life. Her old man left her that pretty little house so she didn't have to pay a cent toward it."

"Nick," I say, stepping forward. "If you know who the father of that baby was, then I need to know, too. If you're right and she was manipulating someone, there's a very real chance they're her killer or at least connected."

The smirk on his face is cruel. It's evil and heartless, and I'd bet my newest pair of Jimmy Choos that she wasn't the only manipulator in their relationship.

"She was fucking the mayor," he says quietly, but every word is spit with anger in the most bitter, derogatory way I've heard in a long time. "He fathered that little runt inside her. He spent as much time at that sick club as she did, and he always thought he could get away with it. But he won't. The truth will come out. It always does."

Someday, I will find a dead body in Holly Woods and their murderer will be standing in front of them, ready to be taken to the police station, guilty plea intact.

Someday, someone will slap me and tell me to stop damn well dreaming. Until that day, however, I will sit here at my desk with every one of Natalie's contracts from D.O.M. and read until my eyes bleed.

I'm also gonna eat my cupcake, 'cause, well, yeah. We might have taken a detour to Gigi's in Austin while I called Drake to update him before coming back to the office. As it is, I came back to a stack of contracts with more pages than most standard romance novels waiting for me.

That's an exaggeration. They're not that long. They feel like it, though. I really wish they'd read like it though. These contracts, for all of their clauses about nipple clamps and anal beads and floggers, are really kind of boring. They could use a swoony, long-haired man on the front of a scandalous bodice-ripper.

Oh, who am I kidding? They need a ripped-as-hell guy pulling on some chick's hair. And that's on the cover.

I've read through three of the twenty and haven't found anything about erotic asphyxiation. It's not even mentioned in the list of "acceptable practices" D.O.M. lists in the documents. I think my father was right when he said that it wouldn't be something they'd allow due to the high risks involved with the activity.

Personally, I don't get it. The page on my laptop in front of me mentions the biggest reason for it—to increase pleasure—and the methods used. And those? Hell, those are…worrying. There's the "normal" strangulation with something like the tie that killed Natalie, suffocation with a pillow, but then it goes to solvents, hanging, and using a plastic bag over the head.

Takes the phrase "only if there was a paper bag over their head" to a whole new level, if you ask me. Except that thought is kinda inappropriate, so it's probably a good thing no one *has* asked me.

I break into the cupcake with my fork and scoop the chocolate sponge into my mouth. I'm pretty sure I'm going to have a sugar overdose by the end of the day, but you know.

My phone buzzes and the screen lights up with a text. I hit the notification blindly and swipe to unlock it. I don't care if this thing has fingerprint recognition. I don't have the damn patience to mess around with that every time I need to do something on it. The message is from Drake, and I groan.

Found anything?

I pick my phone up and respond: *Discovered the cure for diabetes and undeniable proof of alien life.*

The reply comes through almost instantly. *I don't know if you're hilarious or just pissing me off.*

I'm pissing you off hilariously.

Are you reading those contracts? The whips sound real tempting right now…

Aren't you supposed to be interviewing the mayor?

He doesn't reply after that.

"Ha!" I fist-pump the air and flick contract number four open. My fork has sunk into my cake once more when my office door sneaks open and a familiar icy-blue eye peeks through the crack. "Oh, piss off," I mutter, ignoring him.

Drake laughs, coming in. "Surprise?"

"Not a good one." I lick the cake off the fork's prongs, and his eyes darken instantly. "Nope." I point my fork at him. "Nope, nope, nope. What do you want now?"

"For you to come do interviews with me."

"Isn't that supposed to be Trent's job?"

"No. Trent's job was to reconstruct the hours before her death, and they've been staring at security tapes for the last six hours." He drops himself onto one of my chairs and runs his fingers through his hair. "Dev was the last to leave Natalie's house at approximately ten a.m., but between then and noon, we don't know where she was. At noon, she checked into the Oleander with campaign materials. At twelve fifteen, she went into her room, and at twelve thirty, Mrs. McDougall knocked on her door and disappeared inside. After that, there's a period where the tapes go fuzzy, but it clearly shows a figure on the floor at one fifteen and another at one forty-five."

"Why would the mayor's wife be visiting her?"

"Work, we assume. She did drop off campaign materials. For all we know, there was an issue Alyssa McDougall needed to discuss."

"I suppose." I pause, scooping more cake onto my fork. When I look back at Drake, I get what he wants. "You want me to interview her."

"Correction: I want you to come with me."

"Why? The mayor told me to basically arrest Nick and not investigate. Questioning his wife isn't the smartest... Wait a minute." I drop my fork, and it clatters against the desk. "You want me to come with you and tell her that we're only interviewing her because the mayor would hate to have her name smeared through the mud if anyone saw her entering the hotel room."

Drake's eyes light up. "Bingo."

"I don't know why I let you talk me into this shit."

"You're blinded by my superior wit and charm."

"The only charm you possess, Detective Nash, is one worthy of being pooped on by seagulls." I sniff and look up at the house in front of us.

Can we say whoa?

Yes we can, as long as you insert a "fucking" before it.

Because fucking whoa.

The mayor's house is huge. It needs to be in Holly*wood*. I didn't even know these kinds of houses existed in small-town Texas, but apparently, they do. The three stories are in a perfect rectangle, and the sculpted, spherical bush-tree-plant thingies lining the drive are begging me to find a branch out of place.

Go on, you annoyingly symmetrical balls. One leaf. That's all I want.

I don't get the leaf.

By the time we pull up in the circle outside the mansion complete with a water fountain, I'm ready to take a match to my own quaint house, say, "Fuck this shit," and move back in with my parents.

Wait. No. That isn't something that's happening on any day of ever.

"Does she know we're coming?"

Drake glances at me. "Possibly."

"Well, that's a no." I sigh when he kills the engine. "Do you have all of your necessary legal crap?"

"Do I have my badge and a search warrant? Yes."

"Does it ever bother you how quickly Judge Barnes signs off on his warrants?"

Drake holds his arms out. "No."

"Shut up." I jab my finger against the doorbell. The very classic ding-dong echoes through the majestically carved front door and toward us. It's loud. Real loud. I guess it has to be when you're knocking on the door of Holly Woods' answer to the White House.

The door opens slowly and Mrs. Alyssa McDougall appears in the gap between the door and the frame. Her brown hair is swept back into an elegant ballerina bun, her hazel eyes lined with mascara that makes her eyelashes pop outward, and her lips are perfectly painted in red lipstick.

"I wondered how long it'd be until y'all showed your faces," she says, her bright-red lips curving. "Come in, Detective Nash, Noelle. Can I get y'all a drink?"

"We're fine. Thank you, ma'am," Drake replies.

Speak for yourself. "Can I have a glass of water, please?" I ask.

"Absolutely. Let's take a seat and one will be brought in to you." She elegantly waves an arm toward a room to her left.

I follow Drake's lead into it. It's exquisitely decorated, from the detailed ceiling to the painted canvases on the walls and the Queen Anne–style furniture.

Shit me. I've stepped into an antique showroom.

"Please, take a seat." Alyssa smooths her pencil skirt down and sits on one of the sofas, crossing one leg over the other. "I'm assuming y'all are here on an official capacity having seen me enter Natalie's room on Saturday, so I'm open to any questions you have."

Her eyes focus on me.

They linger for a moment too long.

"Why did you go to her room?" I ask. "She isn't on the public council payroll."

"She's my daughter's best friend who recently went through a nasty breakup, Noelle. Why wouldn't I see her?"

"Because she owns a house outright and would have, as your daughter's best friend, spent time with Madison since the breakup." No way am I telling her that it isn't what she thinks.

"My daughter and I lead entirely different lives. I see her only when it suits her."

"Except for the fact that she works for your husband, her father, in his building, five days a week, plus overtime, with benefits."

"Just because she does doesn't mean I do, Ms. Bond."

"I was Noelle three minutes ago. What changed?"

"You interrogated me like I'm a common criminal."

I lean forward, ignoring her entitled, affected gaze. "Well, Mrs. McDougall, I don't see that my questioning should bother you. If you have nothing to hide, you have no reason to be offended by my enquiries."

"No, but I can request you have official representation."

"In case that escaped your notice, ma'am, I'm sitting next to the chief of homicide and have your husband's signature on a contract giving me the same powers as the HWPD to investigate Natalie's murder for the sake of your daughter." I pause, watching the annoyance leave her eyes as my words sink in. "So you can tell me what I want to know or I can tell your husband that I recommend Detective Nash and Sheriff Bates put his wife on the official list of suspects. Your choice."

The silence that stretches between us is long and tense.

"Your talent is wasted as a private investigator, Noelle. You should be on the police force and telling your brothers what to do." Alyssa's lips move into a smile.

"You might be correct, but I much prefer being my own boss.

Besides, I get paid far more." I bite my thumbnail. "Can I count on you to tell me what you know, or am I beating my forehead against a brick wall?"

Alyssa sighs, leaning back and linking her fingers. Her outfit miraculously remains uncreased. "Natalie worked for the council on a contractual basis. She was paid for miscellaneous jobs, such as paperwork, reception, design, cleaning, campaign work. On Saturday, she was due to deliver one thousand promotional flyers to me before the debate, but only six hundred turned up. I went to her room to enquire as to the whereabouts of the missing four hundred."

"What did happen to them?"

She shrugs, one arm to the side. "Who knows? She insisted she didn't."

"Did you fight?"

"Physically? No, of course not. Verbally? Words were exchanged, yes."

Fuck, I wanna ask if her if she knew she was sleeping with her husband.

"Was she lying?" I ask, sitting back. "In your personal opinion, of course. Did you feel she was being dishonest about the flyers?"

"Perhaps," she replies cryptically. "I don't count myself well versed in bodily signals regarding honesty."

That explains why she's been married to the mayor for so long.

"Mrs. McDougall," Drake cuts in. "If you have any information about what happened on Saturday, we'd really appreciate it. The police department is very sensitive of the impact this could have on Mayor McDougall's latest campaign. We respect him highly, and I know I speak for us all when I say we'd love to see him stay on for another term as mayor. We're looking to get this case wrapped up as quickly as possible to minimize the possible damage."

"Why, Detective," Alyssa drawls, "that sounds like you read it right off my husband's latest speech."

"He must have excellent taste, ma'am."

I want to throw up.

"Detective Nash, with all due respect," she continues, "I don't trust y'all as far as I can throw you. I can barely throw the dog's tennis ball these days, so I don't fancy my chances against you. While I understand that Ms. Bond is working with y'all, I'd real appreciate it if you could step outside for a moment so I can finish my conversation with her."

Well. Shit.

Drake looks at me. I smile sweetly before mouthing a quick, "Go!" at him.

"Very well, ma'am. I hope you're well."

Alyssa inclines her head toward him, a perfectly polite smile on her face.

What could she want to discuss with me? And does she expect me not to tell them? Because…ugh. If they question me formally, which is something Trent at least would do, then her cats are let out of the bag and free to mate.

The door shuts behind Drake and Alyssa visibly relaxes. "Fucking cops," she sighs.

Double, well, shit.

"Is it awkward if I agree with you?"

Alyssa laughs and stands up, moving around the sofa with several clicks of her heels against the polished wooden floor toward the bar in the back corner. She lifts the bottle of gin, pours a measure into glass, then tops it up with tonic water.

"Can I offer you one?"

What the hell. The glass of water never showed up. "Sure." I join her at the bar as she drops the empty tonic water bottle into the trash can.

Her red, manicured fingernails stand out against the clear liquid in her glass. "Randy was right," she says quietly, referring to her husband. Her eyes creep up to meet mine. "This case should be solved quickly and quietly, and not because of the bullshit propaganda Detective Nash spewed to me. Just because it's worth it to many people for this to be closed quickly and quietly."

"If the person who killed Natalie agreed, her murder would have been staged to be suicide. She would have been made to look responsible for her strangling, not still have been tied to the bed."

She takes a deep breath, sorrow deep in her eyes. "Believe me," she whispers, looking into her glass. "Except my daughter, no one other than me wishes this could be solved perfectly. I'd give any of me to see Natty's killer come to justice, but I don't know how I can help you, Noelle."

"By telling me what you know. Exactly what you know."

She takes a long drink from her glass, draining it, then sets it down. "My husband has long been…adventurous…in our marriage," she admits, her voice cracking at the word *adventurous*. "It sounds like insanity, does it not? That I'd still be here after forty years, allowing him to play his games?"

"Yes," I admit honestly. "I couldn't imagine being with someone who didn't look at me and see his entire universe."

"You're a romantic, honey. I'm a realist. When Randy first cheated, I saw our daughter, the empire we had and were building. It was too much to throw away on simple misdemeanors."

"Simple misdemeanors? You don't classify him spitting on your vows and tearing them apart as deal breakers?"

"At first? Yes. After? No. This isn't an open relationship by any means, Noelle. I know about every little escapade he has with a woman, but I've never once stepped out on him. I know my place in our marriage."

She knows her place? What the fuck is this? The nineteen fucking fifties?

Why has no one told her to leave his cheating son-of-a-bitch ass inside the washing machine she could take him to the cleaners with?

"And your place is at his side as his equal," I say quietly but strongly. "Alyssa, you don't have to take his shit. You don't have to be the doormat he wipes his dick on when he's done with whatever he wants outside of the vows he unequivocally promised you."

She takes a deep breath. Long and audible, she breathes in, finally, drawing her eyes to me from the window. "I know. But it isn't that easy."

I take my purse from the sofa I was sitting on and pull my card from the silver holder. I hand her the thick rectangle containing my details. "Here's my card. If you think of anything, and I mean anything, day or night, pertaining to our investigation, please don't hesitate to call me." I meet her eyes, and I hope I can portray the message I want to. I hope I can tell her that she is worth more than the piece of shit she's married to. "Even if I'm busy, I'll make sure to return your call. My assistant is on there, too, so if it's urgent, she'll be able to contact me immediately."

Alyssa takes my card between her finger and thumb. "Thank

you," she replies softly. "I sure will."

I put my untouched glass on the counter, sling my purse over my shoulder, and make my own way out, all too aware that there's so much crap building up into this investigation that we'll need a miracle to wade through it all.

chapter TEN

THE truth will out.

The truth will out.

What does that even mean?

My mind is full of both Nick's and Alyssa's words. His certainty that everything will come and Alyssa's insistence of her knowledge of her husband's infidelities.

The question, though, is if she knew about Natalie. He may tell her every time he sleeps with someone or goes to D.O.M., but would he really tell her that he was sleeping with their daughter's best friend? There is a line, after all, and that crosses it, doesn't it? It's one thing to sleep with your brother's best friend or your best friend's sister, but your child's best friend?

That's really screwed up.

That's like my Dad sleeping with Bek.

And now, I'm traumatized.

I sip my coffee and flick through another one of Natalie's contracts.

Do Alyssa and Nick know each other? Would they have met at some point during his relationship with Natalie? She was adamant that she only saw her when necessary, but she wouldn't be the first person to have lied here.

I sigh and close the contract. These are going to be dead ends.

That's for sure. If erotic asphyxiation is against the club's rules, it won't be in a contract anywhere. This is a total waste of my time. I could be talking to Madison McDougall right now. I could be drawing up profiles of motivation and opportunity for everyone we've met so far.

Screw it. I'm going to do that instead. It's a far better use of my time than reading this bullshit.

I shove the contracts to one side. One falls on the floor, but I leave it there and grab my whiteboard Sharpie. I wipe off the reminder to myself to order more printer ink and uncap the pen. Then I write four names at the top, separate their columns with lines, and underline the names.

Mayor McDougall. Motive: If he knew about the baby and Natalie wasn't trying to have an abortion and was throwing her pills away instead, then yes, absolutely. Opportunity: Yes, either before or after Alyssa left Natalie's hotel room.

Alyssa McDougall. Motive: If she knew about her husband's affair and that Natalie was pregnant, hell yeah, that's a motive. Opportunity: When she was in her room with her. The second figure could have helped her, whoever it was.

Madison McDougall. Motive: If she knew about her dad's affair and the baby, yes. Opportunity: Well, she was the one who found her. Supposedly. She could have been the unidentifiable figure on the camera.

Nick Lucas. Motive: Goes without saying. Opportunity: Again, could have been the figure on the camera.

I'm really no closer than I was twenty minutes ago. Hm. I cap the pen and walk back, perching on the edge of my desk. Tapping the pen against my lips, I read what I just wrote. I read it again. And again.

"Hey," I call to Carlton, catching him walking past my office.

"What's up?" He hovers by the doorway, his hands in his pockets.

"Do you have any close female friends?"

"Sure. Why?"

"On a scale of one to ten, how pissed off would you be if you found out your dad was sleeping with one of them and had them knocked up?" I glance at him, and upon seeing the horror on his face, I quickly add, "Hypothetically. I swear."

His shoulders drop as he relaxes. "If he was still married to my mom?" I nod. "I dunno. Probably fifty or somethin."

142

I chew on the inside of my cheek. "What if one was totally cool and one hundred was murderous. Would you still be fifty?"

"There's a point to this, yeah? You're not tryna scope me out as a potential murderer?"

I laugh. "No, I swear there's a point."

He shrugs. "Probably. I'd be mad enough to want to throw a rock at his face or somethin', but not mad enough to actually do it. Does that make sense?"

"Sure. One day, I'll introduce you to my grandmother and you'll understand how often I come close to eighty on that scale." I smirk. "Okay, so let's switch this. What if your girlfriend slept with her best friend's father and got pregnant? Then where would you be on the scale?"

"Probably about the same. I dunno. I'm pretty laid-back. I think I'd be more betrayed than angry."

And betrayal leads people to do more impulsive, stupid things than anger does.

"Thanks, Carlton. Hey—I need some records, actually."

"Sure. What do you need?"

"A lot. I need everything you can get on Natalie Owens, Nick Lucas, and the whole McDougall family."

"The mayor's family?"

"Yep." I meet his eyes. "Probably best to keep that one quiet."

"No shit," he mutters. "All right. I'll try to get some to you by the end of the day."

"Thanks. Natalie Owens is most important right now, more specifically her medical records."

He frowns but nods in agreement anyway.

I guess only a handful of people actually know about her being pregnant. I'd rather it stays that way, too.

My eyes drift back to the whiteboard. Speaking to the mayor so early about his relationship with Natalie without any more tangible proof is asking for disaster. And to be fired, which is the last thing I want. Not even because of the money, but because then Drake and my brothers will withhold every bit of information they can. I don't care what Drake says. He's still not happy about this situation.

I pick my phone up and dial Madison's number.

"Hello?" she answers.

"Hi, Madison. This is Noelle Bond. I was wondering if you were free to talk."

"Sure. I'm at the town hall building."

"I'm on my way."

I get out of my car, having squeezed into the tiniest parking space known to man. Why these business guys need big-ass trucks that take up two point five spaces, I'll never know. I assume they'd be too afraid to crease their suits, but maybe it has to do with their egos. Bigger is better and all that.

Such a pissing contest.

I walk in and go to the main reception desk, which was closed last time I was here. "Can you tell me where I can find Madison McDougall?"

The woman barely looks up at me. "Floor three."

"Thank you." I make it across the lobby and into the elevator before the doors shut.

The button for three is already pushed, so I simply wait until it shudders to a stop and announces our arrival at level three. Almost immediately, I spot Madison sitting at a desk and looking incredibly bored.

"Hey," I say quietly, approaching her. "Am I interrupting anything?"

She looks up with a sad smile. "No. Looking at funeral stuff." She takes a deep breath. "She has no one to plan it except me and I…" she trails off as her voice thickens. Then she shakes her head and focuses on me. "Your brother said you'd be by to talk to me soon. What do you need?"

"Do you want to talk here or go somewhere more private?" I look around at the half-empty floor.

"None of these people care," she replies sadly. "They're on minimize-campaign-damage mode. Same with Dad. He hired a new manager to oversee everything since Jane quit after Nat was found. She's in his office now. The new one, I mean. Not Jane."

I nod slowly. "I know my brother already took your statement, so I'm not gonna ask you about Friday. I want to know more about Natalie."

"And Nick?" she asks, her cheeks pinking.

Interesting. "Especially about Nick. Their relationship sounds kinda crazy."

"It was. But Nat... She had her"—Madison pouts, pausing—"things," she finishes lamely. "I don't know how to phrase it. He was cruel about it. He called her a sadomasochistic whore, disgusting, a freak, all sorts of things. He didn't realize why she liked BDSM."

"I don't know much about it, so at the risk of looking like a total asshole, she had a specific relationship with them, right?"

"The guys at the club? Yeah. She was always the submissive."

"How long has she been going there?"

"Since she was twenty-one. They have an age limit. I think she ended up there after a date with one of the guys who goes regularly. Their relationship never made it back out of the club. As far as I know, he was one of the only people she was with regularly."

"What's his name?" I rifle in my purse for a notebook and a pen.

"Vince Fulton," she answers. "Here." She hands me a Post-it and a pen, and I write his name down then hand them back. "He works at the—"

"Building yard just outside town, right? Yeah, I know him. He did my parents' sunroom last year. Thanks." I tuck the note into a zip pocket inside my purse. "What kind of stuff did she do there? I don't want to upset you, but her positioning on Saturday was kind of..."

"Uncomfortable? Painful? Disturbing?" Madison raises an eyebrow. "Take your pick, okay? I don't know. I told her I didn't want to talk about that shit with her. I accepted that she liked to be whipped and chained or whatever, but when she moved into that strangling stuff and pretending that she was being raped, I was done. I only went once and stayed at the bar the whole time because I was too scared to go inside a room."

"Who else would have known about what she liked except for the club members and Nick?"

"Honestly, I have no idea. Their relationship was screwed the moment she told him she was missing that lifestyle. I think she went back to try to get rid of him, but he gave her a compromise she couldn't refuse."

I nod in agreement.

"It was…awkward with them. Sometimes, they got along really well, but when they didn't, they'd both close off and go and sleep with anyone they wanted."

"Did you sleep with Nick?"

Her eyes flick down to the desk, and she rolls up the sticky note on the top of the pile. "Twice," she admits softly. "The first time was an accident."

Did his penis slip and fall into her vagina or something? Did it apologize after?

"How do you sleep with someone by accident?"

"You get drunk," she responds wryly. "He walked out after finding out she'd had a threesome at the club. I was at the bar, escaping my parents never-ending arguments, and we commiserated together. Literally."

"And the second time?"

"I…wish I could give you an explanation. It was one of those things that happened. She told him she was going away to see her cousins in New Mexico, but really, she was going to a swingers weekend there. He came to my place, and you know how the rest of that story goes."

"So, when you say twice, you really mean…"

"Two different occasions." She even looks embarrassed. She should, too. Sleeping with her best friend's boyfriend no matter the state of their relationship is the lowest of the low.

Mind you, so is sleeping with your best friend's dad.

Still, though, if I found out Bek slept with Drake…

Hold the phone. Since when do I refer to him as my boyfriend? My brain and I are gonna have to have ourselves a little chat tonight.

I pull my attention back to Madison. "Right. When was the last time you saw Nick?"

"Right when they broke up. He told me he wanted to be with me and that's why he broke up with her. He said he couldn't deal with her freaky desires."

"What did you say to him then?"

"I told him there was no way we could be together right away. And that I didn't trust him not to cheat on me." She shrugs and picks at a cuticle. "That was the last time we spoke, too. I tried to call him when the hospital let me go home on Friday, but he wouldn't answer."

"Believe me, you're not the only one who had that issue." I wet my lips with my tongue and meet Madison's eyes. "Did you know that Natalie was pregnant?"

She stiffens, her finger and thumb still pinched at the base of a nail on her other hand, and her eyes gloss over with shock. "She—she was? When? How many—oh my God."

I'm gonna go with a *whoops* here.

"Yeah. It came out in the autopsy," I say quietly. "I'm sorry. I thought you knew."

She shakes her head and clears her throat. "How far...how far was she?"

"Not very," I lie. "Only a few weeks. We're trying to find out who the father was."

"So, it wasn't Nick?"

"He says no." I shrug. "Look, I've taken up enough of your time today. I'm sorry." I hand her one of my cards from my wallet. "If you need anything, call me."

Madison nods slowly, taking the card from me with a shaking hand. Maybe I shouldn't have mentioned the baby thing.

"Ms. Bond?"

Ugh. Kill me.

I turn to face the mayor when I stand. "Mayor McDougall. How are you?"

"Well, well," he responds, his gaze flittering between me and his daughter. "What are you doing here?"

I'm fine, thanks. Got a hankering for a cupcake though. "I wanted to make sure Madison was okay and ask her a few things about Natalie's relationship with Nick. I figured, if anyone could help me, it'd be her."

"Excuse me," Madison whispers, getting up and slinking past him.

His nod is slow, his eyes calculating. "And was she helpful?"

"Oh, absolutely. I have a much clearer picture of their relationship. Nick wasn't real helpful on that when I spoke with him."

"So you're coming close to being able to arrest him?" He finally focuses on me.

"I couldn't say, sir. That's up to Detective Nash and Sheriff Bates.

I've been told to keep my bitch in check and get as much information about him as I can. I'm actually off to his apartment building to interview his neighbors about him now," I lie smoothly. "He seems like a waste of oxygen, if I'm honest."

"Indeed. There's actually someone I'd like you to meet. My latest campaign manager has regrettably stepped out following the unfortunate circumstances this weekend." He steps to the side, revealing a stunning brunette wearing a well-fitting skirt-and-blazer set.

The white blouse she's wearing only accentuates her golden skin, and as my gaze crawls upward, her fake smile is the first thing I notice. The deep brown of her eyes is the next, and they hold a serious measure of contempt.

"Ms. Bond, this is Jessica Shearer. She's my newest campaign manager. Ms. Shearer, this is Noelle Bond, owner of Bond Private Investigations. I've hired her to work with the police here to find Natalie's killer."

Jessica steps forward and holds a hand out, her gaze flicking over me from head to toe. "It's a pleasure to meet you, Ms. Bond. I can't wait to hear more about what you've found out so far."

I slide my hand into hers and squeeze a little tighter than she is.

What? Her tone is really fucking annoying me.

"The feeling's mutual, Ms. Shearer. Unfortunately, though, I'm not at liberty to divulge any of the case to anyone outside of the police department. The only person I can discuss it with is Mayor McDougall, and even then, he understands there are limits to the information he can have." I take my hand from hers and grab the strap of my purse. I hold her gaze for a moment longer before turning to the mayor. "I'll finish my interviews and regroup with everyone at the station tomorrow. I'll ask Sheriff Bates if he can give you a small brief, if only to help ease Madison's grief."

His eyes soften momentarily at the mention of her sadness. "Thank you, Ms. Bond. That's appreciated."

Madison sits back down on her chair, pale, with her bangs sticking to her forehead. If I didn't know better, I'd say someone is still suffering from severe shock and just threw up in the bathroom.

"Madison? Are you okay?" Mayor McDougall says, touching her shoulder.

"Dad…" she replies shakily, weakly looking up at him. "Did you know Natalie was pregnant?" Her voice is barely a whisper, but the mayor freezes. "Someone killed her and her baby, Dad. A baby."

"No," Mayor McDougall replies, licking his lips. His gaze darts from her to me. "I had no idea."

"How could someone do that?" she breathes, her eyes filling with tears.

"I should go now," I say softly. "Madison? I'm sorry."

She ignores me though. Even the mayor is more focused on his daughter than on me. The only person who so much as acknowledges my words is Jessica.

She's still staring at me with contempt. Now maybe it's my ripped jean shorts or my flowery tank, or maybe even my lacy flats, but heaven only knows what's so offensive about that.

Whatever. I don't plan on working with her very much anyway. I'll leave that stuff to Drake. He's the cop, after all.

Regardless of that, this visit has given me lots of information, the most important being that the mayor absolutely knew about Natalie's baby.

And he absolutely knew it was his.

chapter ELEVEN

D*INNER tonight?* Drake's message pops up on my phone.
Like a date dinner? Do I have to wash my hair?
...
Can I wear yoga pants then? I try.
Or we could order pizza and watch a movie or something. At least try to look human.
Why? You wanted to date me. You have to accept my yoga pants and three-day-old unwashed hair.
Fine. Wear deodorant.
I guess I can do that. I laugh and grab my car keys from my desk.

After leaving the town hall building, I came straight back to the office and edited my whiteboard. If I'm honest with myself, I'd hoped that talking with Madison would mean that I could wipe her off as a suspect, but I can't. It only strengthens both her and Nick's motives. After all, if Natalie was out of the way, they wouldn't have to wait to begin their relationship, would they?

And as for the mayor... I kind of feel the same way I did with Ryan Perkins when he hired me to find out who killed Lena. Ryan is now, incidentally, living with his pregnant mistress.

Why would the mayor hire me if he killed her to remove the issue of the baby? That would give her considerable power. He'd have to pay her child support, take up his fair share of the childcare to maintain his wholesome family-guy image, and not to mention the baby would become an heir to some of the McDougall empire.

It would also be a huge difference in his marriage. I guess it's one thing to sleep with someone but another thing entirely to knock someone else up.

Funny. I remember saying the same thing about Ryan Perkins.

I lock my office door behind me and poke my head around Carlton's. He's already left, but there's a folder on his desk, and my name is on the piece of paper folded to stand. He's a smart cookie, this one.

I open the sheet of paper and read his note, which tells me that he has everything on Natalie amd Nick and is working on the McDougalls. That'll do.

I wonder if Drake will mind a working date.

Is it a date if I really do wear my yoga pants?

Possibly.

I flick through Nick's information as I walk downstairs, bypassing the basics. Place of birth, schools attended, qualifications, job histo—

Oh my fucking God.

Job history. Escort. The date shows he started right after he came to Austin, and quit after the start of his relationship with Natalie. No wonder he's so bitter toward her. He gave up a—possibly questionable—career which probably made him more money than the tattoo shop ever will to be with her fully, and she couldn't adjust to life without a bit of kink.

Hell, I'd be bitter, too…

I almost walk into the front door, stopping just in time. I set the alarm and lock it before meandering over to my car as I contemplate this new information. As I get in in, something seriously occurs to me: If he was an escort, wouldn't he be familiar with BDSM? Have even participated in it?

I guess he could have specified on his website or whatever that it wasn't his thing, but still. Surely he'd understand sexual desires? Fetishes? Needs? Shouldn't he have been able to deal with that without judging her for her choices?

Is it a choice though? Is it sometimes a compulsion? A need to be dominated or to dominate? Is it always sadist?

Of course, the simple answer here is that I don't know, and I won't likely ever find out unless I suddenly want to explore the world of BDSM for a romance novel. Given that I don't even type up my own contracts and I delegate e-mails where necessary, a novel is never going to happen.

And while I've been contemplating the mysteries of the sexual universe, I've driven right past my house. Fantastic.

My phone vibrates with a call as I'm about to make a U-turn at the end of the street. I pull over without killing the engine and dig it out of my purse. Drake.

"Did I just see you drive straight past your house?"

"How about you shut your mouth?" I mutter, hitting the hands-free button and putting it down in my lap. "How did you see that? You aren't outside my house."

"I was driving past to get pizza."

"You can order that for delivery, you know." I park in my driveway.

"Not real Italian pizza from Giovanni's."

Aw. If I were a total romantic, I'd be melting. Except I'm not, so I ask, "With what on it?"

"One for you with pepperoni and extra mozzarella with a slightly crispy crust, and one for me with pepperoni, ham, chicken, and mushrooms without the crispy crust."

Aw. Okay. Maybe he wins this.

"How long will you be?"

"Maybe thirty minutes. And since my house is closer to Giovanni's and I've been driving around like a NASCAR driver all day, get your ass over there. There's a spare key under the mat." His instant hanging up beats down any of my ideas about arguing that.

I've never been to his house. And I'm definitely not letting myself in. Although spying would be fun. Just to see what kind of a person he really is, you know? Does he have pictures of his family? What about his friends? Does he have friends outside the HWPD? Where are his family? Is it a bachelor pad? How many bedrooms are used as bedrooms and not dumb games rooms or gyms?

Fuck my curiosity. She's such a tempting little bitch.

Without going inside to get my yoga pants like my waist is screaming for, I restart the engine and reverse out of the drive.

Pizza at Drake's. That's normal, right? That's what two people with a still-undefined relationship do, isn't it?

I don't even know.

I've been alone for so long. It's been a good three years since I settled back into Holly Woods full time. Maybe even longer—I couldn't give a date. For at least nine months before that in Dallas, I was single after I found my boyfriend boning a rookie.

Maybe I've forgotten how to be in a relationship. Maybe I'm scared to be.

No, scratch that. I'm definitely a little afraid to be. That means I have to give up a part of me, and I don't want to do that. I want to be. Just me.

Yet I know exactly where Drake lives without ever having been to his house.

I'm going to blame that on small-town living. Totally, completely, one hundred percent.

I love his street. From the cute little bushes blocking off everyone's front yards to the pretty gates closed over every driveway and the redbrick detached houses, it's the house most people dream of owning one day.

When I was nine, I declared I'd buy a house here one day. Yeah, well, I didn't quite have enough money for that when I left Dallas. Although I probably would right now if I stopped spending money on shoes.

What a ridiculous idea.

Wait. What number is your house? I text him after pulling up alongside the curb.

1762, he replies within a minute.

I look at the house to my right and squint. 1780. There isn't a car behind me, so I reverse back to see the number of the house next to it. 1782. Awesome. No awkward mid-road U-turns needed. Thankfully.

I once took the side mirror off another car trying to do that. I left a note.

I pull back onto the street and drive down it at a snail's pace, determined not to miss Drake's house. When I reach 1764, I go even slower until the opening to his driveway appears. Or, rather, his closed gates.

Ugh.

I get out of my car, killing the engine to be safe, and walk up to them. I can flick the thing securing them at the top over and unbolt them no problem, but my issue is the long stick things with handles making sure the gates stay in the ground. The metal poles disappear into the concrete of his driveway, an inch away from my fingertips.

Driveway gates were not made for short people.

I take a deep breath and lean right over the top of them, stretching my fingers as far as possible. I'm still not even close to grasping the poles, so I swing back down onto my feet with a huff.

Fuck tall people.

I glance at the gate again, but let's be honest. Unless I'm wearing heels, I'm simply not reaching those damn bolts. So, instead of making a further fool of myself, I get back into my car to work.

I turn the key so the radio comes on and turn it down to a low hum. *Vince Fulton* stares at me from the top of Natalie's D.O.M. agreement. I should have asked Carlton to get me some information on him earlier, but I was so wrapped up in learning about Natalie and Nick that I forgot.

Bad Noelle. Bad, bad Noelle.

I doubt even Google can help with this. Besides, I know the basics. He graduated with Devin, went straight into an apprenticeship with his old man at Fulton Builders' Inc. and has been there ever since. His sexual preferences weren't something I ever found myself wanting to know.

That's the problem with this job. You find out things that are better left hidden.

Dirty little secrets are always dirty, but they rarely stay little or secrets.

I drop my head back against my seat, groaning. Once again, there are way too many people in too many places. There are too many motives and opportunities for far too little people. Not everyone should have a motive or an opportunity, but yet again in this case, they do.

Small-town living really does have its drawbacks.

"What are you doin'?"

I turn at the sound of Drake's voice, my eyes meeting his through my window. I bring it down a little. "Waiting," I answer.

"Why?" His lips turn up.

"I can't, um, reach the bottom things for your gate," I mutter, looking down.

He hears perfectly if his laugh is anything to go by. "Come on. I bought wine, too."

"Are you attempting to get me drunk?"

"Noelle, if you and wine are in the same room, you don't need me to help you."

I push my door open, grab my things, and follow him to the gates. "I'd take offense to that if I could ever take offense to anything."

"Did your soul get swallowed when you watched Harry Potter, by any chance?" He glances back at me, one eyebrow raised, then reaches over and opens the gate.

Bastard. "No, actually. I think Nonna ate my soul when I came home single, without the faintest prospect of a boyfriend, let alone the husband she expected." I sniff and follow him up the two-car-long driveway. "I think she ate all the fucks I had, too."

Drake laughs. The rich sound sends tingles through me. "Is she giving it back now that you're dating?"

"Oh, this is dating? I thought we were being nice to each other."

"And still fighting on a daily basis."

"Did we fight yesterday?"

"I think so."

"Crap. There goes my alternative explanation." I sigh heavily.

He laughs again, putting his key in the door. He swings it open and steps in, glancing back at me with a small smile.

Okay. So I'm definitely curious.

Is it wrong to say mostly about his bedroom?

No. Definitely not.

I beat down that little crazy desire before it gets too loud and my brain-to-mouth filter goes on a coffee break.

"Take these," Drake instructs, holding two pizza boxes out to me. Bottles clink in the plastic bag on his arm.

"Why?"

"So you can go and put them on the coffee table while I pour you a glass of wine?"

"You're real lucky you followed up that order with 'a glass of wine.'" I sniff and take the boxes into the front room.

Oh. This is pretty. Not girly pretty though. The black leather sofa is broken up by charcoal and cobalt-blue throw cushions, and the bright, fluffy rug beneath the dark, wooden coffee table matches them perfectly. A huge TV is attached to the wall above the black marble fireplace, and blue curtains with a hint of charcoal and black stripes at the top hang by the windows on either side of the room. There isn't much furniture other than a wooden bookcase and side cupboard that match the coffee table.

Pictures sit on top of the cupboard but I don't get to look because Drake comes into the room and sets a glass of wine down onto a coaster.

"Thank you." I look up with a smile as he takes a seat on the sofa next to me, putting his beer on another coaster.

"I don't know if you've ever thanked me before."

"You haven't fucked me hard enough yet."

"Do you like cold pizza? It can be arranged."

"Ignore me," I tell him. Fucking filter. Where is it when I need it? Oh yeah. It saw wine and got thirsty. "I've had a long day and my filter is drunk off the wine fumes."

Drake grins, one that lights up his eyes and makes my stomach flutter. "Then feed it."

"That's one thing it doesn't need." I take the box he's handing me and open it. Cheesy, pepperoni goodness assaults my senses, and I sigh happily. Yes, this is what I need after today. After the crazy revelations by Madison.

"Did you just come?"

My lips thin, and I face him. "Do you want me to shove that beer bottle up your backside?"

"Can I finish it first?" That. Fucking. Grin.

"Sure—once I've tipped you upside down."

"Now that you have to video. You're nothin' compared to me, cupcake. I could flick you and the only thing that'd keep you standin' would be your attitude."

"So my attitude is larger than life." I pick a piece of pepperoni off my slice and raise my eyebrows. "Better than it being smaller than a single sperm."

"Why? Because sperm can procreate?"

"Please. If my attitude were sperm, it'd be the whole thing. The one trillion little things that come out each time."

Drake snorts. "You make ejaculation sound like it's an ant infestation."

"Depends if you want to get pregnant or not. Oh, and contraception. Because if it isn't and you don't, then you're gonna need a super exterminator to get rid of that potential kink in the road."

"You talk far too much when you should be eating." He grabs my hand and shoves my slice of pizza into my mouth.

I gasp as the hot sauce coats my lips. "You bastard!"

"Is that your pet name for me?" He bites into his own pizza and chews. "Because that could be so fucking hot in the right context."

"Like when I'm shoving your beer bottle up your ass?"

"I love it when you threaten me. It's like my cock is keeping tally and the more you do, the harder your next fuck is."

"Your cock keeps tally? What is it? A fucking pencil?"

"Long and hard? There's a good chance."

"I suggest your piece of paper hand takes a break, because as long as your cock keeps tally of my threats, it's getting nowhere near my sharpener."

Drake stops. His grip on his pizza loosens and the slice flops down. Luckily for him, he only just picked it up, so the hot toppings fall into the box and not his lap.

"Did you just refer to your pussy as a sharpener?"

"Did you just agree that your cock is a pencil?"

"Can I change my mind? If it has to be stationery, can it be a permanent marker instead?"

"Why are we comparing our bits to stationary? This is so wrong on so many levels."

"At least we ain't fightin'."

"Yet," I add. "We ain't fightin' yet. It's only been ten minutes."

"Is that all?" he groans, grabbing his beer bottle. "Feels like a fuckin' prison sentence."

"Oh, now, we're about to fight."

"Can you call me a bastard again?"

"I should call your mom and have her change your name on your birth certificate. Heaven knows Bastard would be more appropriate."

"Since when do you have my mom's number?" He looks amusingly alarmed at this.

"I don't." I raise my eyebrows. "But I have my new techie. He could get it faster than you could wrestle me to the ground to stop me."

"I'd never wrestle you. I value my balls too much." He puts the bottle down and reaches for the remote control. "There are several other things I'd do to you, but I don't want to ruin the surprise."

"Spanking might not be a surprise with you anymore."

"Hey—you knock it, but you've never complained. You've moaned plenty though."

I reach forward and smack my palm against his hard upper arm. Sassy son of a bitch.

"And there it is." He laughs, and damn him, I want to hit him again, but all I can do is look down and smile, fighting my own giggles, because he got me.

Total bastard.

I don't know if I'm amused or pissed. I do know that my thumb wants to trail across that stubbly jaw of his until it's numb to the sensation of the rough hair against it. I want to tease my lips across his in barely there kisses until his patience snaps and he takes control.

God, I want this to be something and nothing all at the same time.

I'm not even hungry anymore.

The silence that has settled in the wake of his fading laugh has me taking a deep breath, picking aimlessly at the cheese on the pizza in front of me. I'm alternately licking my lips and grazing my teeth over them, making sure not to look at him. Because this is different.

It's one thing to be on a date in a public place.

It's another to have one at his house.

I swig from my wine glass, letting the alcohol linger in my mouth before swallowing it down. He even got my favorite fucking wine. What kind of sorcery is this bastard pulling with me? His voodoo is so fucking freaky that not even New Orleans would welcome him onto Bourbon Street without dousing his fine ass in sage and asking Roman goddesses for their blessing.

It's easy to banter with Drake. It's easy to fight and argue every second of the day because those are the words that flow easily. Foot stomps and door slams and righteous shoves and grabs are the way we've worked as long as I can remember. They're easy for us.

This? This crazy, comfortable silence mixed with the echo of our laughter and words that aren't insulting but plain old teasing?

158

It's hard.

It's hard to be something other than everything I've ever known us to be.

More than that, it's terrifying. God, it's so fucking terrifying.

Because it is comfortable. To sit here in silence, me picking at my pizza and sipping my wine quicker than should be allowed while he happily gorges down pizza and barely even sniffs his beers. We're not even touching except for the slightest brush of his knee against mine when he reaches for another slice. And I...I don't know. I don't know what to do with this.

I have no idea how to live with this man who makes my blood boil with both anger and desire at the same time.

"Stop thinkin'," he orders, flicking a piece of mushroom into his pizza box. "Bad shit happens when you think, cupcake."

"But murders get solved, too, so it's a win-lose kinda situation, right?" I give up on the pizza and instead drain the rest of my glass. I tilt it toward him in a question.

He nods toward the door that I'm assuming will take me to the kitchen.

I get up, grasping my glass tighter than I should. His eyes are on me as I make the turn from the living room into the hallway and then the kitchen. Charcoal cupboards cover the room, a chrome sink breaking up the black countertops. The stove is black, too, and completely shiny, but the fridge is a brushed chrome that's neither the color of the sink nor remotely close to the cupboards.

But the cooker is black. His appliances aren't coordinated. I'm not sure how I feel about that.

Still...inside one of those appliances is a bottle of wine, and priorities have to win out here.

I'll figure out how to get home once this awkwardness is gone.

I pour my glass a little higher than I should and put the bottle back into the wine rack on the middle shelf of the fridge. So I think most people call it a bottle rack, but it just so happens to be perfectly shaped for wine bottles. So it's a wine rack.

If I'm rambling in my head, perhaps one glass of wine is enough.

I take two steps in the front room and stop. Drake's shirt is undone, every button un-buttoned and the sides falling to his sides so there's chest and tan skin and abs and a very tempting V that dips beneath the waistband of his black pants. And his belt is unbuckled. Invitingly.

I definitely don't need glass two of this wine.

He turns his face toward me and, with his eyes glinting, smirks.

I take it back. I need this glass.

Fuck it. I need the whole damn bottle.

"Problem?"

"Are you seriously asking me if this"—I motion to his exposed body—"is a problem?"

"I'm sensing a flatterin' answer comin' my way."

"Like a fuck, no, put it away?" I take a drink and set my glass down. "Or were you expecting a girly giggle?"

I think my vagina is giggling in the form of a very harsh clench. Nice to know she's easier than the rest of me. No problems with her in the bedroom, huh?

Since when did I start referring to my vagina as a she? Or even a separate entity?

Fuck this all so much.

Clearly, I'm not cut out for dating.

Drake scoops his arm around my waist and throws me back onto the sofa. He moves his body over mine before I've barely even fallen, and I inhale sharply.

"Thinking," he breathes, the heat of his mouth just ghosting mine making me close my eyes. "Too much of it, sweetheart. Stop it."

"Can't," I admit in my own whisper. "This is so crazy. You. Me. This. We're supposed to hate each other."

"I can hate you. I do several times a fuckin' day. I don't have to like you to want to be with you though."

"I know." My eyes open, but I look down. Away from him.

Because he's stronger than I am. He admits what I can't. He admits what he wants, whereas I'm still hiding beneath myself.

He's a better person than I'll ever be.

And maybe… Maybe he deserves someone who can give him as much of them as he can of himself.

"Nope," Drake snaps, covering my mouth with his hand, forcing me to dart my gaze to his. Toward that intense, Antarctic gaze of his. "Stop. Now. Noelle, enough. You're the strongest, sexiest, most confident woman I know. No doubts. Not from you."

I open my mouth, but it's dry, so I close it again. I lick my lips, and I hate this. This feeling. So insecure. Like I'm not good enough.

Here he is, offering me everything on a silver platter, and I'm feeling fucking sorry for myself.

He's fucking insane. I'm insane. This whole damn thing is so insane that there isn't a single psychiatrist in the country who could make sense of this thing we call a relationship.

Except it's all me. He's there. Waiting. Ready. Open. And I'm here. Hesitating. Not ready. Closed.

So wrong. So. Fucking. Wrong.

I hate myself for it.

My palms flatten against his cheeks, my fingers brushing his hair, and I bring his mouth down to mine. If I can't talk, I can feel. And, God, he makes me feel. Everything. So many things I don't want to feel.

His arms wrap around my body, and he adjusts himself until there isn't a breath of space from our mouths right down to our feet. Our bodies are connected entirely, and I can't get enough of this—of him. Of the feeling of his hot weight on top of me or his long fingers deftly massaging my side and my skull. Of his rough stubble as it scratches my jaw. Of his spicy lips as they explore mine thoroughly. Of his tongue as it battles with mine in a war so fierce that I don't know if either of us will ever win it.

"Fuck!" he yells, shoving himself off me and grabbing his phone from his pocket. "What?" he roars into it. "Does it fuckin' matter? … Thought not. Spit it out." A long pause. "You're kiddin' me. You better be fuckin' kiddin' me, Trent."

"Uh-oh," I murmur.

"Fine. We'll be there as soon as we can get across town." Drake takes the phone from his ear and drops it on the table.

It bounces off the pizza box, landing facedown. He spins away from me and leans forward, diving his hands into his hair. The messy curls curve around his fingertips as he slowly runs them through his hair to the base of his neck.

I, too, set my feet on the floor and sit up straight. My blood is still thrumming with the promise of his kiss, but the frustration tightening his shoulders is more than the slither of lust left inside my body.

I slide my butt along the sofa until we touch. Then I reach up, my hand knocking his out of the way as my fingers press onto the sides of his neck. I gently massage it, waiting with a tightly coiled stomach and twitching toes as his silence stretches further and further between us.

Finally, I drop my hand. "Drake."

"Vince Fulton." He looks up, rubs his hand down his face, and sighs. The way he turns his face toward mine seems to take forever, and I'd swear ten new species have been discovered by the time his eyes finally collide with mine. "The guy we were going to interview first thing tomorrow morning. Natalie's regular dom."

The words fall from my lips although I already know the answer. "What about him?"

"He's dead."

chapter TWELVE

THE blue lights sure do help when you need to make it across town in a quick dash.

We get from Drake's house to D.O.M. in a matter of minutes. I did make a request to bring my wine, but he steadfastly refused while buttoning his shirt.

Personally, I think the wine would have been useful. For me, obviously, because what is it with people fucking dying during my investigations?

Our investigations. Whatever.

The dying thing is getting old.

And yes. I'm pissed. I'm really fucking pissed because I know for a fact that Vince Fulton could have provided me with some answers, and there's no way his death was a freak one, even in the exclusive sex club.

Brody meets us as soon as we get out of Drake's squad car and hands us both a pair of gloves. "Identification on him and the manager both confirm Vince Fulton as the deceased. No visible injuries on him aside from a welt on his left upper thigh. Tim is examining him now but assumes a different cause of death than with Natalie."

"They're connected?" Drake questions, holding open the opaque, black glass door for me to pass through.

"Right now, we're saying yes. The connection between him and

Natalie Owens is too deep to pass off as his death being coincidental." Brody holds a second door open, scooting me through it before I can take the club in. "He's been out of town on vacation for a week according to the club's owner, so he had no idea about Natalie. He was due to meet her tonight, but who he got is anyone's guess."

"Vince is a big guy though," I put in. "It would have to be a male at the very least to overpower him."

"Not necessarily." Drake glances back at me. "A regular like Vince could have entered this club without confirming Natalie coming tonight. A woman coming in could have easily convinced him she'd been sent in Natalie's place and taken control."

People swarm the corridor, but all of them are in official uniform except one man who's dressed in a suit.

"Mr. Lawrence?" Drake asks, approaching the man and snapping a glove off. "Detective Nash. Tell me what happened."

The man—Mr. Lawrence—is presumably the owner of the club, and as soon as Drake releases his hand, he wrings them together in front of his stomach. "I wish I could. I came in as soon as I heard myself. From what I can find out, my staff assumed he knew about Natalie and had switched her out for one of his other girls."

"His other girls?"

"Vince has been coming here five nights a week for at least three years. Every night is a different girl. Each one is contracted to the club. He knows the rules, and so do they, Detective. They wouldn't have broken them."

"All due respect, but someone did, because you have a dead man in your club."

Way to be nice, Drake.

"Mr. Lawrence." I step forward, nudging Drake to the side. "Noelle—"

"Bond," he finishes for me, his smile meeting in eyes. "Keep that one quiet, darlin'. I'd bet there ain't a man in this club who hasn't been waitin' for the day you stepped in here."

Brody steps behind me.

"Well, unfortunately for them, my clothes are staying on." I smile tightly.

"I can think of four men in the bar who'd like to convince you otherwise."

Wait for it.

"Enough," Drake snaps, wrapping his hand around my wrist and tugging me behind me. "We're here in investigate a murder, Mr. Lawrence, and she sure as hell ain't here to be hit on."

Holy shit.

Did he just beat my brother to the protective punch?

He did.

Holy. *Shit.*

That's never happened before.

"Any and all security tapes you have from today would be appreciated," Drake continues. "Perhaps you should go and work with your security team to ensure we get those as soon as possible."

By perhaps, he means do it. Now.

See? I do listen. I'm learning.

"Drake?" I prod his arm, seeing Mr. Lawrence walk away. "You can let go of me now. I promise not to run away from the big, scary man in the scary suit, trying to hit on me."

He turns around, narrows his eyes. And without saying a word, he drops my wrist and walks into the room where Vince's dead body is.

I glance at Brody. "What did I do?"

He shrugs. "I'm still pretty stuck on the fact that he told him to fuck off before I could."

"Glad I'm not the only one," I mutter, finally walking into the room.

Oooooeeee.

That's the only thought I have as I focus on it.

Yeah. The men who come here are gonna be waiting a real long time for me to be here naked. Like another fifty lifetimes.

Whips. Chains. Floggers. Lots and lots of things I don't know the names of and would likely give me nightmares if I did.

One particularly scary-looking clamp device makes me shudder. I cannot imagine that being pleasurable on any part of my body.

"Uncomfortable?" Brody smirks.

"Are you not?" I shoot back. "What if that"—I point to the clampy thing—"is meant for your junk?"

He stops. "How about you stop creating new torture devices and get to work?"

"Pussy," I whisper.

He hits me.

Honestly, it's a wonder anyone in this family ever gets any work done when we're together.

I worm my way in between Drake and Trent with a sweet smile. Then I focus on the man lying facedown on the bed in front of me, buck naked. "How long has he been here?"

"That's what we're trying to work out," Trent replies. "No one seems to know exactly what time he got here. Could be ten minutes or since it opened at noon."

"Wouldn't someone have noticed if he'd been in here that long?"

"Not necessarily. By the sounds of it, these guys can be in here for hours at a time because it's more than sex. Apparently, it isn't unheard of for Vince to be locked away with a woman for three hours."

"That's some stamina," I note. "Do they really go that long without eating or drinking and stuff?"

"Not everyone has the same priorities you do, Noelle."

"Hey. I'm taking offense at that."

"Then don't say things I can offend you with," Trent sighs. "Are you here to be productive or get in the way?"

Given that I was hit on within five seconds, pissed Drake off somehow, and now Trent, I'm probably better off not being here.

"You know what? I think I'll go. Y'all can fill me in tomorrow." I turn toward the door.

"Noelle..." Drake starts.

"No, no." I stop in the doorway, meet their eyes, then drop my gaze to the white shape hidden beneath the bed Vince is lying on. "Oh, and before you discount asphyxiation as the cause of death, y'all might want to get that pillow that's under the bed. Now, if you'll excuse me, I'll go before I get in your way any further. God forbid that should happen," I snap, knowing they didn't notice the pillow.

I don't wait for their response.

I'm stepping out into the balmy night air when I spy Drake's squad car and remember that he brought me here, because my car is at his place.

Awesome.

I pull my phone out and call Bek. She arrives within five minutes.

"In," she demands. "Tell me everything."

I drop my head back against the back of the seat and sit down. I recap everything from the start of our date to the interruption to what transpired inside the club.

"And here I was thinkin' you and Drake were going for some kink already," she snorts. "So, you really walked out?"

"Right after pointing out their possible, and likely, murder weapon. That none of them noticed."

"How dare you get in their way?"

"Right? This is exactly why I could never be a cop again. I can't deal with their complexes. I mean, come on. He's so connected to Natalie, so obviously his death would be similar. You wouldn't exactly strangle someone then stab their fuck buddy unless you didn't know about their connection, would you?"

"Well, you would if you didn't want them to be connected by law enforcement."

"If you don't want that, don't kill them within days of each other." I shrug and take a deep breath. "Bek, this is no coincidence. I was only speaking to Madison this morning at the town hall and saw the mayor. She was the one who told me about Vince. And now, he's dead, like, not even twelve hours later? And the mayor knew about Natalie's baby and that it was his? How fucking screwed up is this?"

"Seriously," she admits. "Have you thought about interviewing the mayor?"

"And saying what? 'Hi, Mr. Mayor. Did you kill the girl you knocked up?'" I shake my head. "We have to be so careful. The only way I could speak to him would be to get more information and try to wrap him up in knots so he'd have to spill. He's smarter than that though. He'd know exactly what I was doing."

"Then why don't we follow him?"

"Because I've been hired by him, not for him."

"I didn't say anything about you." She pulls up by Drake's drive and grins, her red hair glinting as his security light flickers on. "I closed my big case this afternoon. I only have two small ones open right now since that one took all of my time. I can keep tabs on him."

I chew the inside of my cheek. I've never had to follow a client before. Except for that time when my client's wife hired me to follow him. That was confusing.

This would help. I can't follow the mayor or even interview him.

If he catches me, he'll fire me. Which, honestly, might not be a bad thing at this point. Look at the trouble this case has caused since I agreed to it. The only person I haven't fought with on the team is Brody, and that's because he's the laid-back one.

But I want to figure this out. I'm in way too deep again—like I was with Lena and then Daniel. I'm so tightly surrounded by the lies the suspects have told that, to get out, I truly will have to unravel every single one.

Long story short, I'm fucked. And I'm being fucked without the promise of an orgasm, too.

"Fine," I tell Bek, my fingers grasping the door handle. "Light surveillance. Get Carlton to see if he can get the mayor's schedule off Ellis Law's computer so you're not risking sitting around and getting caught, okay?"

"Yes, boss." She smiles. "And hey, Noelle?"

"What?"

"Everything will work out," she says quietly. "I believe it will."

"There's nothing to work out," I respond. "It'll always be this way. Maybe it's easier for it to stay this way," I finish quietly and close the door.

I walk up to the driveway as her car rumbles away down the street. Digging in my purse for my keys, I look at Drake's house, sighing as I remember how different things were some measly sixty minutes ago. I hit the button and get into my car, dumping my purse on the passenger's seat.

My chest aches.

It wasn't supposed to be like this, was it? It was supposed to be easier. If I knew how messed up this whole situation would get, I never would have agreed to that first date with Drake, never mind accepting the mayor's contract.

I don't even know why Drake is mad at me. I don't know what I did. Was I supposed to thank him after he went all protective on the manager? Was I supposed to keep my mouth shut and offer him a demure smile and a batter of my eyelids? Maybe a thank-you blow job?

And it's work again. Always work. Always the thing that drives a wedge between us.

It was easier when I hated him. When he hated me. When we

168

only worked together because we had to. It was easier when I could walk away from an hour of being around him and wanting to punch his smug little face in.

Now, I'm afraid that, if I punched him, I'd hand him an ice pack straight after.

I take a deep breath and rub my hands down my face, leaning back fully in my seat.

He's the one thing I have no control over. Not how I feel or how he makes me feel. I can't control anything about that man. I wish I could. I wish I could wipe away every tingle and thought and memory until he's nothing more than the guy whose foot I shot.

Nonna's blind dates don't seem so bad anymore.

I'm jolted as arms scoop beneath my knees and around my back. My neck is stiff, and I swallow a groan as my head lolls onto the hard chest.

"Shh," Drake whispers.

Drake?

Did I fall asleep in my car?

Oh fuck.

Not enough "oh fuck" to wake up properly though.

He carries me smoothly into his house and up the stairs.

"I'm okay," I mutter around a yawn, my eyes still closed. "Two secs and I'll drive home."

"It's two thirty in the mornin'. You're not drivin' home, cupcake." He kicks a door open and softly lays me on a bed.

I yawn and bury my face into a pillow as he pulls my shoes off and tugs the covers out from beneath me. He throws them over me, and hidden, I pull my shorts off and drop them on the floor before rolling over and stretching my legs out.

Doors close after a few minutes, and I'm lingering in an odd, sleepy state. This bed smells like Drake. Rich. Addictive. Warm. Coffee and cupcakes and maybe a hint of gunpowder underlying the caffeinated sweetness that's wrapping itself around me right now.

Another door shuts, and I force my eyes open long enough to see

Drake yanking his tie off and dropping it. He fiddles with two of the buttons on his shirt and pulls it over his head, exposing his skin, his muscles illuminated by the dimly lit room.

I look away as he undoes the belt and pulls his pants down. "I'll drive home," I whisper. Yawning. Again.

"No, you won't."

A drawer opens and closes. The bed dips twice before the light goes out completely and he lies next to me.

"Spare room?" I ask.

"Nope. This is the only bed in my house."

The covers move as he tucks in.

"I'll drive," I repeat, forcing myself up.

Drake grabs me and yanks me across the bed, forcing my back against his chest. "God, shut the fuck up, Noelle," he mutters, curving his arm around my stomach and trapping me against it. "It's two thirty in the fucking morning. I told you that. You're not going anywhere. You're going to sleep right here."

"I can't." I tilt my hips away from him. "You're poking me."

"I'm gonna a whole lot more than poke you if you don't be quiet. I'm pissed as hell at you, so unless you want to disturb the whole neighborhood with a blazing fight, get your ass back against my cock and go to fucking sleep."

I could let him sleep then sneak out, right?

"And don't even think about escaping while I sleep. I might shoot you."

I move back against him, my heart thudding. "That's my line."

"So shoot yourself." He yawns. "Just shut up."

"Okay." A moment passes, and my eyes close as the warmth from his body calls sleep back to me. "Night, Drake," I whisper.

"Night, *bella*." He kisses my hair, and it's the last thing I know before sleep wins.

Sleeping next to Detective Drake Nash is like being a piece of coal inside a blazing fire. My feet have been hanging out of the covers for hours waiting for some alien monster to come and nibble on my toes.

At some point during the night, I rolled over into him and he ended up with both arms around me. I don't know how it happened, but it's probably the reason I'm so warm right now. I need a cold shower or ten.

I tilt my head back to look at him. My fingers twitch where they're resting on his defined stomach, but it's his hair that has a smile creeping onto my face. If I thought it was messy during the day, I was so wrong. It's sticking up in all kinds of directions, one crazy, loose curl brushing his forehead.

God. His hair is the best thing about him.

Well, it isn't, but since that's encased in his underpants and his eyes are closed, his hair wins right now.

His eyelashes are fanned across his cheeks, and his breaths are slow and easy. The only parts of him that aren't relaxed are his fingers. They're holding me just as tight, and I don't think he was kidding when he said last night that he'd shoot me if I tried to get away. He's sleeping so deeply right now that, if I moved, he'd wake up in cop mode and think I was an intruder.

Which means I'm also stuck here next to my personal radiator until he wakes up. Thankfully, the clock on his nightstand reads 6:57 and the alarm icon is flashing next to a 7:00.

I need coffee. And to pee.

I tighten my muscles in case my bladder decides that three— oh, now, two—minutes is too long for her to wait to relieve herself. Really, at twenty-eight, I should have more control over her than she does me, but I did drink two glasses of wine last night before I fell asleep in my car.

In my car. In his driveway. What a dick.

Slowly, I move my hand from his stomach, and he reaches out with ninja reflexes and grabs it. My hand. Not his stomach.

I squeal at his tight grip, and he gazes down at me through barely-opened eyes.

"What are you doing?" he asks, his voice way too clear for someone who just woke up.

"How long have you been awake?"

"Long enough to feel you looking at me like I'm your favorite cupcake."

I purse my lips. "You're a shit."

"A shit who let you sleep in his bed," he answers, closing his eyes again.

The alarm goes off in the form of a radio, and he reaches over and thumps the top of it.

"You know there's a button to shut that up, right?" I say.

"Yep. I'm taking you to the store to see if they can install one on you."

"I can still shoot you if I can't talk, you know."

"I know."

"And you didn't let me sleep here. You made me."

"I know."

"Is that all you're saying?"

"I'm wondering why it's taking you so long to get coffee."

I prop myself up on my elbow. "Because I'm *your* guest and you're still in bed, perhaps?"

He slowly opens his eyes and sighs heavily. "Really? You're my guest?"

"Sorry. Did I say guest? I meant prisoner. Look." I try rolling over, and he smiles lazily, deliberately tightening his grip. "Trapped. You've virtually kidnapped me."

"Why do you think I need a mute button installed on you? It'd be no fun if you could scream."

"You're hard work on a morning," I sigh. "Where's your bathroom?"

"You're hard work all the damn time," he returns, letting me go and sitting up. "That door right there."

"You don't have a spare bedroom but you have an en suite?" I swing my legs out and pause, perched on the edge of his bed.

"Well, yeah. I don't need a spare bedroom, but I have to pee at three a.m. like everyone else." He laughs.

I roll my eyes and reach for my shorts before realizing that putting them on right now is totally useless since I'll have to take them off again in five seconds. So, with a glance over my shoulder, I notice that Drake is sitting on his side, his back to me.

I get up and run into the bathroom.

"I still saw your ass!" he yells as I close the door and slide the lock.

Fucker.

Mind you, judging by the mascara beneath my eyes, his seeing my ass is the least of my problems.

"We need to talk," he says as soon as I leave the bathroom.

I tug my tank down in an effort to cover my panties. "I swear that's our tagline. 'We need to talk.' And yes, we do, but I can't understand anything except yabber-yabber until coffee happens."

"Better get your ass into my kitchen, then, huh?"

I grab my shorts from the floor and pull them up, buttoning them. And this is why I should never wake up next to Drake Nash.

He's pissed me off already.

I lick my thumb and scrub at the circles under my eyes as I stomp downstairs, shoes in hand. My purse on the counter is the first thing I see, and I peek inside to see if everything is there. Since "everything" is kind of a wide term for all the crap that's usually in my purse, I'm going for yes after seeing my phone and keys.

I dig deep for my compact mirror and pull a hand wipe out of the little packet. There's some kid character on the packet, so it's left over from the last time I babysat Silvio and Aria, but hand wipes are wet wipes, and that's exactly what I need.

Drake appears in the doorway, his hair damp and slicked back from his face, curling at the base of his skull. He's dressed in his usual white shirt and black pants with a black tie wrapped around his fist.

"Don't you do makeup in the bathroom?"

"I'm not doing it. I'm removing it." I wipe the last black smudge from my cheek and snap the mirror shut. Then I ball the wipe up and throw it in the trash. "I'm going home to get changed and get coffee. I already know I have to be at the station."

"Eight," Drake confirms. "And I'm coming with you. You're not getting out of this conversation, either, sweetheart."

"I'm not getting out of it. I'm postponing it. There's a huge difference." I slip my shoes on and grab my purse.

"And I'm still coming with you. I'll make coffee while you change. Problem solved."

Maybe for you, I want to say. Not for me though. I don't want to talk about whatever he wants to talk about. I want to be filled in on Vince's death so I can go to my office and do my thing. That's it.

I don't even want this investigation anymore.

It doesn't take me long to drive from Drake's to mine, and I'm not at all surprised when he pulls in behind me before I've even unlocked my front door.

I gather the mail from the mat, throw it on the side table, and hit the switch on my alarm. There's no point closing the door. He can do that. He'll do what he wants anyway.

I close my bedroom door and lean back against it, closing my eyes. This is why I don't want this investigation. I don't want the two sides of my life to mix together. It's too hard. I can't keeping tugging the personal stuff into the professional stuff, because that's where it goes wrong.

All of it.

I pull a black blouse and a red pencil skirt from my closet. I'm so muddled up inside about everything that I need to at least look like I have my shit together. Besides, if I'm dressed well, I'll feel better.

I pull my favorite Louboutins from my shoe rack.

Give a woman the right pair of shoes and not only will she conquer the world, but she'll run it.

And, today, I need to run my little world.

I change, brush my hair out and over one shoulder, and go into the bathroom. Foundation, blush, mascara, red lipstick. And, finally, my shoes.

I slip my feet into them before I join Drake downstairs. There are two mugs of coffee sitting on the table, and I grab the one closest to me.

His eyes are hot on me as he leans against the side of the table. "You wanna tell me what your disappearing act was about yesterday?"

"I was apparently in your way. By the way, did Tim give a cause of death yet?"

"Asphyxiation. Fibers matching the pillow were found on and around his mouth."

"You're welcome," I snap.

He almost looks ashamed.

"Now, how about you tell me what your diva act was about? The manager?"

"Oh, the guy who tried to hit on you in the middle of a sex club? In a place where he insinuated several other men would like to take you to a private room to do things to your body that you know

174

nothing about? In a place you were clearly incredibly uncomfortable to be in?"

Now, it's my turn to feel a little ashamed.

"Yeah." Drake puts his mug down, his eyes filled with a mild annoyance. "We're both fools, Noelle."

I take a deep breath and look down at my hands clasped around the mug. "I'm sorry," I say softly. "I just…"

"You're not used to anyone other than your brothers stepping up and protecting you."

I hate it when he's right. Really, really hate it.

He closes the slight distance between us and gently takes my hands from the mug. "Hey." He touches his fingers to my chin and lifts it, making me look at him. "I get it. I already told you I don't want someone who needs saving. But saving and protecting are two vastly different things, cupcake. I don't care if you need protecting from a killer or some sleazeball hitting on you because he's loaded and wears fancy suits. I'm gonna protect you, whether you like it or not. I'm not afraid to stake my claim where dicks like him are concerned. One-up me on solving murders every day of the week, but don't be mad at me for doing what feels right. Nothing matters more to me than protecting you, *bella*."

Of all the things he calls me, I'll never let him know how much *bella* affects me. Because just about every time he says it, I stop breathing. It's always at *that* moment when my heart is already pounding.

"I know." I raise an eyebrow. "I'm not apologizing again though."

"I'm surprised you said sorry once."

I purse my lips at his wide grin. "It won't happen again."

"I didn't think it would." His eyes spark in amusement. "I'm sorry too, but I can't help it if your badass gene pisses off my alpha complex."

"My badass gene is laughing at you."

"My alpha complex wants to smack your ass."

I grab my purse, put it over my butt, and walk backward. "Nope. That's not how we're starting today."

"You're right." He stalks toward me with a lusty glint in his eye. "We're gonna start it like this instead."

He slams me back against my front door and I drop my purse. He dives his hands into my hair and seals his lips over mine. Fireworks erupt across my skin as I curl my fingers around his neck.

He devours me, plain and simple.

"Now," he breathes, smiling. "Now, we're gonna go and get some work done."

I flick my thumb across his bottom lip, wiping away the smudge of my lipstick. "Now, we are."

He raises his eyebrows, bends for my purse, and pulls me away from the door. I set the alarm, and after we walk out, I take my keys from him and lock the door.

His phone rings, and he hands me my purse so he can answer it. "Detective Nash... What? ... With what? And the mayor? It's too fucking early for that... She's gonna flip... Yeah, all right."

"Who's gonna flip? Me?"

Is it bad that I always assume "she" is me when in that sentence?

"You're gonna get very passionate. The mayor is at the station with his new campaign manager."

"Excellent."

"And Nonna is there. With her wedding scrapbook."

I stop at my car, my fingers freezing over the handle. "With her what?"

No. No, she isn't. It better be for Devin to look at.

"Her Noelle wedding scrapbook." Drake looks like he doesn't know whether to be confused or laugh his ass off.

I cover my eyes with my hand. "We need to get there before she sets us a date or I'll have florists calling me within the hour."

He gets into his car, his laughter winning out, and I get into mine. I quickly check my lips in the mirror and reverse, digging for my lipstick. I uncap it and touch it up as I drive. Drake flashes his lights at me, and I stick my middle finger up at him. It's his fault anyway.

A good thing about a small town is the lack of traffic. Traffic means three cars at a red light. Unfortunately, every light we come to is red and there are almost always three cars in front of Drake's. Which means our drive to the station is three times longer than normal and Nonna is likely recruiting bridesmaids.

I pull up next to his car in the parking lot, and he glances at me as we get out.

"I should give you a ticket for doing your makeup while driving."

"I'm disputing on the grounds that you are the reason it needed doing." I walk past him, throwing him a sassy grin.

It earns me a slap on the ass.

Eh, it was worth it.

"Noella!" Nonna cries. "You-a see-a this-a dress!"

"Is it white?" I ask, pausing by the reception desk.

Charlotte, the receptionist, nods frantically.

"Not interested, Nonna. Sorry."

"You show-a Drake?"

"I really don't think Drake has any interest in your wedding scrapbook for a wedding that isn't happening."

"I'd love to tell you she meant to bring mine, but she didn't," Dev adds, leaning against the desk. "She's on a warpath with you now. She wants a ring on your finger."

"Not happening." I look at Drake. "No offense."

He laughs. "I'm with you. Trust me."

Nonna gasps, holding the book to her chest. "You-a have-a no idea what-a you-a saying!"

"Okay, Nonna. I love you, but I know exactly what I'm saying, and so does Drake. Can we come back to this if I ever actually get married? Because we have work to do." I grab Drake's arm and tug him toward the back of the station.

"This way," he says, taking my arm instead and leading me up the stairs to the briefing room. "She's crazy, isn't she?"

"I want to say 'in the best kind of way,' but right now, I'm not so sure." I shrug. "She wants us all to be happy. She has a hard time remembering that we make our own happiness and that her… enthusiasm…is scary."

"No fucking kidding," he mutters, pushing the door open.

Trent looks at me with wide eyes. Ones that tell me that I should be running right now. I frown at him, and he drops his eyes to Jessica. Yeah, well, she already hates me, so whatever.

"Ah, Detective Nash, Ms. Bond," Sheriff Bates greets us. "Nice of you to join us."

"I was dealing with Nonna." I grimace.

His eyes twinkle. "Thank you for your sacrifice," he jokes. "Ms. Bond, I understand you and Ms. Shearer have met previously." He turns to Drake. "Detective Nash, this is—"

"We've met," Drake replies curtly.

A sly grin spreads across Jessica's face, and she gets up, smoothing her skirt across her thighs as she approaches him. Then she reaches up and kisses his cheek. "Hello, darling. How are you?"

My eyebrows shoot up.

"Jess." Drake's voice is still hard as he rubs her kiss from his cheek. "I'm well. And you?"

"Far better for learning I'll be liaising with you on this unfortunate matter." Her smile is far too bright for someone referring to an "unfortunate matter."

Trent's eyes are now warning me to shut up. Brody looks like he's ready to see me hit her.

I'm hovering somewhere in the middle.

"Well, that's easier for everyone," Sheriff Bates interrupts optimistically. "Let's all take a seat so we can get to work."

"Move," Drake hisses, nudging me in the back.

I resist the urge to knock his hand away from me. *Hello, darling? Hello, fucking darling?*

"Later," Trent warns me on a whisper. "Work," he reminds me.

I nod and sit down, all too aware of Jessica staring at both Drake and me. *Behave, Noelle. Like Trent said, you're at work. You can hit her at recess.*

Wait. I think that rule only applies in kindergarten. That's a shame.

Ugh. What is wrong with me?

"...so whoever was in the room with Vince Fulton yesterday evening was breaking the rules about practicing erotic asphyxiation within the boundaries of the club. This has led Mr. Lawrence to close the club for three days at extreme cost to himself, as he's unwilling for another accident to happen, in his words." Sheriff Bates pauses, glancing over all of us. "The connection Vince has to Natalie is undeniable. Given the latest findings"—he nods to me with a grateful smile—"I'm going to throw out the hypothesis that Vince was murdered by Natalie's killer because of information he possessed. With this in mind, we're offering her ex-boyfriend extra protection, and while the rest of us are here piecing things together and searching their houses, Ms. Bond, I'd like you to use your charm on Mr. Lucas and see what Vince might have known that could get him killed."

Brody snorts when he says "charm."

"Of course," I agree. "He took a shine to Bek when I saw him last. I'll take her because my charm is on vacation today."

Drake breathes in deeply.

Sheriff Bates half smiles. "Ms. Bond, if you have to date the man for a week for that information, you can do what you like. As long as it's legal." *If you're in my building,* is what he doesn't say.

"I wouldn't dream of anything else." I fight my smirk as Trent snorts. "Y'all gettin' a cold? Should I get some tissue?" I say to my brothers.

"Let's move," Sheriff Bates says before we can waste our time bantering.

I stand and hook my purse over my shoulder.

"Drake," Jessica says, darting past the mayor as he goes to talk to the sheriff. "I'd really appreciate if we could talk so I'm up to date on every detail and can adequately control the damage this is doing to the mayor's campaign. Many people think Madison was involved, as she was the one who found her."

"Sure. Two people have been murdered, but let's focus on images, shall we?"

"Noelle," Drake warns. "I can't talk to you right now, Jess. As Noelle just pointed out, two people have been murdered. It's my job to find out who did it, not release to you every detail of my case."

Spin my words, then. I don't mind.

"Are you sure you can't spare a minute?" Her bottom lip protrudes slightly.

"Brody can help you," he offers. "Trent can, too. Ask either of them, but it won't be today."

"I'm sure the mayor would prefer my discussion to be with the lead detective."

"Fine." He turns to me. "Noelle, are you free?"

"Today? No. I have an elusive ex to find and his behind to charm," I reply.

"Funny," Jessica replies. "I was talking about you."

"I know exactly who you were talkin' about, and I said no, I'm busy. My whole team is busy. If you can't work with the information you have right now, then you're gonna have to wait and explain to the mayor that our priority is solving this case. Now, if you'll excuse us…"

He touches my upper back and guides—see: pushes—me toward the door. He walks through it, holding it open without looking back.

I do though. I throw a glance over my shoulder, and Jessica is looking at me like she'd like to spear me through the belly button with her heel.

I'd offer the same look, but my shoes cost too much.

The tension in Drake is obvious by the way he's stomping down the stairs, his shoulders drawn back tight. He slams the door at the bottom of the staircase open, and it moves so fast that I have to wait a moment before grabbing it. His office door is open by the time I get there, and I hesitate before walking in.

I have a bad feeling about all of this.

"Drake?"

"Fuckin' unreal," he spits, kicking his chair out of his way. It spins and knocks into the wall. "Yet so fuckin' typical."

"Who is she?" The words tumble out of me. "She's hated me since the moment she laid eyes on me, and now, it makes sense. You know her. She knows you. And now, I want to know who she is to you."

He runs his fingers through his hair, and when he turns to me, his eyes are full of resignation. They're angry and fiery, but they're dull, too.

"Jessica," he grinds out through a clamped jaw, "is my ex-fiancée."

There's a stab. Right in my chest. Right in my heart.

"Your…ex-fiancée." I lick my lips. "Right."

Oh my God, I can't breathe.

"I think I need to go." I spin on my toes and walk through his door.

"Noelle—"

I shake my head and keep walking, ignoring that stab in my heart, ignoring the twist of my stomach, of that fucking empty feeling hollowing its way through my body. I breathe in the fresh air as I open the glass front doors and turn instantly to the parking lot.

I knew it would never be simple.

We could never be easy.

I don't know what's more fucked—this murder investigation or us.

"Noelle."

"No," I tell him, opening my door. "I need to process this. Like…"

shit, Drake. Shit." I get in and shut the door, starting the engine.
Shit.

His ex-fucking-fiancée.

chapter THIRTEEN

DRIVE straight past Bek's house and onto the road that'll take me to Nick's tattoo studio.

I don't know why I'm so bothered. Because he never mentioned her? Because she's so obnoxious? And hot. God, why are the exes never butt ugly?

I mean, it shouldn't be a big deal. It's not like we've ever sat down to hash out our relationship history with other people. He's never asked. I've never asked. Hell, it's not even like our relationship is that kind of serious. It's not any kind of anything.

It's just kind of…kinda.

God, two people have died and I'm here bitching to myself about his keeping something from me. But what if she hadn't have turned up in town? Would he have ever told me? Would we have ever been something?

Would we? No—I mean, will we? Do I? I don't even know.

Oh my God.

This is so fucking messed up.

Every time. Every damn time we get somewhere, something screws it up. One of us loses our shit or storms off.

Why am I so incapable of being an adult in a relationship? Will it really kill me if he's been in a relationship so serious that he wanted to marry her?

"Argh!" I punch my steering wheel, braking into a parking spot outside the studio.

The worst part is that she knows exactly who I am. She'll have heard that Drake and I are dating. Why else would she have walked up to him so strutty and been all "hello, darling" with a damn peck on the cheek?

I'm a woman. I'm ninety-percent of the sass in Holly Woods. She's playing a game... With me.

I take a deep breath. That's okay, really. She can play the game. She can hold all the cards, because I'll be the fucking dice.

I am Noelle Bond, dammit. I am not a weeping, crying mess kind of girl because something shocks her. I'm a grab-it-by-the-balls, squeeze-out-the-explanation, and get-the-hell-on-with-it kind of girl.

That's my story and I'm sticking to it.

The guy from last time is at the reception counter again, and he smiles when he sees me. "Hey! You're the chick from the other day."

"That's me," I smile sheepishly. "Is Nick here? I need to talk with him."

"He'll be here in five minutes. You want a coffee or something?"

"Oh, no, thank you. Do you mind if I wait?" I motion to the chairs.

"Make yourself at home."

"Thank you." I give him another smile and take a seat on the leather couch. Then I set my purse by my feet, and my mind, instead of returning to Jessica and Drake, focuses on Vince Fulton and what connection he could possibly have to Natalie Owens aside from being her dominant once in a while. If he was killed by asphyxiation, is it easy to assume he was the one who practiced on her? Maybe he was practicing autoerotic asphyxiation on himself.

But that doesn't explain how the pillow got under the bed... And wouldn't you use a pillow for a murder and a tie for yourself?

Unless he was interrupted before he could remove the pillow from his mouth, and someone else finished him off. He did look like he was holding his penis... Or maybe that was simply a ruse from the murderer in the hope that we'd assume it was an accidental death. They're ridiculously common in users of it, after all.

All you need to do, in theory, is knock yourself unconscious, and unless you're found, you're a goner.

"Well, I didn't think you'd be the next Bond I saw," Nick drawls, the door swinging shut behind him. "They haven't given you cuffs, have they?"

I stand, smirking. "Not today, doll. I was hoping to talk to you."

He jerks his head toward the room we spoke in the other day and passes Dreads a coffee cup on the way past the desk. I click the door shut behind me and wait as Nick takes a seat on his stool and sips his coffee.

"Vince Fulton."

"Is a bastard," he replies. "What about him?"

"He's dead."

The shock in his eyes can't be faked. "Fuck off."

"He was found last night," I say quietly.

"The murder at that shithole?"

I nod sharply. "He was Natalie's most regular Dom, wasn't he?"

Nick's lips curve down. "Twice a week she was with him in the end. That's all I know."

"You knew a lot about the mayor. You told me that the truth will out. What does that mean?"

"It means the truth will be found out. You don't strike me as a dim woman, Noelle. Information is there for everyone to find."

"Where were you last night?"

"Excuse me?"

My lips tug to one side. "Seems to me you have the perfect motive to kill both Natalie and Vince. She broke your heart. He was instrumental to her deceit. A still-unidentified male was found going into her room not long before her time of death. We haven't examined the tapes from D.O.M. yet, but I'd say you probably had an opportunity then, too."

"Are you calling me a murderer?"

"No. I'm asking you if you are. After all, your track record is questionable, isn't it? I mean, you were young, but…"

His face hardens, and his eyes narrow into angry slits. "That was a long time ago. What kind of killer would tell you if they are?"

"Someone who answers instantly with a no instead of questioning my reason for asking." I smile as the realization washes over his face. "In all seriousness, where were you last night?"

"Here. I was working on a big back piece for some gym buff from Austin. Ask Niall out there."

Niall? Oh, Dreads. "A copy of your schedule will be fine and a phone number to verify with the gym buff."

"Niall will get you it."

"Great. What else do you know about Vince?"

"He knew about her affair with the mayor. Helped her cover it up."

"How?"

He shrugs. "When I called her out on the baby, Nat lost it, darlin'. She started beggin' me and promised me she had evidence that could destroy the mayor's life and his image. She said she'd threaten him with it, make him pay big, have an abortion, then we could move away."

Hmm. "What kind of evidence? Did she hire someone?"

"She didn't have the money for that. All of her spare cash went to the club." He stands. "Look, that's all I know. If I had the evidence, don't you think I'd give it to you?"

"Do you think the mayor knows about it?"

"The evidence? Probably. Would he kill for it? Couldn't tell ya."

Get that evidence and we've probably found ourselves the killer.

I'm going to use that as my hope right now—that it's that simple. I'm going to ignore that I have no idea what I'm supposed to be looking for when it comes to the evidence or who has it. Or if let's be honest, it really exists.

God. It's Harry and the fucking Horcruxes all over again.

Since my mission today is to find out as much about Vince Fulton as I can, I stop by Melanie's coffee and bookstore. She always has something informative, and I've been here way too many times, promising a date with Brody for information.

I think I might actually have to hold up my end of the deal soon.

"I promise," I say instantly, walking in. "As soon as this case is over."

"Hmm." Melanie smiles anyway. "Vince Fulton, right?"

"You know everything." I smile and sit down.

She holds a strawberry cupcake up, and I sigh with happiness, nodding. A cupcake is exactly what I need. All right, so two cupcakes would be more accurate, but I am trying to curb my intake of them, after all. I'll buy the second and eat it back at the office.

"He was odd, I think." Melanie sets the cupcake in front of me on a small plate with a paper napkin and a fork and leans forward. Thankfully, her high-necked shirt is containing the goods, or I'd have a boob cupcake. She has, after all, won every wet T-shirt competition in Holly Woods since she was fourteen, and she doesn't even enter half the time. "No, not odd. Quiet. He mostly kept to himself, but he came either here or Rosie's once a week for coffee for his whole team on a Friday. It depended which of us were closer—and one week, when he was building on the other side of Austin, he sent us both gift cards to apologize."

"Wow. Did you know he used D.O.M.?"

"Oh, yeah. Everyone knew that. He wasn't shy. I think he tried to work as an escort, but no one really tickled his whip, if you know what I mean."

Am I the only person who didn't know that D.O.M. is a sex club?

"And Natalie Owens?" I ask.

"By all accounts," Melanie says slowly, a coy smile creeping onto her lips, "Natalie Owens was his favorite little play thing. Rumor has it her hard limit was a hard limit."

"What's a hard limit?"

"The things you won't do. Like your hard limit would be giving up cupcakes."

I grin.

"Vince was apparently a total sadist, but so was Natalie. Even at the expense of their relationships. A few of the guys who use the club are perfectly respectable businessmen, but there were more than a few whispers in here about them plotting something. Something to do with money then running away and leaving Holly Woods."

"They're a fucking romance novel, those two, huh?"

"Only if Shakespeare is the author, given the ending." Melanie chortles. "I don't know what was going on. Natalie was an amateur photographer when she wasn't messing around doing design work for the mayor. That's about all I can give you."

I put the last of the cupcake into my mouth and screw up the wrapper before dropping it back onto the plate. "Thanks, Mel." I put a ten down on the counter. "Can I get a raspberry one to go?"

"There's the Noelle I know and love." She winks, laughing, and turns away. "Hey, have you met the mayor's new campaign manager?"

"Oh, yeah. We're best friends."

She throws a smirk over her shoulder. "She's a bitch—and a mean one at that. Told me she's making sure every business has a flyer for the mayor in their window."

"I'll expect her visit."

"Please do. And tell her not to drop anymore around here. They didn't agree with my paper shredder." Mel hands me the cupcake in a small, cute, blue box tied with a silver box. "Try not to sugar overdose, okay?"

"Sugar is my oxygen," I reply, getting up and backing out of the store. "Thanks, Mel!"

"Anytime, doll." She waves and turns to someone bringing a book to the register.

Back to the office it is.

"She's still alive!" Mike laughs, leaning against Grecia's doorframe with a mug of coffee in his hands.

"Alive and kicking and screaming." I throw one arm in the air and pose. "Is everyone here? While I'm here, we may as well have a meeting."

"Nope," he answers. "Dean is out and I'm about to go find out if Finn Hilton's girlfriend is doing the dirty before he hands her a two-carat diamond ring."

"Nice. To the ring, not the doing the dirty. Is that still hot?" I point to the mug, and upon seeing it full and steaming, I extract it from his grip and sip. "Ew. Too much sugar."

"Did you just say, 'Too much sugar'?" Carlton asks. "Aren't you addicted to cupcakes?"

I hide the box behind my back. "What kind of fairytales have y'all been tellin' him, huh?"

"Every one goin'," Mike replies. "But he's so keen on impressin' his new boss that there are four Gigi's cupcakes waiting on your desk."

I narrow my eyes and look at my new kid. "What cupcakes?"

Carlton looks up at the ceiling and ticks them off his fingers. "Triple chocolate torte, lemon, the cookie one, and a champagne one."

"I'm gonna keep you," I tell him, pointing at him. "You're good." I swear he blushes when I turn to Grecia. "I apologize in advance for my messages."

She simply smiles, her dark eyes sparkling as she grabs the stack of cards. "Jessica Shearer stopped by around an hour ago. She wants us to put the mayor's campaign flyer on our window and coffee table. I told her to bring them back when my boss was here because I don't make those decisions."

"Did you kick her on the way out?"

"Whoa, tiger," Mike laughs. "You've met?"

"Oh, we've met."

"And she hates her because she's Drake's ex," Bek adds, walking through the door. "Uh-huh. I spoke to Brody after you stormed out of the station after the briefing."

"I did not storm out," I protest. "And she's his ex-fiancée. And that is not why I hate her. I hate her because she's a smug and obnoxious bitch."

"Well, that's all right, then," Mike snorts.

"Moving on," Grecia interrupts, a small, teasing smile on her lips. "Drake called. Said not to pass on the message because you already know what he's going to say."

We need to talk.

"Yep. Next."

"Nonna called. Asked if you have Amelia's number to talk about Devin's wedding since she clearly isn't getting anywhere with you."

"She's learning."

"And Trent stopped by. Told me to tell you to, ah"—she hesitates—"that you were absolutely right to walk out of the station this morning because a pissed Drake is a productive Drake."

"A pissed Noelle is a productive Noelle, too. Did he say if Drake was pissed at me?"

Bek laughs. "According to Brody, Drake personally escorted

Jessica out of the building and told her to call ahead next time she wants to come by because she's detrimental to the investigation."

Is it bad that I want to whoop with laughter? It is, isn't it? So bad. But hey, I'm already going to hell, so I may as well go with a bang.

I laugh. Loud. "Okay. I'm gonna go write all of this stuff up, call everyone I need to, and hope Jessica comes back in so I can show her a little bit of Holly Woods hospitality."

"So, you're going to wrap her up in toilet paper and throw a water bomb at her head?" Bek questions, an eyebrow raised.

"Do we have either of those things?" Carlton asks, looking a little worried.

"Yeah, do we?" My voice is sadly more hopeful.

"You know, you're a dreadful excuse for a twenty-eight-year-old businessowner." Trent steps through. "No need to call me. I wanna talk to you."

"Can we reschedule? I'm real busy, so…" Again, I hide the cupcake.

He slowly shakes his head, hooking his thumbs through his belt loops.

"Aw, hell. Okay." I walk to the bottom of the stairs and then turn. "Hey, Carlton. Can you get me Vince Fulton's life story?"

He shrugs. "No problem."

"Thanks." I shoot him a beaming smile, but it drops when I see Trent's hard look at me.

Okay. Sheesh. I'm going up the stairs, Dad. Fucking hell.

He follows me into my office and kicks the door shut behind him. I have the feeling this isn't going to be good. Now it could be the tight set of his jaw or the tense way he has his shoulders pulled back, or maybe it's the way his brow is furrowed over his dark eyes glinting with anger.

"I guess your message to Grecia was a load of shit, huh?"

"Not all of it. Just the last part."

"So, you're not here to tell me off for running away?"

He scoffs. "No. You were right to leave. Otherwise, y'all woulda had a blazin' fight and nothin' woulda gotten done today."

And that is, in hindsight, exactly why I left. "So, why are you here looking like you want to ask Mom to ground me for the next week?"

"Because angry Drake is not a fucking nice guy to be around."

"Hey!" I hold my hands up. "I am not the one who didn't tell the person he's seeing about an ex-fucking-fiancée. Or even think to mention it as soon as he saw her. He made me sit there the whole damn time while she was staring at me and I had no idea why she hates me."

"Did you ever ask him about anyone in his past?"

"No, because that isn't my place, Trent. That's something he has to make the decision to share when he's ready to."

"Have you told him why you left Dallas?"

"That is completely different!" I clench my hands into fists. "You know why I left Dallas. You know that wasn't an easy choice. My guilt ripped that choice from me. Don't you dare throw that in my face, because it has nothing to do with Drake."

"Because that's your decision to share it, right?" His eyebrows quirk upward. "Because he's never asked you about it. Yet you're pissed because he didn't tell you about Jessica."

"At the end of our first date, he walked out." I perch on the edge of my desk. "When I asked him about the then-stalker case, he clammed up and got pissed about fidelity and stuff. And even when we talked, he didn't mention it. He's the one pursuing this, Trent. If he wants this, then he should respect me enough to be honest with me if he has issues about trust and things."

"You were cheated on."

"He knows that. But I don't have trust issues."

"That's exactly why you want to punch his ex."

"Again, I want to punch her because she hated me on sight. Now, I want to shoot her. Big difference."

"Women. Y'all are fucked up," he sighs, shaking his head.

"No, we're not. Dude, not all of us can have easy, happy marriages like you have. Not all of us know when we've met the one right away. Nothing about me and Drake is easy. We fight more than anyone I've ever met, and no sooner do we make up than we're fighting again. It's so complicated I don't know where to start with it."

"I'd try talking to him, because family dinner is in four hours, and Nonna is expecting him to be there."

"Then Nonna needs to get over it, because I'm not even going."

"Noelle…"

"No, Trent. I have a job to do. I have work that needs to be done, and I need to decide exactly what I want. I can't think for a second about me and Drake if I have her muttering in my ear about weddings and shit I couldn't care less about. So, if she bitches, tell her I'm right here, in my office, working."

"She'll come down here. You know that, right?"

My phone rings. Grecia's extension is flashing.

"Yep?"

"Ms. Shearer is here to discuss the mayor's flyers with you."

"I'll be right down." I slam the phone down. "Apparently, Jessica is downstairs."

"With the flyers?" Trent asks.

"Jesus, she's gotten around today," I mutter, taking to the staircase.

Sure as hell, she's standing in the middle of the waiting area, a small box deposited on the coffee table. I don't miss the handful of magazines scattered on the floor or the way Carlton and Mike are staring at her like she walked off the front cover of Playboy.

"Carlton? That information I needed? I'm assumin' you have it given that you're standin' around like a lobster waitin' to be boiled."

"Aw, shit," Bek mutters, briefly making eye contact with me.

Carlton snaps out of his apparent haze and jogs past Trent and up to the stairs.

"Mike? Didn't you say you were headed out for surveillance?" I shoot at him.

"I... Yeah." He shuffles out when he sees my hard gaze.

Finally, I turn my attention to Jessica, who's still standing somewhat demurely in the center of the room, an amused smile curving up her perfectly painted pink lips. "Jessica. What can I do for you?"

"I was hoping your assistant would have passed on my message." She glances at Grecia.

"Oh, she told me you called." I offer her my own fake smile. "But I was too busy working my way through the messages pertaining to my investigation and checking on my staff. I'm sure you can forgive her oversight, given the circumstances surrounding that little investigation."

Trent prods me in the back.

"Oh, no, of course. That is the most important thing." She laughs. *Someone take my gun away.* "So, as I said, what can I do for you?"

"I'm handing out campaign flyers for the mayor, and he's requested that everyone puts one in their window to show their support for him, especially during this difficult time for Madison."

Unreal.

"So," she continues, "I have a small box here, maybe two hundred and fifty, and it would be fabulous if you could put them out here on your table, too."

"Can I see them? Do you mind?"

"Not at all." She pulls one out from the open box.

A big picture of the mayor's head stares at me, with a campaign slogan I don't care to read.

"Sorry. No." I hand it back to her.

"No?" She purses her lips and pulls her plucked eyebrows in for a frown. "What do you mean no?"

"I mean no, I'm not putting this in my window or on my table," I explain slowly. "I make it a rule not to have political choices on display in the workplace. This is, of course, a neutral building, and I can't risk having potential clients scared off by my choice. Besides, I have other staff members who might not even plan on voting for the mayor."

"Do you plan on voting for the mayor, Ms. Bond?" she asks scathingly. "Given that he's hired you and is paying you a considerable amount of money for your services?"

I take one step forward. "The council hired me with the mayor as their liaison, and I've asked him for no more money than I charge any other clients of mine. The additional fees were added at his insistence. Please get your facts straight before you throw your inaccurate comments in my face."

"I will inform him of your refusal to display your support for him."

"Please go on and do so. I couldn't give a flyin' shit what you plan on doin'."

Her lips twist in annoyance, but the evil glint in her eye tells me that she has a score to settle in Holly Woods—and it has fuck all to do with the mayor. She bends to pick the box up and ends up two or three steps closer to me. Accidentally, I'm sure.

"I expect you'll be fired within the next twelve hours, Ms. Bond. Then you'll have absolutely no need to work with the HWPD, will you?"

I pull my lips to the side. "Expect all you like, hon. Was that everything?"

"For now."

"Good. Now, Ms. Shearer, get the fuck out of my building before I help you out."

"Are you threatening me?" she squeals. She looks around me at Trent. "She just threatened me!"

Trent moves out and looks at Bek. "You hear a threat, Bek? Grecia?"

They both shake their heads.

My brother looks at Jessica. "My apologies, Ms. Shearer, but all I heard was her offering to help you out of the building. Those shoes are real high, after all."

Jessica scowls at him, marring her usually pretty face, and clicks her way over to the door. Then, with a tight grasp on the handle, she looks back at me. "This isn't over."

The door echoes as it slams behind her.

"Sounded like a war declaration, didn't it?" Bek offers chirpily, breaking through the silence.

I laugh once before heading for the stairs. "She can declare all she likes. Doesn't mean there will be a war—or that she'll even win it. The chick is deluded."

chapter FOURTEEN

'M going to kill my brother for telling on me.

After he left, I got a frantic call from Nonna in Italian so fast that I could barely keep up with it, demanding why I was refusing to go to family dinner tonight. So here I am, at family dinner, with my laptop and notepad.

I'm determined to work. I'm determined to focus on something other than the fact that it's been ten hours since I walked out of the police station and Drake has only called me once.

I've been in my office all day, expecting him to walk in the brash way he normally does and kick my ass. I expected him to storm in, slam my door so hard that the hinges rattle, and pin me against it until I explode and we scream at each other.

That's how we work. Isn't it?

But he didn't. So I ate my cupcake, drew kaleidoscope-esque patterns all over what could now be the new theory of relatively for all the sense it makes, and threw my Sharpie at the wall.

At least I settled on a color for the office's kitchen walls and e-mailed the decorator, I guess.

I've all but crossed Nick off of my suspect list. I think he knows more than he's letting on, but if knowing stuff got Vince killed, then I don't blame Nick for not saying a word. Although I do have to wonder if he knows he has police protection just in case.

194

The evidence is bugging me more than who the murderer is. That's the link. But it could be anything. Evidence can never be pinned down to a single thing. It has to be tangible though. It also has to be something incredibly damning to make Natalie and Vince think they could get a ton of money for it from the mayor.

The obvious answer is, of course, the baby. But since extracting DNA from a fetus is pretty tough, that's ruled out.

Maybe it's text messages or e-mails or the D.O.M. contract the mayor is probably paying to keep under wraps.

Who knows? Mayor McDougall is so corrupt that even Satan will refuse his soul entry to hell. The amount of people he's rumored to have paid off over the last few decades must be as long as Santa's Christmas list. The media, the police... Probably even his own wife. I wouldn't be surprised to find out that he's paying her to stay married to him at this point.

So, what would he pay so much to keep quiet?

"Auntie Noelle!" Aria bursts through the front door while I'm still sitting in my car.

"What's up?" I open my door and swing my legs around.

She crooks her finger for me to lean in and rests her hands on my knees, lifting her mouth to my ear. "Do you love Drake?"

"Whoa. That was random." I pat her little hands and grab my things from the other seat. "And kind of unexpected."

"Well, I saw him earlier, and he said you're beautiful."

"And I think you've been spending too much time with Nonna, little one." I tap her nose and bump my door shut with my bum.

"Ooookaaay," she replies. "But he seemed kind of sad when I asked him if he was coming to dinner. Nonna was buying all the dinner things and invited him, but he said no. Aren't you friends anymore? Because Dad said he's still friends with him."

Thanks, Trent.

I open the front door. "Aria, things happen. We're grownups, and while I love how much you care, Drake and I need to sort out our own problems. You can tell Dad that, too."

"Okay." She runs past. "Dad, Noelle said to mind your own business."

"Apparently, ten-year-olds are excellent at twisting things," I drawl, dropping into a chair and setting my laptop on my legs.

Alison raises her eyebrows. "Y'think?"

"Pfft." I open the computer and flip my notebook to the last page. Ah—the one with my mindless doodles.

We'll skip back a page.

"Noella!" Nonna shuffles into the room as I open my latest document.

"*Si*, Nonna?"

"You-a never speak Italiano. What-a do you-a want-a?"

"To work," I tell her, motioning to my laptop.

"I see-a Drake. He say-a you-a have-a fight-a."

Excellent. I didn't realize my Italian grandmother was secretly the Spanish Inquisition. "It's not a fight," I protest, sighing. Why will no one listen to me? "I left to avoid a fight. I'm so tired of fightin' over everythin' all the damn time."

Nonna rams her cane against the floor, making Silvio jump and his car flip off the track. "Noella!" she yells, her face steadily getting redder. "You walked out on a fight?" she asks in Italian.

"*Si.*"

"*Perché?*"

"Why? Because I'm fed up of fighting. I said that."

"No." She hits the cane against the floor again and lifts one wrinkled finger in my direction. "*Idioto!*"

"What?"

"*Si, idioto!*"

Oh, crap. She's defaulting to Italian.

Everyone in the house should run right now and save themselves. It's too late for me.

Her next sentence is in Italian, too. Fluent, ferocious, angry Italian. "You think you can walk out on a fight? No! You never walk out on a fight. You walk out, you don't care," she rambles, still pointing at me, her cheeks flushing red with their anger. "You're a Bond! You never walk away!"

I slam my laptop shut. "Well, I do if I'm tired, Nonna! I don't want a relationship where I fight all the time. I don't want to be butting heads with my partner all the time. I want to come home and smile, not wonder what I'm gonna have to yell about tonight. I don't want the relationship you and Nonno had!"

"We had-a the best-a one! We-a knew that-a, in-a the end, we'd-a be okay-a! Many fights-a, lots-a shouts. Noella, it was-a not always okay-a. *Si.*" Nonna pauses then reverts back to Italian. "It wasn't okay a lot of the time, but we loved each other. We still do, and I haven't seen him. You love enough to fight for everything. Then you don't ever walk out on that fight."

"I never said—"

"*Giammai!*" she insists. Never. "Love has-a nothing to-a do with-a it. It is-a your-a soul, Noella. Souls are-a stronger than-a love. Hearts, they-a break. Souls? No. Souls-a never break."

Uncertainty runs rife through my veins, pumping its way through with my blood, and I look away from her. God, I wish she weren't so passionate about everything, especially love. I wish her whole life didn't revolve around love and everything that makes it.

No. I don't.

I'm a liar.

If she weren't a romantic, she wouldn't be Nonna. If she didn't fight for each of us to have our happiness, she wouldn't be Nonna. And damn her annoying Italian ass. I love her for it.

"Nonna…" I say quietly.

"No. You-a want him, you-a go get-a him."

I smile, but it's lame. "I'm not you. I can't fight every day for the rest of my life."

"Ah." Her eyes sparkle. "No. You-a, me?" She throws her head back and laughs. "You-a better. You-a Texan-*Italiano*. You have-a the sweetness of-a a Southern *ragazza*, and-a you have-a the fierce-a-ness, too, but you-a have an Italiano *ragazza's* passion. You-a dangerous, Noella." She waggles her eyebrows. "And-a Mamma didn't raise-a no weak *ragazza.*"

"Oh, damn you!" I snap, grabbing my things. "You twisted old lady. I bet you're lovin' this, aren't you? *Cazzo!* Fine!"

I storm past her, her cackling laughter only riling me more, and slam the front door behind me.

Damn her with her fucking stupid philosophies that make total sense.

She's right.

My mama didn't raise no weak girl.

She raised a sweet but fierce Southern girl with a good dose of Italian passion.

How is it that I can stand in front of a woman who fancies herself a threat to me and tell her what to do with herself, but I can't go out and grab the thing she thinks she threatens?

Because I'm a fucking coward. That's why.

He makes me weak. He makes me completely and utterly soft. He cuts through my hard outer shell until he's found the softness inside, and he takes hold of that and he doesn't let it go. He forces emotions I don't want to feel and realities I don't want to exist.

Drake Nash makes me a coward.

Of the very best kind.

I throw my laptop onto the backseat and put my foot down, going into reverse. I swing back onto the street faster than I'm allowed to, and I have to lift my foot as I turn off my parents' street and the speed limit really slows.

He lives closer to my parents than he does to me.

I have no idea what I'm even thinking when I get out of my car again and storm through his open gates and up his drive.

I have no idea when I'm thinking when my fist raps on his door four times.

"Noelle," he says as soon as he opens it.

I take him in—his unruly, dark hair, the shadows beneath his eyes from his lack of sleep, his tightly set jaw—and say, "We need to talk."

His lips twitch. Just a little. "You stole my line."

"Well, I never said I was completely original. Can we? Talk?"

He steps to the side and opens the door. "Sure."

I have no idea what I'm going to say when I step over the threshold and enter his house.

He pushes the door shut behind me and undoes another button on his shirt. He's still dressed from work, and I'd guess he's barely been home thirty minutes. He brings his eyes to mine, one of his eyebrows lifting in question.

And I'm shaking. I can't focus properly because all I can think of is that Nonna is so right and it would have been easier to fight with him. When I'm fighting with him, his eyes don't look nearly as bright or penetrating or bone-shakingly powerful as they do right now. As the silence lingers, my breath hitching every other inhale, and my heart beating triple time, it's harder and harder to force the words

out.

"I'm not mad at you," I manage eventually, swallowing hard and wrapping my arms around my stomach. "I want to be. I thought I was. But I'm not. I'm mad I didn't know anything about your past. I'm pissed I never asked, but that's my fault, not yours. I never wanted to know, so I didn't. And she blindsided me. I didn't run out because I was angry. I ran out because I didn't want to be angry. I didn't want to fight anymore, but then I get forced to dinner tonight, and unsurprisingly, Nonna tells me that, if I don't fight, I don't care, and God, I'm so confused about everything. You're so open—well, except for about Jessica—and I'm not that. I didn't even know that I did care until today."

I take a deep breath and look away.

"I don't even know what I'm saying. How stupid is that? How fucking ridiculous is it that I have to be surprised by you once loving someone so much that you almost married them before I realize I actually really do want to try at this? At us?" I cover my face and press on the inside corners of my eyes. "How damn dumb is it that I don't even know what I'm saying right now although I can't stop fucking talking and want to punch myself in the face?"

"I didn't almost marry her." Drake runs his hand through his hair, his eyes never leaving mine. "Fiancée is such a loose term. I met her while I was training. She worked at this coffee place we used to go to, and we didn't even get together properly for the best part of a year. It fell apart when I graduated from the academy and she realized I wasn't stayin' in Austin, but comin' home."

"But Austin is an hour away. It's not like you were moving across the country. Or even to Dallas or something."

"She didn't care. She didn't get it. She wanted me to be there with her all the time, but when she realized I wanted to be more than a beat cop—that I wanted to be head of homicide and command a whole, albeit small, team, she freaked the fuck out. I thought I loved her, so I proposed. I was young. I don't think I knew what I was doing." He rubs his hand across his face, shrugs, and finds my eyes again. "I think she thought I'd be back for her every night. That I'd commute into town every day from Austin. I didn't, and then I started workin' longer and longer hours to show the sheriff I was serious and wanted to be someone in his force. Simply, she couldn't hack it, and on nights when I worked late and didn't go to her place after my shift was done, she was with someone else."

Oh, shit. "Drake," I whisper before running my teeth across my bottom lip.

"I didn't care at that point. I was betrayed, but not upset. Honestly? I was glad she did it. It gave me a reason to end that pathetic excuse for a relationship." He shrugs. "I've seen her a handful of times since then, but I've never stopped to talk to her except for once. She obviously found out that I've gotten where I wanted to be, and she's interested again."

"Are you?" I swallow before my voice cracks. "In her?"

"I'd rather drink a smoothie full of my own sperm than look at her that way again."

"Well, then."

He laughs and waves me over to him. We end up meeting in the middle of his living room, and he frames my face with his hands.

"No," he says firmly, clearly, completely honestly. "I have absolutely no interest in her. And this is everything I was going to tell you before you ran out on me."

"I didn't run out," I protest. "Okay, kind of, but I was mad. I thought I might shoot her," I admit. "In hindsight, I would have shot her."

"You need to get that trigger finger under control."

"I don't think so. I think she… I… Well, um." Now, how to tell him that essentially the beginning of a female pissing contest has begun. What's that called? An ovulating contest or something?

He takes two steps back, dropping his hands. His voice is flat when he asks, "What did you do?"

"Nothing! Maybe a little something." I pinch my finger and thumb together in front of my face, a small gap between the tips. "Well, she shouldn't have come into my office all fucking righteous and bitchy, should she?"

"You threatened her, didn't you?"

"I quote Detective Trent Bond when I say it was offering to help her leave the building."

"I don't know if I should laugh or not."

"It was pretty funny. It's actually on camera if you want to laugh." I chew the inside of my cheek. "And she might have told me it isn't over."

"You shot her then, didn't you? Jesus."

"No! I didn't shoot her! Yet."

"Noelle…"

"Like I said. She shouldn't have come in with her bitch face on. My bitch face outweighs hers any day of the week." I sniff and glance away for a second. "She doesn't know who she's messing with."

"Now that I agree with." He shakes his head, his eyes reflecting the amusement curving his lips. "What the fuck am I gonna do with you, huh?"

"Just don't…" I hesitate, my stomach coiling nervously. God, I'm hot all over. Why is it so hard to stop it?

"Just don't what?"

You're a Bond, Noelle. Your mama didn't raise a weak girl, and your nonna didn't influence a pathetic one.

I take a step toward him and curl my fingers around the loose openings of his shirt. He rests his hands on my waist, his thumbs brushing across my skin, and I look up at him.

"Us," I whisper. "Please don't let her come between us."

"You admitting there's an us?" he murmurs, his lips ghosting across mine in a kiss that's barely featherlight.

"Yes." My hands creep up to his neck, where my arms wrap around it, and his easily slip around my body. "I want there to be. Even if we fight every day. If it isn't easy, it isn't worth it."

"It won't be easy," he warns, his voice low. "She won't let it be. She'll make your life hell."

"Then that's real unfortunate for her, because I'm the woman the devil is scared of."

"You mean you aren't Satan incarnate?"

"Shush. I think he's secretly my father. Don't tell Nonna."

Drake's hand cups the back of my head, and he smiles, our foreheads resting together. "The day I tell her that is the day I sign my death warrant," he laughs softly. "But honestly, Noelle. It was ten years ago and I still remember how nightmarish she made my life. She'll be here long after the closing of this case."

I slowly brush my lips across his, taking strength from the warmth of the kiss.

It's the first time I've ever kissed him.

This now—this moment. I know, in that fleeting touch, everything changes.

"I'm not scared of her," I whisper to him. "You? I'm fucking terrified of you. You and me is the scariest thing I've ever encountered, but if I can finally pull my head from my ass and face us, then I can sure as hell take your shitty little bitch of a ex."

"You really do want to shoot her, huh?"

"What gave it away?" I pull back and meet his eyes. My smile dies.

The intensity in his gaze quite frankly takes my breath away. It's hope and resolve and desire and steadfast determination mixed with the kind of protective warmth I know I'll never see again.

It's the way you're only ever looked at once in a lifetime.

"I want to be yours." My words are so quiet, and I stroke my thumb down the side of his neck. "I want it so badly."

"Then be mine," he murmurs. "It's that simple, *bella*."

"Make me," I murmur back. "Make me yours."

He creeps his hand down to the hem of the light dress I threw on before dinner as he pushes me backward, finally lowering his mouth to mine and taking it in a kiss that makes me as breathless as always. I feel his kiss and his touch everywhere as he hikes my dress above my ass and it bumps into the edge of a table.

Oh, shit.

Here we go again.

As he lifts me onto the table, bunching my dress up further, kissing me harder I flatten a hand against it. Drake drops his mouth my neck, and his lips shoot sparks from every single little kiss across it. Each touch is heavier than the last, more teasing, and I swear each one makes me want to beg a little more than the last.

His hands probe my thighs and pull me against him. His hard cock is a jolt of pleasure against my clit, even through the layers of fabric separating us. There's nothing but him as he explores my body, each touch deftly sweeping my skin as if he owns my body.

And right now, on fire from him, I'd swear he does.

He bends, the hot breath that was coasting across my breasts now teasing my thighs.

"You have a thing for tables."

Drake looks up at me, smirking. "I was taught to always eat at the table."

Then, just like that, he hooks my panties to the side, pushes me back, and closes his mouth over my clit.

"Well," I gasp, closing my eyes and dropping my head back. "Manners are important."

"And you'll be thanking me long before the main course." He pauses long enough to say those words. As soon as the final one has left his mouth, he's focused entirely on what he's doing.

Licking my pussy.

And I'm focused on that, too.

I think he has my clitoris on speed dial.

He finds it instantly and wastes no time working it with the very tip of his tongue. And God, God, God. It's so fucking lucky I'm mute from pleasure right now or he'd think I was renaming him.

Still... He isn't shy about this. Neither am I. I want him to do this. A part of me, the biggest part, wants him to own me and possess me so thoroughly that the only thing on my mind as he's inside me is his name.

I want that, too, though. The rest of me. I want him to finally end this are-they-aren't-they bullshit that's been spiraling in my mind for days.

I want him to own me.

I want the most vulnerable part of me to belong to him without hesitation.

And it happens as he pushes me over the brink with his tongue and fingers combined.

He's right. I'm breathing his name before he's even freed his cock from his pants.

He grasps the back of my neck with his hand and forces my face toward his. "Say it," he demands.

No more fighting unless it matters.

"Yours." I tilt my hips toward him.

He teases me by brushing the head of his cock against the opening of my wet pussy. "All of it. Every fuckin' word, Noelle. Because my cock won't be inside you until you've said it."

"Yours," I repeat again. "I'm yours."

He pushes into me in one long, easy thrust.

And I throw my head back again. I want to hold this, this

moment. I want to keep it forever. The moment where everything changes and I finally stop and give myself to him the way he wants. Even if it means fighting every day and rarely seeing eye to eye but always needing the other at the end of the day.

This. Me. Drake.

It's so right that I don't know how I ever thought it was wrong.

His grasp on me is so hard and desperate, and my fingers twine in his hair so deeply as he moves me even closer to him and his hips grind faster and deeper and he's so buried in me that there's nothing but the way my pussy hugs him as he lingers inside me for seconds that aren't really seconds but are nothing more than fleeting moments in time.

And this… This is everything. Our bodies together. Skin on skin. Fingers grasping and mouths gasping. It's insanity and perfection and the one level of oblivion that should be added to dreams.

It's fast and desperate and furious and intense. It's just us, us, all over. It's head-buttingly intense and so fucking crazy that I can't tell his fingertips from the pleasure that coats my skin as he pushes me closer to the brink of the orgasm I know he'll give me.

Everything.

Heartstopping.

Skin-tingling.

Lung-constricting.

Stomach-somersaulting.

Breathtaking.

It's everything and more as his name leaves my lips in a long, breathy cry that isn't worthy of the pleasure accompanying it. It's pathetic and useless compared to the sensations unashamedly assaulting my body in this very moment.

"Mine." He growls it. That deep, rough growl that gets me every time.

"Caveman," I respond breathlessly. "I'm not food."

"She says after being eaten on a table," he laughs into my collarbone.

Bastard. "Shut it." My responding laugh is breathless and barely distinguishable as one. Because him.

God, just him.

Slowly, he pulls out of me and pushes my panties back into place.

204

"Sorry about that."

"The sex or my underwear?"

"That's a tough one. I don't think I should be sorry about either, judging by your response."

"It's okay. I might have packed an overnight bag in case I decided to blow my family off and come here to kick your ass."

"Hate to tell you, cupcake, but not much ass-kickin' happened."

I sigh, still on the table. "I know."

"Does this mean you'll stay with me tonight?" he asks, touching his hand to my cheek. "Again?"

"Do you want me to?" I hold my breath as I look into his eyes.

"Do you need to ask me?"

"Okay," I agree, turning my face into his palm. "Just keep your cock on your side of the bed. It's real distracting at four a.m."

Drake laughs, and I can't help but smile. "Got it." He touches his mouth to mine softly. "There's wine in my fridge."

"You know me so well," I mumble.

He pulls me off the table. "Grab your shit from your car, and by the time you get back, there'll be a wine glass on the coffee table."

"And you'll clean the dining table, right?"

His answering smirk is both cocky and amused. "You got it, cupcake."

"So, to sum up," Drake says, rolling onto his side and looking down at me, "we have no idea what we're looking for."

"That would be an accurate explanation." I wince. "Because the only people who knew about it are now dead."

"So we need to go back into their houses and search for something that could incriminate the mayor."

"Why didn't I think of that?" I grumble and sit up, holding the covers over my bare chest. "When can we do that? Are we even allowed to do that?"

Drake gets out of bed and walks toward the bathroom. He's completely naked, and if I were a less mature woman, I'd laugh at how pale his butt is compared to the rest of him.

"Didn't stop you before, did it?" he asks.

"I have absolutely no idea what you mean," I lie.

"Oh, so you didn't break into Ryan and Lena Perkins's apartment."

"It's not breaking in if the door is unlocked!" I call, grabbing my bra from… Uh… I glance around and find it hanging off the lamp.

Because all good table lamps should have a bra hanging off them.

"But it's still illegally entering." The toilet flushes, and he walks back into his room.

Still naked.

"Have we already reached the toilet conversation stage in this? I'm not sure I'm ready for that," I tease him, pulling a clean pair of panties from my bag and putting them on. "And if we have, I'm drawing the line at poop-talks."

"How have you been single for years?"

"You're a cocky bastard." I grab my dress, lay it on the bed, and dig in my bag. I know I put a roll of string in here yesterday.

"What are you doin'? Not that I'm upset about the view."

"I'm pretty sure my ass is your favorite part of me," I mutter, locating the string under my hairbrush and pulling it out.

"No, seriously." Drake frowns and pauses with his hands on the button of his jeans. "What are you doin'?"

I grin and snap a long piece of string off with my teeth. Then I thread one end through the hole in my zipper. Back zippers are a woman's nemesis, and ever since I saw this trick on one of those stupid "30 Life Hack" articles that are irresistible reading while on the toilet, my life has been so much easier.

I tie the ends of the string together with Drake still watching me. At least he's done his button up now. Actually, on second thought, I kind of preferred it open.

I step into my dress, wriggle it up my body, put my arms in the holes, and sweep my hair around to one side. Drake's now looking at me like the circus let their freak show go somewhere between now and last night. I reach behind me to the base of my back, grab the tied end of the string, and pull it up. The zipper makes that light buzzing sound as it moves up to where I can reach behind me and grab it.

"And that," I tell him, one eyebrow lifted, reaching behind me to snap the string off, "is how an independent woman puts her dress on."

206

"I'm kind of impressed. But what are you gonna do if someone unzips it like…this." He moves quicker than I do, and I swing my fist toward him as he grabs my zipper and pulls it right down into that awkward part of your back where you can reach it but not move it.

"You total dick!"

He laughs, crawling over the bed to the other side of the room. "Zippers on dresses are better left undone."

"Not when you have to go outside," I cry.

Oh, God. Now I'm contorting my arms in ways they aren't meant to be contorted in to reach this zipper.

Holy crap. I can't even reach it.

"I cannot believe you did that."

He pulls his shirt over his head, still laughing at me. "You know you look like a puppy chasing its tail, right?"

"Did you just call me a bitch?"

"If the shoe fits…"

"Then it's probably going up your ass."

He runs his tongue across his top lip, grinning, and crawls across the bed again. This time toward me. He grabs the hem of my dress and tugs me back so I'm sitting on the edge of the bed in front of him. His fingers brush across my skin as he carefully moves all of my hair away from the path of the zipper, only to replace his hand with his mouth.

I shiver.

He smiles.

Bastard.

He grazes his nose down my spine to where his fingers are clasping the zipper pull, and every second he's touching me, tingles are erupting across my skin. He slowly moves the zipper up, each quiet crackle of the teeth coming together preceded by the barest of kisses traveling upward.

"And that," he murmurs into my ear, "is how independent women with someone to pull up their zipper do it."

My lips twist to the side, but I turn my face toward his anyway. "Touché, sir."

He smiles and kisses the corner of my mouth. "I'm going to make coffee. You finish doing whatever else it is you do to turn yourself human."

"I can't even be offended by that because I'd imagine I look like I stepped out of *The Walking Dead*."

Drake gets off the bed, looks at me, and grimaces. "Noelle, you *are* the walking dead."

I throw the pillow at him. He catches it with a bark of laughter and throws it right back at me before turning and leaving me to get ready. I do it in record speed, thankful this time that I did bring some actual face wipes and the character kid hand wipes can stay nice and buried in my purse.

Pretty sure only moms should have those in their purses. I really need to give it to Alison before they get stuck inside my Chucks and forgotten or something.

"Come on," he says, handing me a travel cup of coffee as soon as I take a step inside the kitchen door. "We have some investigating to do."

"We're going to do that now? Like right now? I don't think I have the shoes for it." I suck my bottom lip into my mouth and release it with a *smack*. "Unless three-inch wedge heels are acceptable for that."

"Your dress isn't exactly suitable, either, but as long as you're aware that, if one of us needs to bend over to look at somethin', it'll be you, then it's okay."

"Are you allowed to perv on me while we work?"

His half grin gives me butterflies. "If not, then I should have been fired several times over by now."

Oh, boy. This is gonna be a long day.

chapter
FIFTEEN

M
Y family think I'm crazy. More specifically, my brothers.

On the way to Natalie's house, I called Trent, who told me that he was having his first day off in over a week and he'd tell Silvio to poop on my floor next time I babysit if I tried to make him work.

He won.

Then I called Devin, who agreed to help only because, in the drama of everything yesterday at family dinner, Nonna didn't corner Amelia—who was coming to her first dinner in weeks because of work—and make her look through her scrapbook cover to cover.

I also called Brody right after, and he agreed to help if I didn't ask him to go on a date with Melanie until the next favor I need from her.

I doubt I'll get another favor, but whatever. Desperate times and all that.

So here we are, standing in the hallway of Natalie's house, and all three guys are staring at me like I've grown another head. Even Drake, and he knew from the start.

Damn crowd-pleaser.

"You don't know what we're looking for," Brody surmises, his tone flat. "Are you serious? I could be doing something that's actually useful right now."

"This is useful," I argue. Kinda lamely. "There has to be something here."

He's right though. It is pretty useless because we're searching for a needle in a haystack that might not even exist.

"Noelle," Devin groans, wiping his hand across his face. "Don't you think that, if there were, her stalker would have broken in and gotten it by now?"

"Or her murderer, and that's why Vince was killed?" Brody continues. "If you find anything in either of their houses, I'll take over all of your babysitting favors for Trent for the rest of the year."

Yeah. He thinks I'm trying to catch a mole with a fishing rod.

I shrug a shoulder and look around her house, resting my hands on my hips. "You can't hide everything. If there is something here, there's no saying it was found if anyone broke in. Maybe that's why Vince was killed, too. Because they thought Natalie had given it to him."

"That's what Nick said," Drake points out, and my stomach sinks as it hits me—Brody and Trent have convinced him there's nothing here. "He said Vince had it, whatever it is."

"There could be more." My argument is seriously weak right now. "Copies of something. I don't know, okay? I know there's something here."

"So we're going to spend a whole day searching two houses for 'something' from your gut feeling?" Devin raises an eyebrow.

"Okay, I'm going to," I remedy. "Y'all go on ahead and come up with another solution."

They all share a glance.

"Have you ever considered that your gut needs a trip to the loony bin?" Brody questions me. "Because it comes up with crazy shit."

"My gut also solved your last murder while y'all were twirling on your tiptoes like a bunch of freakin' prima ballerinas." I pull the plastic gloves I took from Drake before we left out of my purse and put them on.

"Your gut got lucky because you were decorating. We almost had it," he protests.

"Yeah, like you almost had all the other case information I gave you," I scoff. "Without me and my team, your police department would still be sitting on their backsides in the briefing room with coffee and stale bagels, tryin' to figure out who did what and where.

Face it. Now you can either help me or go, 'cause I'm lookin' anyway."

I turn my back to them and start. I pull out each sofa cushion, sliding my hands down the edges just in case. I come up with twenty-five cents, a gum wrapper, and an old battery. A search of the armchair gives me a sock and another ten cents.

I should probably check my own cushions. With the amount of times I drop change and leave it there, I'll probably find a hundred bucks down the back of the sofa or something. I turn my attention to the coffee table and the drawers there, ignoring the three sets of eyes still focused on me.

If they don't wanna help, that's fine. If I don't find anything, then that's fine, too. I want to try. I'd rather try and fail than wait and always wonder.

"Ever think she's too much like Nonna for her own good?" Brody quietly asks Devin. Not fucking quietly enough.

"You mean like, when she gets an idea in her head, there's no talkin' her outta it?"

"Yeah. Then she has the motivation and determination of a colony of rabbits in mating season."

"I can hear you, you know," I remind them, moving to the rack of DVDs. I pull them out one by one, opening and closing each one in case something was slipped inside.

"Thorough," Drake notes.

"Obsessive," Brody counters. "Although it's real fun to watch."

"I can still hear you." After finishing with the DVDs, I check in and around the entertainment stand.

"How badly is she going to hurt us if we don't help?" Dev laughs. "And do I have to be here?"

"No," Drake replies, his attention still on me as I move into the kitchen. "I'm not your superior, so you can do what you want, and I can't make Brody stay until his shift officially starts at three. The only one who has to stay is me."

I open what appears to be the pots cabinet. It stretches right back, and I poke my head in to see if there's anything stuffed down there. That's where I'd hide something. In that little nook no one can ever get anything in or out of unless it's a straw.

"You could easily delegate this to her," Dev laughs again. "You're only stayin' 'cause she's your girlfriend."

Waitwhatnow?

"Ow! Fuck!" My head collides with the shelf, and I scoot backwards, keeping my head down, before I sit up. Ouch. That really hurt.

"Are you all right?" Drake asks, coming into the kitchen flanked by my brothers.

"Fine," I lie, rubbing the back of my head. "I misjudged where the shelf ended and space started."

"More like you heard me say the word 'girlfriend,'" Dev teases.

"Or I could shut your mouth for you." I smile sweetly and close the cabinet door.

Drake takes a deep breath and looks at them. "I have to stay because she's a danger to herself. She's probably given herself a concussion and she's only been doing it for fifteen minutes."

"I have not given myself a concussion." I hope. "It's a little knock. People bang their heads all the time." Just not on cabinet shelves because they're trying to find…something. "Y'all are distractin' me with your chitchat. I mean it: Help me or go."

Drake pulls some gloves from his pockets and snaps them with a sigh. I shoot him a glare as Dev groans and holds his hand out toward Drake.

"I'll help," he says with reluctance. "She'll probably lock herself in a closet or somethin'."

"Or fall over a roll of toilet paper," Brody adds, taking a pair from Drake, too.

I smile sweetly, making sure to meet each of their gazes. "Well, aren't y'all sweet?"

Devin points a latex-clad finger at me. "This is the Italian blood deciding that helping family is more important than going home and having sex with my fiancée. Don't think I'm bein' nice."

"I appreciate your sacrifice," I return dryly. *Too much information, brother. Ew.*

"All right," Drake says, pulling his shoulders back and taking charge.

So much for this being my bright idea. He always has to be the king of every search. Pain in the damn ass.

"Before we dive right in blindly," he goes on, shooting an amused but fond look my way, "let's narrow down our options to realistic somethings."

"Nah. I like my somethings the way most men like women's legs. Wide open." I grin. "I'm going upstairs to search. You narrow down your somethings while I go somewhere I can't hurt myself."

"You could drown in the bathroom," Brody offers helpfully.

"Yeah… Or I could flush your head down the toilet. Stay away. I'm dangerous." I make an X with my fingers before going upstairs as quickly as my shoes will allow me.

The low hum of the guys talking downstairs fills the empty space up here. I'm thankful for it because there's something incredibly freaky about going into the bedroom of a dead person. It's not even like I believe in ghosts, so I'm not going to get possessed or something, but ah.

I've never liked this part of investigating. Bedrooms are so very personal. From panties and pictures to vibrators.

Her bedroom door is ajar, so I push on it slowly. It creaks, making this all the more ominous. Damn, maybe there is a ghost. That stuff happens in movies, right?

I did not get enough sleep last night. Or enough coffee this morning.

I smack my lips together as I cast my eyes over her bedroom. Cute. White with accents of lilac and light blue. In actuality, there's nothing special about it. There's a bed with a headboard, a dresser, a vanity littered with jewelry holders, and a three-door closet with mirrors.

I crouch a little to see if there are any boxes under the bed. Once I see the empty space, I turn my attention to the vanity. She had good taste in jewelry. I can spy several of the new collection from Alex and Ani I'll neither confirm nor deny that I've been adding and removing to my basket for two weeks.

The dresser holds photo after photo, and it feels intrusive and cliché, but if the evidence is a note or photo, then it's a foolproof place to hide it. Carefully, I lay each framed photo down on top of the dresser and turn the little clasps.

My phone vibrates from its home inside my bra with a text. I secure the back of one photo, stand the frame up, and pull out my phone. As I tap at the screen, it occurs to me that my phone can't sense my thumb, so I pull my glove off and open the message. I don't know the number, and I frown at the words.

You're wasting your time.

Then the bang happens.

Glass shatters as the booming sound of a two gunshots echoes through the air. I clap my hand over my mouth and drop to the floor, crawling around the side of the dresser. I pull my gun from the holster on my thigh with one hand and help myself back up with the other, staying low. The bedroom window has been shot at, a single bullet hole piercing the lower left corner, and despite the pane being covered with cracks, it's still intact and safely left in the window frame.

The bullet, however, is in the wall, about two inches down from the ceiling.

What kind of an idiot shoots through an upstairs window and expects to fucking hit someone?

Bitch, please. We're not all LeBron James.

I go downstairs quietly, but the sound of Devin's hard voice on the phone requesting an ambulance has my heart jumping out of my chest.

That better be a fucking window ambulance he's calling.

My chest is tight as I get down the last couple of stairs, my gun still in my hand. I follow the sounds of their voices into the study at the front of the house.

My baby brother is sitting against the wall, sweat dripping down his pale face, his hand on his side. Drake pulls his shirt over his head and balls it up to press against him.

I see the blood seeping onto Brody's light-blue T-shirt before Drake can cover it up. "Brody!"

"I'm fine," he grinds out, his eyes screwed shut.

"Yeah, all right." I kneel down next to him and put my gun on the floor. "What happened?"

"We were in here searching. Then the bullets came flying in. One here, one somewhere else," Drake explains.

"The bedroom," I explain. "Went straight into the wall. Right after I got a text saying we're wasting our time."

Drake's face hardens as Brody cries out.

"Shh," I whisper, turning to my baby brother and cupping his face with my hands. "You're gonna be okay, Brodes. I promise."

He nods, and tears spring to my eyes. Jesus, I've never seen him in this much pain.

"Stay with me. Don't you dare pass out." I lightly slap his cheeks, and he forces his eyes open. "Okay. You can't sleep yet. The ambulance is coming. You're not allowed to go anywhere."

He nods again, but this time, it's much jerkier than before. His fist clenches against the floor, and I touch my forehead to his before dropping a kiss against his clammy skin.

Please, God. If you're real and you can hear this and you aren't fed up of me taking your name in vain ten times a day or my nonna's endless requests, please make sure my baby brother is okay.

And for the first time in my life, sirens are welcome.

The lights flash through the window, and Drake climbs over Brody's legs without nudging him.

"Hear that, Brodes? The ambulance is here."

He doesn't acknowledge my words.

"Brody?"

"Noelle," Drake whispers, taking my hands from his face as paramedics arrive in the room. "Let them do their job."

"He isn't talking," I whisper hoarsely. "Why isn't he talking to me?"

Oh God—Brody. The tears spill over my eyes as an angry sadness like nothing I've ever felt fills my body. From my head to my toes, I'm torn between sobbing hysterically or getting in a car and driving around to find the motherfucker who shot my brother.

But I'm shaking. Everything. And nothing makes it better. Not Drake's arms wrapping around me from behind to hold me back or feeling Devin take my hand or seeing the paramedics ease my unconscious and bleeding brother onto a stretcher.

The oxygen mask doesn't make it better.

Nothing does.

My muscles are so tense and I'm breathing through my tears, but it doesn't matter because it's nothing compared to what he's feeling.

My baby brother.

My *baby brother.*

My best fucking friend, even above Bek. My tormentor and the little macho guy who always fancied himself my protector, even when I didn't need protecting.

Brody.

He's wheeled out. I don't know how long it's been. But he's still not awake. He's still bleeding. He's still shot and bleeding and unconscious and completely and utterly defenseless.

Defenseless.

Something he's never been.

I cover my face with my face, and my knees buckle. I'd go down if it weren't for Drake's already steady hold on me. He grips me tighter and turns me into him, and my face buries into his chest, and the fear inside me breaks free.

Hold a gun to my face and I won't tremble. Put your finger on the trigger and I won't run. Shoot me and I won't cry.

But my brother? My family?

No. Fuck. No.

I push away from Drake and press my palms against my cheeks, begging the tears to stop. Drake refuses to let me go, instead touching my back. I'm thankful because my legs are weak. They're Jell-O and ready to break at any point, but instead of letting them go, I find my brother's eyes.

Devin looks how I feel. His cheeks are red, and even he has the glint of a tear in his eye. But his fists are clenched, his shoulders drawn back, his jaw tight. Behind those tears hovering in his dark eyes is anger. Just anger. The kind of anger any sane person would run from.

It doesn't scare me.

I feel it too.

I feel that inhuman anger that makes you see everything with a tinge of red, that makes you want to act on your impulses no matter the consequences.

The kind of anger that would make murder possible.

After all, *la famiglia è tutto.* Family is everything.

Fuck with me. Don't fuck with my family.

And certainly not my little brother.

"I'm calling Dad," Dev manages to croak out. He storms out of the room as the first police car pulls up outside.

"Noelle," Drake says quietly, stepping in front of me. "We ain't goin' near Vince's. Whatever this is, it's gonna have to find us, cupcake. No way am I riskin' anyone else gettin' hurt."

"I know. I wasn't even thinkin' of it."

216

"Sweetheart." He whispers it, touching the side of my face and bringing my eyes to his. "He'll be okay. He's one of the three toughest guys I know, and all of them have the same surname."

"I know. But that's...Brody," I finish lamely. "I couldn't protect him. I should protect him."

Which is exactly why Dev is pissed the hell off, too.

"Hey, no. Hey." He forces my eyes back to his. "No. No guilt. I'll take you to the hospital and you can meet your family there."

"I'll go later. When I know he's okay." I blow out a long, quiet breath. "This... Finding out who did this is important. I have a crazy grandmother who will want to know their address within the next thirty minutes so she can dish out some good ol' revenge, Italian-style."

"You need to be with your family."

"No." This time, I meet his eyes with steely determination. "I need to find out who did this, because this shit just got fuckin' personal."

chapter SIXTEEN

*"*W*HY* are you here?"

I look up at Bek, a deep breath filling my lungs. "Because I can't be at that hospital. I can't sit there in those goddamn stale, white rooms and wait to hear what's wrong with my brother."

"So, you'd rather be here, at seven p.m., waiting for a phonecall?"

Slowly, I nod. I would be. Not because I don't love my brother or care. I do. God, I've cried four times this afternoon since Drake reluctantly brought me here. That was before he drove to his house, brought my car to me, then walked back to get his car again.

It's easier to be here and focus on work. Focus on this goddamn something that got my brother hurt—the same something that makes me want to drive out to Nick's studio and pin his sorry-son-of-a-bitch ass against the wall until he spills exactly what could lead to us solving this murder.

I wish I could be at the hospital. I wish I could be there, holding their hands, waiting like they are, but I know that, the second Brody wakes up—if he wakes up from the surgery they took him into five hours ago—he'd look at me and ask me what the hell I was doing at the hospital and didn't I have shoes to buy?

Although I do agree. It's strange that I'm not there. I've done nothing but flick through the same pages and try to drink the same cold coffee for the last two and a half hours. My phone is on ring for the first time in weeks, and it's plugged into a charger and lying screen up on my desk.

Every time it lights up, my heart stops.

I should be at the hospital. I should be waiting there. I should know exactly what's happening and where everyone is and how he is.

But I still think he'd yell at me and ask me why I'm hanging around there.

So this... This isn't for me. These lame hours I'm spending in limbo, waiting for a word from my family, are for him. Every useless page flip and mouse click and lift of a mug of cold coffee.

It's easier.

I have to keep repeating that. It's easier. I have to keep telling myself that because then I might believe it. I might believe that it really is easier to be miles away from him when he's suffering so badly and fighting so hard to wake up.

I have to tell myself that, too. That he's fighting to wake up. That he's fighting for everything, because I don't know where that bullet hit. It could have skimmed arteries or pierced his major organs.

I. Don't. Know.

"Noelle!" Bek snaps. "You need to go there. Let me drive you to the hospital."

I shake my head and bury my face in my hands. "I have to figure this out, Bek. I have to make this right. I have to find who did this to Brody and Natalie and Vince."

"Tomorrow," she urges me, slamming her fist onto my desk. "They'll still be here tomorrow. The white Cadillac the neighbors said they saw was found in the woods outside of town an hour ago. The cops are running DNA testing on it and hoping the plate will trigger the minds of some neighbors. There's nothing you can do sitting here and staring into space."

I've never wanted Drake to storm into my office more than I do right in this second.

But he doesn't.

"Okay," I whisper, giving in. "Take me."

Bek walks around my desk and takes my hands, helping me up. I feel completely exhausted and lame. There isn't a part of me not burning with worry for Brody.

I rub my hand down my face in an effort to wake myself up before we reach the top of the stairs. Bek, being the best friend ever, already brought me flat shoes so I don't have to worry about takking a sleepy tumble down the stairs and into her car.

"Oh, here's your mail from today. This one was delivered late." She stops us by Grecia's office. "I told her I'd give it to you before I sent her home," she explains, handing me the pile.

"This one?" I point to the letter on top with hand-scrawled letters.

"Yeah. Maybe around four? But I told her not to disturb you. I thought you were sleeping."

I smile, but it's weak. No, around then, I was picturing my brother's pain-stricken face as he realized what had happened to him.

"Let's go." Bek wraps her arm around my shoulders, my purse somehow magically slung over her other arm, and guides me outside.

My hands are shaking so badly that I can barely turn the key. I have no idea how I've lasted ten hours since Brody was shot.

To be fair, I think I've spent eight of them in shock.

Angry shock, albeit, but still shock.

I climb into her car and drop the tied-up mail bundle into my purse when she hands me it. Then I pull out my phone, which has somehow made its way into it, and bring up Drake's name. I hit message.

Going to the hospital... I text.

His reply is quick. *Let me know. How you doing?*

Okay, and nope, I reply. That's how I feel right now. No. Just no.

Talk to you later, cupcake.

I sigh, rest my head back on the headrest, and close my eyes.

"Noelle?" Bek says my name, softly shaking my arm.

"I'm awake." I pinch the top of my nose and blink harshly when I open my eyes. "Are we here?"

She smiles. "Yeah, and we aren't the only ones."

I pull my eyebrows together in a frown, but she doesn't elaborate as she gets out of the car. The only damn elaboration is the growth in her smile.

I'm glad she can smile.

220

She takes my hand and tugs me toward the entrance. A lone figure is standing by the doors, their face initially obscured by the brightness of the lights streaming out from the hospital. It only takes a few steps before I realize it though.

"Drake?" I whisper, covering my mouth with my hand.

"Yep," Bek replies, squeezing the hand still clasped in hers. "He called me when you were sleeping. I love you, Noelle, but I ain't gonna hug your fiesty ass all damn night. Or let you cry on me, for that matter. This shirt was expensive."

My best friend really is the best.

I hug her tight. "I hate how well you know me."

"No you don't. You love it, you silly bitch."

That smile I didn't think I could raise? Yeah. It doesn't matter how badly you're hurting inside as long as you have the people who are your rock-hard pillars of strength around you.

I let Bek go and turn to Drake. He holds his hands out to his sides in a *well?* motion, and I take the few steps between us, running, and all but throw myself at him. My arms tangle around his neck, and his wrap around me so tight that I can barely breathe as I bury my face into his neck.

"Thank you," I whisper against him.

"He's important to you. He's important to me. You're important to me. Like I wouldn't be here," he rumbles back against the side of my head, kissing it when he finishes speaking. "He's on the sixth floor and about to come out of surgery, so you'll know within fifteen minutes how he is."

I pull back, taking a breath so deep that I feel the oxygen spilling right down to my toes. "We will? How do you know?"

Drake nods. Then, with a slight smile, he pulls his something out of his pocket, flips it open, and taps the gold badge exposed to me. "This was my VIP ticket tonight."

"Of course." I smile and look down before extracting myself from his arms to look at Bek. "Coming?" I ask her, warmth flooding me as Drake slips his fingers through mine and squeezes.

"It's okay," Bek replies, but I can see the worry in her eyes. She isn't fooling me.

"Come," I demand, holding my free hand out to her, my purse on that shoulder. "Now."

221

"Yes, boss." She tries for another smile, but it's a pathetic attempt at one.

She does, however, take my hand, tightly curling her fingers around mine. The three of us, with Drake slightly in the lead, enter the hospital, and I look down so the bright lights don't blind me. I wouldn't put it past this place, you know.

Drake lightly squeezes my hand as the elevator doors open, and we step in after everyone has emptied it. I can't remember the last time I felt this weak, honestly. Not knowing how Brody is really is a hole inside me, and the tears lingering behind my eyes aren't playing any games. If they make their way to the front, they're gonna go, and I'm gonna lose it. I'm hoping, and maybe even somewhere deep down I'm praying, that I won't have to.

Floor six is intensive care.

Every part of me tenses.

The man in front of me is as powerful as ever, though, as he rings the buzzer to get in and explains who we are. The doors are clicked open, but it does nothing for my tightly wound stomach as the stench of sterility and illness winds its way around me.

"This way." Drake leads me straight down the hall.

I tug Bek after me. Her hand is covering her mouth, and I wish I could do the same. Instead, I simply look down, burying my face as far into my shoulder as I can. I've never been this terrified in my life. I've never felt such acute fear rocking its way through my bloodstream unapologetically the way it is right now.

I really, really hate hospitals.

We stop outside a room with a plaque on the door marking it *Family Waiting Area*.

Awesome. We have to wait with another family with their own pain. Because, with the size of ours, there won't be enough.

Drake pushes the door open, and I'm thankful for his strength. For everything I am, I don't even think I can twitch a finger knowing that knowledge is imminent.

The room is empty except for my family.

Mom is sitting in the corner, her head on Trent's shoulder. Devin is the other side of her, his arm looped through hers, but his head is resting back against the wall as he stares at the ceiling. Trent is leaning against Mom, his hand clasped in hers. His other is curled around Alison's thigh. The absence of the kids tells me that they dropped them by her parents' before they came here.

Nonna is sitting in front of the window next to Dad. Both of them are on their knees, knelt up, their hands held together in front of them. Even as the slowly setting sun sends cascading waves of orange and red over their faces, they look into it, their noses tilted up, their eyes closed. Nonna's lips are moving quickly, but her words are completely silent. Her rosary beads are hooked over her thumb, and she rubs them gently, in her own world.

I'd bet she's been there for hours. Praying. Believing. Begging.

Guilt hits me at the way they've been here, vigiliantly, while I've been hiding.

That guilt drives me to let go of both Drake and Bekah, walk across the room, and kneel next to Nonna. She squeezes my knee, refusing to let go of her rosary, and still speaking. Now, I'm so close that I can hear her, and it's all in Italian. Her mother tongue has always been her own source of strength, and I breathe in deeply, close my hands in front of me, and shut my eyes like she has, just to listen to her.

She's always done this—spoken Italian in hard times. I wonder if she knows we've all noticed. That even Mom will sit and listen to her as she hands her hopes and dreams over to her Lord's hands.

I do this now. I listen. I want to feel the comfort of her still-thick accent and romantically fluent words flow over me.

"Bless this child," she whispers, each word flowing into the next in perfectly smooth Italian. "Give him the strength he needs to keep his spirit on this Earth. Bless his laughter and his smile. Lend him your bravery so he may fight this obstacle that's been thrown into his path. Bless his sweet disposition and selflessness. Allow him to draw on your everlasting knowledge so that he may give himself everything, so that his soul and his mind may align as one to give him the power he so desperately needs. Lord, I beg of you to give your son all that he gives to you without asking you for a single thing."

My eyes sting. Her ability to trust something she'll never have validity of is overwhelming. But it's like Father Luiz said to me only weeks ago. Belief is relative.

She repeats that, over and over, never faltering in her whispering. Never a single syllable of Italian stepping into the wrong. Her whispers are melodic and rhythmic. I'm thankful for every single one as her words continue to wrap me in their warm embrace borne of the kind of belief and faith I don't know I'll ever experience myself.

The movement of a body next to me has me glancing over. Drake. He's kneeling with us, too, his eyes closed. And Alison next to him. Then Trent. And Bek. And Dev. And Mom.

Mom.

"Speak up, Nonna," I murmur loud enough for only her to hear. "You have an audience, and we're not all hard of hearing yet."

I glance at her in time to see her smile stretch across her face.

"Ah, Noella," she replies, her voice thick. "You-a all-a know what I'm-a saying. You-a don't need me. You need-a your hearts. Believe." She closes her eyes once more "Me? I-a believe that-a the Lord will-a bless-a Brody. He will-a give-a him his heart. Believe," she repeats once more. "It's-a all about-a belief."

And don't you know, that crazy old lady has a point.

Once you believe, you can do anything.

The door opens, and we all turn our heads toward it. The man in the doorframe is wearing green scrubs, a hair cap in his hands.

"I don't mean to intrude," he says in a thick Texan accent. "I'll come back if y'all need a moment."

"No," Nonna says, standing before any of us despite her age. She's facing I'm guessing is the surgeon before we're all on our feet.

For as long as she lives, she'll be the head of this family. That's for sure.

"We are-a ready." She pulls her pashmina over her shoulders and takes the seat closest to the door.

Devin hands her her cane, and she winks at him, but the lines in her face seem to have deepened since I saw her yesterday. Dad takes both of my hands and helps me stand. Then he immediately deposits me in the closest chair. Trent does the same with Mom and then Alison. Bek takes her seat next to Alison, and Drake stands next to me.

If this isn't the strongest group of people I've ever met...

"Mrs. Bond," the surgeon says, looking at Mom.

"*Si*," Nonna says, her eyes going to Mom. "There are-a two of us. Antonio, move-a over." She hauls herself up with the help of her cane and hobbles across the room.

I bite the inside of my lip as Nonna takes the seat next to Mom and takes her younger hand into her much older, darker, wrinklier one.

"We-a are ready," Nonna informs the surgeon.

Twenty-eight years and, although my heart is so hollow, it's oddly never been fuller.

The surgeon holds his hands out. "Well, Mrs. Bond...s," he adds, glancing at Alison, too. "I don't know what to tell you. Our intial tests showed the bullet inside his kidney, but when we got him on the operating table, it'd barely grazed it. Brody Bond has either skin of steel or the luck of an angel."

"He's okay?" I gasp, grabbing the edge of my seat and sitting forward. He's okay.

"Yes, ma'am. He's out for tonight to allow himself to sleep through the pain, but I'm gonna tell y'all that he'll be right as rain soon enough."

I cover my mouth with my hand yet again, but it isn't enough, because those tears that threatened earlier are making their appearance. Mom grabs me into her, and I find my face against her shoulder, and Nonna's hand reaches across Mom's legs to find mine.

Find mine it does. And she squeezes. Hard.

Maybe there's something to her beliefs after all.

Soon enough, every Bond in the room has been tugged in to this huge family celebratory hug. My eyes clear enough to see Alison reach out and tug Bek in. My best friend has tears in her eyes, too, and it's an easy enough swoop from her gaze to Drake.

I think he's the only one in the room not crying. But his smile? That half smile that only lightens the relief in his eyes and radiates the happiness he's really feeling? That's the best part of this post-Brody's-okay moment.

And instead of joining us, he simply leans forward and touches his lips to the top of my head.

Somehow, it's better than a hug.

chapter SEVENTEEN

M om called first thing this morning to tell me that, since the bullet never hit any major organs and they're leaving Brody to wake up in his own time, which they think will be any time now, they're taking him out of intensive care and putting him on a normal ward.

Which is exactly why I'm sitting cross-legged on my office floor, in my yoga pants, with one hundred Post-it notes scattered in front of me in a pink-orange-yellow-and-green rainbow. Okay, one hundred might be an exaggeration. Then again, maybe not. Scribbling on the sticky notes is so addictive.

So is adjusting them so they make pretty patterns.

So far I've made a heart, a boat, and a cupcake.

There is method to my madness. Kind of. Each of the notes has a different aspect of the case written on them, and aside from my, ahem, procrastination designs, they're all grouped together in my best shot at chronological order to see if there's anything I've missed. Anything that might help figure this out.

I scan my eyes over each note, but the move is redundant. There's nothing I've missed that I haven't already looked at this morning.

I sigh and fall backward, throwing my arm over my eyes. Ugh. I roll to the side and reach for my purse. Yesterday's mail is still sitting inside it, untouched, and I'm pretty sure there was a bill I should probably open in there somewhere.

I sit up again and pull the small stack out, removing the elastic band holding the envelopes together. The electric bill slips out of the pile, but my eyes catch the top envelope.

There's no stamp. No postage. Just my name and the address of the building.

Handwritten. Hand-delivered.

Damn. These letters are never good in the movies.

Still, it has piqued my curiosity. Hell, it's gone well above the peak. It's the Everest of curiosities.

I slip my pinkie finger into the small hole by the corner of the flap and use my nail to ease it open. A piece of paper is folded in half inside, so I pinch the creased side and pull it out, but that isn't the only thing inside the envelope.

Small photos fall out from the paper, and I reach for one as I open the note. They're grainy and not the best quality, but what's on them is obvious.

Two people are having sex. The woman's hands are bound to a headboard, short, blond hair splaying around her face. The man has her legs hooked over his shoulders in this one, but in another, it's vastly different.

I drop that photo and pick another up. In this one, the woman is attached to a large cross and the man is holding a whip.

In another, she's on all fours and he's coming at her from behind.

In another, her hands are bound behind her back and a tie is knotted around her neck. She's on top of him, her head thrown back, and he's pulling the tie on.

Holy shit.

These are pictures of Natalie.

And I'd recognise that smug face contorted with pleasure and the receding hairline anywhere.

These are pictures of Natalie...and the mayor.

Bile rises up my throat, and it's only stopped from being vomited out by the lump that's formed and refuses to be swallowed. This... Oh my God.

This is the something.

I turn back to the note and lift it to my eyes. Handwritten again. Whoever sent me this isn't afraid to be found out. They must know that even the HWPD has access to someone who can recognize the

....

handwriting.

There are more. Lots more. And it doesn't stop in the photos. It doesn't stop with you. He isn't as safe as he thinks he is.

Oh my God.

It doesn't stop in the photos.

The something, the one thing we've been searching for, Vince was probably killed for is a sex tape.

My very first instinct.

"Oh, *shit*."

"Miss Noelle?" Dean pokes his head around my office door. "Is everythin' all right?"

"Fine." I gather the photos and stuff them into the envelope. "Hey, can you call the station and find out if Detective Nash is there? And Trent?"

"No problem." He disappears as suddenly as he appeared.

I make my way into Carlton's office without knocking and slap the envelope down on his desk. "Scan these images onto the computer and save them. Copy them to a flash drive, too, and give the drive to Grecia for safekeeping. Mark it 'Owens photos.' Wear these." I throw gloves at him, all too aware that I didn't take the same safety measures.

"What are the pictures?" he asks, picking up a glove and looking at it skeptically.

"At the risk of shattering your innocence... Sex photos."

One light-brown eyebrow rises. "Excuse me?"

"Not mine," I add hurriedly. "Trust me. If anyone ever made those, I'd be burning them, not requiring copies. I'm gonna tell you not to look too hard because it's, uh, interesting."

"Uh, okay." He pulls the gloves on, then takes the envelopes and moves to the three-in-one printer in the corner. "Are these the something you've been mumbling about for a few days?"

"Kinda. God, this case is a nightmare. What time is it?"

He glances at his watch. "Eleven."

"Okay. Are they done?"

"Almost."

"Be right back." I run back into my office and pull an empty USB stick from my drawer. Then I go back to Carlton. "Here. Don't forget to label it or Grecia will have a coronary when I ask her to file them all next month."

"Is that all? Just saving them and making copies?" He brings me the stack of photos back. "And you're right. They are interesting."

"Thank you. And no. It's not everything." I slide them back into the envelope and hug it to my chest. "These were hand-delivered yesterday. I have a suspicion I know who sent them, but I need you to find me something. It's probably going to be hard, if not impossible."

"Sure," he asks. "What is it?"

"They're both at the station, Miss Noelle. They're waiting for you and requested Rosie's coffee," Dean interrupts. "Sorry. Excuse me."

"No, you're fine. Thanks, Dean." I smile at him then turn back to Carlton. "I need you to find me the sex tape these images belong to. There may even be more than one."

"I'll try. Who's in them?"

"Natalie Owens and Mayor McDougall."

"Oh, fucking hell."

"Sums it up pretty good, kid." I tap his desk and turn. "You can get me on my cell. I'm out."

I grab my purse from my office and run down the stairs, thankful that I'm actually wearing sneakers for once. This way, I can at least pretend that running all over town today will be a workout.

I go out to my car and get in. Drake and Trent have a point. Rosie's coffee will definitely help. So will her pie. And cupcakes.

Cupcakes in yoga pants. Sounds like a perfect combination to me.

I pull up outside the little cafe and make sure the photos are well hidden in my purse before getting out and taking them with me. No way am I leaving these babies unattended.

"Noelle!" Rosie says, wiping her hands on a cloth. The bell over the door is still ringing as I approach the counter. "How are you? And Brody? How is he?"

"He'll be okay. He has a couple of weeks of recovery ahead of him, but he won't be kept down. Thank you for asking." I smile.

"Oh, good." She presses her hand against her chest. "I was real worried when I heard. I'll get a batch of his favorite peanut butter cookies made up and sent to your mama for him."

"That's very sweet of you, Miss Rosie. Thank you." My heart is full right now. "I'm sure he'll appreciate that."

"Not a problem. Now, what can I get you? I can see that you're on some kind of mission by the look in your eye." She winks, and I have to laugh.

"Sure am. Can I get two coffees for Drake and Trent and a vanilla latte for me, please? Oh, and a slice of cherry pie, a torte cupcake, and a peanut butter cupcake."

"No problem." Another wink, and she turns and gets to work. She has the coffees made masterfully in minutes and sets the three steaming cups in a holder.

I purse my lips as she pulls a piece of cherry pie from the new pie. "Actually, make that two. In, er, seperate boxes." I smile sweetly as a smile of her own touches her lips.

"You got it, sugar."

She serves another piece into a box then sees to the cupcakes. When that's done, she stacks the boxes expertly. No idea how I'm gonna carry all of this. This is what happens when I get greedy and want pie and cake.

God. I'd say I'm gonna have to eat salads for the next week, but I like pasta and pizza too much to even think about torturing myself that way. Maybe I'll have a salad with them. That's much more preferable than instead of.

I hand Rosie thirty dollars and instruct her to keep the change. She raises her eyebrows, because she's always hated getting tips, but I awkwardly grab my things and turn before she can even think of giving it back.

Just as I step out the door, I hear her drop it into her charity box. That woman.

Now, with the goodies and coffee nestled onto my passenger's seat, I drive to the station. The parking lot is almost full, and I drive for a moment before I find a spot on the other side of it. Ugh. I text Drake and tell him to come get his coffee because I can't carry everything.

He comes out two minutes later and opens my passenger's door. "That's a lot of boxes for coffee. Wait. Do I smell chocolate?"

I slap his hand as he reaches for the box with our cupcakes. "No. Coffee. I carry the cake."

"Possessive."

I give him the finger then take the boxes and my purse. Then I

230

kick my door shut, awkwardly hit the fob to lock it, and follow Drake into the building.

"What are you doing here today? I thought you were sleeping in. And you're in yoga pants. Did you actually work out? Doesn't your cupcake cancel that out?"

"How about you kiss my ass, you dick?" I mutter. "My brain had a workout and I'm rewarding her with sugar, okay?"

"The ass-kissing can be arranged." He shoots me a sexy grin.

"Is that all you think about?"

"And guns. And food. And sports. Oh, and murderers."

"You sounded like the typical guy until you added the murderers," I sigh.

"Well, what do you think about?" he counters, his eyebrow raised as he opens his office door.

"Shoes. And clothes. And cake." I pause. "And guns and murderers."

"You sounded like the typical chick until you added the murderers—and the guns."

"Oh, shut up." I flounce past him, put the boxes on the desk, and then text Trent.

I have coffee and pie.

He appears in record time. "I read pie?" He holds his phone up, my message displayed on the screen.

"Cherry pie," I tell him, sitting down and pulling my cupcake from the box.

"You're my favorite sister," he groans, grabbing for the box and attacking the slice like a rabid animal.

"I'm your only sister, idiot. And I'm not here for pie and coffee, you know. I actually have something very important to tell you." I lick some frosting off my pinkie finger.

"If it's that Coach has a sale on, Alison already mentioned it. Something about it being her birthday in two weeks."

"Coach has a sale on?" I blink. "Wait, stop distracting me!" *But thanks for the birthday present idea, bro.* I was wondering to buy her. "Here." I pull the envelope out of my purse and hold it up.

"What is that?" Drake asks, a bit of chocolate frosting on the corner of his mouth.

Is it wrong that I want to lick it off?

"This is my something." I suck the remaining gooeyness from my hand before I pull the photos out again and drop them onto the desk.

Both the guys reach for them and grab at them. Their expressions turn identical as they realize what they're looking at.

It's a funny kind of look. Somewhere between surprise, shock, confusion, and, finally, realization.

"Explain," Drake demands.

"These were delivered to me yesterday. I didn't open them because Bek took me to the hospital." I hesitate. "So I opened them this morning because my sticky notes weren't helping. I only opened it because it was handwritten and didn't look like a bill." I shrug.

"You're never gonna use five words where you can fit fifty in, are you?" he asks me wryly.

"You're always gonna interrupt me when you could stay quiet, aren't you?" I counter. "Thought so. Now, hush a minute." I show them the letter. "This came with them."

Trent reads it then hands it to Drake with a smidgen of cherry juice on the side of it.

I mean, seriously. He's not two.

"What does this mean?" he asks me. "Do you have any idea who sent them?"

I chew the mouthful of cake I've bitten off and shake my head in the negative. "But," I mumble quickly, swallowing my food before I choke on it. "I have a suspicion."

"Well?" Drake asks. "Are you gonna share that with us or are we gonna get an explanation on how you came to the conclusion before you tell us who?"

"Hey! There's a method to my madness. And this is the something y'all didn't think existed." I sniff. "I think it was Alyssa."

"McDougall? The mayor's wife? Why would she do this?" He holds the picture of Natalie cuffed to the cross up. "Have you even thought about that?"

"She knew!" I stand up to stop myself from rolling my eyes. With my hands on my hips, I continue. "When she kicked you out of our talk, she admitted to me that she knows about every single one of the mayor's trysts after they happen. She was too afraid to leave him. We already know he's been paying people off for years. There's just never been any tangible proof. What would he have done to her?"

"So..."

"So I told her that, if she ever needed help, she could contact me. I think his and Natalie's was the one affair he never told her about, but she found out, and this was her way of documenting evidence against him."

"Okay, so just pictures?"

"No. I think there's a video. Or videos. But to find out, I need to talk to her when the mayor isn't around."

"He's out of town this weekend," Trent supplies. "I heard Sheriff telling Dad that the mayor was taking a few days off to distance himself from these murders. He apparently hired Jessica and has thrown everything onto her shoulders."

Good. I hope it crushes her. "Well, then. We're going to see Alyssa McDougall."

"Right now?" Trent asks, looking at his pie.

Drake has the same solemn look on his face as he glances at his cupcake.

And everyone says that I'm the one with the dessert problem.

"Bring them and eat them while I talk to her." I stand up. "Come on."

I climb out of the backseat of Drake's truck. Apparently, he decided that it wouldn't be great if a police car was seen outside of the mayor's house. My suggestion that his truck was just as obvious was met with a stony silence, so I held my hands up and took my relegated seat in the back.

There's only one thing a backseat should be used for aside from children, and since I am neither a child nor coming down from an orgasm, I'm not happy about the seating arrangements.

Should have driven myself and left them in the station with their treats.

I ring the bell of the McDougall family mansion. A maid opens the door and lets me in. Then she leads me to the very same room I spoke to Alyssa in last time I was here.

"Mrs. McDougall? Noelle Bond is here to see you, ma'am."

Alyssa turns, and if she's surprised, her face doesn't show it. "Thank you. Noelle, please come in."

I do as she said, holding tight onto the straps of my purse.

She waits until the door has closed before she speaks. "I wondered how long it would take you to figure it out."

"I opened your letter this morning," I reply. "Why did you send them?"

"Your brother was shot while you were looking for them," she replies simply. "I'm very sorry about that, by the way. I hope it's not serious."

I shake my head. "He was very lucky. How did you know we were at Natalie's house looking for them?"

"I am...contact...with Nick Lucas."

Huh. "What kind of contact?"

"That's a very personal question, Noelle." She turns to face me, pushing her hair from her face. "It's nothing intimate. Let's say that the both of us stand to gain from my husband's fall as the sweetheart of the Holly Woods council."

"Are you saying that you and Nick are involved in Natalie's and Vince's deaths?"

She laughs. "God, no. What would I gain from killing them and exposing my husband? Besides, Vince is the one who made the footage. Natalie knew they existed, but she insisted that their relationship be kept secret from me. And, well, my husband isn't the only one who knows how exploit people's weaknessess." She leans against the fireplace and clasps her hands in front of her. "Vince's business was failing. I told him that, if he gave me the information and continued to document their activities, I'd be a silent partner in his business and supply the necessary funds to keep him afloat."

"And he agreed."

"Of course he agreed. He knew Natalie could no more exploit my husband than she could abort his baby."

Ah. So she knew.

"Vince told me everything. He knew that his position was stronger if he worked with me."

"So it was all about money."

"Darling, everything is about money." She moves to the bar and opens the gin bottle. "I can't divorce Randy without proof. He's paid too much money to too many people to cover his own back. His biggest fear is that I would leave him and his integrity as a wholesome family man would be called into doubt."

"And the images are the proof you need to get the settlement you deserve."

"You say it like it's a bad thing." She smirks. "This marriage is oppressive. I've lived miserably for years, keeping my nose clean, all while he's been out dilly-dallying around with whoever he likes."

"And this weekend? Is that where he is?"

"Ah, I assume so. I do happen to be aware that his darling new campaign manager flew to Dallas this morning where he's supposed to be." She knocks the gin back. "So the natural progression there is that he'll raise her wages if he can screw her, too."

"Boy, I sure hope you don't mean the darling part," I mutter.

"About as much as my husband meant his wedding vows," she snorts. "Jessica Shearer is one of the biggest bitches I've ever met. She's spent the last few days with her nose so far up Randy's backside she can smell last week's dinner. I, for one, cannot stand her."

High five, sister. "So these pictures," I say, bringing the conversation back around. "What are you doing with them? And the tapes? Are they there for silent bribery in the hope that you can end things reasonably amicably?"

"That was the plan." She shrugs. "But he got my daughter's best friend pregnant and continues on with his antics although he knows he must be being investigated some way or another. No. Vince handed the tapes to someone in the media before he was killed. There were never copies."

This in the media is the last thing we need. Randy McDougall isn't exactly a quiet figure in Texas politics.

Holly Woods doesn't need to be a circus right now.

"Where are they now? The tapes?"

"My husband was made aware of them, likely by Natalie before she died. However, there's no indication that he has any idea that I know they exist." She runs a finger around the top of her glass. "He's meeting someone tonight, by the old 7-11 store just outside town. He's flying into Austin to be here by midnight to get the tapes, and then he's flying back out immediately after."

"He's paying them? The media? To keep it quiet?"

"Three hundred thousand dollars are on hold in his private bank account. The one where he pays everyone from." She crosses the room to the large desk in the corner and pulls a book from the case next to it. She opens the book, removes something that looks like a key from the middle of it, and inserts it into one of the drawers.

Wow. I didn't think people actually did that.

Alyssa crosses the room to me with a small pile of papers all stapled together. "These are the transactions he's made over the last two years. They're all over the place. To the media, his assistant Ellis, and several sex clubs around the country, including D.O.M. It's all corruption to protect himself. There's even a payment he made to Nick when he realized that Nick knew about him and Natalie. He paid him to keep quiet."

"He didn't," I tell her, taking the statements from her.

"I know. I paid him not to." Her lips curve to the side. "And I paid him more."

Oh, to have money to throw away like that.

"Take them." She taps the papers. "I'm certain my husband isn't the person you're looking for—he's an asshole, but he isn't evil. Unravel his ridiculousness and I'm sure you'll find yourself one step closer." She takes a deep breath, regret fluttering across her face. "I'm sorry I can't tell you more about the tapes. Your photos are copies of mine. That's all I need to divorce him."

"Thank you," I say quietly, slotting them into my purse. "I'm sorry you have to do this."

"Don't be. I'm not. I'm sorry I married a bastard."

chapter EIGHTEEN

THIS is fucked up.

The level of corruption the mayor has been working at is far higher than anyone ever suspected. The amount of money he's paid to sex clubs to remove his details from their system and keep quiet about his attendance and sexual appetite is way into the millions. I think the last count was hovering around two million, and that's in two years.

How often does this man travel to have something different? How far is he willing to go to escape the confines of D.O.M.? Is he traveling so he can practice erotic asphyxiation in other places? It's obvious now that he was Natalie's partner in that particular area of their desires. As well as Vince, of course. And the person who killed both of them had to be aware of that.

Was the mayor attracted to men, too?

Ah—but that wouldn't make sense, would it? Surely he wouldn't have time to get down to his briefing with his campaign team if he'd killed Natalie. Besides, the figure on the tape doesn't match his.

I think we're looking at a guy—someone who could have overpowered Vince. Devin did see a figure on the D.O.M. tapes enter Vince's room and stay for approximately two hours. To be that level of intimate, the guy would have had to be bisexual. Unless, of course, it was more about pleasure through pain than penetration.

Which brings me right back to Nick. Paid by the mayor to keep quiet. Paid by the mayor's wife to essentially do what he wants. Nick still has the best motives to kill them both as far as I'm concerned. He hated Natalie because she'd betrayed him and he hated Vince because Vince was the reason she'd done it. And he wanted to be with Madison but not have her relationship with Natalie affected, so this killed two birds with one stone.

Uh... I probably shouldn't use that phrase again while discussing this case.

The only flaw in the Nick plan is that the guy despises their lifestyle. The last time I saw a disgust like that was...well, never. I also can't imagine him as a guy who's attracted to guys. There is the saying that it's always the hot ones, I know, but I don't think anyone can fake his distaste of BDSM.

Which basically means that, even with the discovery of the tapes, I still have nothing, and I'm not counting on the mayor's bank statements to give us much of anything.

I press the heels of my hands into my eyes. This is Lena and Daniel's case all over again. Twist after twist that all throw each other off course.

For the first time, I'm doubting my ability to solve this case. I was so certain that the discovery of the pictures and tapes would make everything fall into place. I mean, a little DNA would be helpful, too. Even just from the car. It's the one time when sharing a lab with the Austin PD really fucking sucks. They're right there, bugging the hell out of their forensics team so everything is done first and we're their afterthought.

"You're allowed to look somewhere other than at this case file, you know."

I rest my cheek on my hand and meet Drake's eyes. "It's really, really pissing me off. And so is the fact that you won't let me go and investigate tonight."

"Sweetheart, you'll likely shoot them both to get your information. I can't deal with any more dead bodies right now."

"You say that like I'm trigger happy," I grumble. "I'm enthusiastic, okay? I haven't shot anyone for weeks now, and that was only because he was going to shoot me first."

Drake leans forward, his shirt stretching over his muscles. "I don't think Marshall would have shot you."

"Really? Because he poisoned and tortured two people and tried to do it a third time, and one of them was his own stepmother," I remind him, the memory making me shudder. "You didn't see him. He looked absolutely feral. I think he would have shot me without a second thought."

"You know, it always bothered me that he tried to shoot you."

"Well, funnily enough, I find myself somewhat bothered by that, too."

He snorts. "No, not that kind of bothered. Well, that kind of bothered, too, but it always bugged me that he poisoned the others but tried to shoot you. Why would he do that?"

I frown. "Because he poisoned them with salads and everyone knows I don't eat salad."

The curve of his lips is slow. "Is that your new life advice? Stay alive, don't eat salad!"

"Uh, yeah. I'm actually considering writing a book and the first piece of advice will be: Eat pizza. We're going to die anyway. Why risk a salad?"

"It occurs to me that, if you didn't have tits and a vagina and a ridiculous shoe obsession, you could be a man."

I press my lips together and look side to side for a moment. "I'm not sure if I should be offended by that. I think I should. Maybe. Where are you goin' with that, huh?"

"Nowhere!" Drake leans back in his chair, laughing, and holds his hands up. "I'm just sayin'."

"Hey—we haven't fought once today. Don't ruin it now."

Wow. We've almost gone a whole day without fighting. Go us.

"Maybe this is what happens when we work together instead of against each other." His eyes glitter.

"And when your ex-fiancée isn't in town."

"That sure helps, too."

I bite the inside of my lip. "I'm sorry. I shouldn't have brought her up."

"Apologizing again? Twice in one week? Are you sick?"

I open my mouth and close it again when I see the teasing smirk of his lips. "Shut up," I mutter. "Can we get back to work now? Please?"

Drake stands, nudging the chair as he does, and walks around my desk. My heart stutters as he stalks toward me, a devilish glint that matches the sexy upturn of his lips in his eye.

"Sure," he murmurs. "In a minute."

He spins me until I'm facing him then leans down, grasping the arms of my chair. My eyelids drop as he moves in so close that is mouth is barely hovering above mine, so close that the slightest twitch from either of us will have our lips touching.

I wait, my breathing speeding up, my stomach erupting in butterflies, for that touch. For that one little brush of his mouth across mine.

It doesn't come.

"You're right," he whispers, instead sweeping his mouth across my cheek as he turns his head toward my ear. "We should work right now."

I tightly set my jaw as annoyance over his sly move flits through me.

"Uh, Noelle?" Carlton appears in the doorway a second after Drake straightens.

"Yes." I hurriedly turn to him, swallowing my frustration at Drake's antics. "What's up?"

He holds a USB stick up. "I found the videos."

"I think I'm scarred for life."

"Huh? It's just kinky porn. And not sexy at all."

I frown at Drake. "I'm so glad you added that last part. If you were turned on right now, we'd be breaking up."

"Oh, we can break up?"

I kick him. "Inappropriate," I mutter. "In all seriousness, I can see why this would be deterimental to the mayor's image."

"Aside from the fact that he's fucking someone who ain't his wife?"

"You're Captain fucking Obvious, aren't you?"

"Just saying." He grins.

I roll my eyes and bite my thumbnail. The video is actually seven videos linked together in a compliation, but when I texted Carlton and asked him, he said that anyone who knew what they were doing would be able to split them at the end of each. Thus giving the beholder seven instances of potential blackmail, I guess.

Each video had a different form of erotic asphyxiation in them, leaving me with absolutely no doubt that that was Natalie and the mayor's *thing*. Since all the videos have been taped outside D.O.M., seemingly in hotels, you don't need a brain to figure out how Vince got them.

"You look confused, cupcake."

"Not...confused." I stand and grab my whiteboard pen before going over to it. I wipe everything off it and scribble my thoughts as I say them out loud. Sometimes, retracing your steps until your feet are blistered and painful is the only way to find what you've lost. "Natalie sleeps with Vince but stops when she dates Nick. A year or so in, she revisits the club and her sexual relationship with Vince, still dating Nick. Nick starts sleeping around."

"Where are you going with this?"

"Shh." I draw a line under that on the board. "Natalie breaks the agreement she has with Nick—"

"According to him."

"And that's all I have," I reply. "Natalie breaks the agreement she has with Nick, which, thanks to the files Carlton found, corresponds approximately with the beginning of her relationship with the mayor. She's still sleeping with Vince. But around this time, Nick sleeps with Madison McDougall for the first time. Then, somewhere around here, Mayor Randy McDougall stops telling his wife about his trysts, which leads to her peeking. Alyssa McDougall pays Vince to get evidence of Natalie and Randy together, which, luckily for her, leads in with Natalie's obscure plan of gathering evidence to blackmail the mayor with, especially when she finds out she's pregnant and the baby is his."

Drake opens his mouth, but I hold my finger up, on a roll.

"Vince agrees with Natalie to video, which works doubly well for Alyssa. In the middle of this, unbeknownst to everyone, Madison and Nick spend a weekend together when both the mayor and Natalie are out of town. Together, they make plans to be in a real relationship. When Natalie comes back, Nick breaks up with Natalie." I draw another line under that. "Almost immediately after, Natalie is stalked. Two weeks later, she hires me. Twenty-four hours after that, her home is almost broken into. And not even twelve hours later, she's dead."

"Her stalker and killer are two different people."

I point my pen at him. "Possibly. In fact, I'd say it's likely. Her stalker didn't want to hurt her. They wanted to scare her. Shake her up. Make her think she was in danger. The mayor knew she was pregnant. I'd bet anything he was behind the stalking."

"With what purpose?" Drake's eyes follow me as I walk to the window. "Make her leave town? Scare her into keeping quiet?"

"Either. Both." I perch on the windowsill and bite the end of my pen. "He wouldn't have wanted to pay her off. She was different than the other people he messed with. She was his daughter's best friend, although paying her a large sum probably would have avoided this mess. Then again..."

"Say you're right. Say we are looking at two different people—now what? Who attempted to break into her house? Her stalker or her killer?"

"Her stalker," I say certainly. "Think about it, Drake. If you're breaking into someone's house to kill them, would you really try to break a window? In a quiet neighborhood? No. You'd pick their lock or knock out the whole pane. You wouldn't throw a brick at their house."

"Let's work of the assumption that the mayor did hire someone to shake her up." He stands, but then he paces back and forth. "They wanted her to think they were trying to break in. That makes me think he was trying to get her to leave town. Face it—she wouldn't have known that he was behind it. What if it was both? What if he was trying to get her to leave town then give her the financial aid to do it? He could have promised to pay her a monthly child support fee under the guise of her working for him and his whole problem—the baby—would have been eliminated."

"Yes!" I cry a little too excitedly. "That makes perfect sense. I asked Bek to get Carlton to look into his bank accounts more in depth, and it turns out that more payments have been made to Nick since the first one. I thought it was simply part of the initial agreement to be paid in installments the longer he stayed quiet, but what if Nick agreed to do it? And those payments were what he was owed for stalking her?"

"How much were they?"

"Ten to fifteen thousand a time."

"That has to be it." Drake stops, looks at me, and grins. "He paid him to stalk her and wired money as soon as Nick reported back with each threat. He was never to hurt her, only scare her so badly she left Holly Woods. And it worked in two ways, because the longer and more Nick was paid, the more likely he was to stay quiet. You!" He crosses my office in seconds, frames my face with his hands, and plants a huge kiss on me. "You're fuckin' brilliant, Noelle."

A flame rises in my cheeks. "Well, it's simple logic, really."

"Let's go." He grabs my hand and pulls his phone out of his pocket.

"Where to?" I barely have time to grab my phone and purse before he pulls me out of the room and toward the staircase.

"I'm calling in backup. Then we're going to pick him up."

Oh, well. Okay, then.

The more I think about it, the more I'm glad that I'm not still a cop. I'm essentially acting as a cop now, and I'm realizing more and more that I like the freedom that owning my own investigative company brings me. For example, I don't have to sit suspects in a ten-by-ten room with nothing more than a table, four chairs, and a voice recorder inside it.

Interviews are suffocating. I hate the stiff, formal way they need to be conducted. I hate the way questions are twisted and manipulated to catch the other person up. I hate how my eyes skim the suspect's body like they're a puzzle that has one piece you can't locate out of place. I hate how every part of their reaction to every single question is an open book to me.

Like right now—Nick is sitting in his chair next to his lawyer, stone-faced. His shoulders are pulled back in defiance, and his eyes are dead set on Drake, his jaw tight. Yet this isn't because he's hiding something. He's angry, pure and simple. He's angry that, after the conversations he and I have had, he's been brought in for questioning.

And that's something that needs to be stressed. He hasn't been arrested.

Yet.

Although it's only a matter of time with the way Drake is tearing him apart.

"Where were you on the night of the eighth?"

"I already told you," Nick snaps, "I was tattooing a client."

"Yet you can't provide me with anything that'll prove it."

"Because I don't have security cameras. I don't need them."

"Every business needs security cameras, Mr. Lucas." Drake taps his pen against his papers. "Were you stalking Ms. Owens? She seemed very insistent to Ms. Bond that you were the person behind her plight. The messages, the phone calls..."

"Believe me, Detective Nash"—Nick all but spits his name—"I'd rather go to fuckin' hell than stalk that crazy bitch. I wanted nothin' to do with her freaky ass when she was alive, and I sure as shit don't want it now."

I run my tongue over my lips. "Tell me again where you were the night Natalie's house was almost broken into."

He slides his eyes from Drake to me. "My studio. With a client." Sweat beads on his upper lip.

"What were you tattooing?"

"A back piece. A pheonix."

"Not a dragon, then?"

"What are you insinuating?"

I walk across the small room from where I've been leaning against the wall and clasp the back of both Drake's and Trent's chairs. "I'm insinuating that, when you told me this information only a couple of days ago, you were tattooing a back piece, except it was a dragon. Now, it's a pheonix. Not creatures you can mix up. So, while I fully believe you were at your studio, I'm insinuating, Mr. Lucas, that you weren't tattooing at all. So, who were you with?"

His eyes narrow until they're barely slits. "I thought you weren't a cop?"

"I'm not. But as long as the mayor's signature is on my contract, I can interrogate you until you lose your voice. And believe me when I say I will. So, who were you with? Why won't you tell me? What's the big issue with honesty?"

"You don't have to answer anything," his lawyer instructs.

"Correct. He doesn't," Trent adds. "But there's more than enough

244

circumstancial evidence against him that, if he doesn't tell us the truth, we're going to arrest him on stalking charges and he'll be in the dock tomorrow morning, explaining himself to Judge Barnes."

"Circumstancial evidence?" Nick looks at both of the guys in front of me before his eyes rest on me. "What do you mean circumstancial evidence?"

"There are several payments to an account in your name from Randy McDougall's private account," I explain. "We have reason to believe that he hired you to harrass Natalie Owens and issued you a payment every time you reported back to him. Unless you tell us the truth, we're assuming that's the case."

"He didn't pay me a damn penny. You can check my bank details with his right now."

"That'd be great, thanks," Drake says. "Here. Write down your bank details and turn over your card for photocopying and I'll get someone on that right now."

He does it.

Because he isn't lying about being paid. He's lying about what he was doing the night before Natalie called me out about the attempted break in, but this? No. He never saw a penny from Randy McDougall except for the initial payment.

"The eighth," Trent continues after Nick's card has been handed to Drake, despite his lawyer motioning for him not to. Ugh, what a dick. "That night. Was it a pheonix or a dragon? A tiger? A fairy, Mr. Lucas?"

He doesn't say a word.

"Perhaps you had an adult coloring book and don't want everyone to know you have a penchant for coloring in pretty pictures," my brother continues. "Or you really were at Natalie Owens's house, a brick in your hand, ready to smash her window in."

"I was with Madison!" Nick snarls. "Okay? I was with her. We went for dinner in Austin then came back to my apartment. We spent the night together, and she left the next morning."

Bingo.

Drake fights his smile as he slides his chair back. "Thank you, Mr. Lucas. I'll get these bank details checked out and inform you of our next move as soon as possible. Someone will be in soon to escort you and Mr. Jenkins to a more comfortable waiting area."

Trent calls the end of the interview and hits the button on the recorder before pulling the tape out. He slips it into his pocket, and I open the door and slip out first.

"Well?" Drake asks me. "What was he lyin' about?"

"Apart from the tattoo? Nothing. I'd bet my next purchase of Louboutins that those account numbers won't match up with the ones on the payment records." I shrug a shoulder. "Do y'all have coffee in this place? My brain is about to give up."

"Hey." Drake grabs Dev as he walks into the station. "I need you to check something for me."

When Dev replies in the affirmitive, Drake hands him the card and scribbled details.

"Check these against the payments that were made to Nick Lucas. He swears he didn't see a cent after the first one."

"Got it."

"Oh, and get your sister some damn coffee before she kills me," he adds, pushing his office door open.

I punch his arm.

Yeah. I might have just validated his statement. Fuck it.

"Like coffee will stop me." I follow him into the room.

"I know," he replies, "but it'll buy me some time at least, and I'll use that time to convince you why you shouldn't kill me."

I shut the door behind me. "Seriously? Two of my brothers are right out there. They don't need to hear that."

"I was talking about cooking you dinner..." Drake pauses, his eyes belying his innocent answer. "What were you thinking about?"

"Shut up." I drop onto a chair in front of his desk, and he laughs.

"You're cute when you pout."

"I don't pout."

"I beg to differ." He flicks his thumb over my bottom lip. "Pouty lips."

"You're really not doing well with your time-buying. In case you were wondering." I fold my arms. "Hey, isn't it almost time for the mayor to get his tapes? Who's there?"

"You're still not going," he insists, stepping back as the door opens. "Sheriff Bates is there with a few other guys. They're not looking to arrest him, before you get excited. Just to see if it's true."

Dev hands me coffee before I can protest. "I got a message that they're all in place and a black Range Rover is parked up outside the old gas station."

"Please, can I go? Please?"

"No," Drake repeats. "That's the end of it."

"You're not my boss," I argue.

"I can be." His eyes spark.

Devin gags, leaving the room.

"I'd like to see you try," I counter, ignoring my brother's childishness. "What would you do if I walked out that door right now?"

"I'd sling you over my fucking shoulder and carry you down to the cells."

Well, that wasn't nearly as sexy as I thought it would be. So much for that train of thought.

"And here I thought you'd bring out the handcuffs."

"You want me to cuff you?" Drake quirks an eyebrow. "That can be arranged. Within seconds."

"Uh, are you gonna take me home before you cuff me?" I scoot out of the chair and skirt around it to the door. "'Cause, if not, I'd prefer to keep my hands free."

His lips match the amusement in his eyes. "Well, my work is done here, and I do think you need supervisin' tonight to make sure you don't run off down to the sheriff's stakeout."

"I didn't mean right now. And don't you have to tell Nick what happens with his card?"

Drake slowly approaches me, and I walk backward until I'm against the wall, my hands flattened on either side of me.

"No," he says quietly. "My shift ended thirty minutes ago. Trent's here until one. He'll deal with him."

"So, you're taking me home?" I ask, tilting my head to the side. "To my house."

"Yep." He takes one step closer to me then cups my chin. "Except I ain't leavin' after."

chapter NINETEEN

I F it isn't Nick, who is it?

This is the question that's been bugging me since five a.m. I managed to lie around in bed for thirty minutes before I sneaked my way out from Drake's sleepy hold and crept downstairs in my bathrobe.

Now, curled in the corner of my sofa, I realize I've asked myself the question "Who is it?" more this year than I planned to in the next decade.

We're missing something. I'm almost positive of it.

Now, it's almost eight in the morning and I have the urge to talk to do the one person we haven't interviewed yet. The mayor himself.

That could cost me everything though, and Drake definitely can't know. If the mayor suspects for a second that he knows about my desire to ask him every question in existence, then Drake's fired. For sure.

Even though the mayor is in Dallas, I call his office anyway.

"Mayor McDougall's office."

"Ellis? Is that you?"

"Yep." She yawns. "Who's this?"

"Noelle—Noelle Bond. Sorry. Is Mayor McDougall there?"

"Nope, sorry. He's out of town until tomorrow. Can I take a me-message?" Another yawn.

"Nah, it's okay. I was hoping to catch him before meetings, but if he's out, no worries. Have a good day!" I hang up and drop my phone on the coffee table.

Damn.

That girl sounds like she needs a coffee or ten.

I swing my legs off the sofa and carry my empty mug to the kitchen. I rinse it out under the sink, looking out at my yard. Needs flowers.

"Mornin'." Drake yawns.

I turn. He's still yawning, his hand buried deep in his hair. He's wearing nothing but the pants he wore to work yesterday, and they're slung low on his lips.

"Morning," I reply absently, half distracted by my mind and half distracted by those little dent things at the bottom of his stomach that disappear beneath his waistband.

"My face is up here, Noelle." He grins and walks toward me, hugging me from the side and kissing the side of my head.

"Sorry. I'm...thinking."

"Already?"

"Hush. I've been up since five." I set my mug in the sink and rest my elbows on the edge of the counter. "Just...thinking."

His eyebrows draw together. "About the case?"

"Hmm." I nibble on the side of my thumb, focusing on my yard once more. "It's bugging me."

I feel like I've said that a thousand damn times in the last few days. Probably because I have. God only knows how many times I've thought it, too.

"Did you ever find out what happened last night?"

"The tape thing?" Drake grimaces. "Yeah. The mayor got it, but they couldn't get any kind of ID on the other person. All they got was a similar profile to the guy we got on camera in the hotel and the club."

"So, it could be the same person? Couldn't we tell the mayor that we found some stuff at Natalie's house and know he was meeting someone last night and ask him?"

"If we want to lose our jobs, sure."

"Ugh." I drop my head down. "Can't we lie and say it'll help us arrest Nick?"

"If we want to be shot."

"Oh my God, you're so dramatic!" I stand up and huff my way to the stairs.

Seriously. If I didn't know he was being deadly serious, I'd be calling the mayor's private line right now.

I'm halfway up when my phone rings from the living room. I cannot catch a break here, can I?

"Hello?" I snap into the phone.

"Uh…" Carlton's voice travels hesitantly down the line. "Did I wake you?"

"No," I reply, softening my voice. "You didn't. I'm sorry. I didn't sleep well. What's up?"

"Can you go to the office to meet me? I did some more research last night and, uh, found something else."

"Something else?" I frown as Drake appears in the living room doorway. "What something else?"

"You really need to see it."

"See what?"

"There's another video of the mayor," Carlton replies after a long moment. "But, um, Natalie isn't the girl in it."

"I'll be there in ten minutes." I hang up and throw it on the sofa. Then I fight my yawn as I look at the ceiling. "Fuck me."

"Noelle?"

"There's another video." I throw my arms out to the sides. "But fuck knows who the chick in it is."

Drake's face hardens. "Let's go."

My sentiments exactly, Detective. Not that I needed him to say it out loud, of course. Captain Obvious strikes again and all that. I should probably get him a cape with that on for his birthday or something. Except it'll have to say Detective Obvious.

Ha. That's it. His new nickname. Detective Obvious. I won't be saying it out loud any time soon, because as hot as he looks buttoning that shirt while his muscles do that flex thing, I think he's kinda pissed.

And hey. We did manage one whole day without fighting. As much as I like this new nice us, I'm kind of bored. And pissing him off is fun. Aw, hell. I'm gonna end up blurting that out by the end of the day. Then he'll threaten to spank me or cuff me or something along those lines.

Wait. That's an excellent reason to piss him off. One of these day, I'll do it so much that he'll simply have to follow through on his threats.

"Noelle. Focus." He snaps his fingers in front of my face, jolting me back to reality.

"What?"

"You've been fondling that pair of panties for minutes. What the fuck's wrong with you this morning?"

I look down at the blue thong in my hand. "I don't know. It's like my brain is broken from all of my epiphanies yesterday. I can't focus on anything for longer than a few minutes." I tap the side of my head. "Seriously, it's like fucking kindergarten up in here."

"Well, try to focus, yeah? We need to get to your office to see this video."

"Video? Oh—right. That video," I add when he looks like he wants grab my ankles, tip me upside down, and give me a good shake.

I put the underwear on and pull a dress from the closet. The red is bright and the skirt is full, probably not made for a day of running around like a fool like it seems like I could be doing today, but what the hell.

The dress is pretty.

And here I go again with the tangent.

I get dressed and quickly apply my makeup before my mind decides to waltz with a peanut or something. Honestly, I should video myself spewing out every random thought I have so that, next time I wake up at five in the morning and decide that it's a good idea to get out of bed, I can watch it and remember why I need to roll the hell back over and go the fuck back to sleep.

Even that thought was way longer than it should have been.

Ugh, Drake was right. I really won't use five words if I can use fifty. Or even five hundred.

Oh my God. I'm doing it again.

I need to be knocked out. Stat.

"Noelle!"

"I'm coming!" I yell, tugging my cowboy boots on, not even bothering to fully slide my feet into the bottoms before I run toward the stairs. I almost trip over my own feet, so I grab the banister and make sure my feet are in them properly before I run downstairs.

"What the hell is wrong with you today?" Drake asks me, handing me my phone and my purse.

"Ask me what's right with me. It's a shorter answer." I set the alarm and follow him out.

"That's always the shorter answer where you're concerned," he mutters, pulling his keys from his pocket as I throw mine into the depths of my purse. "I was hopin' you could give me a definitive answer on the wrong side for once."

"You know," I say, getting into his truck, "I'm about to attach my gun to my person. It'd be a real shame if my finger accidentally played with the trigger."

"And you're back to normal. Your version of it, anyway."

I take a deep breath and come to the conclusion that my gun should stay in my purse for a little while longer.

I'm pretty sure Drake breaks just about every speeding limit in town as he fights to get us to my office. My spacing out earlier has put us behind, and by the time he pulls up in the parking lot, Carlton is already waiting outside the front door.

"What've you got for me?" I ask before I've even put the key in the lock.

"If I knew the chick, I'd tell you." He shrugs, holding his laptop tightly under his arm.

"All right." I push the door open and stalk inside.

He and Drake follow me to the meeting room, and I sit on the table.

Carlton takes the chair next to where I'm sitting and opens his laptop. He clicks a few times then says, "Here." He turns the screen toward me, and I bend forward to watch it.

It's definitely the mayor, and the images are the same grainy quality as before. Vince must have gotten these, too, maybe thinking Natalie would be meeting him? Who knows? It's the same hotel room, the same layout of sex toys on the sofa, and the mayor is wearing the same old Y-front underpants as he was at the start of the other video.

But the girl is definitely not Natalie, and my heart stops when she walks on screen.

"Holy shit." I grab Drake's forearm. "Holy shit."

Of course. Of course. Of. Fucking. Course.

I jump off the table and run to the stairs, storming up them, leaving two confused faces behind me. Thankfully, the door to my office is unlocked, so I quickly get inside and head straight for the case file.

"Pictures, pictures," I mutter to myself, flicking through every sheet.

"You're like a fuckin' chihuahua today," Drake grumbles. "Now what's wrong?"

"Shut up a minute." I pull out one security image from the hotel then the one from the club. They're the clearest ones they could get, and they match. Almost perfectly. "Come back down. I need to check something. Oh, grab that file."

"Seriously," he mutters, and I hear the sound of the papers shuffling as he gets it.

I run back into the meeting room and stop right behind Carlton. "Turn it back to the beginning. The very start when the woman walks in."

He rewinds it then hits play. The first two minutes are all the mayor, but then she walks out of the bathroom.

"Pause it."

She's every inch a woman—except for her haircut.

Her short, pixie-style cut. The one that, on security camera photos, could easily be mistaken for that of a guy, especially if the woman wasn't wearing a particularly feminine outfit.

"It's Ellis," I breathe, dropping the photos onto the keyboard.

"In the video?" Drake questions.

"All of it." My voice is a whisper. She was yawning on the phone this morning—because she'd been up late. "The stalking, the murders, the exchange with the mayor last night... All of it is her. Ellis Law. She's our killer."

chapter TWENTY

"WHY would she kill Natalie? What does she have to stand to gain from that?" Sheriff Bates asks me, pacing the length of the briefing room.

"I have no idea. But look at the images. You can't argue with it, and it's totally plausible. She has the opportunity, and if we don't have a motive, that's important. She would have been at the hotel prior to the mayor's talk, and if she was a member of D.O.M., no one would question her being in the club at the time Vince died. I bet the account numbers on the fake transactions to Nick will match hers."

"What about shooting Brody?"

"The rental company lists the car as being rented by a Stacey Ellis-Law," Trent throws out there. "I never made the connection, but this does make sense."

"We need to find her." I bite the inside of my cheek then release it. "I doubt she'll be at the office anymore. She knows I'm looking for the mayor."

"Do you think he knows about this?" Drake asks. "He knows about everything else."

"There would have been a payoff somewhere if he did," Sheriff Bates responds. "Find Ellis Law. Or Stacey, whatever her damn name is. Find her and bring her in for questioning. I want alibis for every damn thing we have on record, and I want them now."

"Yes, sir." Drake stands, grabs my hand, and tugs me up with him. Trent follows after us as we leave the room. "Where do we start?"

"We split up," Drake replies through a tight jaw. "I'll drive Noelle back to her place to get her car. Then we'll try to find her. Trent, go to her house first. I'll check the bank. Noelle, you know women. Check wherever."

"Like, what? The hair salon? The nail salon? The cupcake store? The shoe store? The clothing store? Why do I get all the female places?"

"Because you're a female," Trent sighs in exasperation. "I'll take the shoe store. You're only gonna get distracted going in there."

"Or you could try getting her car registration details and put local stations on standby in case she tries to leave town." I shrug. "But hey, what do I know?"

"That's the first sensible thing I've heard you say this morning." Drake opens the door to his truck, grabs my waist, and hauls me into the passenger's side seat.

I oomph as he signals to Trent to do what I suggested.

Honestly, am I working with them or am I their new boss?

"Do y'all actually think of your own ideas or do you just wait for me to tell you what to do?"

Drake gives a harsh turn on the keys then shoots me the biggest, smuggest grin I've ever seen. "We wait for you, sweetheart. We figure that, if you keep thinkin' of these awesome ideas, you'll be too tired to talk."

"I swear to God, when we find Ellis and you arrest her, I'm going to beat your cocky ass into next week."

"Sounds like a date." His laughter is drowned out by the revving of his engine, and he pulls away from the station like he's a fucking NASCAR driver and not a cop.

I'm pretty sure we're in the wrong car to be doing these speeds, but hey, I've just about exhausted my bright ideas for today.

Where is Ellis?

And are we going to find her?

My purse is sitting between my feet, and I reach down into it. My fingers find my thigh holster buried beneath my wallet, and I pull it out then hike it over my left foot and up my leg. I have to slouch in the seat and pull my dress up to get it to where it belongs, and if the tingling feeling worming its way across my skin is anything to go by, Drake's noticed.

"What are you doin'?" Yep, he noticed.

"Accessorizing."

"With your gun?"

I pull my favorite Tiffany-blue Glock out of its case in my purse and hold it up, smiling innocently over the top of it. "Yes. Although my color coordination leaves a lot to be desired." I hike my dress up a little further and secure my gun.

"I hate it when you wear that thing like it's a damn bracelet."

"Hey, this is me being sensible. If you haven't realized, I haven't worn my gun for, like, two whole days. Okay, one. But whatever." I wave my hand dismissively. "I'm actually being sensible instead of paranoid this time."

"For a damn change." He steers into my driveway.

I shift in my seat so I'm facing him, and he cuts his eyes to mine.

"The last time I came face-to-face with a murderer," I say, "I thought he was going to kill me, too. I didn't know what weapon he had then, either. This time, I do. If I find Ellis before all y'all do, I know she has a gun, and I know she'll use it. I'm not afraid to do it again to protect myself."

His jaw tightens, and his answering nod is a sharp dip of his chin.

I lean across the center console and kiss his cheek. He's not going to reply. I can see it. His brain is whirring in macho-man-alpha mode, where all he can see is the danger he's potentially allowing me to walk in to. But…whatever. I have to do this, too. I can't sit around and do nothing while she's running around with a gun in her pants and a heart of stone.

I pull my car door open and throw my purse in, but then there's the distinctive slam of Drake's truck door. I turn as he stops in front of me.

His hands clasp on either side of my neck, his thumbs curving up over my jaw and brushing my lower cheek, and his mouth comes down onto mine in a kiss that is equal parts fear and frustration. The resignation is in his following sigh.

"Letting you go and do this goes against every fuckin' instinct in my body."

I curl my fingers around his lower arm, tilting my face down into his touch as I meet his eyes. They're icier than I've ever seen them, yet there isn't an ounce of coldness in his gaze.

"You're not letting me. I'm choosing to go."

"I know." He grinds his teeth. "But that doesn't mean I don't feel sick at the thought of you getting hurt."

"Then find her first," I say simply.

He touches his forehead to mine. "We both know you're a killer magnet. If you find her, do what you did before and call me and leave the line on, okay?"

I nod. "I promise."

He takes a deep breath and moves to step back, but I grab his collar and pull his mouth down to mine. He freezes for all but a second before he returns it. The kiss is fierce. It's desperate and frustrated, and each brush of our lips is my fear mingling with his.

But it's still more. Still everything. Still every breath we are struggling to take and every touch we wish we could give.

When he pulls back, my heart is pounding inside my chest, and I think he's transferred all of his worry into me.

"Be safe, cupcake," he whispers, resting his forehead against mine again. "Just don't get yourself fucking killed, okay?"

"Believe me. Not getting myself killed is at the top of my to-do list. And then, when I survive, you're second on it." I smile.

He does, too, and a little bit of the tension disappears.

"Now, go," I demand, pulling his hands from my face. "And be safe yourself, okay? Because, if you get shot, you're getting bumped down my list."

"Got it. Now, since there's no way I can stop you, go let your badass gene out to play."

Nothing in the town hall building. Nothing in the hair salon. Nothing in the nail salon. Rosie hasn't seen her, and neither has Melanie or old Mr. Beatty, who runs the hardware store next to the bookshop. My whole team is on the lookout as they do their own jobs, and I've driven past enough cop cars to know that Sheriff Bates has pulled out all the stops and has almost the whole department out on this wild-goose chase.

I can't believe she disappeared so quickly. It's barely been two hours since I called her, yet she's absolutely nowhere to be found in Holly Woods. Drake has checked her house and her parents' place, while Trent searched the town hall top to bottom immediately after I did.

She's all but vanished into thin air, yet there's no proof of her even leaving town. And if she tries to, she's getting caught there, too, because Sheriff Bates called in some favors from the Austin PD to bolster town security, and there are more than one or two cars on every road in and out of Holly Woods.

Sure. We can't be absolutely certain that it's her on paper, but my gut says it is. And my gut is never wrong.

Apart from right now, when it's telling me that I need a cupcake. I don't have time for that, but I happen to have a big bag of crispy M&Ms stashed in my glove box, so I reach forward and tug them out, opening them. Hey, I'm parked.

I throw a handful into my mouth and chew. Running around like a six-headed chicken on steroids washed down with vodka isn't going to get me anywhere. It's not going to get any of us anywhere.

One of the most important lessons my nonno taught me when I was eight and fell in love with Sherlock Holmes was that, to catch a killer, you need to think like a killer. And, he said, unless your killer is psychotic, then the chances of you finding them without a plan are nothing. Someone who kills for a reason will always have a plan, and in that plan, you'll find every reason a hundred times.

I take another handful of M&Ms.

One can only assume that Ellis killed Natalie because Ellis found out about the video and assumed Natalie had evidence. That would tie in to the break-in, too. She tried to get in and out but got desperate, for a reason I'm unaware of. Then, like most members of D.O.M., she was aware of Nat's close relationship with Vince and correctly assumed that Vince would be the next obvious target.

Wait. Mr. Lawrence said that Vince had several girls he could have swapped her out for without knowing. What if Ellis was of his partners, too? What if he'd accidentally let slip about the videos and that's how she knew? Then it would be completely plausible that she was in the room when it should have been Natalie.

So, by this reasoning, her motive is the knowledge of the video. Meaning that her next target…

Oh, shit.

Her next target would be the only other person who knows that the tapes exist.

Alyssa McDougall.

I wrench my hand out of the bright-green bag so fast that it falls to the floor and scatters the colorful candies across the black carpet. Simultaneously, I start my engine and dial Alyssa's number. When it goes to voicemail, I use voice control to call her again. But it happens again.

"Call Drake," I tell my phone.

"Dialing Drake," it responds. Two rings, and then, "What?"

"Alyssa!" I shout, beeping my horn at someone driving too slowly. I move into the next lane, overtake them, then cut back in front with my foot down. "She's the only other person who knows about the tapes and she isn't answering her phone!"

"Where are you?"

"Like two minutes away from her house. If that. And I think I just ran a red."

"Don't worry about that now. Get to the house, and if you can get inside and confirm Ellis is there, do it. But try to stay out of sight until we get there. I'm calling the sheriff now." Then, he hangs up, and I pull up outside the huge house thirty seconds later.

Apparently, I was driving faster than I thought. I wonder if I can charge the red light and speeding tickets to the mayor on account of potentially saving his wife and all.

I leave my purse in the car, but I take my keys so I can lock it. My keys end up in my bra, because, well, I have nowhere else to put them where they won't jingle.

My heartbeat is racing while my stomach does some kind of anxious shimmy as I approach the front door. It's ajar, and that only sends my heartbeat skyrocketing even higher. The silence of the house as I step on the top step, though, has my badass gene kicking into action. My adrenaline spikes, and although I know I should probably hide and wait for the police, my curiosity is stronger, and I slide through the gap in the door.

Drake's gonna kill me. So is Trent. Probably Nonna, too, actually.

A floorboard creaks to my immediate left, and I turn, my head instantly reaching up my dress for my gun. I meet the eyes of a timid girl no more than twenty and hold my finger against my lips.

"Upstairs," she mouths.

"Go out the front door now," I whisper to her, that one word confirming everything. Like the fact that I should go back outside. "The police are on their way."

She nods quickly, hugging herself so tight that her knuckles are white.

I'm guessing that Alyssa sent the staff "home" at Ellis's request—except most on them live on site or in a separate part of the house.

I remove my gun from its holster, thinking this is my best bet for safety right now. Except leaving.

Jesus, I'm not going to let her scare me out of here. Besides, the bitch shot my brother.

I keep to the edge of the stairs as I take each one tentatively. It's too quiet in this house. Yet another reason why I should turn around and go.

Damn feet take another few steps upward.

"Oh, come on!" Ellis yells out of nowhere. "You have to know where it is!"

I pause at the top of the stairs, just able to see inside the room they're in. The same one as before again. I wonder if Alyssa lives in this room. Mind you, there was a wall pretty much lined with books. I'd probably live in that room, too.

"Trust me, darling," Alyssa replies, sitting at one edge of the couch, her legs crossed like a lady. "If I knew where it was, I'd happily hand it to you."

To anyone else, she'd look as calm as a puddle of water after a storm, but I can see the tremble of her fingers as they rest on her knee, and her rapid blinking hints at her fear.

"Madison has to know," Ellis growls.

"I don't even know what you're talking about!" Madison protests.

I lean to the right and catch sight of her. Tears are slowly falling down her cheeks, and her bottom lip is quivering. My view of her is interrupted when Ellis steps forward with a gun in her hand.

Oh, joy.

And she points it toward Alyssa.

"Ellis," tumbles from my lips. Aw, fuck it. *Brain-to-mouth filter, you bastard.* "She doesn't know," I say softly. "She has no idea about her parents' relationship."

Ellis turns to me, her gun still on Madison. "She knew about us though, didn't she? Me and Natalie?"

I'm sorry, what?

"I didn't until I saw you!" Madison cries, and Alyssa squeezes her hand. "I was trying to scare her into going away so I could be with Nick! I didn't know you were with her!"

"You're her stalker?" I ask Madison. "You?"

Madison squeezes her eyes shut and nods. "I wanted her to leave. I thought she'd be alone. I didn't even know she was bisexual until Ellis came downstairs with her."

Oh, fuck me.

"She wasn't bi. She was a fucking liar!" Ellis yells. "She lied to everyone. I loved her and I loved him, but she lied."

"She was doing what was best for her baby," Alyssa says softly. "As wrong as it was."

"No. She was messing with everyone. I was nothing more than her scapegoat!" Tears fill her eyes. "And then she got herself killed!"

"Why did you do it, Ellis?" I ask. "And Vince, too? Was it just the video?"

"They wouldn't give it to me," she hisses, turning to me. With her hair spiked and her cheeks flushed, she looks anything but angry. She looks deafeated and helpless. "They were going to use it to blackmail that cheating bastard further, to get even more money for themselves."

"Vince never was. He was videoing Natalie for Alyssa. He had no reason to video you. Yours exists because of Natalie, I'm sure."

"No! He was working with her all along. Even when he was fucking me, he was thinking of her!" Her voice is shrill now, and her hand is shaking so violently that, if she relinquished her grip on that gun for half a second, it would clatter to the floor.

She isn't a cold-blooded killer. She's a young woman who had her heart broken and her trust betrayed by someone she loved more than anything. She didn't act out of spite. It was desperation.

"Ellis, listen to me," I breathe.

"I didn't mean to kill her!" she screams, grabbing the gun with her other hand. "I just meant to push her. I wanted her to beg me for mercy, but it was too late. She was already dead. Vince too. I wanted him to know that it was his fault she died. I wanted him to ask me to let him live. But I knew he'd tell. And it was a little harder. I pushed down, and he was weak. He didn't deserve her! I did! But now, she's gone and I don't have her at all."

"Honey, please," I plead, seeing Alyssa pull Madison behind Ellis. "The police will be here any minute."

Alyssa and Madison skirt around the room until they reach me, and I pull them both behind my body. Hey, I have the gun if she tries it.

The tears are falling out of Ellis's eyes quicker than she can control them, and every part of her is tense. Even her breathing is speeding up, and she's gasping now, harshly and painfully.

"Put your gun down, Ellis. Please. It doesn't have to be this way."

Her smile is jittery and weak, and she drops one hand from the gun and holds the muzzle against her temple, angling it in such a way that one bullet would... Well.

"It does," she whispers as footsteps thunder up toward us. "I'm sorry."

Oh, hell no.

I lift my gun and squeeze the trigger before she can. My bullet flies into her elbow, and she screams, dropping her gun. It discharges, her bullet soaring into the window and smashing it. Ellis falls to the floor, clutching her arm, and I take a few steps forward and kick her gun out of her reach.

I'm sorry she was so desperate, but I'm not sorry for her. Justice is justice, and she has a fuck-ton of it coming her way.

Cops storm past Alyssa and Madison standing in the doorway. Alyssa's arms are tight around her daughter, and through the crowd of officers, most in uniform, I find Drake's eyes. Trent is right behind him, and after I give him a nod, he walks straight to Ellis and demands that someone call him an ambulance, cuffing her uninjured wrist.

"Madison," I tell Drake as he stops in front of me, glancing at her. "She was our stalker. It was a childish move. I don't think she'll be a problem in an interview."

He nods and grabs Detective Johnson, relaying exactly what I just told him. He walks over to her, exchanges a few words with her, and I look away as Madison holds her hands out to be cuffed.

Drake touches two fingers to my chin and raises it. "You're okay?" he questions.

"Yeah. I'm fine."

"What happened?"

"The short version is that, apparently, crazy in love is a real thing, and you can die of a broken heart. Or want to, at least. So Ellis Law might not have much of an elbow left, but it's easier than cleaning up a brain. So." I shrug a shoulder. "Plus, that was for Brody. You'd rather me get revenge than Nonna."

Drake smiles slowly, pressing his thumb to my lower lip. "Excellent work, Ms. Bond."

"Why thank you, Detective."

chapter
TWENTY-ONE

"WHY am I not surprised that you shot her for me?"

I roll my eyes. "Honestly, Brodes, you say it like you were expecting me to do something that crazy."

He snorts then winces, pressing his hand against his side.

"Noella! Are you-a bugging him-a?" Nonna storms into the front room, her cane clacking like she needs the announcement. "He need-a his-a rest!"

Oh, yeah. If Brody's recovering from a gunshot wound isn't enough, Nonna won't hear of him going home until he can use the bathroom alone—and that's one of her criteria. Since he got let out this morning, he's in it for the long haul. Being the good sister I am, I thought I'd stop by and fill him in on what happened at the McDougalls' yesterday.

"I'm not bugging him! I'm letting him know what happened."

"So you-a bugging him."

"Trust me, Nonna. No one could bug him more than you."

"Hey, Nonna. Can I have a glass of water?" Brody cranes his neck around to look at her. "And maybe you can make garlic bread for dinner?"

"Of-a course." She kisses the top of his head and hobbles back out.

"Dunno why you can't get along," Brody mutters, closing his eyes.

264

"'Cause she pisses me off." I laugh. "Anyway, Ellis is in the hospital, guarded. I almost shattered her elbow, but apparently, Trent got a confession out of her this morning. Madison was questioned and charged last night, and her hearing for bail is this afternoon."

"She'll get a fine and a community service order. Mayor's daughter and all that. What's Alyssa doing?"

"I think they're flying to Dallas to stay with her parents for a while. Madison is somewhat of a sensitive soul."

"Not everyone has to be a granite-hearted bitch."

"Hey now. I felt sorry for Ellis until I remembered she shot you. Then I felt sorrier for you." I pat his hand. "You're tired. I'll leave you to sleep. Do you need me to get you anything?"

He shakes his head, and I reach down and cover him with the blanket. He curves his lips into a small smile and mouths, "Thank you."

God. It's hard seeing my strong, confident little brother kind of broken.

I close the front door and get into my car, breathing out a sigh of relief. Despite Brody's obvious pain, he's still himself, and he's definitely going to be okay. The only reason he was allowed home is because Nonna likely annoyed every staff member she came across until they let him out. It's like they said though—despite the extensive surgery to find the bullet, he was actually completely fine. If you don't count the hole in his side.

He was right about what he said about Madison, I think as I pull away from the house. She'll be unlucky to get a fine and a community service order. Her father will pull out all the stops for her to walk away with a slap on the hand—but then again, as soon as Alyssa files divorce proceedings and his council finds out how much of a smily snake he is, I suppose he'll try to save his reputation by insisting she get a substantial punishment so she learns the consequences of her actions.

I still don't understand what Madison did, why she'd harass her best friend. I doubt I ever will. Nick is a nice guy. Don't get me wrong. But he isn't *that* nice, least of all trustworthy.

And as for Ellis… That I'm never going to understand. I'm not even going to try to. The whole thing is a mystery, so I'll leave the people who should be figuring it out to figure it out.

I park outside the office and grab my purse from the backseat before I walk in. Grecia is sitting in her office, alternately filing her nails and typing. Mike is humming in the kitchen, the clatter of cups the giveaway that he's making coffee. I'll bet it's his third cup.

I throw Grecia a wave and head for the stairs, but she stops me.

"Mrs McDougall is waiting in your office. I hope you don't mind. She wanted some space to herself while she waited."

"Not at all. Has she been waiting long?"

"Five minutes. I knew you were with Brody. Is he okay?"

"He's getting there. Thanks." I smile and resume my journey upstairs to my office.

Alyssa is sitting in one of my red chairs, facing the window that overlooks the park. Her hair is swept back into a loose chignon, and somehow, she still looks perfectly elegant. The only thing that belies her compsure is the redness around her eyes.

"Thank you," she says calmly, standing up and coming to take my hands. "For coming in when you did. And for saving her life."

"I doubt she'd express the same sentiments." I squeeze her fingers. "What can I help you with?"

"Madison has posted bail and we're going to visit my parents, like I mentioned yesterday. I think it's best for both of us to be out of town when her father returns tonight. This way, I can tell her what's going to happen without us fighting."

"That's probably for the best."

"Which means…" She reaches for the small, black purse hanging off her shoulder and removes her wallet. Two long, rectangular pieces of paper are handed to me. "Two checks. One which should more than cover your expenses incurred for your work, as I understand Randy paid you all up front."

"Yes, ma'am, he did. This isn't necessary."

"He agreed to pay extras. This is that." She puts that down on the desk and gently lays the second on top of it. "The second is for your brother. He was injured while chasing after my harebrained husband, and Randy and I are both in agreement that, for once, he should pay someone who needs it instead of paying someone off. He spoke with his insurance company on an advisory basis, and the amount on the check should cover Brody's medical costs and allow him to take unpaid leave instead of using his vacation days after his sick days are exhausted."

"I—Alyssa, you—"

Oh. My. God.

"You don't need to do that," I manage, swallowing hard.

"We do. My husband has a lot to repent for, and let's say that, if he'd like certain private images to remain private, he's willing to take some of my advice." She winks and stands. "Thank you, Ms. Bond. I'll see myself out."

She turns to the door, leaving me dumbstruck and staring after her, and shuts it behind her.

I'm not even going to look at that amount. I don't want to know what she's done, but I know that my mom is gonna need her own medical attention when she finds out. Although the police provide insurance for Brody, I know that the Holly Woods PD doesn't have that much money to go around for serious injuries. I suspect Alyssa McDougall knew that, too.

And I wouldn't be surprised if there's a sudden rise in funding for them after this.

I take a deep breath, turn the checks over, and zip them safely into my wallet for cashing tomorrow.

I uncap the jar of sauce and drop it over the chicken, bacon, and broccoli. God forbid if Nonna ever saw me using jarred pasta sauce. I'd be kidnapped and locked in her kitchen until I made the perfect marinara.

I mean, I can make a pretty good marinara. I just have to want to do it. And after the last few days, I most definitely do not want to do it.

Drake sets a glass of wine down next to the stove and kisses my shoulder. "You look tired."

"That's a polite way of telling someone they look like shit."

He laughs and opens the drawer, pulling the bottle opener out. He uncaps his beer and drops the opener onto the counter. I make a pfft kind of noise, grab it, and deposit back into its home. The drawer.

The counter is not where utensils belong unless they are being used.

"You want me to tell you that you look like shit?"

"Do you want me to break your balls?"

"Depends on your method of breaking them. Will you be naked while you do it?"

"Trust me when I say that, if you tell me I look like shit, I'll most definitely not be naked."

"Ah, well. Can't blame me for tryin'." He laughs and sits at the kitchen table. "Brody seems better."

I tilt my head to the side. "I think he's milking Nonna for all of her cooking skills at this point. When I left earlier, he mentioned garlic bread and she took off like a bat out of Hell. I have to promise to name my firstborn after her for a glass of water."

"That's 'cause y'all fight all the time."

"Hey now. We fight all the time and you pour me wine." I hold the glass up and sip. "Thank you, by the way."

"You're welcome."

I turn the stove off after stirring the pasta one last time and put the colander in the sink so I can drain it. It feels really odd cooking for Drake in my own kitchen, but his other suggestion was that we go to Giovanni's. He spent three hours with the mayor this afternoon, and despite my understanding his need to unwind, my need for my yoga pants was slightly stronger, so I agreed to cook.

It feels a little too homey to be completely comfortable though.

I spoon pasta onto two plates and then add the chicken and sauce on top of it. The parmesan is already in a small bowl in the center of the table along with the cutlery, so I move the pans to the sink before going for the plates.

Drake steps up behind me and beats me to it. He takes a plate in each hand with a chuckle and steps back, sweeping them around me. I shake my head even as I smile. Maybe he's not a total asshole all the time.

I settle for grabbing my wine glass. I have a feeling he knew exactly what my priority tonight was.

"So we got a little more out of Ellis," he says, swallowing some food. "Turns out she'd been seeing Natalie for a long time, and when she and Nick broke up, she thought she'd come out as bisexual. When she didn't, they fought a lot, but because of the nature of their relationship with Ellis being the dominant one, she effectively punished her through sex."

I wrinkle my face, stabbing a pasta shell. "That is…unusual."

Drake shrugs. "You'd think. Along with that, Ellis assumed their relationship would be exclusive. Natalie had said as much, so when it didn't happen and she found the video of her and the mayor on Natalie's laptop, she realized Natalie was using her to exploit the mayor and was destroyed. And the rest she already told you. It was a crime of passion."

"Wow. Imagine loving someone that much that you'd kill them." I pause and point my fork at him. "Actually, no, don't. That's kind of a horrific thought."

"I agree. Besides, I don't need to be in love with you to want to kill you on a regular basis."

"If I didn't feel the exact same way, I'd be real offended right now." I smile over the top of my glass.

Drake's eyes glitter with laughter. "You know, it occurs to me that I still owe you a do-over of the first date."

"Are you still gonna insist on that? Really? Don't you think we're past that now that we're officially doing the dating thing?"

"You only call it dating to appease Nonna," he points out, a wry smile on his lips. "But no. So, now that this case is done, we're going to do a real date. Hopefully out of town."

Of course. With the return of the mayor is the return of Jessica.

Ugh. I almost forgot about her, too.

I cast my eyes toward my plate and swirl a piece of pasta around my plate. This will never be easy. I knew that. I *know* that. We'll always be antagonistic and a completely crazy kind of match. Except I'm kind of convinced that maybe it could work, even if we do have to solve cases together.

Except I'm more than a little worried about her.

"Nope." Drake gets up, his chair scraping across the floor. He takes my fork from me then clasps my hands and pulls me up.

My lips part as my front comes flush with his and he wraps a firm arm around my waist, holding me against him.

"You aren't doing this. We aren't doing this," he says quietly but certainly. His eyes are so bright and compelling that I can't look away even though my chest is tight. "She's my ex for a reason, Noelle.

Actually, several reasons."

I smile and rest my hands on his waist. "I know. But she's obnoxious and pushy and—"

"So she's an uglier you."

"Um." I lean back and raise an eyebrow. "I'll have you know that I have a special brand of bitch, and I own its copyright. Take that back before I kick you."

He laughs and tightens his arms around me. "She's an uglier wannabe you," he corrects himself. "How's that?"

"It'll do, I suppose."

"Right." He leans his face in toward mine and our noses brush. "Again, she's my ex. She's only here now to get under my skin and convince me that breaking up with her all of those years ago was a mistake because she's realized what she's lost."

"Whoa now, Detective. You need to be able to walk out of my front door. You know that, right? Keep singing your own praises like that and your ego is gonna get stuck right here in this kitchen."

"I'm pretty sure you're incapable of shutting up, especially when you get uncomfortable."

"And I'm pretty sure you have that exactly right," I confirm, grinning. Or trying to. Because I am uncomfortable. A little.

Okay, a lot.

Drake covers my mouth with his hand. "Problem solved. Now—"

I interrupt him by licking his palm. "You were saying?" I ask with an innocent smirk after he removes it.

He clicks his tongue against the roof of his mouth. "I was saying," he continues, wiping his palm—the one I just licked—down my cheek.

"Ew!" I squeal, batting him away from me and swiping at my cheek. "That's vile!"

He answers by laughing and grabbing me back. "Now, for the love for God, shut the fuck up a minute so I can finish what I've been trying to say for five minutes!"

"Oh my God, okay," I groan, making it extra dramatic.

He opens his mouth,then stops. "I don't even remember what I was saying."

"All of that for nothing," I sigh, extracting myself from his arms and reaching for my wine glass.

He grabs me from behind, his arms pinning mine to my sides, and I squeal again when he squeezes me tight, rubbing his jaw across mine. It makes me squirm, but equally, the roughness is kind of hot even though he's only playing.

"I was saying that you shouldn't give her another damn thought, because she'll never be half the woman you are. And I need a real kind of woman. And let's face it, sweetheart. There isn't another guy in this town who could handle your special kind of pain in the fucking ass."

I'd be so offended by that if it weren't true.

"Uh, okay," I mumble as he replaces his stubble with his lips.

They brush across the top of my neck, and I bend my arms up so my fingers curl around his forearms.

"I think I can take that kind of explanation. Even if you did just call me a pain in the fucking ass."

He smiles against my skin. "But you're my pain in the ass, and that makes a huge difference."

I tilt my face toward him. "Yeah. I guess it kinda does."

Then he spins me and kisses me fully, and somehow, everything makes sense.

At least, for today.

The End

Until early September...

about the AUTHOR

By day, New York Times and USA Today bestselling New Adult author Emma Hart dons a cape and calls herself Super Mum to two beautiful little monsters. By night, she drops the cape, pours a glass of whatever she fancies - usually wine - and writes books. Emma is working on Top Secret projects she will share with her followers and fans at every available opportunity. Naturally, all Top Secret projects involve a dashingly hot guy who likes to forget to wear a shirt, a sprinkling (or several) of hold-onto-your-panties hot scenes, and a whole lotta love. She likes to be busy - unless busy involves doing the dishes, but that seems to be when all the ideas come to life.

Find her online at:

Facebook: www.facebook.com/emmahartbooks or www.facebook.com/emma.evelyn
Twitter: www.twitter.com/emmahartauthor
Instagram: www.instagram.com/emmahartauthor
Pinterest: www.pinterest.com/authoremmahart
Website: www.emmahart.org

30892366R00173

Made in the USA
San Bernardino, CA
25 February 2016